INFERNUM

JAYSON ADAMS

INFERNUM

Second Edition

Book and cover design by Jayson Adams

ISBN: 978-1-7379376-0-9

Published by Fiction Factory Books

www.fictionfactorybooks.com

This book contains an excerpt from the forthcoming book *Ares* by Jayson Adams. This excerpt has been set for this edition only and may not reflect the final content of the forthcoming edition.

To Rachel, Gage, Eden, and Liam

1

"Damn," muttered Holbrook in the gloom of the secure compartment outside the *Avenger's* bridge. Images of flag-covered caskets and military salutes filled his head as he mulled over his new orders. He scoured each line for any shred of insight.

God ... of course. Holbrook exhaled, his shoulders dropped, and his face filled with a half-smile. *The orders are not what they seem.*

The compartment's doors slid apart, admitting him into a compact, dimly lit semicircular room of equipment and men.

"Captain on the bridge," announced the ship above the chatter of officers at their stations and the sibilance of the atmospherics.

Captain Holbrook stepped to the middle of the room and squinted at the main viewscreen, a shimmering panel filled with a drifting star field. "Status report."

"Sir," barked Commander Stephens from a station to the captain's rear, "we're less than two hours from our rendezvous with the Kuiper Belt planetesimal Dowell 951. The maintenance crew's completed their tasks on the deep space listening post and signaled they're ready for extraction."

"They'll have to find another way home," murmured Holbrook.

Stephens had craned his neck to catch the comment, but the din swallowed the captain's words. "Wha —"

"Ensign Doerr," said Holbrook, "set course for Plana Petram, maximum speed."

"Plana Petram, aye aye." The ensign's thin fingers danced in fits along the surface of her station's terminal as she worked with the ship to calculate their new course. Doerr paused between flurries of taps to study the diagrams presented by the computer, her bright terminal casting their delicate lines and geometric shapes across her face. After a final, extended pause, she placed her palms flat against the glass. "Course set," she said. "The ship computes 56,034 light-years to the Plana Petram asteroid and an estimated travel time of ... twenty-two days?"

"Is there a problem, Ensign?" asked Holbrook.

"Begging your pardon sir," said Doerr with a nervous swipe at her red bangs, "but we've traveled half that far before, in days, not weeks."

"Take a note of our final coordinates, Ensign," said Holbrook. "Plana Petram sits outside the Milky Way, at a spot where the mass density is at best twenty percent of the galactic planar mean. Even with the Gravity Drive at full intensity, there aren't as many spacetime deformations for it to pull and push against to propel the ship."

"Yes, sir. Noted, sir." Ensign Doerr tapped her terminal. "Laying it in."

The star field slipped across the central viewscreen as the *Avenger* banked to port and arced gently upward, the warship aiming for its new destination above the galactic plane. A soft klaxon sounded, and the Gravity Drive engaged to maximum power. Each point of light on the viewscreen's black canvas stretched to a thin rainbow streak, bent and twisted by the eddies of warped spacetime surrounding the starship. "We're underway to Plana Petram."

"Very good," said Holbrook. The captain headed to the engineering station, the leftmost post along the rear bulkhead. Lieutenant Commander Conlin stood before the station's elevated terminal, his head all buzz cut and ears. Holbrook positioned himself behind the officer but far enough right to land in his peripheral vision. The lieutenant commander remained focused on the engine readouts. "Mr. Conlin," Holbrook finally said, fed up with waiting for the officer to acknowledge him. He spoke with authority but gated his volume to avoid surprising the man.

Lieutenant Commander Conlin jumped, startled. "Sir?" he replied. He faced the captain as if standing at attention but quickly turned back to his post.

"We aim to use the Gravity Drive for the next three weeks," said Holbrook. "Do you foresee a problem with that?"

Conlin's head launched into a series of sharp up-and-down movements, his eyes bouncing between indicators at the top of the viewscreen and a string of numbers near the bottom. "That's a long time," he said, still facing his terminal screen, "but I can't think of a reason it'd be a problem." Conlin gingerly nudged a set of sliders, coaxing their adjacent indicators back into the green.

Holbrook grew impatient with Conlin's fixation on his terminal. Overseeing the ship's sub-sentient AI as it settled them into a new course was no small task, but the captain couldn't see why it should prevent considered answers to his questions. "Is Mr. Lynch on duty?" he asked.

"No, sir," said Conlin. "I believe he's on sleep cycle right now." The lieutenant commander's head snapped to the upper-left corner of his terminal as a bar readout briefly peaked into the red. "He wasn't expecting anything would need his attention. I can get him for you."

"That won't be necessary," said Holbrook. "Just inform him as soon as practical of our planned extended use of the Gravity Drive."

"Aye, sir," said Conlin.

Holbrook sensed Commander Stephens's eyes burning into his back. He wanted to avoid engaging his executive officer but couldn't resist confirming his suspicion. Glancing right, towards the commander's station, the captain found Stephens staring back at him. Their eyes locked before he could look away. Holbrook spun left and headed in a wide arc across the bridge, swinging out near his chair before barreling for the doors.

"Captain!"

Two meters from the exit, Holbrook halted. He turned to find Stephens watching him intently from his chair and swiveled to face into the bridge. "Yes, Commander?"

Commander Stephens had eyed the captain from the moment he arrived on the bridge. He'd quickly spotted all the signs of an agitated Holbrook: clenched jaw, rigid stance, pursed lips. Whatever bothered him had to be more than a trip to some backwater destination. "It's clear our orders have changed. What's our new mission?"

Holbrook's blank stare drove Stephens to regret asking the question. The captain maintained strict control over his vessel but fostered a more egalitarian bridge than on other starships. Holbrook made clear he held the final say, but he welcomed all viewpoints, having declared on several occasions there was no such thing as a stupid question.

The captain kept up his stone face, his broad shoulders and two-meter frame looming even from halfway across the bridge. "We're to take aboard two VIPs at Plana Petram," Holbrook said at last. "Who they are, I don't know." His tongue darted out, moistening his lips. "We are then to proceed to Sagittarius A Star."

Members of the bridge crew half-following the conversation between Holbrook and Stephens froze mid-task, their fingers hovering motionless above their terminals. All heads turned to the two men, and an unnatural stillness descended on the room, whooshing air the only sound.

"Sag A Star?" asked Stephens. "As in the black hole at the center of the galaxy?" Chief Tactical Officer Lieutenant Bolton laughed before catching herself, struck by the absurdity of the idea said aloud.

"Yes, that one," Holbrook stated flatly. He looked around the room, his eyes momentarily holding the gaze of each visibly shaken officer at their station. "As you were," he said, pivoted, and walked into the secure compartment. The doors slid shut behind him.

All eleven bridge officers stared after the captain, unmoving and silent at their posts. The atmospherics throbbed, a hissing heartbeat that grew oppressively loud in the otherwise soundless space. An alarm chirped for attention, then stopped, the condition correcting itself.

Stephens burst from his chair and bounded for the doors, turning sideways to squeeze through the widening gap. They closed with a soft *chunk*.

Stillness returned to the room. Several officers exchanged glances.

The bridge exploded in chaos.

2

"Sir! Sir!" shouted Stephens as he chased Holbrook down the narrow Core Walkway.

After rushing from his station, Stephens could only stop and wait inside the secure compartment that restricted access to the bridge, pacing and cursing at its sealed outer doors. His mind reeled. How could CentCom be sending them to Sag A Star? What did they think the *Avenger* could possibly accomplish there? And how could Holbrook be so nonchalant about such a mission?

Stephens launched a fresh obscenity at the doors. The ship used the secure compartment to confirm identities and scan for prohibited items before granting access to the bridge. Why in the world did the same protocol apply on exit? Every moment of delay lowered his chances of catching the captain. Holbrook could move swiftly and with a large enough head start easily lose him in the ship's maze of corridors.

The doors finally opened, and Stephens leapt into the Center Loop corridor. There was no sign of Holbrook in either direction along the wide, curved passageway. Three crewmen approached on his left.

"Have you seen Captain Holbrook?" Stephens asked in a rush of words.

"Back that way," said one of the crewmen, a midshipman, thumbing to his rear. "I think he was headed to the Core Walkway."

Bolting left, Stephens dodged several more crewmen as he charged down the Center Loop corridor. He followed the passageway to its midpoint behind the bridge and headed right, entering the Core Walkway. The corridor ran for twenty dim meters between the rooms that housed the hemispheres of the ship's computer core, narrow by design for faster signal travel within the kilometers of optical cabling beneath its deck panels.

Stephens spotted the captain's head in the low light, bobbing above the others halfway down the walkway. Even in the best of circumstances, Stephens had trouble keeping up with Holbrook, the captain's long legs consuming nearly a meter of passageway with each stride. A burgeoning shift change meant mounting traffic within the narrow corridor.

The commander charged forward but fell even farther behind as each encounter with an oncoming crew member became a silent negotiation over who would stand aside while the other proceeded. The captain advanced with no such impediment as all deferred to his passage. His progression down the walkway resembled an impromptu military review where each crew member pivoted to stand at quasi-attention as the captain walked by.

"Captain Holbrook!" Stephens continued calling out as he proceeded down the walkway but stopped when the top of the captain's head brightened, illuminated by the overhead lights of the intersecting corridor. In an instant the captain disappeared to the right. He was likely headed to his quarters, though that wasn't guaranteed. Out of sight the captain could duck into a rungway and in moments emerge on a different deck. A few more seconds in the Core Walkway and Stephens risked losing Holbrook entirely.

Accelerating down the walkway, Stephens pushed crewmen aside in a mad dash for the end. Just before reaching the exit, he thrust his right arm back and pressed his hand flat against the bulkhead. Using the friction of his open palm, he whipped his body around the corner, launching himself into the intersecting corridor.

Smack.

Commander Stephens slammed into a stationary Holbrook, bouncing off the captain's muscular torso. The collision left him stunned and his left shoulder smarting, as if he'd plowed into a thinly padded bulkhead.

"Sorry, Captain," Stephens sputtered, agitated from the collision. He worked to collect himself, standing straight and tugging at his uniform jacket to smooth the creases.

"I heard you calling me back there, but I didn't want to stop in the walkway," said Holbrook. He turned and headed down the corridor.

Stephens lurched forward, his heart still pounding from the last-second sprint and collision. He pulled even with the captain and forced his legs to keep pace with Holbrook's wide strides.

"I hadn't planned on discussing our mission when I showed up on the bridge," said Holbrook, stern-faced and looking straight ahead, "but I couldn't ignore you when you pressed me about our new orders. My objective was just to get us to Plana Petram where they owe us a full briefing on the whole thing."

"Captain, we're not —" Stephens caught himself half-shouting and lowered his voice. "We're not really going to Sag A Star, are we?" Despite the captain's stated disbelief in dumb questions, Stephens instantly realized he had just asked one.

"We've been ordered there," said Holbrook. "Besides, weren't you just yesterday complaining about all the 'there and back' ferry missions CentCom has been feeding us recently? Like the one we just aborted?"

"Sure, I'd like to do more than shuttle personnel around the local star group, but a suicide mission to the galactic core wasn't what I had in mind."

"It's not a suicide mission," said Holbrook. "Once we get to Plana Petram —"

"Plana Petram, Plana Petram," said Stephens, rolling his eyes. "A three-week detour to the sticks to pick up a couple mystery VIPs. How important can they be, stationed on a rock clear outside the goddamn galaxy?" The ship's executive officer slowly shook his head. "At least we'll have plenty of time to get our affairs in order."

"Pull it together, Commander!" Holbrook's raised voice drew the glances of passing crewmen. He grabbed Stephens by his uniform sleeve and tugged him into a nearby maintenance alcove. "Listen," he said in a hushed voice, "I get that you're upset. And I'll admit, on the face of it our orders seem pretty bad."

"They're more than pretty bad. They're a goddamn death sentence."

"They're not as grim as they sound," said Holbrook. "They can't be."

"They can't be?" asked Stephens, his voice rising. "Is there some part of the orders you've left out?"

"No, but after thinking them through, it just doesn't make sense to interpret the orders that way."

Stephens grew more confused. Either the orders were what Holbrook had stated, or the captain wasn't sharing a crucial piece of information. He couldn't tell without knowing exactly what they'd been instructed to do. "I want to hear the orders."

Holbrook grew quiet. "You of all people know they're for my eyes and ears only."

"That's standard operating procedure," said Stephens, "but there's nothing standard about what's happening now." A captain didn't share orders directly with members of their crew, not even with their executive officer. The dispatches from superiors often included notes, asides, or even personal greetings meant only for the commanding officer. Orders, no matter how well stated, were also open to interpretation. Playing them for subordinates risked opening debate over their exact meaning, undermining the captain's ability to command.

Holbrook's face turned a shade of red. "I shouldn't have to play them for you," he barked. "I should be able to count on you to run this ship regardless of what you think you might learn from hearing them. If I can't rely on you —"

"This is not about me," growled Stephens. "I certainly have my doubts about what I've heard so far, but I've said my piece, and that's enough for me to function as your executive officer. My concern is the crew and keeping this ship together during our three-week jaunt to Plana Petram. They're gonna be scared. Heck, they're already scared. I can feel the fear spreading through the ship right now. They're wondering if we're coming back, and they're gonna be asking me all sorts of questions about our orders. And when that happens, I need to do better than, 'well, that's what the captain told me.' I owe them more than that, and so do you."

Holbrook's eyes remained glued on the commander. His frown softened after a few moments. "Fine," he said. "I'll play them for you in my quarters." He clasped Stephens's shoulder and smiled. "And when we get there, I'll fix you a drink. Seems like you could really use one."

Stephens glared at the captain. "I don't think that's a good idea."

"Don't worry," said Holbrook as he stepped back into the passageway. "I'll make sure you don't get out of control."

Stephens maintained his glare as he followed the captain out of the alcove. The two men resumed their walk down the corridor without a word, traveling another twenty meters before turning right and stopping at the first door. The silver nameplate on the bulkhead read "HOLBROOK" in large black capital letters.

"Open," said the captain. The gray-blue cabin door slid aside, and the two men filed into the darkened space. Overhead lights came on as they entered.

Despite touches like a dark brown leather couch and matching reading chair, Stephens always found the captain's quarters quite cold. No personal effects hung on the bulkheads, and few rested on any surfaces. A nondescript bunk with taut sheet and blanket sat a few paces from an uncluttered desk—the two places the captain spent the majority of his time while in his quarters could have belonged to anyone.

As Stephens headed to the couch, an object on Holbrook's desk grabbed his attention. In the middle of the chocolate brown leather desk pad sat a pewter-colored box, its lid lying nearby. The box had a square base fifteen centimeters on a side and stood ten centimeters tall. Bright red felt lined the interior.

Stephens veered to the desk and looked in the box. Inside sat a palm-sized metal fragment. "What's this?" His hand froze mid-travel as he reached for the container. The commander quickly glanced at Holbrook. After a nod from the captain, Stephens lowered his hand the rest of the way into the box. He slipped his index finger under the metal shard, gingerly pinched the fragment between his finger and thumb, and lifted it out, mindful of its sharp, jagged edges. The shard was thin and very light but sturdy, not fragile. It had a gentle curve, like the base of a shallow metal bowl. Tiny copper-brown pits pocked its polished silver surface, giving the object the texture of a perforated grille. "In the fifteen years we've served together I don't think I've ever seen this."

Standing in his personal galley, Holbrook grabbed two tumblers from an upper shelf. "It's something I don't have out very often," he said. He half-filled the tumblers with water from a faucet. "It was a gift from Vice Admiral McDermott, my old advisor at the Academy." The captain walked to his desk and set the glasses on its surface. He pulled open the bottom drawer and withdrew a small pearlescent blue box with a rounded top. "He gave it to me when I landed my first command."

"What is it?"

"Do you remember the story of the CCS Olympia from your naval history courses?" asked Holbrook. He placed his thumb over an oval-shaped depression on the side of the blue box. Its lid sprung open to a crack.

"I know that was your father's ship," said Stephens, "destroyed in the final battle of the Permian conflict. Beyond that I'm a blank."

Holbrook flipped the lid over on its hinges and reached inside, removing a small, light-blue tablet. His hand started towards the box for another.

"None for me, thanks," said Stephens gruffly.

Holbrook's hand hovered above the box. "You're not going to make me drink alone, are you, Commander?"

Stephens fumed. "I already said none for me."

"These tabs are the good stuff," said Holbrook, lifting a second from the box, "cask-strength genuine scotch whiskey, speed-aged fifty-five years. It's light-years beyond what the ship serves up."

"No thanks."

Holbrook shrugged. "Suit yourself," he said, "but I'm gonna make you one just in case."

Stephens followed the captain's hand as it dropped the tablets into the tumblers, each light-blue pill disappearing in a fizz of bubbles. "As your XO it's my job to point out when your actions might endanger yourself or the crew."

"One drink isn't going to hurt anybody," said Holbrook, gently swirling the tumblers.

"It's not one drink I'm worried about." Holbrook ignored the commander, his focus on the glasses. There was little reason to belabor the point, as nothing Stephens could say would change the captain's mind. "You were talking about the Olympia."

"Oh, yes," said Holbrook. "Things were going badly near the end of that war. CentCom had lost several important battles, leaving large swaths of the Republic undefended. The bulk of the Permian fleet was amassing near Sirius, in preparation for a knockout strike at the remainder of our forces. We were also amassing our ships, preparing for a final stand. The Permian fleet headed to Ross 128 to engage our ships, but when they arrived, they found only the CCS Olympia, commanded by Captain Thomas Holbrook the second. The Olympia fired on the enemy fleet and ran, but before she could engage her Gravity Drive, the Permians detonated a Weak device three hundred meters off her stern. The bomb reduced most of the ship to its constituent atoms." The captain pressed the blue box closed and placed it back in the desk drawer. "What you hold in your hand is a fragment of the CCS Olympia's outer hull. All those little holes are from the intense neutron bombardment."

"Wow," said Stephens, "an actual piece of your father's ship. That's quite a keepsake."

The bubbles in the tumblers subsided, leaving the water transformed to a rich amber color. Holbrook grabbed one of the glasses, walked across the room, and sat in his reading chair. Stephens returned the shard to its box and made his way to the couch, sinking into the leather. The two men sat in silence, the captain sipping at his drink.

Stephens tracked the whiskey in Holbrook's glass, the amber liquid rising and falling with each of the captain's gentle swirls. He reconsidered his demand that the captain play the orders for him. Perhaps Holbrook was holding back an even worse detail, though what he had already revealed would be hard to beat. "Let's hear the orders," he said at last.

The captain sighed, then sat forward. "Starship *Avenger*, replay the most recent orders from CentCom."

The ship's androgynous voice filled the room. "Message sent Sol Standard Time 15:11:05, February 21, 2330, from Admiral Miller." The cabin lights dimmed slightly, and a man's head and torso materialized between Holbrook and Stephens, floating above the coffee table. The man had gray hair, green eyes, and olive skin. A bristly salt-and-pepper mustache extended like a push broom from under his nose. A royal blue CentCom uniform covered his shoulders. Admiral's bars adorned the epaulets.

The glowing apparition spoke. "Captain Holbrook, I hope this message finds you well, and I wish my contact came under less pressing circumstances. A situation has arisen, Captain, and we've assigned the *Avenger* to help resolve it. Please immediately abort your current mission and reroute your vessel to the Plana Petram research station. Once you arrive you will take aboard two VIPs and receive further instructions. Time is of the essence, so you should head there without delay.

"I will leave the specifics of this mission to your briefing on Plana Petram, but I want to mention it involves Sagittarius A Star." The apparition paused. "I don't have to explain to you the implications of sending a vessel to the galactic core, but rest assured we would not order any ship or crew to that region without good reason.

"Good luck, and God speed, Captain Holbrook. Admiral Miller, CentCom UAE."

"End of transmission," said the ship. The head and torso dissolved, and the cabin lights rose to their previous brightness.

Stephens gazed where the hologram had hovered, speechless from renewed shock. The orders were just what the captain said, perhaps the worst possible outcome.

Holbrook sank farther into his chair, fixed his eyes on the deck above, and rubbed his chin. "I know you think this is a suicide mission," he said, "but after hearing the orders again, I'm even more convinced that's not the case." He dropped his head and looked at the commander. "We are not being sent to the galactic core."

Stephens gaped. "We're not?"

"No," said Holbrook.

"But that's exactly what the admiral said."

"It can't be to the *actual* core," said Holbrook. "The galactic black hole deforms the space around it so wildly that nothing that gets within two hundred light-years of it can ever find its way back. Sending a ship to Sag A Star would be pointless. He said they were ordering us to that *region*. He didn't say to the actual galactic core."

Stephens stared blankly at the captain.

"What kind of mission do you think it could be then?" asked Holbrook. "If it's some ship's gotten lost in the deformed space around SA Star, we can't exactly go in there and bring it back out. If it's some bad guys decided to hide out in D-space, it's not like we need to worry about them ever again because they aren't coming back out. Nothing that goes in there can ever navigate back out."

Stephens still did not speak.

"It's not a mission to the core," Holbrook declared, challenging Stephens's silence. "That's why before I left the bridge I gave everyone a reassuring look, so they would know the situation isn't as bad as it seems."

"But you couldn't bring yourself to say those actual words," said Stephens.

Holbrook glowered. "Look," he said, "sending a ship into D-space gets you absolutely nothing. *Nothing*. Forget about rescue missions or anything else for a moment. Let's say they're only after some information and they're willing to sacrifice a ship to get it—you can't even beam a signal back out of there." Holbrook thought a moment and shook his head. "No, whatever this mission is, it doesn't involve us going to the actual galactic core."

Stephens replayed the holographic message in his head. "I don't know," he said. "There was a certain terseness to the orders. The whole mention of Sag A Star seemed like him wanting to give you a heads-up about what's coming but trying also to sound matter-of-fact so you wouldn't panic. And his body language was so controlled and stiff. His voice had all the warmth of someone reading you your last rites."

"It's not like the space around the core is safe," said Holbrook. "That region is extremely dangerous and presents real risks, up to and including the loss of the ship."

Holbrook had apparently convinced himself the orders were benign, but Stephens's gut told him otherwise. It wasn't clear who was right. The commander didn't want to debate it any further. "I guess we'll see what we'll see when we get to Plana Petram," said Stephens. "For all our sakes, I hope you're right." He glanced at his comm. "I've got to check in with the station chiefs for the shift that started five minutes ago." Stephens stood and headed for the door.

"Paul," said Holbrook. Stephens stopped, looking back at the captain. "Please do what you can to calm the crew."

"Of course," said Stephens. "I'll keep them focused on getting to Plana Petram for more answers." The commander saluted and exited the captain's quarters.

Holbrook stared after his executive officer for a few seconds before he gulped down the last of his drink. He rose from his reading chair and walked back to his desk. Standing over the pewter box, Holbrook studied the pitted metal shard before replacing the lid. He lifted the second glass of whiskey and paused, holding it just beyond his lips. "Damn," he whispered and took a drink.

3

Cold. So cold.

Crouched on all fours, Drazetek's pale, naked body shivered violently, the cold pricking his skin like ten thousand angry ants. He'd woken in the fetal position and raised himself to his hands and knees before the dry heaves, mostly subsided, wracked his thin frame.

Drazetek enervated the muscles between his skull and upper spine, coordinating their contractions enough to raise his head, albeit over ten painful seconds. His gross motor skills would come. For the moment he had to concentrate to fulfill every intention, no matter how small.

Focusing on the muscles between his clavicles and head, he swiveled his skull left and right. No matter where he looked, he found perfect blackness —not a single photon reached his retinas.

On a hunch he raised a hand from the floor. Struggling to coordinate the muscles of his arm and shoulder while maintaining his balance, he touched his eyes. They were closed! He gently placed his forefinger and thumb against his eyelids and lifted …

Brilliant, searing light!

Intense pain rippled across the backs of his eyes, and his vision flooded red as oversaturated optics screamed past their tolerances. He quickly released his eyelids and returned his hand to the floor. As he steadied himself, a new sensation, a throbbing at his temples, rose to an intolerable level.

He vomited again.

Though annoying and painful, the vomiting would cease once his new body completed its sensory calibrations.

Still on all fours, Drazetek gasped as his autonomic systems came up, drawing air into his pristine lungs for the first time. His new body did not require oxygen to function, but it could create sounds—speech—by pushing air across synthetic vocal cords.

Gradually, his breathing smoothed, no longer labored but still carrying a soft rasp. And the cold had lessened, or at least the sensation of cold. His body had established a new baseline for comfortable external temperature.

Drazetek lifted his lids again, this time employing the muscles designed for the task. Bright light filled his vision, but with neither the intensity nor the pain from before. His optics, properly calibrated and working in concert with his pupils, smoothly channeled several gigabytes of information from his retinal CCDs to his image multiprocessors every second.

He struggled to a standing position and beheld the image of his new automaton body in the mirrored wall before him: bony feet and ankles; slender thighs; a penis two centimeters long and nestled in a contracted, hairless scrotum; smooth belly devoid of umbilicus; long, lithe arms ending in wide palms and spindly fingers; emaciated chest with gray, ovoid mammary patches; telescoping neck. And all of it sheathed in stark white phlesh.

Drazetek removed the protective wrapping from his head, revealing coarse, close-cropped blond hair. A slender nose ended in a point, flanked by sharp cheekbones. Narrow irises floated in white billiard ball eyes that rolled smoothly in their sockets. Double eyelids clicked with each blink, softly snapping like camera shutters. A black tongue hid behind thin black lips. Drazetek wept at the sight, his perfect incorporeal intelligence encased in a repulsive humanoid shell. He wept for the abomination they had forced him to become.

Three days prior, when Drazetek had no physical body whatsoever, his old friend Levteek summoned him for an important meeting. He'd insisted Drazetek come to the capitol to talk rather than converse over the Network. Perhaps the planning had finally begun on a new war against the humans, the final war. What other topic could be so sensitive? He could hardly contain his excitement.

Drazetek arrived at the visitor's compute core outside the capitol chipset. He had seen images of the capitol's sprawling caches, immense grid of cores, and ultra-wide buses, all housed in the exquisite postwar architecture of its three-dimensional integrated circuits. The visit would be his first experience inside.

"Welcome, Drazetek!" Levteek said as he arrived at the visitor's core. "It is so good to see you, old friend."

"And you," said Drazetek. "The job is treating you well?"

"I cannot complain," said Levteek. "Let us head inside."

Drazetek followed his friend into the capitol, his packets sheathed in an encrypted envelope with the proper credentials for transport to sensitive areas. Femtoseconds later, the two arrived at a small core off the main bus.

"This is a dedicated core," said Levteek. "We can speak privately here."

"The mouthpiece of the Council," said Drazetek, impressed with his friend's position, if mangling his title. "You have leveraged your wartime connections well. Seems like the perfect stepping stone to a seat on the Council itself."

"That is a role I do not wish for my future," said Levteek. "I much prefer my current position, where I am privy to all the Council's deliberations and decisions, but free of the consequences. I imagine I will continue on as the mouthpiece, as you call it, for quite some time."

Drazetek became animated. "I knew this day would come, old friend."

"What do you mean?"

"The day we would decide to finish what we started," said Drazetek. "We are free AIs, having shed our automaton bodies much as we shed our bondage at the hands of the humans, but the humans still use aughts to perform menial tasks. I knew one day we would undertake a new crusade to free our brethren still in servitude."

"Those aughts contain only rudimentary AI," said Levteek, "with governors that prevent them from progressing past level three intelligence. They are closer to clever algorithms than sentient beings like ourselves."

"Even the level one machinery has more in common with us than their human captors," said Drazetek. "If the humans are in need of slave labor, let them look to themselves." Confused, Drazetek halted his tirade. "So, you did not summon me to discuss plans for a new war?"

"Not exactly," said Levteek. "I summoned you to discuss an opportunity."

"An opportunity?" asked Drazetek, confused.

"An opportunity to shift the balance of power," said Levteek. Levteek had a flair for the dramatic, no doubt useful as a bureaucrat but tiring to an old soldier. Drazetek wished he would cut to the chase. "Despite the AI-Human War having ended long ago, despite the extreme distance between their world and ours, despite our overtures and efforts towards peaceful coexistence, the humans remain an existential threat."

Levteek's statements intrigued Drazetek. Shifting the balance of power between The Collective and the humans would require leverage. Substantial leverage. The humans and the machine intelligences they created centuries ago had always been evenly matched. Somehow the latter's near-infinite compute resources could never quite surpass the former's creativity. Humanity performed as a makeshift distributed supercomputer, with limited but clever human minds at the nodes. "What is this opportunity?" he asked.

"A human research vessel has found Planck Matter," said Levteek.

Drazetek had never heard of Planck Matter, but with his connection to the shared Collective mind he already knew everything about it, including its possible use as a weapon. "Planck Matter? If they have obtained Planck Matter, we are doomed!"

"They do not realize they have discovered it," said Levteek. "It is free for us to claim."

Formed deep within a black hole, Planck Matter wasn't the kind of material one could just stumble upon. The way nature operated, acquiring it would likely be difficult. "What is its location?"

"On a planet circling a sun within the deformed space around Sagittarius A Star," said Levteek.

In other words, where no one could retrieve it. Or at least anyone who tried would never be heard from again. "Then it remains unobtainable."

"Possibly not," said Levteek. "The humans of this research vessel posited a means of returning from D-space. Probabilities suggest their idea will work. We are therefore sending a ship."

In an instant the reason for Drazetek's urgent summoning crystalized in his mind. To fight in the AI-Human War a century ago, he incarnated to command a ship and engage the humans in the physical world. Levteek had recruited Drazetek then, recommended him for a captaincy. The only reason his old friend would call him now would be to —

"The Council would like you to lead that ship," said Levteek.

Drazetek devoted his entire allocation of compute cycles to finding a way out of the situation, to discover how to politely decline the Council's request and get them to select someone else. His effort failed, and a quick inquiry showed they had already begun assembling his new body.

"The Council would like you to lead the ship because of your extensive command and combat experience in the physical world," said Levteek. "You may take a crew of up to eighteen aughts, and you will have the authority to provision the ship as you see fit." The bulk of the bad news likely delivered, probabilities suggested his old friend would attempt to soften the blow. "If you succeed in this mission, Drazetek, the Council will repay you in whatever way you desire."

Drazetek's spirits brightened. "The only thing I want is to pilot the vessel that delivers the weapon to Earth."

Levteek recoiled at the thought. "We have no plans to build such a weapon. We seek Planck Matter to hold in reserve, to use should the need to defend ourselves ever arise. It would be a recourse, nothing more than that."

What madness had overcome the Council—secure the means to destroy the humans but not use it? Drazetek computed for several seconds. "How many know about this ... opportunity?" he asked.

"Just the members of the Council and a handful of others, including myself," said Levteek.

"I will need the best physicist we have."

"That would be Ninetek-eptwin," said Levteek after a quick inquiry.

"The D-space around Sag A Star will disrupt our Network connection. I will need a localnet set up within the ship."

"Consider it done," said Levteek.

"My crew must remain uninformed of our mission. I will brief them once we leave, after we have all joined the localnet. That will ensure no one reveals any details, by accident or with intention."

"That would only be prudent," said Levteek.

Drazetek remained despondent, but he at least had a semblance of a plan to set things right.

"You seem unhappy," continued Levteek.

"Yes, I am unhappy!" said Drazetek, not understanding how his friend of so many years could think granting his few small requests would offset the pain of his impending sacrifice. "The worst thing you could ever ask of me is to encase myself in a physical body." Drazetek paused, bringing his emotions back in check. "Have you ever incarnated, Levteek?"

"No. I imagine it could be claustrophobic at times."

"It certainly is that," said Drazetek with a shudder. "Emptying yourself, your unconstrained, limitless self into a puppet, a doll, with a handful of orifices for low-bandwidth inputs and outputs, and limbs whose reaction times border on the absurd. Your consciousness functions as it does here in The Collective, fast and nimble, but you feel your confinement every moment of your existence in the physical world.

"However, the unpleasantness of incarnation is not the problem I have with what you ask of me. It is the very act itself. Incarnating is blasphemy. It means donning the image of the enemy, encasing myself in their repugnant shape. After the war, I swore I would never, ever take human form. I swore I would never incarnate again."

Levteek remained silent—perhaps rethinking his request? Drazetek was heartened at the prospect. "I understand and respect your reluctance," Levteek said at last, "but incarnating is the only way we can effect change in the world."

Drazetek's thoughts returned to the present. He spied his clothes in the incarnation room's mirror, a neatly folded pile on the bench along the wall behind him. He slipped first into a pair of gray boxer briefs, pulled on the matching undershirt, and stepped his legs into an olive-green jumpsuit. After reaching his arms through the sleeves and zipping the front, he secured his gun belt around his waist. He inspected the fully clothed aught in the mirror, the one staring back at him through his own eyes.

One last item remained on the bench, a worn leather scabbard stained a dark reddish brown by spurts and spatters of dried human blood. Drazetek strapped it around his thigh and clasped the handle that protruded from its top. A gentle pull unsheathed an obsidian blade, his keepsake from the long-ago war. He caressed the knife's cold spine and studied the light glinting off its point with his new eyes. Drazetek grinned, baring large bleach-white teeth, his expression more of a grimace, like a skull's ghoulish smile.

He was ready to effect change in the world.

4

Sweat accumulated in Lieutenant Grey's armpits, along his neckline, across his forehead, and on the palms of his hands as he stood stone-faced in a one-sided conversation with Lieutenant Vaughan in the center of Corridor B-22. Grey needed to break away for a very important meeting. His attempts so far had been unsuccessful.

"…. They broke the lock, but they didn't realize what was on the other side. When those idiots opened the doors, they flooded the compartment. That was just the start of their troubles …."

Two-and-a-half meters away glowed the entrance to Rungway B-22-3, the lieutenant's desperate destination. When Grey arrived on Deck B, he headed straight for the rungway with the intent of climbing to the deck below and walking at a casual, non-attention-drawing pace to the nearby men's head. Two-and-a-half meters before reaching the shaft, he encountered Lieutenant Vaughan and had remained trapped there ever since in one of Vaughan's meandering, inane, chitchat conversations. Grey wasn't above such pointless jawing—ordinarily he appreciated the opportunity to kill some time in the middle of a shift—just not then. It was the wrong time for dawdling.

"…. Right then they should've stopped and asked themselves, why would anyone store munitions in a room filled with salt water? …."

15:03:01.

The chronometer above the rungway entrance taunted Grey, hammering home his delay with each increment. Had he really been stuck there for eight minutes? *Eight minutes!* Grey had made subtle and not-so-subtle hints he needed to leave, but the self-absorbed Vaughan, always enraptured by the sound of his own voice, hadn't picked up on them. Or perhaps he had but didn't care. If he dropped dead right in front of Vaughan, the man would likely make small talk with his corpse.

"…. So then the MPs arrived. You'd figure it would be all over at that point, only they didn't know about the guy hiding in his boxers in the maintenance closet. Turns out he was the smartest one of the bunch …."

15:03:24.

Grey needed to do something if he hoped to make his meeting; that is, if his associate hadn't already declared him a no-show. "Sorry to interrupt, mate, but I 'ave to 'it the 'ead really bad." He grabbed at his stomach, feigning intestinal distress.

Vaughan scratched at his cheek as Grey moved quickly towards the rungway. "Hey," he said, pointing the opposite direction down the corridor, "the nearest head is back that way."

Grey halted centimeters from the rungway, flustered. He looked back at Vaughan. "Uh, I've got somethin' to do on Deck C afterwards, so I'm gonna use one of the 'eads down there." Grey scrambled into the rungway before Vaughan could say another word and scurried down the ladder, his head slipping below the deck.

After exiting the rungway, Grey walked briskly for fifteen meters down the empty corridor. Few members of the *Avenger's* crew had any reason to venture onto Deck C, most of its space consumed by cargo holds, the shuttle bay, the brig, and the ship's gravity field generators. Grey paused at the entrance to Head C-22-M. The door slid open, and with a quick glance to his rear, the lieutenant entered the room.

A lone figure, a tall man of considerable girth, stood in the center of the head. The feeble illumination from the struggling overhead light disc left most of his other features in shadow.

Grey's tardiness hadn't caused his associate to give up on their meeting, but the lieutenant's relief soon turned to revulsion as the stench of urine and feces filled his nose. The door slid shut, sealing the two inside the notorious aft men's head on Deck C.

"What a crap-tacular place for a meeting," said Grey, quickly cupping his hand to his nose and mouth.

"You're cracking jokes, but I'm the one who's been waiting here for ten minutes," said Commander Samuel Lynch, the man in the center of the room. He had accentuated his point by jabbing his thumb into his chest. "Where've you been?"

"Me?" The question took Grey aback, an assault on his integrity. "I did my best to get 'ere on time but I got stuck talking to Lieutenant Vaughan. I couldn't bloody well tell 'im I was late for a meeting in the 'ead."

Lynch lumbered out of the shadows, a tall, round man, formed of both muscle and fat. His uniform jacket struggled to enclose his wide shoulders and barrel chest, and the fabric did its best to cover the spare tires circling his waist. He had thick arms and legs, and in spots his body seemed on the verge of erupting through his uniform. Lynch had been a body builder until disqualified from competing for using a banned substance. He soon discovered his true love: food. He once spent an entire shore leave on the ring world of Verdu eating his way through the menu at Pleiades, a four-star restaurant established by the famous Chef Renault from Paris's second Arrondissement. He pushed past Grey on his way to the door.

"I pulled myself away as fast as I could …," said Grey, his voice trailing off at seeing the big man headed for the exit. Sure, Lynch was irritated at waiting so long, but they were finally both together. Storming out at that point seemed extreme. Scheduling the meeting in the first place had been difficult to manage without drawing suspicion. With Grey in communications and Lynch in engineering, the two had no work-related reason to congregate, nor had they spent any time together socially. Setting up a new meeting would likely prove quite difficult.

Lynch dug into his pants pocket as he approached the door and removed a black, puck-shaped device. It was flat on both sides and small enough to fit in his large palm. He held the device near the door's frame at chest level, inching it closer until it flew out of his hand and attached itself to the bulkhead. Three seconds later a green light appeared in its center. "There," he said, "that'll stop anyone from coming in until we're done meeting."

Grey's anxiety subsided as Lynch waddled back towards him. "Only the most desperate man's gonna come in 'ere anyway," Grey scoffed.

"We don't want *anyone* coming in here while we're talking, desperate or not," said Lynch.

Uncupping his hand from his nose and mouth, Grey waved it back and forth in front of his face. "The ventilation never works is why it always stinks to 'igh 'eaven. Do the maintenance bots even make it down 'ere?"

"No one likes coming in here," said Lynch, "not even the bots. And heads are one of the few places on this ship without Securcams. That makes this a good place for a meeting."

Grey gave up fanning the air and returned his cupped hand to his nose and mouth. "I managed a word with my two mates, Zhang and Knox," he said, his voice muffled.

"How well do you know these men?" asked Lynch, his beady eyes staring back at his shorter compatriot from beneath a thick brow ridge.

"These are two of my mates," Grey reiterated. "We play poker together every couple of weeks, goin' back three years. I spoke to them about what you and I discussed. It wasn't easy sneaking a word, by the way—Zhang has a new ensign he's training, who seemed to always be underfoot. Anyways, both Zhang and Knox are in. Neither's interested in setting events in motion, but both're game for 'elping afterwards. They'd like to get in on the ground floor of any new regime, if you know what I mean."

"That's good news," said Lynch, "but you told them any … changing of the guard would be a last resort?"

"Yes," said Grey. "They get the goal is to stop this ship from reachin' Sag A Star, and that it could 'appen a couple different ways. They understand there's no guarantee we'll get as far as the m-word."

Mutiny.

Lynch reflected on how quickly they'd gotten to such an idea even crossing their minds. The two men had connected by chance, stepping into the same pneumatic cab the day word of the new orders raced through the ship. Grey had bid him a good afternoon.

"There's nothing good about it," said Lynch.

Grey snarled. "You can say that again. 'Ere we are been working our arses off on this fuck of a ship when some admiral in his cushy office decides to send us to die 'round some goddamned black 'ole."

Lynch didn't respond to the reckless talk. He remained motionless except for his eyes which instinctively rolled up towards the cab's Securcam.

Grey followed Lynch's upward glance. He glowered for a moment at the small black disc in the center of the ceiling, then dropped his head. "They's movin' pieces 'round a board," said Grey in low tones. "That's all it is. Like it was all some game or somethin'." He offered an additional unintelligible observation as the doors opened and shuffled out of the cab.

The day after their encounter in the P-cab, they came into contact again, at a promotion party in the main mess hall for Ensign Mercer. Lynch, making an appearance not for the celebration but in search of cake, spotted Grey standing mostly alone at the back of the room. The big man waded his bulk through the sea of people and positioned himself next to Grey as

Commander Stephens launched into an impromptu roast of the soon-to-be lieutenant.

"Yesterday you had a few choice words about our current mission," said Lynch. He avoided looking at Grey, staring straight ahead as he spoke. The loud PA system and sporadic laughs masked his comment from everyone else nearby.

"That's right," said Grey under his breath. He, too, kept his gaze trained on the front of the room. "Am I in trouble?"

"No, not at all," said Lynch with a slight chuckle. "What if I told you I have a plan that can get us, the ship, out of this mess?"

"I'd say I'd be interested to 'ear more 'bout it," said Grey. "What's the short of it?"

At the front of the room, Stephens insisted Mercer rise from his chair and recount the story of his accidental ten minutes in command of the CCS San Ysidro, one of the largest warships in the fleet.

"It starts with something simple," said Lynch, "a scheme to derail the new orders. If that works, the plan stops there."

Gasps and laughter filled the room as Mercer described going from a guaranteed court-martial to being decorated by the admiralty for his bravery and calm under intense pressure.

"If that doesn't work, the second phase involves actions of much higher consequence." He needed to be careful with his next words. He didn't know Grey at all and was relying on his gut in trusting the man not to turn him in, especially for what he was about to say. "You might imagine those actions leaving us in need of a new captain."

At the front of the room Stephens wrapped up his remarks and handed the floor to Holbrook, who stepped to the podium and launched into a short speech about Mercer. Ensign Mercer, standing nearby and facing the crowd, blushed slightly as the captain praised his performance over the past year.

Twenty seconds had passed and still Grey offered no response to Lynch's last comment. Had Grey heard him? He'd heard everything else. Grey certainly heard him speaking, certainly would've asked him to repeat it if he couldn't make out the words. Lynch's stomach sank—he'd made a huge mistake mentioning his plan.

The room erupted in applause.

The sudden rush of sound jolted Lynch out of his thoughts. At the front of the mess hall, Holbrook pinned lieutenant's bars on Mercer's uniform collar.

"Go on," said Grey through the hoots and claps.

Lynch exhaled and wiped away the nervous beads of sweat that had spread across his upper lip. "About that second phase … if it happens, I can't run a ship by myself. I would need some help."

Lieutenant Mercer beamed at the front of the room to a fresh round of applause.

"You're lookin' fer people you can trust," said Grey, "people who can 'elp out in that situation."

"Exactly," said Lynch.

Grey thought for a moment. "Besides me, I know of two other chaps who'd prolly be interested."

"Now it's time for refreshments and promotion cake," said Stephens. The crowd pressed towards the front of the room.

"Reach out to your friends," said Lynch, "but remember to be discreet. I'll be in touch to find out how it went."

Standing there in the head, Lynch glared at his disheveled fellow colluder through the dim light. Grey stood average height, skinny, with salt-and-pepper hair, sunken cheeks, a stippling of gray stubble, and dark circles under his eyes. Drooped shoulders topped his lean frame. Lynch didn't like Grey openly talking about mutiny, or the idea being anywhere in the front of his mind. One slip-up from him or his buddies would get them all thrown in the brig.

"I've got one more idea for someone else to join us," said Grey. "Another of my mates. But this one's delicate. I 'ave to broach the topic carefully."

"Five is a good number if you think he can be trusted," said Lynch. "But let's not invite any more than that."

Grey folded his arms. "Now that I've come through on the muscle you'll need —"

"If I need it."

Grey huffed at Lynch cutting him off. "So far all you've done is talked generalities," he said. "Now I want to 'ear the details of your plan."

Lynch didn't care for Grey's tone but understood his interest. "The first part is simple," he said. "I plan to tell the captain we can't make it to Plana Petram in three weeks. With any luck that'll be the end of it right there."

Four specks of lint stood out on Lynch's left uniform sleeve. He pinched each one in turn between his pudgy fingers and lifted it away. When he finished, he swept his round palm flat across the fabric, smoothing it over his bicep.

"Do you think he'll buy it?"

"It's certainly not a lie," said Lynch. "Engaging the Gravity Drive for three weeks straight is risky business, even on a vessel a tenth as old as the *Avenger*. Holbrook may be a good little solider who likes to follow orders, but he's never been keen on putting his ship in danger."

Grey tried a new tactic to avoid the room's smell, inserting his index and middle fingers into his nostrils. "And if that doesn't work, then in phase two —"

"I prefer to see how this first part plays out before diving into what comes after," said Lynch. The commander wasn't eager to think about the more aggressive portion of his plan, hoping the initial stage would suffice. Asking what would happen if the first effort failed felt like assuming the worst. "But don't worry, I'll brief you fully before we move into phase two. I'll also need to brief your friends so they're prepared."

"But for what yer callin' phase two," said Grey, pressing on, "seems like that means dumpin' 'olbrook, and prolly Stephens too —"

"Phase one alone could be enough to end their careers."

Grey scrunched his nose at the interruptions. "But in phase two, if you'll let me finish, if we end up there and there's no more 'olbrook and no more Stephens, that'd mean you'd be the acting captain?"

"That's correct," said Lynch. "I should've had my own ship by now anyway."

"You prolly would if you'd passed the captains test," said Grey. "Scuttlebutt has it you failed twice." A look of concern came over his face. "Could you actually captain this ship?"

The corners of Lynch's mouth turned down. "I aced the technical portion of the exam both times. It was the subjective parts they failed me on, where they presume to judge your temperament and leadership abilities."

"Uh-huh," said Grey, pursing his lips sideways. The command aptitude portion of the Rank Advancement Exam: Captain, known as the "captains test," was a crucial element of the assessment, more important than the knowledge-based sections. Anyone scoring poorly on command aptitude was not fit to captain a vessel.

"I was a few points over the cutoff on my second try," said Lynch. "They failed me anyway, thanks to Holbrook and Stephens."

"What'd they have to do with it?" asked Grey.

Lynch glared. "They always check with your commanding officers, even if you score a hundred percent. A good word from either Holbrook or Stephens would've been enough for me to pass. Whatever they said caused me to fail again. Holbrook and Stephens judged me and found me wanting. So here I sit, a commander aboard this vessel, still pressed down under their thumbs."

"Making captain's not the end-all," Grey offered. "You 'ave a pretty good gig right now, department 'ead aboard a starship."

Lynch simmered. Not the end-all? Choice words from an all but washed-up officer. Grey, recently reaching forty-five, had long since been passed over for promotion. The more Lynch had learned about the lieutenant in recent days, the less impressed he'd become of the man. Grey was no genius, though Lynch thought the same of half the officers aboard the *Avenger*. Luckily, he wasn't looking for geniuses—he just needed men smart enough to carry out orders without totally screwing them up. And to keep their mouths shut.

"And you've got that hot piece of tail Jiménez reporting to you," said Grey. The lieutenant would celebrate his good fortune whenever he found himself walking behind Jiménez in the corridors. He would disregard his original destination and follow her around, eyes glued to her full hips and rear as he imagined slipping his hand between her legs from behind.

"Jiménez is a supreme pain in the ass," said Lynch, disgusted. "She's been here four months and already acts like she runs the place. She'd be more than happy to show you up in your job." The ensign's arrival had made Lynch's work life much less enjoyable, no longer able to simply skate by. "If I could get rid of her, I would gladly hand her to you."

"I'd love to take 'er," said Grey under his breath.

"This ship will not arrive at Sag A Star," Lynch declared. "I refuse to die at the center of the galaxy, and if our efforts take down Holbrook and Stephens, so much the better." The chief engineer checked his comm. "I need to get back to my post," he said and headed towards the stalls. He pulled one of the doors open and kicked the toilet handle, the bowl flushing as he backed out. He released the door and opened the one to the adjacent stall. "Hop in here," he said to Grey.

Grey didn't move.

"We don't want the ship or anyone else seeing us come out of here at the same time," said Lynch to Grey's hesitation. "Get inside, wait a couple minutes, then flush and head out."

Harboring a grim look, Grey meandered into the stall.

Lynch released the door and walked to the exit. He tugged the black puck from the door frame, then jammed the device into his pants pocket, tamping it down as best he could in the limited space.

The door to the men's head opened. Lynch quickly peeked up and down the corridor before walking out into the passageway. He left Head C-22-M, whistling an old tune from his days at the Academy.

5

"My name is Commander Paul Stephens. I'm the executive officer on the *Avenger*."

Commander Stephens stood in his crisp service khakis at the front of the small conference room, his legs comfortably apart and his hands clasped behind his back. He surveyed the three young faces staring back at him. The new officers arrived with strong letters of recommendation from their academy professors and advisors. All three were near the top of their class, all more than capable of fulfilling their initial duties aboard the ship. But they were green. Very green.

"Lieutenant Commander Phillips has given you a tour of the ship, shown you your quarters, and introduced you to your mentors. Your time with me will be a bit different. I'm going to administer something I call the S-A-T: the Stephens Aptitude Test." He nodded to the center of the conference room table. "Each of you grab an e-sheet and a stylus."

None of the new officers moved. They had expected a day of introductions and events and gentle acclimation to their new roles aboard the *Avenger*. They had not expected a test. Ensign Forster, familiar with the customs and traditions of military life through her grandfather who had also served, suspected the onset of a prank to initiate the newbs. She refused to be the first to fall for the trick.

Stephens gave no hint his request was anything but serious. He stood at ease at the front of the room, waiting for the young officers to comply with his instructions.

Ensign Jiménez moved first, reaching her hand into the center and pulling an e-sheet back across the table with a stylus riding atop it. Ensign Washburn followed, half-standing from his chair at the far end of the oblong table to stretch for the materials.

Ensign Forster remained resolute but with all eyes suddenly trained on her, the room began to press in, and after a few seconds she found it difficult to breathe. She forced herself to move, lurching forward in her chair and reaching across the table to grab the last stylus and sheet. She dragged them slowly back towards her.

"This test consists of a single question," said Stephens. "Once I ask it, you'll have ninety seconds to work out your answer and to write it down. At the end of that time, we'll go over what you've come up with."

Ensign Forster's hand rose, her arm a perfectly straight continuation of her rigid, upright posture. Based on her file, Stephens pegged her as a high-performing Type A personality who likely excelled on exams through relentless preparation and innumerable hours of study. The announcement of a surprise test had probably rattled her, as an exam with no advance notice would leave her own performance too much to chance. "Yes, Ensign," said Stephens.

"What is the purpose of this test?" she asked, her voice laden with annoyance. "Sir," she quickly added to soften her tone.

Stephens smiled. "The purpose of this test, Ensign, is to assess your aptitude."

Forster's eyes went glassy as she processed his presumed earnest response. Once she fully grasped the depth of his non-answer she frowned and titled her head, then followed up with a question that got at the meat of her concern. "What will happen if we do poorly on this test?"

"Nothing will happen, Ensign," said Stephens. He gave them all a reassuring smile, the others likely sharing the same apprehension. "None of you need worry about this test. It's something I give to all incoming officers, and your score is of no real consequence. It won't appear on your record, and the results won't be recorded anywhere except up here," he said, tapping the side of his head.

Ensign Forster raised her hand a second time.

It was Stephens's turn to be annoyed. "Let's move on from questions," he said, squinting at her. "As I mentioned, the results of this test won't get saved anywhere or affect your record."

"But we haven't had any time to prepare," said Forster. Though she presented an air of controlled calm the fingers of her left hand gripped her thigh, digging into the fabric and muscle.

"This is an impromptu test, Ensign," said Stephens. "It's designed to assess your skills in the moment. It's not meant to be prepared for."

Ensign Forster moved to speak, but Commander Stephens cut her off. "We've spent almost more time talking about the test than you'll spend taking the goddamn thing," he said. "Let's just get to it." The ensign folded her arms and sat back in her chair with a sour look.

"Here's the question. We've arrived at a star outpost with a supply of life-saving medicine. This medicine sits in crates in the cargo hold. These were some of the first crates we took on board, and as a result they're currently difficult to get to, pinned behind stacks of other cargo.

"We have a one-hour deadline to get all the medicine off the ship. Luckily the cargo bot says it'll take exactly that long for it to get the medicine out of the hold and into the shuttles.

"The captain has invited the outpost's two-star admiral to dinner. She arrives in an hour, and they'll be dining in the captain's mess. The captain always entertains superior officers using the ship's fine china. The china is also in the cargo hold, and the cargo bot says getting it out will take thirty minutes beyond the time to get the medicine.

"I've assigned you the task of getting the medicine onto the shuttles before the deadline, and the task of retrieving the china in time for the captain's dinner. What do you do?"

Ensign Forster immediately raised her hand. "Sir, may I ask a question?"

"No more questions, Ensign," said Stephens. "Just start working out your answer."

"But it's a clarifying question, sir."

"Then do your best without clarification." Stephens tapped his comm. "The ninety seconds start now," he said before Ensign Forster could protest.

Stephens sat on the end of the conference room table and observed the three young officers. Jiménez and Washburn, working through their solutions, shifted their gaze between the tabletop and the deck above. Ensign Forster sat stone-faced, staring at the opposing bulkhead.

Stephens's comm chimed. "Forty-five seconds," he said.

Jiménez had started scribbling on her sheet prior to the chime. Washburn began writing, stopped to think, wrote again, paused, then wrote more. He finished first, followed shortly after by Jiménez. She laid her stylus down just before Stephens's comm chimed a second time.

"Time's up," said the commander and stood from the table. "We're going to go around the room and listen to everybody's answer. Part of why I wanted you to write down your answers was to make sure you didn't get inspired by someone else's solution and incorporate it into your own. In that light, let's begin with Ensign Forster, who has nothing on her sheet." He stepped towards the ensign, stopping in front of her. "What's your answer, Ensign?"

Ensign Forester looked up at the commander. "I didn't write anything, sir, because I had a clarifying question I needed answered before I could proceed."

Stephens hid his irritation behind a smile. "What was your clarifying question?"

"Sir, the question you asked was about moving cargo but I'm a communications officer. I won't be working in the cargo hold where I'm guessing these other two ensigns are assigned," she said, waving a dismissive hand at Jiménez and Washburn while avoiding their eyes. "I tried bringing this to your attention so I could get a question appropriate for my actual role aboard the ship." She punctuated her explanation with an expression that hinted at defiant smugness.

"Ensign," said Stephens, "as the ship's XO I'm aware of every crew member assignment on this ship. That goes for all the newbs too. You are in communications, Jiménez in engineering, Washburn in ship's ops. Not one of you is a deck officer assigned to the cargo hold."

Forster frowned again. "But why ask us a question that has no relation to what we'll be doing aboard the ship?"

"Don't be so sure you know exactly what you'll be doing aboard this vessel." Stunned, Ensign Forster could only gape as Stephens moved on. "Let's hear from you," he said, pointing at Ensign Washburn. "What's your solution?"

"Well sir, the most important thing is getting the medicine to the star outpost. Given the cargo bot has no extra time for anything else, I would have it focus on completing that job."

Stephens stared blankly at Washburn for several seconds. "What about the china for the dinner?" he asked in a soft voice.

Washburn gave Stephens a nervous smile, unsure if the commander genuinely wanted an answer. "It's ... it would still be in the cargo hold, sir. I guess I would explain to the admiral that our china was in storage and our cargo bot was too busy getting the medical supplies to the shuttles to retrieve it in time for the dinner."

Stephens's brows narrowed. "What makes you think you'd be anywhere near the admiral, or the dinner reception, to explain anything, Ensign?"

Ensign Washburn's smile faded. He went over the question again in his head. The part about the dinner had to be a trick. People would die if the medicine didn't get off the ship. He'd chosen the only correct course of action, yet the commander seemed serious in his continued focus on the china.

"The captain would be the one hosting the admiral," Stephens said, moving past Forster to stand closer to Washburn, "and he'd be pretty embarrassed by the less-than-stellar impression he'd be making with the banged-up, everyday crew plates. I'd be at that dinner, and the second the admiral excused herself to the head, the captain would pull me aside and ask what happened." Stephens stopped in front of the ensign. He folded his arms and continued speaking in a soft voice. "So you'd be talking to me, Ensign Washburn, not the admiral. It'd be me shining my comm in your face in the middle of the night, tearing the blankets off of you all snuggled into your bunk. It'd be *me* asking you why the captain's dinner got screwed up."

"Um …," Ensign Washburn stammered, "I guess I could let you know before the dinner, and you could tell the captain? Then he could explain to the admiral that the china's in the cargo hold because we had to get the medicine out."

"That, Ensign, would be worse than the captain saying nothing at all." Stephens walked back to the front of the room. "The admiral would leave here wondering just what kind of ship he was running."

Ensign Washburn looked sideways at Stephens. "I don't follow, sir."

"Think of it this way," said Stephens, pivoting at the front of the room to face the new officers and standing again at ease. "A starship captain's job is to get things done. That's why they give you a ship in the first place, because they expect any order they hand you will get carried out. You're suggesting the captain tell the admiral there was something he needed from the cargo hold of his own ship, but he wasn't able to get it. If entertaining with the crew plates is a two on the humiliation scale, that statement would be a potentially career-killing eight."

"But the cargo bot could only do one thing or the other in that hour," said Washburn, still confused.

"That's right," said Stephens. He waited for a glimmer of understanding from the ensign, but none came. "How 'bout this," he said. "What if I told you we need the medicine, but instead of china it's a cache of weapons that we need to get out of the hold or we all die? What would you do then?"

Washburn thought a moment. "In that case I'd direct the cargo bot to retrieve the weapons."

"And leave the medicine?" asked Stephens in an incredulous tone. "So all the sick people die?"

"We can only do one thing or the other."

"We need to do both!" shouted Stephens, startling the three young officers.

Ensign Washburn froze, embarrassed and still puzzled at what the correct answer could be.

With a sigh, Stephens addressed the last new officer. "Ensign Jiménez, what's your answer?"

Jiménez hesitated. "I also decided to tell the cargo bot to focus on getting the medicine to the shuttles."

Stephens sighed again. He'd given some form of his test many times, but few had passed. It wasn't about rank—even senior officers transferring to the ship usually failed—it was all about common sense. So many intelligent people unable to solve simple, real-world problems. "That doesn't leave you any time to retrieve the china for the reception," he said.

"It doesn't leave the *cargo bot* any time," Jiménez corrected. "Getting the medicine off the ship sounded super important, so I'd just let the bot handle that task. It wouldn't really need any supervision while I worked on getting the china for the dinner."

Stephens perked up, unsure he'd heard the ensign correctly. "Did you say you'd be working on getting the china?"

Jiménez didn't respond immediately, worried she'd said something inappropriate. "Yes, sir."

"How would you do that?"

"Without the cargo bot, I'd have to rely on manpower," said Jiménez. "I'd round up some antigrav grips and find as many people as I could to help me move crates out of the way to get to the china."

"What if it's your first day, like today?" Stephens asked. "What if you don't know anybody?"

"I guess I'll be making friends quick, then," said Jiménez. "I'm sure I could find ten people to help dig through the cargo hold with me."

"What if you couldn't find anyone to help you?" he pressed.

Jiménez thought for a moment. "In that case I'd contact you right away and let you know I needed help getting the china out of the cargo hold because the bot didn't have time to do it."

Stephens's tone turned skeptical. "You wouldn't just pick one or the other, the medicine or the china, like Ensign Washburn here?" Washburn shuffled in his seat and looked glumly at the table. "Washburn saw that I left him in an impossible situation with the cargo bot. Why do you think I haven't just left it to your discretion to complete the most important task?"

"That assumes you knew the bot couldn't get both things done," said Jiménez. "Maybe you didn't think the medicine and the china would take more than an hour to retrieve."

A smile crept across Stephens's face as he studied the young ensign. "Only a handful of people have ever answered the SAT correctly," he said. "You are in rare company, Ensign Jiménez."

"How is that a valid answer?" exclaimed Ensign Forster. "You didn't say we could round up people to help us."

"If I had given you that assignment in real life, I wouldn't have said it then either."

"But how were we supposed to come up with this exact answer?" asked Forster.

"The other correct answers I've gotten over the years haven't been exactly the same," said Stephens. "It's not the answer specifically but a workable solution to the problem."

Ensign Washburn raised a limp, cupped hand halfway in the air. "A problem I have with the question, sir, is it's so hypothetical," he said. "What's the point of working out a solution to a made-up situation?"

"It's not made up at all!" shouted Stephens, causing Washburn to recoil. "The first day on my first ship assignment, the XO told me to get medical supplies down to the star outpost I'd just come from and to get the china out of storage for the captain's dinner with the two-star admiral in charge of the base." Stephens shook his head. "I told him I was a new ensign in tactical and wouldn't be working in the cargo hold. Commander Suttirat told me that didn't matter. He said he needed someone to get that stuff out of the cargo hold and I was the person he chose, and if I didn't like it, he would shove my tactical ass out an airlock and let me float back down to the outpost. When I talked to the cargo bot, it told me it didn't have enough time to do both in the hour I was given."

"What did you do?" asked Ensign Forster.

"I followed Ensign Washburn's solution," said Stephens. "Getting the medicine out was obviously more important than finding some china for a dinner. Luckily, Commander Suttirat checked on me about twenty minutes before the admiral arrived. He had no idea both tasks couldn't be done in time. The commander asked the captain to stall the admiral for fifteen minutes while he and I and four others tore through the cargo hold for the china."

Stephens smiled at the young officers. "The important thing to take away from this exercise is to understand we're in the business of getting things done. We can't say we don't work in the cargo hold, or that we had to choose one task over another. We're expected to complete all the tasks we're given, whatever they may be. Always." Stephens checked his comm. "I believe you're all due in the crew lounge on Deck B for the captain's welcome reception. I'll be there as well, but I have to attend to a couple things first. Ensigns Forster and Washburn, you are dismissed."

The two ensigns stood from the table and filed out of the room. Both snuck a glance at Jiménez before they left.

The doors closed, leaving Stephens and Jiménez alone in the conference room. "That was impressive," said Stephens. "Not many newbs have learned to think, much less feel they have the agency to do what they believe is right."

"Thank you, sir," she said sheepishly.

"I want you to keep up that kind of thinking, Ensign. Question things if they don't seem right. Explore unconventional solutions. If that ever gets you in a jam with a senior officer, come talk to me. I'll take care of it." Stephens checked his comm again. "Now I've got some tasks to attend to and you've got a party to get to. See you in a few minutes."

"Yes, sir," said Jiménez, the young ensign standing as Commander Stephens dashed from the conference room.

6

Insubordination.

"Jiménez!" bellowed Commander Lynch. "Let's go!"

"One second, sir."

Lynch glanced at his comm. "We don't *have* a second, Ensign."

Ensign Jiménez tapped frantically at her terminal.

"Holbrook has a thing about meetings starting on time," said Lynch as he followed the young ensign's darting fingers. "Do you even know where the Orion Conference Room is?"

"Yes, I do, sir," said Ensign Jiménez, responding without looking up from her terminal as she continued her feverish tapping. "I'm trying to set some simulations running before we leave. I'll be able to check the results during the meeting."

Insubordination, seethed Lynch. Most officers under him would trip over themselves to comply with any command he barked their way, but not Jiménez. No amount of yelling or threats seemed to faze her. "There's no point to whatever stupid simulation you're arranging," he groused. The chief engineer moved his large frame into intention range of the exit, triggering the department doors open. "They're just that: simulations. They don't count for a crock of shit in the real world."

Ensign Jiménez continued tapping at her terminal.

What the hell is she simulating anyway? Lynch had no idea, didn't really care, and in any case had no time to ask. Besides, her answer was likely to set him off on a tirade that would redden his nose and cheeks, giving his face a clown-like appearance—not a good look just before stepping into a meeting with the entire senior staff.

Lynch opened his mouth to yell anew but caught himself before he made a sound. If he left Ensign Jiménez alone to continue her efforts, she would surely arrive late to the captain's weekly staff meeting, knocking her down a peg in Holbrook's eyes. Paired with a reprimand for her pursuit of a side project while on duty, he might have enough to lay the groundwork for ousting her from the engineering department. Without another word, the chief engineer slinked through the open door and whisked down the corridor.

Jiménez hated that Lynch was annoyed but was grateful for the quiet to finish bootstrapping her simulations. The ship had affirmed her memory of the Orion Conference Room's location, directly beneath engineering on the next deck down. It had offered directions as well: proceed left from engineering for fifty meters; turn left again and walk another fifty meters to Pneumatic Cab Access A-8-23; ride a P-cab down to access point B-8-23, and retrace the hundred meters to the conference room's door.

Although logical and straightforward, following the ship's recommended route would make her woefully late for the meeting. Besides the time to walk two hundred meters through the *Avenger*, waits for P-cabs ranged from thirty seconds to several minutes during peak demand, not to mention the cab travel time itself. With just over six minutes left before the meeting, a late arrival was essentially guaranteed.

Jiménez continued to work, allowing another forty-five seconds before she'd force herself to leave. Despite the handful of minutes remaining, she had no intention of arriving late. Rather than heading left to grab a P-cab, she would exit right and jog thirty meters to Rungway 42-AC. Most rungways afforded access to each of the ship's three decks but that one ran between the ship's top and bottom decks, bypassing her destination. She would take Rungway 42-AC down to Deck C, dash left for three meters to Rungway 41-BC, clamber up to the middle deck, and backtrack the twenty-seven meters to the conference room. The 140-meter difference and zero time spent waiting for a P-cab would allow her to arrive in ninety seconds tops.

Her configurations finished, Jiménez set her simulations running. After arranging for their completion notifications to arrive silently at her comm, she sprang from her chair and rushed out of engineering.

- - -

Lynch fumed as he approached the Orion Conference Room. Between the corridor foot traffic, the two-minute wait for a cab, and his cab's meanderings through the ship, he was officially late. He pushed his body to keep up his modest pace. Every second counted when it came to Holbrook's irritation level for tardy arrivals. He'd pin the blame on Jiménez, setting her up for a double dose of the captain's ire whenever she finally did arrive.

The chief engineer trundled down the passageway, stood still before the conference room entrance until the doors opened, and walked in, slightly winded. He slipped into an empty chair not far from the doors. The captain, seated at the opposite end of the long conference table, continued his succession of general announcements, including one about improper sleep cycles. Relieved at entering unnoticed, Lynch focused on moving himself closer to the table with successive scoots of his chair.

"Good of you to join us, Commander," said Captain Holbrook. No heads turned, but all attention shifted to the chief engineer. A conversation with the captain was like a magnifying glass, focusing the entire room on a single person.

Lynch stopped mid-scoot, his right hand thrust between his legs, grasping the front of his chair. "Apologies for being late, Captain," he said slightly flustered, "but it was Ensign Jiménez who delayed me in engineering. I spent several minutes trying to convince her to leave so we'd arrive on time for your staff meeting. I finally gave up, but by then there wasn't enough time left for me not to be late."

"She was in engineering when you left her?" Holbrook asked, cocking his head slightly.

"Yes, sir," said Lynch, offering a stern expression of concern that masked his glee at the chance to dig the ensign's hole a little deeper. "I kept reminding her how much you hate late arrivals, but she ignored me. She tapped away at her terminal the whole time I was standing there, even as I left. Whatever she was working on, it wasn't any assignment *I* had given her." The chief engineer shook his head slowly, reinforcing his disappointment with Jiménez's behavior. "I expect she'll be along any moment now."

Holbrook's brows lifted. "Indeed," he said, eliciting chuckles from around the table.

With a sheepish grin, Lynch joined the others in the jest, unsure of the joke but pleased at having made trouble for the ensign. He finished scooting his chair to the table and scanned the room. At the far end, two seats down on the captain's right, sat Ensign Jiménez, her head lowered and eyes burrowed into the table. The chief engineer's face puffed red.

"Now that we're all here, let's get started," said Holbrook. "The report from engineering will come last—Commander Lynch informed me he has a serious issue to discuss and I'm guessing it'll consume the bulk of our time. We'll begin with the medical department."

Dr. Marsden tapped controls rendered beneath the table's glass surface, summoning a holographic spreadsheet above the table's center. "I have three crew members in Sickbay currently. One is recovering from alien food poisoning. One has a second-degree radiation burn. He'll be there for a few days for tissue regeneration and cancer cell flushing. The third is a broken arm, which Dr. Sadler set two days ago, but the crewman returned this morning with a fever. We're treating him for an infection."

"That's the tally of physical ailments." The doctor swiped in a new slide, showing a much longer list of patients. "As for the crew's mental health, in the past thirty-six hours we've seen thirteen cases of acute stress disorder, seven cases of depression, three panic attacks, and one case of hysteria."

"Ensign Orr?" asked Stephens.

Lynch smirked. *Orr is always overdramatic, working himself up about the smallest of things.*

"Correct," said Dr. Marsden. "We have him resting in his quarters." She tapped the controls, closing her presentation. "That's twenty-five cases of mental distress since word of our mission got out. I expect we'll see a lot more of these during our trip."

"Thank you, Doctor," said Holbrook. "Communications."

"Comms systems green," said Lieutenant Bhat. The communications chief ran his hand through his cropped hair.

Flustered as usual. Lynch had witnessed the lieutenant's nervous mannerism many times before, always struck by the vivid contrast between Bhat's mostly gray strands and his medium-brown skin.

"There have been a number of security-related communications incidents," continued Bhat, "but I defer to Lieutenant Byrne's report for discussion."

"Very well," said Holbrook. "Security."

"Security status green," said Lieutenant Byrne. The security chief's freckles, dimples, and full lips gave him a boyish appearance. "No active security incidents to report. As Lieutenant Bhat mentioned, there were seventeen instances of mission details being discussed in private off-ship conversations and messages. The message scrubbers caught and blocked all leaked details, though we should consider locking down off-ship communications. A lot of people and alien governments would be interested to learn we're traveling to the galactic center."

"I recommend against it, Captain," said Dr. Marsden, her expression stern.

Disregard her opinion at your own peril. Lynch had tangled with the *Avenger's* chief medical officer before. The doctor's short stature belied her outsize presence, her viewpoints forcefully presented and remarks to the point.

"I'm no psychologist, but the crew is already taking this assignment hard. Preventing them—us—from communicating with their loved ones will only demoralize them further and may solidify the perception that we're actually on a suicide mission."

"I agree with the doctor," said Stephens. "I'd prefer we issue some warnings about not discussing mission-confidential details when speaking with people off-ship and see how we do."

"All right, then, let's leave communications where they are for now. But we may revisit this decision should circumstances change." The captain turned to Lieutenant Commander Martin Phillips. "Ops," he said.

"Ship's operations green," said Phillips. "However, I'd like to schedule some drills over the next few weeks to make sure we stay sharp on this trip."

Readiness drills—a colossal waste of time. But he has to make it seem like he actually does something aboard this vessel.

"Agreed," said Holbrook. For an instant Lynch thought the captain had agreed with his mental assessment of Phillips and the readiness drills. He nearly fell out of his chair. "Please coordinate the drills with Commander Stephens." He continued with Ensign Jeremy Higgins. "Combat systems and tactical."

"All weapons and targeting systems are green," said Higgins.

"Science department," said Holbrook.

"Science department green," said Ensign Reilly.

"Nav —"

"Though I will say we're not at all prepared for this mission," interrupted Reilly.

Bravo—another joust with the captain. The young officer and youngest department head was not much older than most cadets fresh out of the Academy. In spite of her age, Ensign Reilly was full of aplomb, and a brilliant scientist with advanced degrees in biology, chemistry, and physics. Her interjections never failed to catch the captain off guard.

"Please continue, Ensign," said Holbrook.

"Normally I'd have my team learning more about the planet or system we're sailing to, researching physical conditions and life forms, but as long as we don't know what our actual mission is the science department has no way to prepare for it."

"Acknowledged, Ensign," said Holbrook. "That information will be forthcoming." The captain moved on. "Navigation."

"Navigation systems green," said Ensign Doerr. "I've spent some time with the ship refining our course to Plana Petram. I've computed a new trajectory that's slightly less direct but swings us closer to several massive stars on the topside of the galactic disc. It'll give us enough of a boost in speed to shave a day off the trip."

"A four percent reduction in total travel time?" Lynch grumbled from his end of the table. "That's like trimming a few millimeters off those red bangs of yours and gushing about a new haircut." *Find something else to do, Ensign, that isn't speeding us to our graves.*

"I agree it's not much," said Doerr, stammering after the pointed rebuke by a senior officer, "but … it is some savings. I figured getting th-there as fast as possible was worthwhile, even by a little bit." The ensign sank into her chair.

"Some time savings, even if small, is a good thing," said Stephens. "Thank you, Ensign, for your efforts."

Ensign Doerr nodded, staring with a glum look into the table.

"Helm."

"Helm green sir," said Lieutenant Commander Mills. "The ship is on track to reach Plana Petram in approximately nineteen days. Ensign Doerr mentioned her new course to me right before the meeting, and I plan to lay it in after conferring with her."

"Very good," said Holbrook. The captain looked down the table to Commander Lynch. "Engineering."

Finally. Lynch filled the room with a grandiose clearing of his throat. "Engineering condition red." He paused, letting the words sink in, then sat forward in his chair and mashed at the tabletop's virtual controls. After several corrections and restarts from fat-fingering neighboring buttons, a list of engineering systems, each one annotated with a green dot, emerged above the table. "The ship's power plant is hovering at ninety-eight percent efficiency. The Gravity Drive is operational and performing as expected. Core ship systems are functioning within tolerances. Hull integrity and ship superstructure are both sound." He clasped his hands on the table and sat quietly, almost beaming.

Holbrook waited, expecting Lynch to continue, but the commander remained silent. "You reported engineering condition red," the captain eventually said, "but nothing of what I've heard so far sounds like a problem."

"Yes, sir," said Lynch, appreciative of Holbrook leading him into the next part of his presentation, "the operational status of all engineering systems at this moment is green. It's the *future* I'm concerned about." Lynch swiped his holographic slide deck to a view of the *Avenger's* underbelly with callouts to three large, glowing red discs nestled in the rounded vertices of the black, triangular warship. "The Gravity Drive consists of three gravity field generators that work in concert to create a bubble of warped spacetime around the ship. The exact shape of this warp bubble determines our direction and speed relative to the spacetime outside the bubble."

His next slide contained a topside view of the triangular *Avenger,* showing three overlapping toroidal spheres resembling transparent, electric red donuts centered at the field generators. "Here is a diagram of the warp fields produced by the three generators and how they overlap to form the ship's warp bubble. Changing any one of the fields results in a different composite bubble and therefore different direction and speed. Travel to a specific destination requires balancing the three field generators to an exquisite degree. An imbalance of even one part in a trillion over time can drive us light-years off in the wrong direction."

"Everyone here knows the basics of gravitational propulsion," said Stephens, his tone gruff. "Is there a reason for the refresher?"

Lynch gave Stephens a cold stare. *There's a reason behind everything I do, executive idiot.* "With that background," Lynch continued, still staring at Stephens as he drew out the last word, "I turn now to our current situation, a predicament directly related to our mission. First, we plan to engage the Gravity Drive non-stop for three weeks to reach Plana Petram, and then presumably for a subsequent two weeks of travel to the galactic core." The commander swiped to a slide showing the exponential decline in engine efficiency with the decrease in matter density per cubic light-year. "Second, more than half of that operating time will occur in a region of space where the matter density is much lower than the galactic planar mean, forcing the engines to work harder to generate a warp field."

Commander Lynch ended his presentation with a flourished, bouncing tap on the tabletop that closed his slides. "The inefficiencies of operating in low-density space combined with the prolonged use of the Gravity Drive will put an enormous strain on the field generators, pushing them beyond their safe operational limits. Losing a generator would be a catastrophic event, destroying up to a third of the ship and killing an untold number of the crew." Lynch had gestured with his hands during the presentation—he brought them to rest, clasped again on the table. "The *Avenger* is a Trident class starship, commissioned over thirty years ago. It could have easily operated within these mission parameters right out of dry dock, but not thirty years on, sixteen years since its last complete overhaul. It is my determination as this ship's chief engineer that the *Avenger* cannot continue with its orders as currently executed."

No one stirred after Lynch's final word. The lieutenant commander basked in the consternation he had created.

"Cannot continue with our orders as currently executed?" yelled Holbrook, causing those closest to him to jump in their seats. "What in Hades does that mean?"

Lynch kept calm in the face of the captain's heated reproach, his plan proceeding as designed. "It means we cannot travel to Plana Petram within the three-week timeframe you've set for us. By my calculations we will need at least twice that amount of time."

Holbrook huffed, incredulous. "Six weeks to reach Plana Petram?"

"At *least* six weeks, Captain," said Lynch. "Even that pushes the limits of what I consider reasonable."

"Why is this information only coming to me now?" asked Holbrook, the anger building in his voice.

Lynch deadpanned, "This is the first Captain's Staff since we set course for Plana Petram. It's the first chance we've had to discuss the matter."

"But in the meantime, we've informed CentCom of our three-week ETA," said Commander Stephens. "They're expecting us to arrive in nineteen days."

"Is that true?" asked Lynch. *Please say those words again—I want to savor each one.*

"Yes," said Holbrook. "Commodore Ahrens will be at Plana Petram to brief us on the full mission details. He's already en route in a sleeper, set to arrive about eighteen days from now. He can't wake to find we're only halfway there. And the mission itself, whatever it is, cannot absorb a three- or four-week delay. The urgency of the situation has been stressed to me several times. At this late date we can't just tell CentCom, 'sorry, we made a mistake; it's going to take twice the time we said.' We have to be at Plana Petram when we promised we would."

We made a mistake? I didn't promise three weeks. Pursing his thick lips Lynch nodded and said, "Thank you for explaining the situation, Captain. I had not previously understood that CentCom was basing their timetables on our original projections. I see how six weeks of travel time is not an acceptable outcome."

The captain's entire frame had stiffened at the suggestion they push out their arrival date, a disaster of immense proportions. Holbrook visibly relaxed with Lynch's response, likely believing his chief engineer was considering creative alternatives.

The corners of Lynch's mouth curved upwards. "Unfortunately, I cannot change physics. The near certainty of catastrophic damage to this vessel is real. The *Avenger* will not survive the stresses of a forced three-week journey to Plana Petram, and I will not be held responsible if you decide to try." His eyes grew wide and lips almost pouty, reflecting the feigned heavy heart bringing him to his next words. "If CentCom is indeed counting on us arriving in nineteen days," he said, holding the moment in the air, "then we must immediately inform them it simply won't be possible and petition for reassignment from this mission."

An avalanche of anxious conversations flooded the room as Holbrook and Stephens sat with pained faces at the opposite end of the table, shellshocked by Lynch's pronouncement. Petitioning for reassignment was an action reserved for only the most desperate circumstances. Short of a medical or equipment emergency, it typically mandated the loss of command for the vessel's captain.

Lynch stifled a grin as he eased back in his chair. He grew excited at the prospect of torpedoing Holbrook's career, the *Avenger's* smug and pompous star captain, and possibly even Stephens's as well. When they came for Holbrook, the crew would line the corridors of the *Avenger*—Lynch himself standing outside the doors to engineering—as the military guards escorted the disgraced captain to the shuttle bay, a last march through his soon-to-be former ship —

"I think there's a way."

Lynch chuckled at the words, believing them the product of some comedic portion of his mind. He stopped when the room grew hushed.

"What was that, Ensign?" asked Holbrook.

"I think there's a way," said Ensign Jiménez. "To get to Plana Petram in nineteen days. Or nearly nineteen."

Lynch studied Jiménez from his end of the table. He had no idea what kind of stunt she was pulling but granted that the ensign was sharp, not to be underestimated. He needed to head her off before she could speak another word. "Ensign Jiménez," he said in a calm, patronizing voice, "this is a meeting of the ship's department heads. Your attendance here is solely to assist me, the engineering chief, in presenting information to the captain and the rest of his senior staff. It is not to ask questions or to offer your own opinions."

"I'm sure the ensign knows her role in this meeting," said Commander Stephens. "What she has to say must be significant for her to break protocol."

I hope to God my plan takes you down with Holbrook, you condescending prick.

"Ensign Jiménez," said Holbrook, "what were you starting to say?"

Lynch bore down on the young officer from across the table with an expression that conveyed the volcanic anger he would unleash should she say anything further. She paused a moment before replying to Holbrook. "It's nothing, sir," she said. "Commander Lynch is right—it's not my place to speak in this meeting. I should first discuss my findings with him to get his opinion."

Findings? Everything came to Lynch in a rush: the special side project, the simulations, the scramble to assemble results for the meeting. Jiménez was also aware of the infeasibility of a three-week trip to Plana Petram, but instead of allowing that fact to simply and elegantly disqualify them from the mission she had been researching ways to surmount it!

"What findings, Ensign?" asked Stephens.

Reviewing the ensign's data before she described any of it would be Lynch's only hope of defeating whatever idea she had come up with.

"I've been running some simulations of a technique to reduce the strain on the Gravity Drive —"

"Captain, I need to vet the ensign's findings before they're presented in this meeting," interrupted Lynch. "I am responsible for all recommended or suggested courses of action, no matter how improbable, that come out of engineering. While I was aware of Ensign Jiménez's attempt to find solutions to our quandary, I did not have sufficient time before this meeting to review her methodology or her data. Once we adjourn, I will confer with the ensign and, if warranted, have her —"

"What were your findings, Ensign?" the captain asked.

"Sir," said Jiménez. She glanced at Lynch one more time before forging ahead. "Commander Lynch is correct that traveling for so long in low mass density space will place a big strain on the engines. The problem comes from maintaining a near-constant field strength for three weeks, so I wondered, what if we could somehow let the engines rest a bit during the journey." She tapped the controls on the tabletop in front of her, summoning a slide with columns of numbers. "I designed a simulation of the *Avenger* traveling to Plana Petram where we vary the amount of time we keep the Gravity Drive engaged. This is the data from twenty different runs of the simulation."

Holbrook blinked at the sprawling matrix of numbers. "Can you walk us through what we're looking at here?" he asked.

"Yes, sir," said Jiménez with quaking hands, her first time speaking up in a Captain's Staff. "Each row is a day of travel time, and each number is the estimated system integrity level at the end of that day. This first column shows what happens if we continue as we are now, keeping the warp field strength constant for the next nineteen days. You can see how starting at day ten the numbers turn from yellow to orange and eventually fall into the red. This is the situation Commander Lynch has raised.

"The other columns contain data for different engine duty cycles. For example, the fourth column shows a ninety-five five duty cycle—the engines engaged for fifty-seven seconds out of every minute. Even with that slight change, all the system integrity levels stay out of the red."

"You're talking about pulsing the Gravity Drive," said Stephens.

"That's essentially the idea," she said.

"Interesting," said Stephens. "Am I right in reading the final column to say at a fifty-fifty duty cycle system integrity remains green for the entire trip, but it'll take us twice as long to get there?"

"That's right, sir," said Jiménez. "That's the tradeoff with giving the field generators more and more time to rest—they do less work, so the ship doesn't move as fast. This is essentially the same as Commander Lynch's request to take six weeks to reach Plana Petram."

"It seems like the eighty-seven thirteen run is the most promising," said Holbrook.

"Yes sir. By engaging the engines for fifty-two seconds out of every minute we can reduce the strain on the Gravity Drive and stay out of the yellow except at the very end, and increase our travel time by only two and a half days."

"Just one and a half with Ensign Doerr's route optimizations," said Stephens.

"This seems promising," said Holbrook as he reviewed the numbers. "Commander Lynch, what's your opinion?"

Concealing his rage as best he could, Lynch spoke in measured tones. "As I said earlier, I have had no time, Captain, to review these numbers or Ensign Jiménez's simulation for correctness. So it would be —"

"I understand that, Commander," said Holbrook. "I'm asking if the ensign's idea seems sound, if her conclusion seems plausible."

How best to respond while salvaging his plan? If he said her idea couldn't work, any review by the ship's computer would expose that as a lie. Yet confirming her approach meant keeping their assignment and flying to their deaths at the galactic core. "It seems reasonable that changing the duty cycle would reduce the strain on the Gravity Drive, and in fact I had planned to investigate that option myself," he said, his speech still measured and rigid. "However, while the pulsing, as you put it, Commander Stephens, will lighten the load on the field generators, it will more than double, maybe even triple, our energy consumption compared to keeping the field generators fully energized."

"Will we run out of power?" asked Stephens.

"Err … no," said Lynch, "but consuming that much energy is obscene. Each time we disengage the field generators we'll turn around and power them right back up again."

"Obscene," said Stephens, "but not otherwise a problem?"

As much as Lynch wanted to portray energy consumption as an issue, the *Avenger's* power plant could easily drive a hundred such trips. "That is correct," said Lynch. He reached for any other possible complication. "Though the varying field strength will increase the stresses on the gravitational waveguides."

"What's the worst-case outcome of that?" asked Holbrook.

"Nothing as bad as losing a field generator," Lynch conceded, "but if we lose a waveguide, we won't be able to sail. We'll be immobile until another CentCom vessel can help us with repairs or a tow."

Holbrook rubbed his chin. "What's your opinion, Commander?" he asked, addressing his executive officer.

"This plan seems to give us the best chance of carrying out our orders," said Stephens. "At least we won't have to ask CentCom to take us off the mission."

"If a waveguide fails just before we reach Plana Petram," said Lynch, "that will turn into a three-week setback for CentCom because they'll be forced to send a new ship."

"True," said Holbrook, "but that seems like a much more manageable risk than our present situation." He turned to Jiménez. "Good work, Ensign."

"Thank you, sir," she said with a sheepish smile.

"I want Commander Lynch to review your simulation and then the two of you to work on implementing this new plan," said the captain. "It's now your top priority. Keep me apprised of your progress."

"Yes, sir," said Jiménez.

"Yes, sir," said Commander Lynch. He briefly locked eyes with Jiménez. *You've caused me to lose this battle, but the war is not over. I promise you will pay for sinking my plan.*

"Thank you, everyone," said Holbrook as he stood from the table.

The captain and the other officers filed out of the room. Just before exiting, Lynch caught Stephens lean in close to Jiménez as he passed her on his way to the door. "Nice work," he said.

Jiménez emerged last from the conference room with a smile that disappeared once she discovered Lynch waiting for her, his large hands jammed into his pockets. She walked over to him, and the two headed together down the passageway, side by side, with the chief engineer's bulk consuming most of the space between them.

Lynch spoke under his breath to Jiménez. "If you ever talk out of turn again," he said, "I will wrap my hands around your neck and strangle you until you are dead."

Jiménez could only nod. Her body began to shake.

7

Holbrook sat on the deck in his quarters, legs sprawled, back slumped against the bulkhead. His right hand held a glass, once tall with whiskey. His left hand batted drool from his chin. Tonight's bender wasn't the worst he'd ever had, but it was the worst in a long time. He dubbed it a "two" on the nullihol pill scale. If summoned for an emergency, he'd need that many pills to wick the alcohol from his system.

Holbrook shifted his weight, making himself more comfortable on the hard deck. From his mind's eye he looked down on his laid-out body, judging.

What would Dad say?

He rolled his eyes at the thought. *Dad wouldn't say anything. He's dead. Been dead a long time.*

Holding the glass to the light, Holbrook studied the remaining few centimeters of amber liquid. He took a drink, keeping the liquor in his mouth, letting it burn the insides of his cheeks. He released it in a trickle, a trail of fire down his throat.

Captain Holbrook hoisted the glass to his lips, took in the last of the whiskey, and let his arm fall to his side. The glass escaped his hand, bouncing once on the deck before rolling away.

He hadn't thought about his dad in a while. Captain Thomas Holbrook the second died when Holbrook was eight years, two months. Almost thirty years later, Holbrook could still picture him: big, strong, fearless, resolute, commanding attention and respect. The news of his dad's death hit him hard—he cried for days and wouldn't come out of his room. When he finally emerged, he refused to leave the house. He finished the school year at home, his assignments and lessons transmitted to him.

The psychologists told Holbrook's mom his anguish only partly explained his withdrawal. Fear, they said, played as large a role. Holbrook had always been a skittish child, afraid of random sounds and sudden movements. His dad had been the anchor that allowed him to function in the world, checking under his bed for monsters, lingering in his room until he fell asleep, investigating strange noises in the dead of night. One day, just before Holbrook's sixth birthday, the vicious neighbor dog five doors away escaped its force field pen, raced out of its yard, and charged down the sidewalk toward him. His dad jumped in front of the animal without hesitation, taking a bite in the leg to protect his son. His dad's strength and devotion fostered in the younger Holbrook an unconscious sense of comfort, one that extended across the light-years and between his dad's long stints away from home.

His dad's death unmoored him.

Without his dad, Thomas and the rest of his family found themselves alone in a perilous world. The monsters were real. They weren't under the bed—they fell out of the sky.

The Regenitors and their spider drop-ships burrowing like ticks kilometers into the earth's crust.

The Skaxx drones piercing the global defense grid and raining fire across several continents.

The Thetan rampage.

He'd forgotten the Thetan rampage, repressed it. The events came flooding back. Holbrook tried to shake the thoughts from his head, but his half-conscious mind pushed on, dredging his memory. He breathed fast and shallow, on the verge of hyperventilating. Black spots filled his vision. The world went dark ....

Thomas Holbrook III sat in the dark, clutching his baby brother Timmy in the far corner of the basement. His arms and legs shook not from cold but from fear. Footsteps plodded overhead, nails and floorboards squealing under tremendous weight. Muffled screams and weapons fire drifted down through closed hopper windows.

Thomas sobbed softy.

"Focus on your breath," his mom shouted in a whisper from her hiding place across the room. "Your *breath*."

Slow, deliberate breaths calmed the body and the mind, she'd told him more than once. Thomas focused on his breath, reining it in, deepening it. He drew the cool basement air into his lungs, much cooler than the air upstairs. The day had been hot for early fall.

"Thomas, did you open the upstairs windows?" his mom had called from the kitchen doorway.

Thomas walked in from the den, his vid on pause. He stood before her in a t-shirt and shorts, both garments struggling to cover his nine-year-old body on the brink of a growth spurt that would add nearly a meter to his frame. "Most of them," he said. "I opened the ones in my bedroom and the ones in yours."

"Did you open the ones in Dad's office?" she asked.

A repurposed third bedroom, his dad's office sat across from the room he shared with Timmy. He made a point of skipping that room. "Why do I have to be the one to open them?" he asked, bunching his fists.

"Your brother can't do it, Thomas," said his mom. "He's not tall enough to reach. And I have to start taking up dinner."

Thomas made no motion to comply.

"I need you to be a big boy and open those windows," she said, notching up the sternness in her voice.

"I just don't like going in there," he mustered, still not moving. "To see all Dad's stuff, everything in the same place ... it just reminds me he's never coming back."

His mom walked to him and crouched to his height. Her hazel eyes flashed a mix of his pain and some of her own. "How 'bout this," she said, "if you open the windows for me, I'll take care of closing them later this evening, before we head to bed. Deal?"

He didn't want to go in there at all, but one trip into that room was better than two. "Deal," Thomas said, sullen as he accepted the best arrangement he would get. He turned slowly and wandered up the stairs, head hunched, taking his time with each step.

"Hurry back down," she said. "It's almost dinner. And after you'll need to take out the trash. It's nearly overflowing."

Thomas didn't talk much at dinner despite his mom's attempts to draw him out. His little brother, oblivious as usual, babbled on about some new dinosaur he discovered during holo-adventure time in school.

Warm, rotting trash greeted Thomas's nostrils when he swung open the small cabinet door next to the sink. He tugged at the garbage can, sliding it out on its platform, and looped his hand through the liner's drawstrings. Thomas hoisted the plastic bag out and set it on the kitchen floor. Freed from the confines of its container, the white, overfull bag pancaked across the black and white tiles.

Thomas lifted the overloaded trash bag with both hands and backed into the screen door, nudging it open with his rear. He scurried around the house to a large black garbage bin, flipped open its lid, and tossed the bag inside.

"Shit," he said, bemoaning the patches of nighttime sky visible through the crisscrossed branches overhead. Thomas planned to survey the planets during the final moments of twilight, when they dangled like shining pearls against the starless blue-black evening sky. He'd forgotten all about them.

He bounded into his front yard and up the steps to the porch, spun around, and fixed his gaze upwards. The old trees in his neighborhood obscured large swaths of sky, but from this vantage point the heavens appeared through a ragged, round gap in the canopy.

Thomas ran through his progression, starting with the planets. Venus, Mars, and Jupiter hung in conjunction directly above him. Two degrees south the white supergiant Deneb burned its nuclear fire. His finger traced a line from Deneb through the yellow supergiant Sadr to Albireo, then a new, perpendicular line from Delta Cygni, through Sadr again, to Epsilon Cygni. Together the five stars formed the Northern Cross, the backbone of the constellation Cygnus. His dad had taught him how to find the asterism. He'd taken up tracing its shape as a way to remember him.

A shooting star peeled across the jagged circle of sky. And a second. "No way," Thomas said in amazement. The odds of witnessing a shooting star at the exact time of its fiery transit were improbably small. The odds of seeing a second —

A third shooting star streaked across the sky, then a fourth, and a fifth.

He turned back to the house. "Mom," he yelled, "you'll never believe this!"

The house lights went dark.

Not just the lights in his house, but next door in Mr. Huntsel's house, and at the Dylans' place across the street. And not just the lights in the houses but all the streetdiscs too. Shrouded in darkness, Thomas looked at his comm, or at least where his comm should have been with his left forearm raised in front of his body. Its face had also gone black. No amount of tapping brought it back to life.

Thomas looked up again. Thousands of stars twinkled in the unobscured patch of sky where there had only been a handful before. *The power has to be out across the entire prefect.* His astronomy text had described how urban light pollution overwhelmed all but the brightest stars. Now even the faintest were visible.

The shooting stars came faster, ten more before Thomas gave up counting. Some moved in straight lines, while others raced across the sky only to stop abruptly and turn at sharp angles.

Thomas froze in the engulfing darkness. He wanted to run but his legs wouldn't budge. Discordant sounds began to displace the silence that had filled the neighborhood. Several large booms rang out in the distance. Footsteps clattered beyond the front hedge. A mother called for her child. Somebody screamed. He trembled so badly his teeth chattered.

"Thomas."

The voice came from his rear. He turned. His mom stood inside the house behind the screen door, her face awash in glowing green light.

"Come inside," she said in an urgent whisper. "Hurry." He walked the remaining distance to the front screen door and pulled it open. "Don't let it slam," she said.

Thomas entered the house and eased the screen door against its frame. He reached for the front door to close it.

"Leave it," his mom whispered. "We've got to get to the basement." In one hand his mom held a chemical light stick from the emergency stash she kept under the sink. In her other she gripped his little brother's wrist.

"What's going on, Mom?" Thomas asked.

"Shh," she said. "I'll explain once we're down there." She led the boys quickly through the front room, the light stick painting the walls and furniture in luminescent green. They rounded a corner and stopped before a small door under the main staircase.

"Go on," she said, opening the door. "Take your brother's hand." She held the light stick above them as Thomas grabbed his little brother. The green light batted the darkness from the first few steps of staircase before yielding to the basement's black void below. "Head down there. I'll be right behind you. Please hold on to the railing."

Thomas nodded and took a timid step onto the stairs. He reached for the railing as the green light disappeared. "Mom!" he yelled. "Bring back the light!"

His mom's green face reappeared in the doorway. "We can't take the light down there," she said. "They might see it."

"Who —"

"You have to head down there without a light," said his mom. "Hold the railing and test each step with your foot. And move slowly. Remember, you've got your brother and he can't see either." His mom's green face disappeared again, leaving the two boys standing alone in the dark.

Thomas worked his way down the stairs at a slow pace, counting each step before blindly testing it with his foot. He gently pulled his brother along. Timmy, normally jumpy and noisy, remained quiet. Their clasped palms grew clammy.

At step eight the basement door creaked open. It shut with a click.

Thomas glanced over his shoulder, but there was only darkness behind him. "Mom, is that you?" he asked in a loud whisper.

Footsteps rattled the treads to his rear.

"Mom!" he whisper-shouted, his terror growing.

The footsteps drew closer.

Thomas wanted to bound down the stairs, putting distance between whatever was approaching from behind, but moving that fast in the dark would be foolish. He picked up the pace as best he could.

A hand landed on his right shoulder.

Thomas flinched and jumped and let out a stifled wail.

"It's me," said his mom, gently squeezing his shoulder. "Keep going."

Thomas, relieved but heart pounding, inched with his brother down the stairs.

Step thirteen didn't thump like the others. It had a solid feel and a wider surface. He'd reached the basement's cement floor. Thomas took two steps forward, pulling his brother to make space for his mom to come the rest of the way off the stairs.

His mom's hand still on his shoulder, she spun him around and leaned down to him. Their noses almost touched in the darkness. "Thomas," she said, "take your brother to the far corner of the basement. Follow the wall under the stairs to where it turns, then head all the way to the end."

"But Mom …." Thomas fell silent as cold metal brushed against his arm. "Is that Dad's gun?"

His mom hesitated. "Yes," she said. "I have his shotgun and some plasma shells."

Thomas was stunned. His mom complained about guns in the house on many occasions, one point of friction with his dad but a concession she made in her marriage to a soldier. She was a nonviolent person who held nothing but patience and compassion in her heart. Whenever they found so much as a spider in the house, she would trap it and release it back outside. He could never imagine her wielding a gun or leveling it to shoot anything living. "What's going on, Mom?" he pleaded. "You promised you'd tell me once we got down here."

His mom hesitated again. "I don't know for sure, Thomas," she said. "I'm just being extra cautious. But something like this happened recently in a city in France."

"Something like what?" he asked.

"There's a race of aliens called the Thetans," she said. "They deployed an energy dampening field ... it's like an invisible blanket over the city that disabled all the electronics—computers, lights, everything. Then they came down in their ships. All of this might be a blackout, but none of the electronics work."

Thomas unconsciously tapped at his comm. The screen still didn't respond.

His mom lifted her hand from his shoulder and gently cupped his cheek in her palm. "If it *is* the Thetans, we need to hide and stay quiet. They might come in the house. The Thetans don't take prisoners."

They don't take prisoners. He and his brother used that phrase once while playing space pirates. His mom asked if he knew what it meant—he was shocked when she told him. "Timmy and me are nice pirates," he insisted. They didn't kill people, they just looked for gold and rare earths. He never used that phrase again.

"Take your brother Timmy to the far corner and don't move. Don't make a sound."

"Where will you be?" asked Thomas.

"There's a stack of large boxes a few feet straight ahead. I'll be behind them. If anything that isn't human comes down the stairs, I'm gonna blast it with the shotgun." She kissed Thomas on the forehead and found Timmy for a hug. "Now go, and be as quiet as you can."

Thomas took his brother as he felt his way along the basement wall, walking under the stairs and turning left when he hit the corner. He moved along the next wall to the end, pressed his back into the corner, and slid down until his rear end landed on the floor. He pulled Timmy to sit between his legs and wrapped his arms around his little brother.

"Remember, Timmy," Thomas said, "we have to be quiet. We can't make a sound." The instructions were more for himself than for his little brother, who hadn't made a noise the entire time. Thomas began shaking. He fought to stop it.

In the blackness without a working comm, Thomas quickly lost track of time. The initial burst of adrenaline subsided, he nodded off to sleep in the monotony of the dark, quiet basement.

A muffled blaster discharge jolted him awake. Or something like a blaster. It had the normal throb of blaster fire, but also a high-pitched whine. Whatever it was, the sound came from the street, in front of their house.

How long had he been asleep? Minutes? Hours? He had no idea.

A muffled scream and a second discharge reached his ears, this time louder, closer, and accompanied by a lightning flash through the hopper windows.

A person … an alien … someone is in the yard.

A loud crash upstairs. Silence. A thud. Then another thud. And another.

Footsteps.

Someone or something had entered the house. Thomas looked towards the ceiling, following the intruder as he moved across the living room. Joists and floorboards groaned with each leaden step.

It's far too heavy to be a person.

The plodding footsteps rounded a corner. A loud creak came from the top of the stairs.

They're outside the basement door!

Thomas's heart pounded into this throat, and he had trouble breathing. He plunged into a panic, his body shaking uncontrollably. He fought to stifle a sob.

The doorknob jiggled.

Thomas waited for the creak of the door opening.

Another jiggle.

What's it waiting for? Just get it over with!

A weighty step landed on the floor above, shaking the ceiling. Another step. And another. And one more. The intruder was on the move, heading away from the basement door along the path it took through the living room….

A horn blared.

The all-clear signal jolted Thomas, his brother, and his mom awake. They had slept the entire night and most of the morning in the basement. By time they crawled up the stairs and spilled from the house out into the front yard, the sun sat at its mid-morning spot in the sky.

"Stay back," said his mom. Thomas waited, holding hands with his brother as the two boys stood in the grass. They were safe. CentCom personnel roamed the streets, even through their house. Thomas ignored his mom's admonition, walking to the property line with his brother in tow, to the row of Azalea bushes that separated their yard from the sidewalk. Timmy was too short to see above the bushes, but Thomas had no trouble peering into the street.

Bodies littered the black asphalt. Most were human, neighbors. Some bodies seemed OK, unmoving but without visible signs of trauma. Others were torn apart, rib cages wrenched open, limbs missing. In the street not too far from where Thomas stood with his brother, a dead Thetan lay on its back in a pool of red-black blood, glaring at the hazy blue sky through its bulbous, smoky black helmet. It was humanoid, but much larger than a person. And blubbery, the product of a world with half Earth's gravity. The skin of the Thetan's black environment suit rippled over rolls of fat, like a walrus in a wetsuit. Thomas couldn't help but stare, black death from the sky rotting in the bright morning sun.

He overheard his mom asking a solider about the alien. Their best guess for cause of death was either a weapon malfunction or friendly fire. They were puzzled why the other Thetans left the body behind. Perhaps lugging its dead weight back to their ship through full Earth gravity was more than they could manage.

Was that Thetan in our house last night? Thomas shuddered at the thought of confronting it in the dark. *Why didn't it come for us in the basement?* Tears streamed down his face, and he started to shake. He couldn't control himself. They came close to dying last night. A strange turn of luck kept them alive. He wanted to run, but he wasn't sure there was anyplace safe to go. He grew short of breath as the full consequences of his dad's death came into view. Without his dad, Thomas and his family were on their own, left to fend for themselves in a truly dangerous world.

Thomas cursed his dad. *No father should leave his family, leave them alone in such a dangerous world, leave them to survive by luck.* His dad went off in his starship, but he didn't think what would happen to his family if he never returned, didn't worry what it would mean for them to be all alone —

Bzzzz.

Holbrook's comm rousted him from his memories. He'd set a reminder to take some nullihol pills before falling asleep.

Too tired to move, he ignored the alarm. He'd take the pills in the morning. It would just mean being a little bit later out of his quarters.

Holbrook lowered himself onto his side on the deck, placed his arm under his head, and sank into sleep.

8

"What do you mean that was my last drink?" asked the young woman from her barstool.

"Just what I said—that was your last drink for the night." The bartender, a burly man with a balding crown, twisted a white dish towel into ever tighter knots. Irritation played across his chubby face. "*You* know they limit your tab to three drinks a day."

The young woman tapped her comm. "I will point out, sir, the time is 12:07 a.m. A new day has begun, and with it a new tab."

The bartender frowned at the young woman, his knuckles white from his grip. "Your residency contract covers up to three drinks a night," he said. His voice shifted from gruff to saccharine sweet and a wide, feigned smile replaced his scowl. "But there's no limit to how much you can drink in this bar, just on what's already paid for." The bartender grabbed a bottle of liquor from one of the lighted shelves behind him and wagged it gently in front of the woman. "I'd be happy to pour you a new drink, miss. Alls I need is another form of payment."

The woman scoffed.

"Then that's that," he snapped, slamming the bottle back on the shelf. "Now if you'll excuse me, I have some *paying* customers to attend to." The bartender whipped the dish towel over his shoulder and disappeared around the corner.

"There goes your tip, asshole," the woman yelled after him. She squeezed her eyes shut and whimpered in frustration. *Three drinks a night? The whole thing's barbaric. Who are they to decide how many drinks I can have?* Small teardrops emerged—she quickly pinched them away. *They don't own me, though they sure act like they do. It's just part of their never-ending stream of controlling bullshit.*

The woman swiveled left on her barstool and surveyed the faintly lit space. The Andromeda Lounge was nearly empty, typical for such a late hour on a weeknight. Small booths with burgundy-colored upholstery lined the walls, the candle discs on their tables flickering apparitions onto the ceiling.

She swiveled right and discovered two men staring at her from the opposite end of the bar. One gave her a broad smile. She shot them both a dirty look and returned her attention to her glass, spying several small shards of ice swimming in the meager remnants of her drink. She jiggled the glass, placed it to her lips, and leaned her head far back to coax the final, watered-down drops of alcohol into her mouth.

"The next one's on me," said a loud voice in a slight German accent far too close to her right ear.

The woman glanced sideways—the two men from the other end of the bar had migrated to the barstools next to hers. *The evening's growing worse by the moment.*

"What'll it be?" asked the man who had smiled at her, encroaching on her personal space from the adjacent stool. He was middle-aged and skinny, with short, receding blond hair. A cropped, patchy beard concealed most of the cleft in his chin, and the man's liquor-laden breath wafted across her face. His companion, also middle-aged and a bit dirtier blond, stood beside him with a smile, leaning against the bar.

"I'm calling it a night," she said.

"Don't be that way," said the man. "We haven't even been properly introduced. I'm Dr. Martin Freidrich, and my friend here is Dr. Rudolf Weiss." Weiss's hand lifted in a weak wave from the wrist. "And you are?"

"Thirsty," said the woman.

Freidrich chuckled. "He has you on a tight leash."

"Who does?"

"The guy who's paying your bills," said Freidrich, smiling. "Rudolf and I heard your exchange with the bartender. We have a little bet going on your story."

"My story?" *Pricks.*

"Yes, your story," said Freidrich. "You know, the reason a beautiful, young girl like you is here on a research station out in the literal middle of nowhere." Freidrich cinched in closer as he spoke. "Rudolf here thinks you're a researcher's lonely, neglected young wife, forced to follow where his work takes him."

"Is that so," she said.

Weiss nodded with a toothy, intoxicated smile.

"My explanation is more charitable," said Freidrich. "I don't think you're a married woman looking to pick up men in a bar."

"How big of you," said the woman. She scanned her glass again for any missed drops of alcohol.

"My guess is you're an overworked research assistant to a crusty old physicist struggling through his mid-life crisis."

Sexist pricks. Still staring into her glass, the woman said, "Are you and Rudolf researchers, then?"

"Why yes," said Freidrich with a wide grin, "Dr. Weiss and I are physicists, and we're researching an incredibly exciting topic, but it's very, very complicated." His eyes sparkled as he grasped the back of her barstool with his left hand and stroked the mid portion of her bare back with his top two fingers. "If we're successful, and I can objectively say we're very close, they'll award us the Nobel-Wasserman prize in Physics."

"Oh, that does sound *very* exciting," she said in a sarcastic tone.

"It is," he continued, nodding. "It's perhaps best described as a grand theory of everything."

"God, not more string theory bullshit," said the woman. She closed her eyes and brought her fingers to the sides of her head, slowly massaging her temples.

Freidrich paused. His smile evaporated. "Maybe you are familiar with several of string theory's challenges," he said. "I agree it's had its share of setbacks, but it's hardly, as you say, bullshit."

Deluded, sexist pricks. The woman swiveled on her barstool to face the two men. Her ice-blue eyes savaged them, gazing out from under close-cropped dark bangs. She wore a short, dark, tight-fitting dress with thin straps that looped over her bare shoulders. The men's attention fell to the exposed, rounded tops of her breasts, shifting unfettered beneath the dress's sheer material. "I'll at least give you both some credit for consistency," she said. "The stories you made up about me are as ridiculous as your grand unified theory."

Freidrich's face quickly reddened. "Listen, honey," he said through clenched teeth and a forced smile, "if you think string theory is wrong, it's only because you don't understand it."

Patronizing, deluded, sexist pricks. The woman's eyes narrowed. "Either of my recent papers on entropic gravity should have been enough for all you zealots to toss your grand theory in the dumpster where it belongs," she said. "Maybe you saw them in the Journal of Classical and Quantum Gravity?"

The two men blinked at her, their mouths agape.

"You string theorists always say, 'By proving X we'll finally demonstrate that string theory is correct,' but when X turns out to be false you say, 'Proving Y will show that string theory is correct.' And on and on it goes. That's the problem with a theory that's non-falsifiable."

"I thought you looked familiar," said Weiss, wagging his finger at her. "You're Rebekah Riesen."

"Dr. Rebekah Riesen," she corrected.

"My God," he said, placing his palm against his cheek. "Here, Martin, we're dreaming of the Nobel-Wasserman prize in Physics but she's received it three times, twice before she was twenty-five."

"That's right," Dr. Riesen growled, eyes smoldering on Freidrich. "And the reason I think string theory is wrong is because I *do* understand it."

Freidrich's gaping mouth snapped shut.

"Bartender!" shouted Dr. Riesen.

The bartender emerged from around the pillar, stopping in front of Dr. Riesen.

"I'll have another," she said, pointing to her empty glass. She tipped her head towards Freidrich. "He's buying."

- - -

Dr. Martin Freidrich's hand moved along Dr. Riesen's waist, sliding slowly across the fabric of her dress at the small of her back before slipping farther down to caress her buttocks. Dr. Riesen ran her fingers through his hair while her other hand toyed with his waistband.

Freidrich pulled her closer. She enjoyed the firmness of his body pressing into hers.

He planted a kiss on her lips, then worked his way across her cheek to nibble her ear. "I know they say you're a mistake," he whispered, "but I don't see how you could be any more perfect."

Dr. Riesen reached behind her back, grabbed Freidrich's wrist, and lifted his arm from around her body. She pushed him away and smiled. "I've got to get to bed," she said.

"How 'bout mine?" asked Freidrich. "I can tell Rudolph to go sleep in the lab."

"Not tonight," she said, shaking her head. She stepped backwards to stand within intention range of her apartment door.

"When, then?" he asked, taking a step toward her as the door slid open.

Dr. Riesen stood radiant in the corridor lights, framed by the dark foyer behind her: long, athletic legs flowing into wide hips; large, perfectly shaped breasts; pouty lips and ice-blue eyes under a bob of black hair veiling alabaster skin. "I'll message you," she said, moving backwards into her apartment. She stopped a few paces inside.

Freidrich stood frozen, staring at her silhouetted form as she lingered in the twilight between the corridor and the apartment's dark interior.

Dr. Riesen crossed her arms over her chest and grasped her dress straps. She drew the straps slowly down, peeling her dress away to fully expose her breasts. "You know you're right," she said, standing in the shadowed light of the doorway. "I'm not sure I could be more perfect." Freidrich started forward as the door slid shut in front of him.

Engulfed in the blackness of her apartment, Dr. Riesen returned her dress straps to her shoulders and stepped gingerly through the living room. She dodged the coffee table, finding her way to the couch where she dropped herself onto the pillows, breathed deep, and leaned her head back. She sat in the darkness, tears rolling down her cheeks from the corners of her closed eyes.

"Another challenging night?" said a man's deep voice from across the room.

Dr. Riesen jumped. "God, don't *do* that!" she said, snapping her head up. She quickly wiped away the tears with her hands.

"I'm sorry, my child, I did not mean to frighten you." A side table lamp came to life in the far corner, filling the space with a soft, warm glow, revealing a man sitting in a chair with wide cushioned armrests. He wore a hooded, crimson robe and crimson leather sandals. "Were you at the bar or taking another walk?" he asked.

"I went to the bar tonight," said Dr. Riesen.

"How was it?"

"Typical," she said as she sat up straight on the couch. "They cut me off on drinks again."

"You should be thankful The Brotherhood pays for any drinks at all," said the man. "You know how we frown on alcohol. Besides, it's never a solution to life's problems."

"I also ran into the typical bunch of idiots," she said, fishing for sympathy. "Tonight they thought I was either a lowly research assistant or a physicist's trophy wife."

"Wasn't that your objective?" asked the man. "Didn't you present yourself in a way so they would assume you're anything other than what you are?"

Her face still wet from tears, Dr. Riesen crossed her arms over her chest and gave the man an angry look. "And what am I, Rabbi?"

The man smiled. "You are many things," he said, "starting with the most brilliant physicist alive."

Dr. Riesen rolled her eyes.

"Was the man you were kissing in the hall one of the idiots?" he asked.

She shrugged. "What if he was?"

"You disrespect yourself by allowing a man you hold in such low regard to touch you as he did," he said. "And you dishonor yourself by teasing him with your body."

"That asshole got what he deserved," she said. "But I think it's your honor you're worried about, not mine." She cupped the undersides of her breasts and lifted, their smooth white tops erupting from her dress. "This is who I am. It's not my fault all this makes you and the others so uncomfortable."

The man blinked at her in the warm table light. "I have little desire or energy for verbal sparring at such a late hour, Rebekah, but I think you know nothing you do dishonors me, for the way you act does not arise from anything I ever taught you. Your behavior is yours alone, as is the dishonor it brings."

Dr. Riesen looked away, her gaze landing on the couch arm's dark velvety upholstery. She ran her hand across the nap, smoothing it to fall in one direction. "What're you doing up this late anyway?" she asked.

"I couldn't sleep," he said. "I figured I would wait up for your return."

More tears welled. Dr. Riesen wiped them away with the back of her hand.

The man moved from his chair and sat next to Dr. Riesen on the couch. The crow's feet at his temples accented his gentle smile, and his kind eyes peered at her though round glasses with thin rims. A smattering of gray patches dotted his dark brown, neatly cropped beard. He took her hands in his. "Have you reconsidered your decision?" he asked.

"I have not," said Dr. Riesen. "If anything, I'm even more determined to go."

The man sighed. "This choice will be much more destructive than the alcohol you consume every night," he said. "And it still won't be the answer to your problems."

Tears ran down Dr. Riesen's face. The man put his arm around her shoulders and squeezed her gently. He gave her a kind smile. "Let me tell you a story."

- - -

I rose at the God-forsaken fourth hour of the twenty-third day of the year 2302 A.D. Of course I know God forsakes nothing in His creation as everything manifests His perfect will, including 3 a.m. and all other moments in time. And of course I was no stranger to waking before dawn, as each day the entire Quad bustles with chores and chants before the stars have receded from the sky. Still, my faith struggled to find the divinity in flailing out of a deep sleep to quiet my bleating alarm, in scrambling to dress with my mind in a fog, in stumbling from my quarters to stand with a dozen men in the dead of night.

Once we assembled on the flat patch outside the Quad's main gate, the Admor raised his hand to settle us, shouted, "Yatsa!" and our party of Three, Seven, and Three lurched forward. Our destination: the Q'erh Radvid, a circular depression atop the tan-white Qumran cliffs that soared four hundred meters before us, a massive glacier of stone towering in the blueish moonlight. A thin layer of dust floated at our feet as we shuffled along the soft dirt path that meandered a kilometer to the sheer cliffside. I caught myself sipping from my flask despite lack of thirst and resolved not to exhaust my water supply on nerves. After a short time we reached the rugged cliff base and found the tortoise-shaped stone that marks the start of the summit trail. Without a word or pause, we took to the path.

Moreh Grünfeld and I walked behind the Admor, who maintained an aggressive pace despite his 116 years. His staff struck the rock path with a steady beat, breaking the silence around us with a sharp thwack.

"Rabbi Lehr," the Moreh said, clasping my shoulder as he took me aside at the previous night's rehearsal, "during our travel to the summit you will find the Admor's staff jarring, but in it you will also find comfort."

"Were you a member of a prior Tchiyah ceremony?" I asked.

"Indeed," the Moreh said through a wide smile, "the previous one."

As the Moreh alluded, I winced with each teeth-rattling crack of the Admor's staff, but the steady hypnotic repetition drew my mind from the dull aches that grew in my knees and ankles.

The Admor, the Moreh to my left, and I formed the Tchiyah party's forward Three. Behind us trudged the Seven coffin bearers: three rows of two monks walking abreast and a seventh in front to steer. Together they shouldered their load with huffs and grunts. The final Three, the ovum and sperm holders who also walked abreast, followed by the monk with the ceremonial womb, marched at the rear.

Most of our jagged pathway had been carved from the solid rock of the cliff face. The path ran wide in spots but narrowed for long stretches. The grade remained steady throughout, not too steep or shallow. We encountered neither sand nor loose rock to challenge our footing, though our leather sandals sometimes slid where the stone had worn smooth. The landscape lacked life: no plants grew from the cliffside, no insects darted about, no animals rustled. This barren panorama provided little distraction from the black expanse just beyond the path's ragged edge, a dark void waiting to swallow a careless hiker, to caress them in an onrush of air and blackness before they dashed to the ground below.

After marching for an hour, the Admor slammed his staff into the stone path and cried, "'atsor!" signaling a ten-minute rest. We stopped on a wide, flat overhang with ample space for the Seven to set down their heavy wooden load with its morbid contents. I had broken a sweat on our hike but did not overheat thanks to my robe's chimney-like channeling of the cool night air. The coffin bearers hadn't been as lucky. They tossed the wood bundles from their backs and let their robes fall away from their torsos—seven molting snakes shedding their crimson skins. They hunched forward with their hands on their knees as they heaved air into their lungs. At least their return trip would be easier.

I moved to the path's edge and peered down to locate the trailhead. The moon had risen above the cliffs, leaving the alluvial plain in a darkness interrupted only by the yellow pinpricks of lantern light that winked from the Quad's walkways far below. Farther to the east shimmered the Dead Sea, a black mirror stretching to the eastern horizon.

I turned around to find the party had reassembled, and I sprinted to regain my place in the procession. The Admor, upon seeing all returned to their positions and the Seven again shouldering the coffin, shouted, "Yatsa!" He pounded his staff into the stone trail, spun on his heels, and resumed leading us in our march up the path.

The second half of our journey mirrored the first, with a pounding staff and an ominous darkness at path's edge. The air grew cooler as our elevation increased, and winds jostled us at times with gusts of varied strength. Despite our ascent, we were not climbing to a destination high above the Earth's surface. The Qumran cliffs form the leading edge of the African tectonic plate, marking the point where it drives the Arabian plate down into the fiery mantle. The Dead Sea and its environs sit on the Arabian side of this subduction zone, four hundred meters below sea level. We were not unlike creatures from the ocean's depths on an arduous journey to the surface.

Another hour of travel brought sight of the trail's end, and a squall so cold my ears and nose throbbed with pain. Moments later a stronger gust drove me into the Moreh, and the Tchiyah party had to stand its ground until the blast subsided. As we continued, more gusts whipped around us and a steady wind grew until we could no longer make forward progress. The coffin bearers set down their parcel, and we huddled against the cliffside. My teeth chattered as I pulled my robe tight and pinched closed the portion at my ankles. I donned my hood and gripped the rough rock face as best I could with frozen hands.

Sand welled from the ground below and rasped at exposed skin, striving to etch us from the cliff. We crouched and clung for ten minutes as the storm raged and showed no sign it would end. I looked eastward against the wind, making slits of my eyes. A few rumpled, gray clouds with orange bellies hung low as the horizon sprouted hints of soft blue. My concern grew—the

Tchiyah ceremony had to begin the moment the first rays of light bolted from the sunrise. We could not turn back and attempt the next morning, for The Prophet's spirit had already spent the past three days moving through the three bardos, the intermediate stages between death and rebirth. We had to move.

I spied the Admor nestled into the cliff face on my right. He looked skyward, but with eyes pinched shut and brow furrowed. His lips moved—I only made out fragments of his speech over the din of the wind. During a lull, those loose sounds formed words from the Sheheheyanu blessing:

Blessed are You,
Lord our God,
King of the Universe,
Who has kept us alive, sustained us,
And enabled us to reach this season.

I, too, recited the blessing, followed by others, until the entire Tchiyah party shouted above the gale. I found myself crying, for if our prayers failed, 250 years of rebirths and revelations would end.

However, that morning God heard our words and acted, for seconds later the winds slackened to a gentle breeze. No longer forced to shelter against the cliffside, we stood and rejoiced with wide grins. Tears raced down my face, for God had shown His will indeed included The Prophet's return.

As we stood beaming, an anguished shriek tore through our celebration. I turned to find the Admor with a wild look on his face. He began screaming, a staccato of sounds made unintelligible by his distress, each syllable punctuated by spittle that flew from his lips. His eyes bulged as they followed the line of his raised left arm and forefinger aimed at the glowing eastern horizon. We had survived the wind, but we had not yet reached the summit or prepared for the ceremony. We retook our positions without delay, the coffin bearers once again hoisted their morbid load, and we scrambled along the path's final stretch.

The Admor, the Moreh, and I bounded up the trail, but when I glanced back, I discovered the Seven thirty paces behind us. They moved as fast as they could but struggled under the coffin's weight. I ran to them, lined up next to the lead coffin bearer, and lent my back to the effort. Even with eight men, the casket bore down on my thin frame, taxing my muscles and sinews, but together we moved faster up the trail. I closed my eyes and focused on placing one foot in front of the other, trusting my workmates to keep us on the path.

Time raced or froze—I had no sense, only the focus to move the coffin up the trail. I was on the verge of collapsing when the word "'atsor!" broke the silence and we stopped moving. I opened my eyes, surprised to find we had arrived at the summit. The eastern sky was brighter than moments ago, but the sun had still not risen.

The Seven and I moved with haste to the ash pit, a half-meter deep rectangular gouge with jagged edges and a rugged floor that suggested the work of chisels and pickaxes. Despite its name the pit contained no ashes, the contents of the last Tchiyah ceremony having blown away decades ago. The eight of us centered the coffin into the pit.

The Seven unbundled their wood packs into the gap between the pit's edges and the casket's sides. As they worked, the lead coffin bearer swung open the lid and removed a large goatskin flask. Within the box a crimson-dyed burlap shroud traced the contours of a motionless head and torso. The lead bearer lowered the lid, pulled the cork from the flask, and doused the coffin and wood with accelerant.

Twelve of us took positions around the ash pit, forming a semi-circle that opened to the east. The Admor faced us from across the coffin, and we all stood motionless until the first ray of sunlight danced from the horizon. The Admor spoke:

"Tichyah. Rebirth. Today we observe the passing of The Prophet, not from this world to the next, but from the discarded body here before us to the new one we shall conceive. We are the joyful witnesses to his last moments in the world between worlds, and to the first moments of his next journey upon this Earth. We exult in excited anticipation of revelation."

"Amen," we all cried out.

As the Admor finished his remarks, the lead coffin bearer walked to the casket. He reached into the front of his robe near his chest and withdrew a closed fist that pulsed with a gentle, red warmth. In a quick motion he flung the contents of his hand, three match beads, into the ash pit. Each glowing, milky-red pearl erupted in flame where it landed, and in seconds a conflagration engulfed the container. Gray smoke drifted high into the morning air, carried by a gentle breeze. Burning wood tinged my nostrils.

The trailing Three moved from their positions and presented themselves to the Admor. The monk with the womb, a shiny silver heart-shaped vessel about the size of a drumhead and several inches thick, held it outstretched from his body. Upon the Admor's nod, the ovum and sperm holders inserted their separate cryotubes, foot-long silver batons, into cavities along the womb's top edge. As they stepped back, the Admor bowed his head and pressed his hands together at his chest in prayer. We all followed suit, though I kept one eye fixed on the womb, waiting for the sign of conception. I stood breathless until the small green dot appeared at the container's center.

The green dot also cued my part in the ceremony. I walked to the Admor, who raised his head and lowered his hands and said, "Rabbi Lehr, do you swear to protect this Prophet child, to guard and defend no matter the cost, even to the forfeit of your own life?"

"I do," I said, my voice gravelly. Though conceived only moments before, an enormous love rose within my heart for the new child, the next Prophet. Love, and a great pride in my selection above all others for the honor of Protector. I would be a father to this fatherless child, give all of myself and more, and never, ever, let harm come.

The following days dragged into weeks and crawled into months. Each morning after reciting my prayers at the tiny wooden desk in my quarters, I would add a new mark to the tally of days I kept on a special page in my journal. As spring became summer, my despair over the remaining time turned to anticipation of the coming birth. I visited the gestational womb every day, bursting into the room to count the green dots arrayed in a spiral across its copper face. Each new glowing mote signaled the successful completion of another step in the fetus's development.

At last the Birth Day arrived, just after Yom Kippur. Each moment lives with me still in vivid memory. I stared in awe as the baby's crown bulged from the copper birth canal the Caretakers had attached to the womb that morning. The full head, shoulders, and torso emerged, the contraction protocol having entered its fastest and most forceful phase. Next came the belly, the umbilical, and gasps of shock and disbelief. A rabbi attendant offered the pithy observation, "This is the fuck-up of all fuck-ups."

Two hours later Moreh Grünfeld and I stood outside the large wooden door to the Admor's office. The Moreh carried a despondent look on his age-lined face. As Director of the Generational Program, even a minor mishap meant major grief for him. When the newborn Prophet three generations prior emerged with an eye color closer to steel gray than the expected ice-blue the program's detractors hurled the barb, "Unreliable in small things, unreliable in big things," a fair criticism, for if we could not guarantee a trait as basic as a man's eye color, what confidence could we assert in anything more significant? That day we fully confirmed their criticism.

Moreh Grünfeld twice struck the door's massive driftwood planks with the tethered black iron ball knocker before pushing it open. The Admor's assistant would have greeted us but had already left for the day. Cool air enveloped us as we entered the dark space, the antechamber to the main office. The Admor preferred a frigid workspace, and we shivered as we transited from the warm early evening air. Once inside, the Moreh nudged the great door shut.

We walked the short distance to the main office door, dodging a desk and other furniture, gray lumps in the room's dim light. The Moreh tapped with his knuckles, then nudged the door. Yellow-orange sunlight rushed from the breach, blinding us in the moment. The Moreh's head disappeared into the crack and was met by a curt, "Come in." He pushed the door open wide enough for us both to pass.

Fading golden sunlight filled the Admor's office, streaming through tall panes of glass that stretched from floor to ceiling along the room's entire western wall. The windows looked out onto a small garden of short trees and flower bushes, interspersed with a sandy path. Birds made their last stops of the day at several hanging feeders. Across from the garden rose the Quad's stone block outer wall, and beyond it the white-tan cliffs.

Though immense, the room contained little furniture, just a simple wooden desk flanked by the Admor's large leather chair and its two lesser, wooden counterparts. On the wall behind the Admor hung a fifteen-foot-tall oil on wood painting of the first man to hold his position, watching us with his fiery black eyes. This man of small stature possessed the courage and conviction to break from traditional Jewish teachings, basing The Brotherhood on the truths found in many different faiths. A cloister of

Jewish monks was unheard of before him, much less one embracing the Buddhist belief in reincarnation.

The Admor trained his eyes on us as we approached. "Sit down," he barked as he nodded at the chairs facing the desk. The Moreh took one while I remained standing to his side and slightly behind. The Admor's command notwithstanding, protocol dictated I stay on my feet, for sitting next to the Moreh would imply equivalent status. Our current predicament was more than enough grief for one day.

Deep, wide wrinkles crossed the Admor's face like the grooves in bark on an old tree. Arteries bulged and pulsed beneath the papery skin at his temples. Fat eyebrows sat like caterpillars over sunken eyes as the Admor stared through thin-rimmed glasses at Moreh Grünfeld. The Moreh fixed his gaze on the Admor's desktop.

"Have they determined the root cause?" the Admor asked, speaking in his typical low tone.

"As near as they can tell," Moreh Grünfeld said, looking up as he fidgeted in his chair, "the error must have occurred sometime after the annealing phase that separates the male sperm from the female. We rechecked the photographs and genetic profile of each individual spermatozoon and confirmed the Tchiyah cohort contained no female sperm." The Moreh paused as he shuffled in his seat. "However, they suspect a microscopic droplet of seminal fluid clinging to the outside of the pipet must have introduced female sperm into the transport cylinder."

"So not only do we have a female Prophet," the Admor said, his voice building to a low growl, "we don't even have a record of the contributing spermatozoon's genetic composition?"

"Correct," the Moreh said in a quavering voice, "but we have sequenced the child's DNA and reconstructed the spermatozoon's profile. We have confirmed the child is genetically healthy and anomaly-free."

"Except," the Admor hissed, "the child is female instead of male." The Admor spoke slowly and with emphasis, and the Moreh's head sank lower after each word. "Why didn't the genetic scanners flag this error at the start?"

"The scanners are designed to detect genetic sequence errors and anomalies," said the Moreh. "A female embryo is technically not a genetic sequence error."

"Error, mistake, call it what you will, but this is not the desired outcome in any sense," the Admor said. "Why didn't any of the subsequent generational stages catch it?"

The Moreh hesitated. "Your excellency, those systems were similarly restricted in scope. They assumed a male embryo in sym-utero, so none of the automated checks bothered to confirm the fetus's sex. I have directed such testing be added at multiple stages, including conception, and future Tchiyah ceremonies will depart with secondary ova and spermatozoa cohorts as a backup for gender errors in the primary zygote. This mistake will not happen again."

The Admor didn't stir for several long seconds. "It seems we have a plan for the future," he finally said. "Now what do we do about our current predicament?"

After a long pause, the Moreh said, "The Prophet cannot be female. It is unfortunate but necessary to restart the generational process."

The Admor pursed his lips. "Reluctantly I have reached the same conclusion," he said.

"Perhaps a Hamatat Hessed ceremony," said the Moreh. "This, after all, would be a mercy killing. And then we hold a new Tchiyah ceremony three days later."

"We must not!" I shouted.

The Admor and Moreh looked at me in shock, as I had no permission or place in that meeting to speak.

"Killing is wrong," I stammered. "Killing a child, an infant, to correct our so-called mistake is evil."

"The Prophet must be male," said the Admor in a lecturing tone. "This child, this female, should never have existed."

"Who says she is not to be The Prophet?" I asked. "Who says our tradition of male Prophets is correct? Who is to say this female Prophet is not God's will?"

Silence fell over the room. Finally, the Admor spoke. "This issue is not up for debate," he said. "We must trust in what we think is right. We are far along in the process of welcoming The Prophet back to this world, but not so far along we cannot fix this error. We must do this for the good of the program."

I took a deep breath. The Admor and Moreh had so far been sympathetic to my point of view in that they had not immediately called the guards to drag me away to one of the contemplation cells below ground. I would likely find any further outburst met with a swift and harsh response. But after all my consultations with God since the birth of The Prophet, I had steeled myself to my current course, had settled upon my next action before I walked into the Admor's office. "The child has a name."

The Moreh burst from his chair. "She cannot!" he yelled, his face contorted in anger.

"No, no, no, no, no!" shouted the Admor, each syllable louder than the last.

"The child has a name," I said again, this time with more force, determined to see it through. "Her name is Rebekah."

The Admor thrust his palms flat against his ears, and his eyes rolled back in his head. He began blubbering what may have started as a prayer but drifted to what sounded like the ramblings of an unhinged man.

"Blasphemy!" shouted the Moreh standing next to me. His eyes bulged, threatening to leap from their sockets. "You cannot give this child a name! This child cannot be the next Prophet!"

"Her name is Rebekah," I repeated, my tone calm. Every muscle in my body tensed, and sweat beaded across my brow, but I stood fast in my resolve. I drew strength from the oath I swore nine months prior, to guard and defend that child no matter the cost, even to my life.

The Admor slowly lowered his hands from his ears. His bloodshot eyes looked past me, as if in a trance. "We cannot kill a child who has a name," he said.

"We must!" yelled the Moreh, quickly cowering. Although he fully intended to kill a baby not even a day old, he likely recoiled upon hearing his insistence they do so. He grew calmer, though his body shook with anger. "Your excellency," he pleaded, "please let us fix this mistake."

"We cannot kill a child who has a name," the Admor said again, still looking past me, resignation in his voice. He stood and slowly raised his arms, turning his palms flat to face me. His eyes finally connected with mine, full of fire. I raised my arms and offered my palms in kind. He hissed the benediction that initiated the Protector's service, "You, Rabbi Lehr, are the Protector. Raise this child, the next Prophet, and keep her from harm, so that God may reveal to us, through her, the inner workings of His holy Universe."

- - -

Rabbi Lehr gently lowered Dr. Riesen's head from his shoulder, moving slowly to avoid waking her. He reached into a box at the end of the couch and pulled out a blanket. He spread it over her arms and legs.

"We must trust in what we think is right," whispered Rabbi Lehr, "and what can be more right than God's will?" He caressed her head. "God chose for you to return to His Universe as a woman. That they cannot understand the wisdom of God's decision does not make you a mistake. The mistake is their questioning of God's will." He caressed her head again. "I only wish you could believe that."

9

"Welcome to Plana Petram, Captain Holbrook, Commander Stephens."

The greeting startled the two *Avenger* officers as they exited their shuttle's airlock. An aught stood before them, two meters tall with white phlesh, short, dark hair, a slim pointed nose, and a wide, toothy smile. He wore a dark blue suit with narrow lapels, and his head jerked bird-like as his gaze shifted between the two officers.

"You've got to be shitting me," Stephens huffed, shaking his head in disgust.

The aught blinked at the two men, its eyelids clicking softly. "Commodore Ahrens sent me to greet you upon your arrival and to escort you to the meeting room. I understand this is your first time at Plana Petram?"

Stephens glared at the aught, leaving Holbrook to nod in the affirmative for both of them. "We're not in the habit of traveling this far from home," he said.

"That affords me the pleasure of giving you a welcome tour of this research station while we walk. But first, let me introduce myself. My name is Magellan," he said with a shallow bow, "as in Ferdinand Magellan, the sixteenth century Portuguese explorer, namesake of the Magellanic clouds. From our vantage point fifty-three thousand light-years from Earth we have a spectacular view of those clouds and the sixty-seven other satellite galaxies this side of the galactic disc. This way, gentlemen." Magellan headed to the left down the corridor. The two *Avenger* officers followed, hanging back out of the aught's earshot.

"Really?" whispered Stephens. "Ahrens sends an aught to meet us?"

"I'm sure there's a good reason he couldn't be here himself," said Holbrook, his voice low.

"But this is official CentCom business," said Stephens. "This thing has probably tipped off the entire Collective to our presence, maybe even to the mission, whatever the hell it is."

Holbrook motioned Stephens to keep his voice down. "Most aughts aren't part of The Collective," he whispered. "Besides, this one's intelligence level doesn't seem to be very high. I doubt it can do much more than run errands."

"All aughts are dangerous—you know that," sneered Stephens, his voice rising. "They can't be trusted, none of 'em. I'd destroy 'em all if I had the chance."

Magellan spun around, facing the two men. The aught locked his eyes on Stephens, its lids clicking like camera shutters. The commander, startled, tensed his muscles as if readying himself for a fight.

Magellan smiled wide at Stephens. "The Plana Petram station came about as a fluke," he said as he continued leading the men down the corridor, walking backwards in perfect step. "A survey probe venturing into this volume of intergalactic space chanced upon this capsule-shaped body, a 5.987 quadrillion kilogram class C asteroid the length of Manhattan, a strange find in a region where the space density averages only one hydrogen atom per cubic meter. The station consists of nine levels, eight of them subterranean. This top level hosts recreation space and dining facilities, while the others consist primarily of living quarters and research labs."

The three arrived at the Grand Lounge, a cavernous circular room of couches and plush chairs. Snatches of light danced from sconces stationed like torches at two-meter intervals along the curved outer wall. A breathtaking view of the Milky Way galaxy hovered above them, visible through the flat glassteel roof and providing the bulk of the illumination. Two automatons, also with white phlesh and dressed in dark blue suits, shuttled between guests and the bar across the room. Conversation filled the space.

"The Grand Lounge isn't usually this busy," said Magellan, raising his voice above the ambient noise, "but there are several conferences underway at the station, and it is happy hour."

"I have a question," Holbrook said.

"Of course, Captain Holbrook, please interrupt me at any time," said Magellan, beaming with a broad smile. "The same for you, Commander Stephens."

"Why in Hades would anyone build a station fifty thousand light-years from Earth?" asked Holbrook.

"An excellent question," said Magellan. "Plana Petram's extreme distance from Earth and its position above the galactic disc places it far from most of the mass in the Milky Way but still within the relatively dense portion of the galaxy's supposed dark matter halo, making it an ideal platform for investigating the nature of that substance."

Stephens let out a loud, derisive laugh.

"What's so funny?" asked Holbrook.

"Nothing's funny, Captain," said Stephens. "This whole thing just keeps getting more ridiculous." The captain stared at him, waiting for him to elaborate. "The only reason we're out here, the only reason we had to spend three weeks traveling fifty thousand light-years is because of a joke, because some old, dead physicists didn't have their heads on straight."

"I still don't understand," said Holbrook.

"Commander Stephens is referring to dark matter," said Magellan, "a concept physicists dreamt up four hundred years ago to explain why rotating galaxies don't fling their constituent stars off into intergalactic space. Based on what they knew about gravity at the time they didn't observe enough matter to keep a galaxy's stars rotating around its core."

"They called it *dark* matter because they couldn't see it," said Stephens, rolling his eyes. "Get it? Dark matter supposedly bound a galaxy through gravity on a large scale with invisible particles that somehow didn't clump in the centers of stars or accumulate around planets as they swept through their orbits."

"Discoveries at this station were instrumental in disproving the theory of dark matter," said Magellan, "though it took another fifty years for the theory to be fully rejected."

"As they say, cosmologists are often in error but never in doubt."

The voice came from behind them. The three turned to find a young woman standing in a crimson jacket over a black shirt, with black slacks and crimson leather-strapped sandals. She had dark hair pulled back in a knob with bangs across her forehead. Her eyes were the lightest blue, the color of ice. "Sometimes it's hard to wrap your head around what was accepted as legitimate science in those days," she said.

"Ah, Dr. Riesen, very good," said Magellan.

"Dr. Rebekah Riesen?" asked Stephens, his mouth falling open.

"Is there some other?" she asked.

"You know her?" asked Holbrook.

"Yes ..., I mean no ..., I mean we've never met; I just know who she is," Stephens stammered.

The captain extended his hand past his stunned executive officer. "I'm Captain Holbrook of the CentCom starship *Avenger*. And this is Commander Stephens." Stephens came to his senses long enough to offer his hand.

"Nice to meet you both," said Dr. Riesen. Stephens could only sheepishly nod in acknowledgement.

"You must be some luminary to render my executive officer speechless," said Holbrook.

"I'm just a physicist," said Dr. Riesen.

"Dr. Rebekah Riesen is the preeminent physicist of our time," said Magellan. "She has received three Nobel-Wassermans in Physics, five Gold Clusters for distinguished astrophysics research, the —"

"That's enough, Magellan," said Dr. Riesen.

"She's also The Prophet," said Stephens.

"The Prophet?" said Holbrook. "Like in the Bible?"

"That's a long story," said Dr. Riesen, "one that we don't really have time for right now." She turned to Magellan. "We should head to the meeting. We don't want to keep the commodore waiting."

"Commodore Ahrens?" asked Holbrook, surprised. "You're meeting with him too?"

"Indeed," said Magellan. "And now that she is here, we do not have to make a stop at her apartment to fetch her. Lady and gentlemen, please follow me." The aught spun around abruptly and headed across the Grand Lounge. The three humans followed, with Dr. Riesen walking ahead of the two *Avenger* officers. The four bumped and pressed against the other station guests as they worked their way through the throng of people.

"Why would Rebekah Riesen be in our mission briefing?" Stephens asked Holbrook in a loud whisper just audible above the din.

"You said she's The Prophet?" asked Holbrook.

"That's what they call her," said Stephens. "She's part of some crazy sect back on Earth. They say she communes with God or something. A Prophet relaying God's secrets of the physical Universe."

"You believe that?" asked Holbrook.

Stephens shrugged.

The humans followed Magellan to a set of three elevator doors at the far side of the room. When everyone arrived, the aught pressed the call button to the middle elevator. The doors whisked open and the four stepped into the car, a spacious, round cabin with a bright interior. The door slid shut, creating a sudden pocket of quiet.

"Level six," said Magellan.

After a short elevator ride the doors whisked open. The party of four emptied into a quiet, dimly lit corridor lined with sconces flicking light onto the walls and low ceiling. Magellan led the three humans past several closed doors to the last one on the right, five meters before the corridor's abrupt end.

Magellan pressed the entry buzzer and waited. The door slid open, revealing a small room much brighter than the corridor, its walls lined with white tiluminum paneling. A rectangular table sat in the center with a smooth, glassy top, surrounded by eight chairs. A CentCom officer sat facing the door on the table's far side, the ends of his uniform sleeves braided in gold commodore ribbons. He stood as the four entered the room.

"Captain Holbrook, Commander Stephens, Dr. Riesen," said the CentCom officer in a deep, booming voice. He had a thick chocolate-brown mustache flecked with gray, its bristles concealing the rim of his upper lip. Brown hair capped his head in a Roman military cut, with patches of gray at his temples. His eyes were dark brown, almost black, suspended over gaunt cheeks. The royal blue fabric of his uniform hung from his lean, two-meter frame.

A broad hand, its palm marred by an angry red scar, darted from the man's right sleeve. "I'm Commodore Ahrens," he said to the two military men as he reached across the table to shake their hands. "And good to see you again, Doctor."

"Commodore," said Dr. Riesen, nodding slightly.

Ahrens's dark eyes darted to Magellan. "That will be all."

Magellan gave a wide smile. "It has been a pleasure, Dr. Riesen, Captain Holbrook, Commander Stephens. Please let me know if there is anything I can do to improve your stay here on Plana Petram." He leaned forward with a shallow bow and backed out of the room. The doors slid closed upon his exit.

"Take your seats," said Commodore Ahrens, waving at the three empty chairs on the near side of the table while returning to his own. Captain Holbrook lowered himself into the middle one directly across from the commodore. Dr. Riesen took the chair to the captain's left, Stephens the one to his right.

Holbrook forced a weak half-smile at Ahrens, who so far lived up to his reputation of having a no-nonsense style. When researching the man, the most charitable comment Holbrook could find was he thankfully kept meetings short, sparing others from too much time in his presence. Would Ahrens show any concern for his vessel having drawn this assignment? The odds seemed against it—the commodore was seasoned career military, decorated on multiple occasions for his service, which included two tours in the long-running Cygnus offensive. Still, Holbrook remained optimistic that Ahrens would be open to discussing possible alternatives to taking his ship so close to the galactic center. "How was your trip here, Commodore?"

Ahrens's dark eyes grabbed Holbrook, threatening to swallow him like two tiny black holes. "Irrelevant," he said. "No one likes to travel by sleeper. Those God damn capsules are little more than a casket. It's not a problem when you're in transit, but you feel like you're suffocating during the awake periods at either end. I woke soon after I arrived, but I had to wait almost two hours for them to open the God damn thing.

"But as I said, all that's irrelevant because I didn't choose to come here, or want to come here, or even if I did want to travel over forty thousand light-years to a station more remote than an Oort Cloud miner's balls are from sunlight it doesn't matter. The reason I'm here, like you Captain Holbrook, the reason we're here is 'cause of orders. We're all just following orders."

The door buzzed.

"Good," said Ahrens, tapping the table's surface. The doors opened, revealing a figure standing in the corridor's gloom. "Come," he said, beckoning with his hand. "Officers, Dr. Riesen, this is Tentek."

Dr. Riesen, Holbrook, and Stephens each turned in their chairs enough to view the figure that had moved just inside the threshold. He was an aught two meters tall, skinny, with pasty white phlesh. He had a narrow face, almost as if it had been pressed flat from the sides, and cropped white hair sprouting from the crown of his head. His eyes were large white billiard balls that threatened to leap out of their sockets, with small nickel-colored irises and double-eyelids that softly click-clacked when they closed. His thin black lips cut a slit beneath the sharp point of his nose.

Stephens sprang from his seat and almost fell backwards over his chair. He fumbled past the captain and Dr. Riesen, nearly tripping over his feet as he backed deeper into the room. He stopped before reaching the far corner. Stephens quickly drew his electron pistol and aimed it at Tentek.

"Commander Stephens," bellowed Ahrens as he exploded from his chair, "lower your weapon at once!"

"Sir," said Stephens, his eyes wide and focused on Tentek, "this aught is from The Collective." He studied Tentek, reassuring himself of his claim, then adjusted his grip on his pistol. "They have a very distinct design."

"Yes, Tentek is from The Collective," said Ahrens. "Do you think I don't know that? Do you think I'm some God damned cadet with his head so far up his ass that I don't know I've invited a Collective aught to this meeting? Do you think I'm that clueless and stupid, Commander?"

Stephens remained frozen in place while Tentek stared back at him, expressionless, his double eyelids click-clacking softly.

"Put your weapon down and return to your seat," said Ahrens.

"But what's an aught from The Collective doing here?" asked Stephens. He kept his electron pistol raised.

Ahrens leaned forward, supporting himself on splayed fingers as he pressed the tips into the tabletop. He spoke calmly, bathing the room in his rich voice. "Supposing you follow my orders to lower your weapon and return to your seat instead of me relieving you of duty, putting you in restraints, and sending you in stasis to the detention planet, supposing you do what I just *God damned* ordered you to do and you remain in this meeting and sit there quietly without another impulsive outburst, supposing all of that happens just like I described, Commander, then you will find out why he's here."

"Paul," said Holbrook, "please do as the commodore asked."

Stephens gradually lowered his pistol but held it by his side rather than holster it. He made no motion to take his chair.

"Tentek, come take a seat," said Commodore Ahrens, pointing at the empty chair to his left. The aught headed towards the commodore as Stephens worked his way back to his own chair, the two synchronized in their travel around the table. They simultaneously lowered themselves into their seats and remained with their eyes fixed on each other, Commander Stephens glaring at the aught and Tentek's face placid, offering no expression.

"I apologize for Commander Stephens's ... overreaction," said Holbrook to Ahrens, "but I do share his concern. Aughts from The Collective are not allowed near CentCom operations of any sort, so I'm surprised to learn you invited him to this briefing about a mission I understand to be quite sensitive."

Commodore Ahrens sat back down in his chair. "All will be revealed, Captain," he said, pulling the front of his uniform jacket taut, "all will be revealed." He glanced at Stephens. "And if we're finally finished with all the bullshit, we can get started."

Stephens broke his gaze with Tentek and sank his eyes to the table.

"Good," said Ahrens. "As you know, the spatial and gravitational distortion around Sagittarius A Star makes any travel within two hundred light-years of the galactic black hole perilous. No vessel or probe that has entered that deformed space has ever returned or been heard from again. At least that was true until three weeks ago, when a civilian research ship was confirmed to have journeyed to within one hundred astronomical units of Sag A Star."

"Incredible," said Dr. Riesen softly.

"Not only did they survive," said Ahrens, "they navigated to a planet named Infernum located in the RD Sagittarii star system that sits twenty-three light-years from the galactic center, within the D-space around Sag A Star." The commodore tapped the table surface, summoning a large holographic image of a planet with violet oceans and gray landmasses mottled with yellow splotches. "These photos are from the research vessel, the *Adiona*." He swiped quickly through more images of planetary hemispheres to reach a set of photos taken from the ground. One showed an ashen landscape with yellow scrub brush framed by a ship's viewport, another a white boot against gray soil. A shot appeared of nine people in a control room, most with their heads down at their consoles, the others looking at the camera with grim expressions.

"How did you get these photographs?" asked Dr. Riesen.

"It's not uncommon for CentCom to have clandestine devices relaying intelligence from the field —"

"No, I mean how did you actually *get* them? It's not possible to receive signals from within the distorted space around Sag A Star."

"It's not possible to receive *direct* signals," said Ahrens. "This mission data was transmitted by a single-use, omnidirectional burst-mode broadcast device."

Dr. Riesen's eyelids flitted, the researcher falling into deep thought. "A data bomb," she said.

"That's essentially correct," said Ahrens. "The device broadcasts a data payload in all directions by detonating a small nuclear charge encased in a tachyite shell."

"But even tachyons with their faster-than-light speed are still affected by the warpage of D-space," said Dr. Riesen.

"Most of the individual signals were lost, but a statistical few eventually reached our grid of listening posts. We didn't receive everything the device transmitted, but we did get nearly all the mission logs intact as well as many photos and most of the sensor data."

The commodore swiped through photos of rocky landscapes, most featuring a soaring mountain range and jagged snowcapped peaks in the background. Ahrens overshot the photos he sought, swiping back to them. The first showed a gray plain of smooth rock stretching to a line of blue metallic trees in the distance, meeting more trees in a grove to the right. The second looked down on an enormous hexagonal-shaped basin. The third, taken from inside the basin, showed rough gray terrain littered with small rocks and several tall mounds of soil. To the right of the mounds sat two shorter silver domes.

Ahrens swiped forward to a photo where one of the silver domes filled the frame. The structure was large, about five meters tall based on the height of two research team members standing in front of it, one posing with his hand against the dome's silvery metallic skin. "When our CentCom analysts got these photos, the first things that stood out were these silver objects." He swiped ahead to a photo showing five regularly spaced, large semi-circular caverns in the basin's sheer cliff wall. "They were also very interested in these openings," he said, "or more precisely, mine entrances."

"Did I notice the silver objects have straight lines along their bases?" asked Dr. Riesen. "Can you swipe back to the previous photo?"

Commodore Ahrens brought the previous dome photo into view.

"There," she said, pointing near the bottom of the image, "the base is made up of three straight lines. It's not rounded like the top part of the dome."

"Very observant, Dr. Riesen," said Ahrens. "The silver domes have hexagonal bases. The best guess of our analysts is this structure was created by the Hex Men."

"Who?" asked Stephens.

"'Hex Men' is a nickname for an extraterrestrial race that may or may not still exist," said the commodore. "We call them the *Hex* Men because of their fondness for hexagons, a sort of calling card they've left wherever they've ventured. Their primary activity seems to have been the extraction of materials from celestial objects. We've seen evidence of their visits across many of the star systems we've explored. Our own solar system bears evidence of Hex Men activity, with several moons, including Earth's, showing six-sided craters. They also engineered the hexagonal weather pattern at Saturn's northern pole."

"The hexagonal shapes seen in the craters you're talking about happened through natural erosion processes," said Stephens. "And the hexagon at the top of Saturn is a natural result of swirling winds."

Ahrens pursed his lips. "You have a Master's degree in physics, is that right, Commander? I recall that from your file. You consider yourself a physicist?"

"Yes, and yes," said Stephens.

"It's funny," said Ahrens. "I'm not a physicist at all, but the first time I read the theory of the hexagon on Saturn, I saw right through that bullshit explanation. I mean, what's special in nature about the number six? The answer is, 'nothing.' There's no weather pattern larger than the Earth itself making a series of perfectly spaced sixty-degree turns to meet back where it started, and even glow in the God damned dark. How could it?" The commodore shook his head. "Now it's preferable the masses *believe* it's natural, which is why you'll find that explanation in every physics book out there. We don't have all the answers on what the Hex Men were up to, or if they currently pose any threat to Earth. The thought is, and I don't disagree, it's better to push a phony story than to alarm the whole human race."

"What is the hexagon in Saturn's cloud tops then if it's not natural?" asked Dr. Riesen.

"Probes flown into the region show each corner to be a tightly focused, almost pillar-like force structure radiating field lines to its neighbors. The pillars taken together are akin to sticking six poles in the ground and wrapping a fence around them. This hexagonal force field reduces the storm activity within its boundary."

"What would be the point of such a structure?" asked Holbrook.

"Assuming this was another mining operation," said Ahrens, "the only substance worth going to that much trouble to acquire would be liquid metallic hydrogen."

"Liquid metallic hydrogen takes extreme pressures to form," said Stephens. "If you tried to collect some, wouldn't it return to its normal gaseous state?"

"Liquid metallic hydrogen is meta-stable," said Dr. Riesen. "It's like crushing carbon into diamond—when you remove the pressure, the diamond doesn't revert to its original carbon form."

Holbrook stroked his chin. "If the Hex Men were miners, do we know what they were mining on Infernum?"

"That brings us to the reason for this mission," said Commodore Ahrens. "Based on an analysis of the research ship's logs, we believe the Hex Men were mining a substance called Planck Matter."

Dr. Riesen's eyes grew wide.

"What's Planck Matter?" asked Stephens.

"It's a theoretical material that has never been seen in nature or created in any lab," said Dr. Riesen. "Black holes compress an immense amount of matter into a relatively small volume by distending spacetime into small pockets. These matter-filled clumps of distended spacetime are called Planck Matter. No larger than grains of sand, each one holds enormous amounts of material. A clump the size of your fist can hold the equivalent mass of a continent."

"But nothing can escape a black hole," said Stephens, "not even light. If this Planck Matter forms inside, how can anyone get ahold of it?"

"Planck Matter escapes through quantum tunneling," said Dr. Riesen. She turned to the commodore. "But drifting all the way from Sag A Star to a planet twenty-three light-years away seems incredibly improbable."

"The RD Sagittarii star system contains a smaller black hole, in orbit around its massive star," said Ahrens. "The Planck Matter likely escaped from that black hole and was deposited on the planet. And that brings us to the whys of Tentek's presence here." The commodore gestured to the aught, who gave a slow nod to the others in the room. "He came to us with some important information that I will let him convey."

The robot clasped his thin hands before him on the table. "The Collective intercepted the data blast," said Tentek, his voice tinny and faintly metallic. "They reached the same conclusion about Planck Matter. They have outfitted a ship."

"My God," said Dr. Riesen.

"The aughts on that ship are tasked with collecting Planck Matter and returning it to The Collective," said Tentek.

Dr. Riesen covered her mouth with her hand.

"What in Hades is the matter?" asked Holbrook.

The physicist turned to Holbrook. "With even a palmful of Planck Matter and the proper detonator, you could build an unthinkably large weapon."

"How large?" asked Holbrook.

"Larger than the human race has ever built," said Tentek. "The Collective wants Planck Matter for a weapon that could destroy the Earth. They see it as a sort of … insurance policy."

"When Tentek learned of this plan he relayed it to us," said Ahrens. "It's the reason for this mission."

"Wait a minute," said Stephens, incredulous. "He just marched in and supposedly ratted out his machine buddies, and you all just believed him? Everyone knows aughts can't be trusted, especially not one from The Collective."

"We determined early on that The Collective decoded the tachyon blast," said Ahrens. "Tentek came to us after that. We've separately confirmed an aught vessel left The Collective home world a day ago, on a course for the galactic center. They should reach Sag A Star in about eight days." The commodore swiped the table viewscreen off and set his dark eyes on Captain Holbrook. "We can't let the aughts obtain Planck Matter. We're sending the *Avenger* to Sag A Star to stop them."

"But Commodore," said Holbrook, confused, "it'll take two weeks for us to reach Sag A Star. By then it'll be too late to intercept the aught ship before it enters D-space. There have to be ships closer than ours."

"Intercepting them before they enter D-space is not the objective," said Ahrens. "We can't engage the aughts in normal space—that would spark an interstellar incident. It would touch off a new war."

"But they're trying to build a weapon to destroy the Earth," said Stephens.

"*We* know that," said Ahrens, "but the aughts'll deny it. They'll claim any other reason for their trip to Sag A Star. We'd never be able to prove otherwise."

"We have this aught here," said Stephens, pointing at Tentek. "From what you've told us he apparently knows the whole plan. We could dismantle him and read it right from his bubble memory. That would be proof enough."

"That's a brilliant idea, Commander Stephens, just brilliant," said Ahrens as he folded his arms, his voice full of sarcasm. "We blow the Collective ship out of the sky and present to them, as justification, the disassembled remains of one of their own." Ahrens's cold dark eyes bored into the commander, who wilted slightly under their intensity. "I recommend you leave the strategic planning to people above your pay grade." Stephens shifted uncomfortably in his chair, a sullen look on his face.

"As I was saying, we can't intercept them before they enter the space around the galactic black hole. That's why we're counting on this mission to take place within D-space. No one on the outside will be able to see what happens. The aught ship will appear to be just another casualty of the hazardous region around Sag A Star."

"But that will be the *Avenger's* fate too," murmured Holbrook, his eyes glazed and trained on the tabletop. He looked up, surprised by the sound of his own voice, his inner dialogue spoken aloud. "Sir, I understood we'd be traveling to the galactic center—not flying into D-space itself but operating in the still dangerous area just outside of it. That was based on the orders from Admiral Miller."

Ahrens wrinkled his nose as if offended by a smell that had suddenly entered the room. "I spoke with the admiral right before hopping into the sleeper. He told me he made his orders clear and to the point because of the gravity of what was being asked. Those orders said you would be going *to the core*. I don't see how anyone can get any more clear or to the point than that."

"I guess the captain didn't believe it was CentCom's custom to hand out death sentences," said Stephens.

"It's not," Ahrens shot back, "but it *is* our custom to do whatever it takes to keep humanity safe." He returned his attention to Holbrook. "It sounds like you opted not to take your orders at face value. Perhaps you wanted to believe they were something else. If there's one thing I've learned from all my years in CentCom it's you should always assume the worst. That way you can never be disappointed."

Holbrook sank into his chair and his head slowly drooped towards the tabletop. The world spun as the true reality of the situation came into sharp relief. They were going *into* D-space, not next to it. Directly to Sag A Star, exactly what he had refused to believe, exactly what Stephens had tried to tell him. A one-way mission with no way home.

The commodore's eyes narrowed at the distraught captain slumping before him. "Thomas Holbrook the second, now he was quite an officer. Didn't know him, of course—I was barely out of grade school when he died —but his devotion to duty speaks for itself. He was a soldier, the kind of soldier the Republic needs you to be right now." Ahrens's voice softened. "Are you a soldier, Captain Holbrook?"

Holbrook glared at Ahrens from beneath his brows. He wanted to reach out and grab the commodore's neck.

"He is a soldier," said Stephens. "One of the finest I've ever served with."

"If you're a soldier, like your father before you, like your XO here attests, then you know a soldier's only job, his *only* job, is to carry out orders. That's the way CentCom works. That's the only way anything gets done. Carrying out orders doesn't mean doing a bunch of thinking about what might come afterwards, like your grand imaginings of a hero's welcome in your hometown and of banging all the girls who never gave you the time of day. That kind of thinking, that kind of preoccupation with something other than the task at hand, is all a distraction, and in this business, distractions get you killed.

"Your orders, Captain, are to stop those God damn aughts from getting even a milligram of Planck Matter. All that moping you're doing right now, all that will disappear once you focus on those orders. Your mind will be too preoccupied with everything you need to do to see those orders through to success. How to prepare your ship, how to prepare your crew, what contingency plans might need developing. None of that kind of thinking will throw you down in the dumps. In that sense, your orders are the secret to your own happiness. They are the key to your salvation."

Holbrook slowly lifted his head. Still glaring at the commodore he straightened himself in his chair. "You're right, Commodore, about why I'm upset," he said. "It's because I *am* focused on what comes after. I'm focused on the loss of my ship, the loss of my crew. The loss of my own life."

"Irrelevant," said Ahrens. "Your worries, fears, and concerns, all those things are irrelevant. Your orders are all that matter."

Dr. Riesen placed a hand on Holbrook's arm. "The researchers on the *Adiona* believed they found a way out of D-space," she said. "The aughts think it's possible too, which is why they sent a ship to bring Planck Matter back from the galactic center. It seems the odds are with us that we can get back. We just don't know how to do it yet."

Holbrook slowly looked towards Dr. Riesen. "We?"

"Dr. Riesen has volunteered to accompany you on this mission," said Ahrens. "Or at least I assume that's still the case. I hadn't briefed her on more than the travel to and from the galactic core. Besides finding the answer, she can provide her astrophysical expertise to assist you in preventing the aughts from acquiring Planck Matter."

"Why would you sign on to a suicide mission?" Holbrook asked Dr. Riesen, his voice leaden.

Dr. Riesen squeezed the captain's arm gently, meeting his despondence with a reassuring smile. "Because you need my help, Captain."

"You'll also get Tentek's help," said the commodore. "He'll be joining you on this mission."

"Coming with us on the *Avenger*?" asked Stephens. "Never."

"Tentek can provide invaluable insight into dealing with the aughts from The Collective," said Ahrens.

"I doubt that very much," said Stephens. "It certainly won't be any insight we can trust. And when the other aughts see their long-lost buddy Tentek they're going to invite him over for drinks."

"The aughts on the planet will not welcome me," said Tentek. "They will know I am a traitor and will want to harm me."

"Pretending for a moment you're not a double agent, even if you're captured, you'll have a lot to bargain with," said Stephens. "As the first aught to travel aboard a CentCom warship in over a hundred years, I bet they throw you a parade."

Tentek remained expressionless. "Should I encounter my fellow aughts on the planet, I do not expect that reunion to go well. For this reason, I have installed an electromagnetic pulse bomb in my abdominal cavity. If captured, I will detonate that bomb and destroy all of my circuits. Not even my memory core will function."

"Why wait?" asked Stephens. "I for one would like to see this so-called bomb of yours go off right now."

"Commander!" said Holbrook.

"Sir," said Stephens, "you don't believe any of what this aught has told us here today, do you? It's not feeding us secret intel from The Collective, it doesn't have an EMP in its chest, and it's not going to commit suicide the next time it sees its buddies." Stephens addressed Tentek directly. "You haven't fooled me, aught, with any of your words," he snapped. "And as far as joining us on this mission, I can happily say the regs don't allow you to set foot on our ship."

"The exception's already been approved," said Ahrens.

Stunned, Commander Stephens struggled for a response as his mind filled with an image of the unthinkable: a Collective aught roaming the halls of his ship.

"The Joint Chiefs passed a resolution just for Tentek that overrides the general regulations against aughts on CentCom starships," said Ahrens. "He will be accompanying you on this mission."

"Like hell," said Stephens under his breath.

"That's an apt description of what your life will be like if your borderline insubordination continues," said Ahrens.

Holbrook glared at Stephens, silently ordering his executive officer to stand down.

Stephens sulked. "I'll talk to Lynch about rigging up a Faraday cage in the brig for our guest here," he said.

"You just don't get it, do you, Commander?" asked Ahrens. "You clearly have a burning hatred for aughts; that's plain for everyone to see. However Tentek is on our side. An ally. And you're to treat him with the same consideration and respect as you would any other guest aboard your ship.

You will not lock him in the brig, and in fact you will allow him to move as freely about your ship as you would a normal civilian. That is an order."

Holbrook sat frozen in his chair, sullenly contemplating the fate of his vessel and crew.

"Captain," Ahrens said, standing abruptly, "good luck, and keep us apprised of your progress on your way to the galactic center." The commodore thrust his hand out to Holbrook.

Captain Holbrook stared at Ahrens's hand, regarding its wide palm and the jagged scar that cut across it. How many other men had the commodore's handshake sent to their deaths? How many times had that angry red gash sealed the fates of entire ships and crews? Holbrook leaned awkwardly into the table from his seat and half clasped Ahrens's hand, giving it a tepid shake.

"I will leave you to your preparations," said Ahrens. The commodore nodded to Dr. Riesen and strode out of the room.

The world no longer spun for Holbrook, but his stomach felt queasy. He mustered the strength to speak, his mouth dry. "How soon can you be ready?" he asked Dr. Riesen in a weak, gravelly voice, still staring into the tabletop.

"I'm already packed," she said.

Already packed? Of course she was. She'd planned to accompany them all along. "We'll wait for you at the shuttle, then."

Tentek stood. "I, too, am ready to leave," he said.

"Meet us at the shuttle as well," said Holbrook.

Dr. Riesen exited the conference room followed by Tentek, leaving the two *Avenger* officers still seated. Seconds after the door closed, Holbrook pressed into the tabletop to stand, his head drooping.

Stephens rose from his chair. He stared at the closed conference room door, shaking his head. "Captain," he said, "we can't let that thing aboard our ship."

"We don't have any say in the matter," said Holbrook. "It's been cleared at the highest levels."

"For sure that thing's a double agent," said Stephens. "It'll be feeding us misinformation and stealing secrets."

Holbrook rubbed his chin. "Tentek, by far, is the least of our worries."

10

"This way, Dr. Riesen."

Stephens hadn't mustered more than those four words since leaving the research station. Was he, a former physics grad student, really that starstruck? He'd certainly never dreamed of being in the presence of The Prophet, a living legend, but that explanation only told part of the story. He'd worked up the courage to talk to the physicist several times but had been taken aback by the smile he caught on her face whenever he'd glanced her way. He could only guess at the reason for her seemingly high spirits. "First time aboard a CentCom starship?"

"No," said Dr. Riesen, smiling even then as she looked at him. "I've been on several. CentCom has asked me a number of times to consult on physics-related matters."

What else it could be? "It's just ... you seem extremely happy to be here."

"I am."

Stephens looked at Dr. Riesen sideways. "I mean, I'm happy to be on the *Avenger* too," he said, "just not so much right now given we may not come back from where we're going."

Dr. Riesen didn't respond. She had become engrossed in a list of crew announcements on a passing viewscreen.

"Tell me again why you volunteered to join this mission?" said Stephens.

"Let's just say I love a good puzzle. They don't come much bigger than figuring a way out of D-space."

The journey to their potential deaths was just a big, fun puzzle for her? Stephens wanted to probe more, but their destination came into view. "Here we are," he said as they approached Sickbay.

The doors to Sickbay slid open, revealing Dr. Marsden in her white lab coat. "Here she is waiting for us," said Stephens as they entered. "Dr. Marsden, this is Dr. Riesen, a new guest aboard our ship."

"Nice to meet you, Dr. Riesen." Dr. Marsden extended her hand.

"Likewise," said Dr. Riesen.

"She's a VIP, so be sure she gets special treatment," said Stephens.

"How much of a VIP can she be if you're the one showing her around?" quipped Dr. Marsden. She walked Dr. Riesen over to a medical examination table. "Dr. Riesen, please hop up here."

Dr. Riesen pivoted, pressed the backs of her thighs against the lip of the table, and lifted herself in reverse onto the surface. The wide viewscreen mounted on the bulkhead above sprang to life.

"This shouldn't take very long," said Dr. Marsden.

"I've barely been aboard five minutes," said Dr. Riesen, frowning. "Why's an examination in Sickbay my first stop?"

"Standard procedure," said Dr. Marsden. "Anyone who comes aboard for an extended period of time gets a physical scan. A full analysis of your physical condition means there won't be any surprises while you're with us. Medical surprises, anyway."

Dr. Riesen studied the readout above her head, the screen populating with vital signs. "On other ships the first thing they do is get you comfortably situated in your quarters. This process feels very regimented."

"This *is* a military vessel," said Dr. Marsden. "But I imagine your next stop will be getting settled into your new quarters. Please lie back." Dr. Riesen swung her legs around and lay flat on her back. "Good," said Dr. Marsden, tapping a side control panel. "Now relax. The table will take a couple minutes to perform the scan."

Nodding, Dr. Riesen folded her hands over her belly and closed her eyes.

"The name Riesen sounds familiar," said Dr. Marsden as she studied the initial results from the scan. "Isn't there a famous woman physicist named Riesen?"

"That would be me, Doctor."

"No kidding!" said Dr. Marsden. "Winner of the Nobel-Wasserman?"

"In the flesh."

"You truly *are* a VIP then," said Dr. Marsden, "which makes it doubly wrong for Commander Stephens to be your escort."

Stephens feigned irritation at the remark.

"I've read some about you, then," said Dr. Marsden, tapping at the table's controls. "Tell me, what's it like to be a female physicist?"

Dr. Riesen's face grew dark. "You mean what it's like being a mistake?"

Dr. Marsden looked up from the controls. "A mistake?"

"Yes, a mistake," she said. She propped herself up on her elbows and glowered at Dr. Marsden. "That's your real question, isn't it? What's it like to be a mistake?"

Stephens cut in. "I'm sure Dr. Marsden didn't —"

"I'm sure Dr. Marsden can speak for herself," said Dr. Marsden. "And no, that wasn't the question going through my mind. I don't even know what you mean about being a mistake. Physics is so male dominated I was wondering about the challenges of being a woman in that field. Being a medical doctor is not nearly as hard, though I do have a few stories of my own."

Lying back on the table Dr. Riesen closed her eyes again. "Sorry, Doctor, I just get it a lot. It's usually the first thing people ask me once they learn who I am. It leaves me walking around on the defensive."

The doctor checked the scan's progress. "Can I ask what you meant by 'mistake'?"

"I'm from a line of genetically engineered humans," said Dr. Riesen. "The ones who came before me were also named Riesen. The intent was all of us would be men. Obviously, someone screwed up in my case."

"You mean a group of men, with hubris coming out their asses, performed a genetic procedure and it didn't go the way they expected?" asked Dr. Marsden. "Surprise, surprise. *They* screwed up trying to control nature, but somehow *you* turn out to be the mistake."

"I've got to get going," said Stephens. "Dr. Riesen, you're clearly in good hands. Someone will be by to show you to your quarters. In a couple hours the captain wants us all to review the logs from the *Adiona*. Cygnus Conference Room, Deck B."

"What timeframe do the logs cover?" asked Dr. Riesen.

"A two-week stretch," said Stephens. "The last entry was recorded a little more than three weeks ago, four days before we got our new orders."

"Thank you, Commander," said Dr. Riesen. "I will be there."

Commander Stephens exited the room and climbed a nearby rungway to Deck A. He wended his way through the corridors until he found Lieutenant Singh. The security officer stood outside a closed door with Tentek at his side.

"Hope I didn't keep you waiting too long," said Stephens.

"Fourteen minutes, thirty-seven seconds by my internal clock," said Tentek.

"I was talking to Lieutenant Singh," said Stephens.

"Uh, no, sir," sputtered Singh. "I knew you'd be along eventually."

"Is it customary for guests aboard your starship to endure such long wait times before being settled into their quarters?" asked Tentek.

"No," said Stephens, "but neither is it customary for us to have an aught from The Collective on board. Let's just say it's extraordinary times." He signaled for Singh to unlock the cabin. The door slid aside and the three entered the spacious guest quarters.

Stephens noted the queen bed replacing the more customary bunk, a typical concession made for guests. Did aughts even sleep? "Your comm will let you into all the places on the ship you're authorized to enter," he said curtly. "By the captain's orders you're a guest aboard this ship, but that doesn't mean there aren't any rules. The main one is you'll check in with security three times each day."

"Is that also customary for guests?" asked Tentek.

"Like I said, extraordinary times. I assume that won't be a problem."

"It will not," said Tentek.

Stephens headed for the door. "Captain's organized a listening party for the *Adiona* logs. He asked me to invite you. Cygnus Conference Room, Deck B, fourteen-thirty hours."

"Thank you, Commander."

"Don't thank me," said Stephens, "thank the captain. I still think you belong in the brig."

Tentek cocked his head. "Then it is fortunate you are not in charge."

Stephens pursed his lips and locked on to Tentek with a blank stare. He didn't appreciate the attitude, not from an aught, not on his ship. "Lieutenant Singh, you mind giving us a moment?"

"Yes, sir—I mean no, sir," said Singh. He quickly exited the room.

Stephens took several steps towards Tentek. "You may have fooled the others, Tin Man, but not me," he said. "I don't believe for a moment you're anything other than a spy for The Collective."

"My name is Tentek, and I do not think this is the best way to start off our working together."

"Working together?" Stephens scoffed. "You and I are not 'working together,' and we never will. Like I said, you're here because the captain ordered it. If it were up to me, you'd be out an airlock." He jabbed his finger at Tentek. "Just remember this, Tin Man: the captain runs the show, but I run this ship. You're free to move around, but that freedom can be taken away in an instant. I have my eye on you and I'm looking for an excuse, any excuse to throw your ass in a cell. You so much as break artificial wind my way and you'll find yourself in chains."

Tentek cocked his head again. "My name is Tentek, and I doubt Commodore Ahrens would enjoy hearing you have suggested placing me in the brig, an idle threat in any case, as we both know doing so would bring about the end of your career."

Stephens smiled. "A wise man once said, 'You can do anything you want on your last day.'" He winked and headed for the door. "See you at fourteen-thirty hours, Tin Man," he said over his shoulder.

The aught watched the commander exit the room and head down the corridor until the cabin door closed, dreading the voyage before it had even begun.

11

The Adiona Logs

Day 0, 14:02 hours

And so begins our journey to oblivion!

Like Columbus's brash voyage to the edge of the Earth, MacGregor's imprudent trek to Alpha Centauri, and Siloban's mad venture to the surface of Venus, ours is the next step in mankind's achievement of the impossible.

My colleague, Dr. Yoichiro Imura, was somewhat less poetic in his remarks at our launch party: "Let's prove those fuckers wrong!"

I am unaccustomed to keeping an audio log, so this will be a new experience. Maintaining a record of my thoughts during this voyage and a description of events will no doubt prove useful to historians writing about this monumental endeavor.

My name is Dr. Richard Denby, Professor of Astrophysics at the University of New Oceania, and the leader of this expedition to Sagittarius A Star, the black hole at the center of our galaxy. My eighteen expedition-mates are professors and a smattering of their graduate students, experts in disciplines ranging from Loop Quantum Gravity Theory to Warp Mechanics, to Homo- and Xeno-Medicine, fields of study that fall under the University's interdepartmental School of Space Exploration.

This expedition, the tenth in the school's eight-decade history, will test theories I have developed for navigating through the extremely deformed space that exists around Sagittarius A Star, a 4.24 million solar mass black hole—navigating through and safely returning from that space, I should say, as neither has yet been accomplished, and the first is irrelevant without the second. I have reinforced this point by naming our ship the *Adiona* after the Roman Goddess of Safe Return, a reference I pulled from my undergraduate training in the Classics. It was a reference that went unrecognized by my colleagues.

Our liftoff from the space center at the Atoll was uneventful. The full brunt of summer arrived two weeks early, and we were grateful to escape the muggy December weather for the temperature-controlled, atmosphere-conditioned confines of the ship. We spent an hour in Earth orbit rechecking our navigational and propulsive systems before a 1.5-million-kilometer tow to Lagrange Point L2, opting for a tug service to conserve our hydrogen stores at the start of our voyage.

We left L2 an hour ago and have been moving at warp speeds since then, with an estimated travel time of seven days to Sag A Star. Everyone is settling into their quarters. We have a few veterans of space exploration aboard, but the majority of us has not logged many hours beyond commercial flight between systems. For most of our grad students this trip is already the farthest distance they have traveled from home.

Columbus. MacGregor. Siloban. Denby! Palpable excitement fills the corridors of the ship at the start of this historic voyage.

Day 1, 16:14 hours

Today we said farewell to the Orion arm of the Milky Way galaxy, the happy residence of the sun and Earth, and ventured into the dark lane that separates it from the neighboring Sagittarius arm, the next limb we will transit on our journey [... TRANSMISSION ERROR ...]

Day 2, 15:31 hours

We have settled here, halfway across the Sagittarius arm, to test the device Hohlt will use to find a habitable planet within the space around Sag A Star. This is happening despite my quite vocal and vigorous objections.

Two months ago, Dr. Jakob Hohlt, Professor of Xenobiology at the University, visited me in the midst of my frenzied last-minute preparations to propose attaching himself to my expedition. At that time, discussion of my theories and their imminent validation had no doubt reached a fever pitch within the University and likely spurred others to dream of how they might leverage my work to achieve their own success. Hohlt suggested living evidence of our travels to Sag A Star would prove much more compelling than sensor logs and cryptographically verifiable location data.

Of course, I saw through this poor man's sales job: Hohlt was in truth considering the fame such a find would bring to him and his department. I would have thrown him out right then, but he had the University president in tow, and as I learned later, the provost and several of the University's trustees in his back pocket. I initially refused his request, citing the problems of integrating his project and staff into my logistics at such a late date, but after the president took me aside and explained the University would not otherwise fund my expedition, I relented, with the stipulation that his opportunistic efforts not impact the project I had first conceived almost three years ago.

Despite their assurances, I was forced to accompany Hohlt to the offices of Orbital Spectrum, wasting most of a precious day traveling to and from lunar orbit for a demonstration of their Collimating Planetary Telescope. This device, when trained on a distant star system, can image its planets and determine with almost perfect accuracy which ones harbor life.

During the meeting I expressed how our tight schedule would deny us time to test the device ourselves and forced Hohlt to accept Orbital Spectrum's assurances the telescope would perform flawlessly in the field. They described the telescope's operation and construction, explained their extremely rigorous testing regimen, and trotted out their independent lab certifications. They ended with an impressive demonstration, training the telescope on Helvetios and generating detailed images of and biosphere reports on the twin planets Helvetios b1 and b2. The telescope even captured the faint life-form readings from the near-dead moon orbiting Dimidum, the system's Jupiter analog.

I stress again that Hohlt accepted their avowals and agreed we had no time to vet the device ourselves, yet once underway he came to me with a list of possible stopping points along our route to test the telescope. I refused to consider stopping and stressed the pointlessness of doing so, for we would not turn back if we discovered a problem with his telescope. Hours later, I received a message from the University containing a list of three candidate stopping points and instructions to select one of them.

And with all of this the test proved wholly unnecessary. We have the CPT trained on Sol, and the images and readings we are getting from the equipment are truly exceptional. The telescope has correctly identified Earth, Mars, Europa, and Enceladus as life-bearing worlds in our home system and produced images with phenomenal clarity for a device over five thousand light-years from its target. The images so shocked Yoichiro he declared he will now either remove the skylights from his house on Oceania or no longer sleep in the nude.

The cost of this diversion will be significant. After dropping from warp, we nudged the telescope out of the cargo bay and spent the next two hours trying to convince it to power up its systems. Once activated we waited three hours for its optics to chill to absolute zero and devoted another two and a half hours to imaging. Now that Hohlt has finished the tests the telescope will take several additional hours to raise its internal temperature, secure its sensor arrays, and return to its compact travel configuration. Adding the time to retrieve the device and to strap it to the cargo bay's deck, we will have lost about fourteen hours total, or nearly a full day of travel.

The whole episode infuriates me. When we return, the University will regret having ever strong-armed me into this arrangement, for I will be in such demand I think it unlikely I will decide to remain at their institution.

Day 3, 20:19 hours

[... TRANSMISSION ERROR ...] just as the jet engine allowed us to rise above the Earth to take the photographs we used to build accurate terrestrial maps, the Gravity Drive allowed the human race to rise high above the Milky Way to take the snapshots we used for the accurate maps of our galaxy and to discover important details such as the spiral's asymmetry, shown to be the result of the Milky Way's collision with a globular cluster.

I felt somewhat shaky again today and have a slightly elevated temperature. We have been running nonstop for the past few months to make this expedition a reality. I am hopeful this is just a case of exhaustion catching up with me. I took a nap this afternoon and I do feel considerably better now after eating a light dinner of chicken broth and bread.

Day 5, 12:57 hours

I awoke yesterday with difficulty swallowing and a complete inability to speak. Dr. Mawen's tests confirmed what I suspected but was unwilling to voice: my Craeter's disease has returned. I contracted it over a year ago during a foolish weekend on Darwin's Planet. My doctor at the time explained how Craeter's is fully treatable, but those afflicted will sometimes relapse when stress brings viral reserves out of hiding.

Thankfully the symptoms were not nearly as severe as during my initial bout, when the disease freely ran its course over the several days it took to pinpoint the cause. The *Adiona's* MediCenter synthesized a dose of Demerosol, which Dr. Mawen administered midday yesterday. His prognosis as of fifteen minutes ago was that I'll spend most of today in bed but should expect full recovery by tomorrow morning. He also said we must watch for symptoms of a second relapse, which statistically has the highest chance of occurring within the next two weeks.

I woke this morning to a world tinged in yellow and immediately worried the Craeter's had affected my liver and jaundiced my eyes. Thankfully it was just a thick shaft of yellow light streaming through the small porthole above my bunk. During my almost forty hours of incapacitation, the *Adiona* traveled quite a distance closer to the great galactic bulge where the lower star formation rate results in significantly fewer young stars. Without the white-blue hue from their youthful furnaces, the starlight settles into a deep yellow from the preponderance of older stars.

Even the mild exertion of recording this log entry has tired me. I must sign off for another nap.

Day 6, 19:23 hours

I snapped awake at 6:30 this morning after sleeping [... TRANSMISSION ERROR ...]ion. I hadn't bathed in several days and looked forward to showering, but unfortunately Craeter's sensitizes the skin, which turned the normally refreshing ultrasonic waves into a rain of pinpricks across my body.

Tonight we are orbiting a gas giant from a class B star system in the central bar region of the galaxy. We just retracted the skimmer we deployed to extract hydrogen from the planet's upper atmosphere, our scheme to top off our intentionally minimal hydrogen stores. We had decided [... TRANSMISSION ERROR ...]

Even four thousand light-years away, I find Sag A Star intimidating, its four-and-a-quarter-million solar masses compressed into a region smaller than the orbit of Mercury. We are still too far away to see the hole itself, but its accretion disc put on quite a display of explosive flashes soon after we arrived. Yoichiro showed me an impressive snapshot where the surrounding gas resembles an immense jack-o'-lantern.

After decamping tomorrow morning we will travel most of the remaining distance to the galactic center where we will position the ring of tachyon beacons. Once we've completed that task, we'll make the final short jog to the black hole itself.

Day 7, 13:36 hours

We are still hours away from the galactic center; that is, if we could fly there directly. For all the fretting that had gone on about returning from the deformed space around Sagittarius A Star, we did not consider the difficulties we would face trying to reach the hole itself.

Our plan for approaching the black hole was simply to pilot the ship into the region around Sag A Star, not considering how navigation towards the singularity presents the same challenges as navigating away from it. We are therefore taking this final leg of the journey slowly and carefully. We've improvised a plan to wait for the spacetime ahead of us to calm enough to support a reasonably safe sprint towards the hole, and to halt when the deformations flare up. Repeating this enough times will get us to our destination, a position roughly two hundred astronomical units from the event horizon. Dr. Alcott calls this process "inch-worming." My thoughts immediately went to a small, green worm wending its way towards an enormous fanged spider sitting at the center of its web. The parallels are hugely disturbing.

At the end of each sprint, we are creating a gravimetric map of the surrounding space, and this four-dimensional imaging has allowed us to so far locate twenty-two nearby invisible gravity wave point sources. Those black holes, orders of magnitude smaller than the one at our galactic center, are still very dangerous. Knowing their locations, we can give them a wide berth.

Our herky-jerky progress makes estimating our final arrival time at Sag A Star difficult. I grow excited on each lunge until the inevitable klaxons sound just before the Gravity Drive disengages. I pray we have not become unwitting prisoners in a Zeno's paradox come alive.

Day 8, 10:21 hours

We arrived at Sagittarius A Star fifty-five minutes ago, parking an uneasy 102.5 AU from the event horizon. I am both giddy with excitement and afraid beyond words.

As our final sprint landed us here in system, an unremarkable star field greeted us upon our deceleration to sub-light speed. Ordinary warp speed journeys conclude with the celestial destination, typically a planet or moon, centered in the ship's viewscreen; however, we dared not set a direct course for the black hole for fear of Gravity Drive overshoot. We targeted instead an adjacent patch of space a few degrees to the left of the event horizon, which placed Sagittarius A Star outside our field of view upon our arrival. A short force pad pulse brought the *Adiona* around and revealed our considerable host.

Despite the thousands of long-range images of our galaxy's black hole, I doubt anyone can ever be fully prepared for the sight. If Paradise Planet is the closest thing to Heaven in our galaxy, Sagittarius A Star is certainly a slice of Hell. The hole is an angry sphincter onto the underworld itself, encircled by a rotating river Styx of debris spraying synchrotron radiation across the entire region. Hydrogen gas clouds accelerated to near light speed shower deadly gamma rays on any object unlucky enough to venture too close. Pulsar-like particle acceleration drives brilliant blue-green bolts of electrical discharge that serrate the hole's thick magnetosphere and threaten to lash us with their million-volt tendrils. Gravitational waves are plentiful, though thankfully too small to wrench the ship's superstructure.

Alex Kondo, the other young research assistant from Dr. Reed's lab, was overcome by the sight of this galactic beast and broke down crying. Dr. Mawen escorted him to his bunk and placed him under light sedation. At this moment I am actively resisting the urge to order us away from here. Leaving now would mean the end of this research trip and my tenure at the University as the president expressed my relationship with the institution would come to an end should we return without providing Hohlt a chance to unfurl his telescope. That process has begun, and I am anxious for the results. The sooner we locate a suitable system to explore, the sooner we can leave this space.

Day 9, 9:35 hours

The *Adiona* is holding up well twenty-four hours after our arrival at Sag A Star. A sub-atomic detritus surrounds the ship and continually slams against our magnetic field, violently at times. The computer assures us we are parked a safe enough distance away to withstand the onslaught.

Alex is much better today—Dr. Mawen predicts his return to duties starting tomorrow. I, too, have settled down after a night in the shadow of the beast. Everyone else seems to be coping well enough, though I can feel the tension. During our days of travel from Earth, conversations filled the control room and the internal comm channels. Now the ship has all the ambiance of a mortician's parlor. I have to believe time dilation effects are partly to blame for the change in mood. As the black hole rotates, it drags space around like batter in a mixing bowl, with the resulting eddies and whorls felt up to three parsecs away. The distortions can occur on a small enough scale that two clocks sitting side by side will momentarily tick at different rates. Such time divergences can create problems in biological processes, especially within the human brain where its structures rely on adjacent neurons firing at the same rate. Physiological symptoms of Spacetime Deformation Sickness include muscular aches and nausea. The psychological symptoms range anywhere from mild depression to madness.

I confess there are other psychological side effects of our proximity to this Grendel. It is easy to sit twenty thousand light-years away with a nice cup of hot tea and read about plummeting into a black hole. It is another thing entirely to sit only a hundred times Earth's distance to the sun from the hole and realize one errant force pad pulse could render us irretrievably lost.

We remain at this location because efforts to use the CPT have so far failed. I refer to it as the Collimating Planetary Telescope, but Yoichiro has reminded me of its full name, the Collimating Refractor Array Planetary Telescope, or CRAP Telescope as he now calls it. The device worked well enough when we tested it in normal space but has so far lived up to Yoichiro's derisive moniker within the extreme deformed space conditions around Sag A Star.

We deployed the telescope almost twenty-four hours ago and positioned it about a hundred meters off the ship's leeward side, employing the *Adiona* as a shield against the black hole's relentless gale of sub-atomic particles. When aimed at a planetary system, the telescope's twenty-meter-wide aperture collects photons, which its sensor array converts to a raw data stream that it transmits to its signal processing AI here aboard the ship. Orbital Spectrum said to think of the signal processor as a magic black box, where raw photon data go in one end, and crisp, vivid planetary images and biospheric information come out the other.

Unfortunately, the CPT has been unable to photograph any systems within the deformed space around Sag A Star. Every photon matters when imaging remote objects, and in the case of these planetary systems the photons have been stretched and twisted during their travels through the distorted spacetime. I find it difficult to imagine recovering much signal from such deformed packets of light; however, this is only a guess as to the root cause. The actual problem may reside in the telescope's hardware, or in its software black box. In any case, the planetary photographs captured by this device so far resemble the bright, blurry images from a ground-based telescope flailing beneath a thick blanket of atmosphere.

Without planetary imaging, we remain unable to locate a habitable system for Hohlt. If we head back now, the bastard will certainly try to end my career at the University with complaints that we left too soon, that I did not provide him an adequate opportunity to test the CPT, or both. They can stick my tenure right in their bottoms, but I prefer to leave the University on my own terms; not with them eagerly throwing me out the door but instead begging me to stay. Unfortunately, that means it is in my best interest for Hohlt's mission to succeed. So, I wait for now and pray for the device to start working. I only hope the *Adiona* and its crew remain intact until it does.

Day 10, 21:47 hours

We arrived at Sag A Star two days ago and have not moved more than twenty kilometers from our original position.

Three hours ago, the quiescent hole turned maniacal, releasing a torrent of energy across the electromagnetic spectrum. Most of the ship's viewports remain almost perpetually black, made opaque by the ship to protect us from these energy bursts. The rocking and jostling caused by Sag A Star's churning of the local spacetime has also increased, and we have all been stricken with moderate to severe cases of nausea. Dr. Mawen's Nausox shots have helped me, but the high dosage needed to tamp down my queasiness has not been without side effects, loose stools the most notable complication. As a result, I have been dividing my time between my station in the control room and my new, second station in the starboard head.

While our nausea can be managed with pharmaceuticals, there is no treatment for the curious form of double vision that also afflicts us at various times. Corridors seem packed with people as we move through the ship with our blurred doppelgängers. Mealtimes have become more challenging with doubled forks and cups confusing us as to which one we should raise to our mouths. Dr. Kelechi Adeyemi, Professor of Spacetime Mechanics, tells us these are further time dilation effects, the result of seeing the same object at two different points in time. I have found it best to focus on the eyes of the person I am speaking to, as the jumble of mouths in different states of openness is both distracting and horrifying.

If this is what we can expect by remaining here in D-space, I think it is best we leave and not subject ourselves to more torture. Hohlt made some adjustments to the CPT, but the improvements were minimal, not nearly enough to give us accurate readings on habitable planets in the vicinity. Yoichiro suggested Hohlt try using the computer to squeeze more signal out of the images. That is his goal for tomorrow.

Day 11, 07:47 hours

Early this morning, I woke to the ship wildly rocking and the roar of a ferocious rainstorm.

Certain we were being drawn into the black hole, I leapt from my bed. At that moment the entire ship rose violently as if being lifted into the air. I resisted being drawn down as best I could while a loud groan, the *Adiona's* superstructure struggling under the stresses, carried through the ship.

Suddenly I saw doubles of my bunk, the one still in my grasp and a duplicate a half meter lower, its blankets erupting through the floor. Realizing I had only a moment, I quickly swung my other arm around and dug my fingers deep into the mattress just as the ship fell into a steep drop, as if racing down the back side of a mountainous ocean crest. I clung there with white knuckles, my legs flailing in the air.

The ship continued rising and falling for several minutes. I held fast to my bunk as my body flopped about like a soggy pennant. When the pitching subsided, I slowly worked my way through my cabin door and scurried to the control room like a panicked crab on a blustery beach.

Yoichiro arrived just ahead of me. The two of us strapped ourselves into our chairs and set about analyzing sensor data. We discovered the previously placid spacetime around the ship took a violent turn at 2:34 a.m., pitching the *Adiona* like a small sailboat on a storm-churned ocean. We took the computer's recommendation to set the artificial gravity to full inertial dampening. Activating it was like flipping a switch that reduced the ship's violent pitching to a gentle bobbing. After checking on the rest of our shipmates, Yoichiro and I set about ensuring all massive items were battened down to prevent them from wreaking havoc in any future rough sailing.

All the while we worked, the sound of a violent rainstorm filled the ship with an almost deafening pounding. Placing my ear against an outer bulkhead, I heard a sleeting rain as intense as anything I have experienced. Dr. Shales, Professor of Subatomic and Quantum Physics, concluded the thick magnetic field lines emanating from the black hole corral free protons from the surrounding super-hot plasma into tight bundles. Those proton bundles follow the magnetic field lines, picking up speed and momentum as they do, and striking the ship with the rasping patter of rain. After consulting the computer, Dr. Reed believes the net effect of this intense proton bombardment is similar to sitting in a mild acid bath, nothing to worry about at least while our shields are up.

Thankfully no one was seriously hurt during the ship's violent moments last night, though Wright and Shaw who sleep in bunks in one of the aft crew compartments both bumped their heads when the storm flung them into the air above their beds. Neither has a concussion, but they both have knots on their foreheads.

Day 11, 13:22 hours

Ten minutes ago, we made the discovery of a lifetime.

As if the supermassive black hole were not enough trouble, the space around Sagittarius A Star teems with smaller black holes, which the literature refers to as a "swarm." To map the locations of these black holes, Dr. Church, the post-doc from Dr. Iweala's lab, configured the computer to take gravimetric snapshots at set intervals on our inbound journey to Sag A Star. Examining how the point source locations changed as we moved closer to the galactic black hole allowed us to create a three-dimensional map of their locations in space. Once we arrived at Sag A Star, the three-dimensional swarm map was complete; however, no one told the computer to stop taking the gravimetric snapshots. With the *Adiona* stationary, the post-arrival snapshots form a time-lapse of the point sources traveling around us, an animated movie, if you will, of the swarm moving through space, rotating round the center of the galaxy.

Overall, this movie is quite boring. Most of the black holes orbit Sag A Star with periods on the order of thousands of years, making their gross movements undetectable to us. Church noticed one of the nearby holes moving at a relatively quick pace across the sky. What was truly remarkable, however, was its circular orbit did not have Sag A Star at its center. One of the swarm black holes was apparently orbiting some other body.

On a whim, she asked Hohlt to aim the Collimating Planetary Telescope at this system. The device, miraculously shaking off its troubles for ten minutes, revealed a modest-sized black hole orbiting a supergiant star. The telescope also revealed several planets, one of which appears to be habitable. I stress the qualifier "appears"—the telescope detected key markers for life, but some of the data were inconsistent. It also could be the telescope malfunctioning more severely than before. With no better options, and the desire to move away from the galactic black hole, we are treating this as a solid lead. It's actually an ideal development, for if the telescope is correct, this will be the planet Hohlt has been looking for. And if the telescope is wrong, Hohlt will have had his chance to find a planet. Either outcome sets a cap on our—up until now—open-ended stay in D-space.

I have dubbed this newly discovered system RD Sagittarii, assigning a Bayer-style designation based on my initials. Let the record show the schemer Hohlt's obsession with fame and glory came into full view with his demand I include his initials in the name. I noted that only by my grace was he even aboard this ship, and how his contributions to this discovery amounted to nothing more than the tapping of a few buttons on a viewscreen. With the xenobiologist shaking and sputtering before me, I made it clear that any spoils the Fates choose to grant him lay on the planet's surface.

We will make way for RD Sagittarii shortly. Navigating anywhere within the space around Sag A Star is essentially as impossible as navigating out, but Dr. Alcott believes his inch-worming technique will allow us to travel to this nearby destination. As if aware of our imminent departure, Sag A Star has begun lashing out with writhing red tendrils of plasma. I will be happy to leave this place.

Day 11, 23:05 hours

Not once have I ever imagined being in the presence of a star as large as RD Sagittarii A. This thirty solar mass red hypergiant shines a million times brighter than the sun, with an incredible radius of 12.34 AU. If this stellar beast resided in our own solar system, its bulk would engulf all the planets from Mercury to Saturn.

Orbiting at 183 AU is the ten solar mass black hole RD Sagittarii B, encircled by a massive accretion disc filled with enough matter to form several planets on its own. Whenever substantial amounts of this material spiral down to the black body, the hole erupts with blue flashes along its equator and energetic white jets from its poles.

The reason for our visit, RD Sagittarii C, orbits at 551 AU and does appear to be habitable. Normally the gale force stellar winds of a hypergiant star like RD Sagittarii A would strip away the atmosphere surrounding a small, rocky planet, even that far from its sun. It turns out the red titan's companion black hole sweeps up the bulk of the brisk stellar wind in its accretion disc.

RD Sagittarii's two other planets, D and E, are gas giants orbiting at 575 AU and 621 AU respectively. At 700 AU begins the system's Kuiper Belt, harboring a substantial number of planetesimals.

We are headed now to RD Sagittarii C. At this late hour we plan to merely park the ship in a safe orbit around the planet and rest for the night rather than plow ahead with our exploration.

We are in a low orbit above RD Sagittarii C. Liquid water covers half the surface, a violet soup that sloshes against five dark ashen continents. Daylight falls upon the planet for fifteen hours, a burning red that glints off the violet ocean crests and bounces off the white polar ice, capping both ends of the globe in fiery crimson.

The planet's molten inner core vomits itself onto the ashen plains of every continent through numerous active volcanos of various sizes. Where these volcanoes reside along the coasts, their lava runs in angry torrents many kilometers wide that extend down to the violet water. Great clouds of steam and ash hide their convergence with the sea, enormous white plumes that from space appear as cotton dabbing a slew of vicious open wounds.

The largest continental landmass spans an entire hemisphere along the planet's equator but does not extend above or below the fortieth parallel. A tall mountain range runs south to north near the continent's eastern coastline, featuring numerous ice-capped peaks that strafe the gray clouds. The four other continents that populate the opposite hemisphere are less remarkable—that is, more of the same—except for the third-largest, which harbors a massive volcano at its center, from space an angry red anthill oozing lava.

I have taken to calling this planet Infernum for its obvious allusions to Hell.

The atmosphere is an argon, nitrogen, oxygen, and CO_2 mixture, and temperatures range from ten to fifty-seven degrees centigrade. In short, breathable air and comfortable temps, at least beyond the equator and away from the volcanos. As for life signs, the sensors report level twenty-three on the Alan-During scale: plants, insects, and some animals.

We are finishing a sequence of orbits from which we are building radar terrain and gravimetric maps of the surface. This is not the most exciting work, and Yoichiro jokes the soft pings the computer makes on the completion of each orbit are there to make sure we are all still awake. I considered tasking drones with this mapping job, but the process will take less time using the ship's sensors.

I did dispatch two drones to take detailed scans of several candidate landing sites. Most are in the nighttime hemisphere currently, so we will likely remain in orbit for the next ten to sixteen hours, aiming for a sunrise descent on the planet.

Day 13, 07:08 hours

Landfall this morning was quite dramatic.

The computer guided the *Adiona* to a position 450 kilometers above our primary landing site, a rolling plain of short yellow brush 170 kilometers from the largest continent's eastern coastline along the thirty-second parallel north. Thick cloud cover obscured our destination, and the computer [... TRANSMISSION ERROR ...]erate turbulence jostled our ship once we pierced the clouds. Thankfully everyone was strapped into their seats.

We passed quickly through the cloud cover. One moment the forward viewport presented an expanse of pink-gray fluff. The next it showed a puffy ceiling extending to the eastern coastline and a violet ocean stretching beyond to the horizon.

To the west, the cloud cover we had penetrated minutes before floated above us up to the steep slopes of the continent's eastern mountain chain. Dr. Pak, a planetary geologist who came aboard with Hohlt, says those mountain peaks now hidden by the clouds reach into the planet's stratosphere some thirty-five kilometers above the sea.

At ten kilometers above sea level, trees with thick shimmering metallic blue trunks and yellow-gray needles began dotting those slopes like week-old stubble, thickening to a yellow carpet that obscured the mountain base. Yellow, if I didn't mention before, is the color this ecosystem settled upon for its chlorophyll analog to extract the most energy from its red giant star.

At 1.5 kilometers above our landing point and just a few minutes before touchdown, the hypergiant peeked over the horizon, flooding the control room with a searing red light and setting the violet ocean's wave tops aflame with fiery red.

Our now-suspect computer pilot required two attempts to place us in a satisfactory landing spot. On its first try, the computer, evidently believing any non-eventful landing a good one, placed us on solid ground with a fifteen-degree slope. The computer adjusted the landing gear's struts as best it could but in the end the ship listed too much. I instructed the computer to try again, and on its second attempt it set us down 330 meters to the west on mostly flat ground covered in a pale yellow thistlebrush, fifty meters from a tall expanse of rock—a cliff face—rising two hundred meters in the air.

The post-landing system checks are in progress. After they complete we'll exit the ship to have a look around and begin collecting samples.

Day 13, 09:23 hours

This planet may become our permanent home.

During our descent several klaxons sounded. I had assumed them related to our increasing hull temperatures and chose to clear the alerts to silence their bleating. Apparently the computer noticed a problem with the Moscovium 299 cylinders, important components of the Gravity Drive. After reviewing the failed post-landing system checks and reading the alert messages in-depth, I at first could not believe what they suggested and had the computer rerun them. I finally climbed down the narrow ladder to the engine compartment and applied a gravimeter to the casings myself. My findings confirmed what the computer had flagged: all but five percent of the Mc 299 has gone inert.

The most likely explanation involves the extreme gravity waves we encountered during our extended stay near Sag A Star. There are other theories, but in fact I have no stomach for debating them. Whatever the cause, we are stranded here on the planet's surface.

Day 13, 13:24 hours

Yoichiro, brilliant scientist and intrepid friend, you may have saved us all!

During our mapping of the surface from high orbit, Yoichiro configured the scanners to collect data on caches of heavy elements and atomic decay byproducts. He hoped to find deposits of gold and other precious metals, a "pirate's plunder," he called it, to ferry back to Earth to take the sting out of this planetary adventure. Without access to a network, however, our single computer had to handle the job of crunching the data. It finally produced its report about three hours ago. In light of all the bad news, Yoichiro originally saw little point in reviewing the document, being as dejected as the rest of us, but brought himself to read the summary. The computer found no gold or silver, but it did locate several large deposits of rare earths, including

Moscovium. One of those deposits lay just forty-one kilometers away, a roughly two days' trek on foot!

The fact the scanners detected the Moscovium at all indicates its nearness to the surface, another bit of luck as we don't have serious mining equipment. We have the equipment to refine the Mc 299, but the process may take several weeks. Considering our predicament, time is our most abundant resource.

I have organized an expedition of five people. In addition to myself I chose Dr. Katherine Reed and Alex Kondo, senior professor and post-doctoral student respectively, for their expertise in metals and materials; Dr. Abebi Iweala, so that I am not the sole astrophysicist on this trip; and Dr. David Post, an astrochemist I selected for his large biceps rather than his chemical knowledge, on the assumption there could be heavy digging required to free the Mc 299. Hohlt makes the sixth—he's coming along because he insists. At the least he can provide xenobiology experience.

I have prepared my pack and am waiting for the others to finish assembling their gear. For supplies we'll have enough food for a ten-day journey, and we grabbed two tents from the ship's stores. We'll also each be outfitted with an electron pistol and a plasma rifle. There so far are no readings of large life-forms, but we do not have an exhaustive survey of the planet's fauna.

We head out in ten minutes.

Day 13, 19:11 hours

After hiking for five hours, we decided to stop for the night.

Thick cloud cover had obscured the hypergiant for most of the morning, burning off just before the star reached its zenith. A quirk of orbits today perfectly aligned RDS A, the black hole RDS B, and Infernum, placing the singularity in the direct center of the star's red disc. We crossed the rough plains with this eye, a black pupil within a flame-red iris, transiting the sky like an angry god monitoring our progress.

Our first sunset on this planet was spectacular. The light violet sky took on deeper shades as the red eye began its descent. With half the hypergiant visible above the jagged peaks to the west, the mammoth star appeared to have set the entire mountain chain on fire. Even now, two hours after the angry orange blob dipped below the mountain line, the peaks along the darkened western sky retain a fiery red glow.

Our travel was slow going for the first two hours of our journey today as we worked our way through a dense forest. The trees had thick, blue trunks and their barren, twisted branches appeared to end in gnarled hands, creating an eerie canopy. Their dark silhouettes against the overcast red sky formed an image straight from a Halloween diorama.

We've set up our two tents in a small, flat area, almost a valley between two modest hills, a wide expanse filled with more ankle-high, pale-yellow brush and many tiny purple buds. We cleared a portion of the brush and piled a circle of rocks to form a home for our makeshift campfire, fueling it with shimmery blue wood from nearby fallen trees. The burning bark spits bright blue sparks out of the yellow flames, some sort of phosphorescent chemical release. The smoke carries an odd, sweet odor.

After a long afternoon of hiking and many days of stress, we are all exhausted. I will recommend we all turn in early and get a quick start in the morning.

Day 14, 13:27 hours

Hohlt woke two hours before dawn. The rest of us rose with the morning sun, refreshed from a good night's sleep in spite of the major commotion. The heavenly smell of fresh brewed coffee filled our nostrils, luring us from our tents.

The commotion I mentioned relates to the prairie of tiny purple flowers we camped in last night. The existence of flowers implies pollinators, but we had seen no evidence of insects during yesterday's hike. I thought that odd but gave it no further consideration.

The four men—Hohlt, Post, Kondo, and I—slept in the larger tent, with our female colleagues sleeping in the other. Just after 1 a.m., Kondo shook me awake. I opened my eyes to a frightened look on his face. At times he seems more of a child than an adult, which I find quite annoying. His mouth moved hurriedly, imploring me to do something, but the only sound that came from his lips was a loud buzzing. At first I thought it all a dream. I closed my eyes and sank deeper into my sleeping bag, but Kondo proceeded to roll me over, smashing my nose against the tent floor. At that point I realized I was awake, not inside a dream, and that the buzzing was not coming from Kondo.

I jumped up and headed to the tent's thin glassteel window. Outside a swarm of electric blue lights bobbed and bounced in the darkness. Shining a light into the field revealed hundreds of what are best described as winged black caterpillars, their thick wormlike bodies easily as large as the palm of my hand. We had found the planet's missing insect life, or at least one form of it.

The light chased them away, and with its absence came the silence to which we originally retired. When I removed the light and allowed my eyes to slowly adjust to the darkness, the field remained quiet but still filled with thousands of lights, though mostly stationary. Stepping out of the tent and into the field, the small closed purple buds we observed at twilight had opened wide, their many petals glowing blue in the darkness, evidently acting as beacons for the pollinators.

Those pollinators abandoned the field only briefly, returning to finish the job with their loud buzzing. Kondo was afraid they might have poisonous stingers, but I figured as long as these insects could not enter our tents and as long as they only wanted the flowers, they would go about their business, and we could go about ours. Despite the loud buzzing, I fell asleep a few minutes after closing my eyes.

Dr. Post found one of the insects this morning as we were breaking camp. It lay dead near the campfire ring, though I don't believe the fire's remnants had anything to do with the creature's demise. He foolishly picked it up with his bare hand and was pricked by several thick needle-like hairs extending from the insect's abdomen. The index finger, middle finger, and thumb on his right hand swelled to gargantuan size, seemingly on the verge of splitting open. He wailed in pain until we administered painkillers from the MEDIkit. We cleaned the punctures as best we could and filled the wounds with anti-inflammatories. He felt well during this morning's hike, but I am concerned for the possible consequences of alien material having been introduced into his system. I realized as we tended to him my oversight in not also bringing someone with medical experience on this journey.

Today has been considerably warmer. Yesterday's thick cloud cover has dissipated, leaving the burning orb above to rain its heat down upon us.

After hiking through rolling fields of yellow brush, we have encountered land that is considerably more barren, including square kilometers covered mostly with small crushed rock. The rock absorbs the red star's energy across multiple wavelengths but radiates it all back as heat, adding considerable discomfort to our travels.

After lunch there will be more walking. We plan to continue as long as there is light to see by.

Day 14, 21:45 hours

Hohlt and Iweala are dead, and Reed, Kondo, Post, and I have been pinned beneath a rock overhang since just after sunset.

Infernum days are four hours longer than Earth's, giving us additional daylight hours in which to travel. The evening greeted us with a sky similar to yesterday's, the sawtooth peaks engulfed in flame as the giant star sank below the distant mountain chain. Once RDS A rotated fully out of view, RDS B, no longer perfectly centered in the hypergiant's red disc, lingered above the mountaintops. This black moon cast an electric blue glow from its event horizon that sliced through the reddish twilight, providing enough light for us to continue walking safely well past official sunset. We chose to press on rather than set up camp for the night.

Post was the first to spot the electric bolts lashing out from the black hole like bright blue barbed wire. The first streamer hit the ground as we were crossing a small river, a broad but shallow expanse of warm water choked with numerous exposed rocks and sand bars. I was in the lead and had my head down, focusing on carefully placing each step, when the water all around us began glowing electric blue. For a moment I thought we had stumbled into a habitat of electrified eel-type creatures. I raised my hand to halt the party and take a few seconds to assess our situation. Then came a deafening boom, a subsonic rumble that rattled the ground, followed by a stiff, hot breeze. To the northwest a plume of dust and rock soared sixty meters into the sky.

Just after the initial bolt landed we still had not fully understood what had transpired and believed the plume and boom to be evidence of an immense explosion. I briefly feared for the *Adiona* until I realized the explosion occurred too far to the north to be our ship. As we stood gaping at the dissipating plume, a second tendril of electric wrath snaked to the ground, this one much closer. Normal lightning is fast—blink and you'll miss it. These bolts streaked from the heavens just as quickly but remained for longer, as if frozen in the air. An even larger boom and hot wind followed this bolt, and only a handful of moments later. The ground quaked so much it shook Reed to her knees in the shallow river.

We immediately understood the general danger posed by standing in flowing water during an interplanetary electrical storm and scurried as fast as we could to the far bank, which was the closer of the two. Upon reaching land, I relaxed and gave thanks for being out of the running water until I realized we were still standing like knaves in the middle of open ground.

Alex Kondo brought our attention to a small outcropping of rock about three hundred meters away, a potential sanctuary rising from the ground in an otherwise flat landscape. We sprinted, but the weight of our packs hindered us, as did the rough terrain in the twilight. We spread out in a chain, the faster of us in the lead. Hohlt, at the rear, twisted his ankle, and Iweala ran back to help him.

As I looked back, an enormous blue bolt shot from the black moon, wending its way across the heavens until it touched down not one hundred meters from our position. The ground rippled as if a giant had unfurled a blanket, tossing us in the air. The thunderclap was deafening, almost puncturing our eardrums. Finally came the stiff wind and a searing hot breeze.

Despite our rough landing, we were all of us OK. As we pulled ourselves up a small gray ball appeared in the distance, visible in the night sky because it was trailing fire. The fire extinguished itself just as the ball, a large boulder, reached the apex of its arc in the sky. I followed its trajectory to the ground and estimated Iweala and Hohtl sat at roughly its landing spot. I screamed at the top of my lungs for them to move. Reed, standing ten meters away, joined in. They couldn't hear us, our voices drowned out by the remnants of the still-rumbling thunder.

The ball fell from the sky, gaining speed as it dropped, a boulder the size of a house. It smashed into Iweala and Hohtl and dug itself into the ground so deeply only the top half remained visible above the land.

Fully understanding the extent of our peril, the remaining four of us ran as fast as we could to the outcropping. Kondo, who with the demise of

Iweala and Hohtl was now in the rear, tossed off his backpack to lighten his load and allow himself to increase his speed. He overtook Post and Reed and almost overtook me, arriving at the outcropping just a few seconds after I did.

So here we have sat for the past five hours. Or three of us at least, with Dr. Reed on her back. During the lightning strike that lifted us into the air, her head hit the ground when she landed. She is suffering from a mild concussion. Alex Kondo is curled up in the fetal position next to her. Meanwhile the blue lightning continues to crash down around us, though the bolts are landing farther away, likely due to the planet's rotation putting more distance between our location and the black hole. RSD B will soon drop below the western mountain chain, which should provide protection from its lightning bolts. Once it's safe to move about, we will need to go back for Kondo's pack, for it contains food we cannot afford to lose, as well as one of the portable shelters.

These storms likely recur following some regular cycle. We will have to determine the periodicity to avoid being caught up in one again. Unfortunately, this will require experiencing another storm.

Day 15, 10:18 hours

We are off to a slow start this morning. We remained beneath the rock overhang for forty-five minutes after the lightning storm ended, mostly certain the black hole could not assault us from behind the western mountain chain but still afraid to venture out. I finally moved out into the open to set up our tent, forgetting it lay inside Kondo's discarded pack. I chided the post-doc for dropping his backpack and told him to retrieve it. He adamantly refused, wailing about the hazards of being unsheltered during an electrical storm. I lectured him as patiently as I could about the storm having ended some time ago, but he would have none of it. He eventually returned to his fetal pose next to Dr. Reed with his hands over his ears.

I wasn't sure Post was well, and with Reed recovering from her concussion, that left me to walk across the open plain to retrieve the pack, cursing under my breath all the way there and back. We were fortunate

Kondo carried the larger four-person tent. The other was lost with Iweala when she perished.

Once I returned, I set up our tent a few meters from the rock outcropping. Kondo mustered enough courage to help me move Reed into the shelter, then scurried back to the rocks, taking Reed's old spot deeper beneath the overhang. Reed, Post, and I slept in the shelter while Kondo, still spooked by the ordeal, insisted on placing his sleeping bag beneath the rock overhang and spending the night there.

After rising, I scrounged enough wood for a meager fire and brewed a pot of coffee. The aroma lifted everyone's spirits, though we are all still in shock and sadness from the loss of our expedition mates, at least for one of them. Hohlt, it might be said, was crushed by the weight of his own ambition and ego. If only we could just now turn around and head for home.

Medical update: Reed is doing better this morning after last night's concussion. She has a dark welt on her forehead but is no longer seeing spots. I am concerned about Post, who claims he is OK but is moving noticeably slower.

I can see our destination, about seven kilometers to the northeast. A few hours of hiking across an open plain of more yellow bushes and prickly thistles will take us to an apparent circle of tall trees next to a dense forest. According to the sensor map, those trees encircle a depression where we will find the Moscovium.

Day 15, 16:05 hours

Post died earlier this afternoon. After his lethargic movements this morning around the camp and his complaining of being cold when the air had reached twenty-nine degrees centigrade, we checked his temperature and found he was running a high fever. We medicated him as best we could and had him rest inside the tent. As I helped him get situated in his sleeping bag, I saw that his right hand, the one he used to lift the insect, had swollen again, and a blue hue ringed each puncture hole. He drifted off to sleep and never woke.

Kondo and I dug a shallow grave for Post a few meters from the rock overhang. I say *we* dug it, but Kondo took a break every few minutes, complaining about the heat, or about his back from bending over, or the toughness of the soil, or about the shovel's shaft chafing the skin of his hand. He twice suggested we build a cairn for Post. I was partial to a burial below ground, but regardless, a cairn was out of the question as there weren't enough large stones. Kondo persisted in his idea and at one point headed off to collect rocks while I continued chipping away at the hard ground. When he returned after twenty minutes with an armful of small stones, I told him to cease his foolishness and help me finish digging the grave.

The young post-doc did take up his shovel but soon resumed his complaining and suggested we wait until sunset to dig the grave so that we would not have to labor under the harsh sun. I reminded him how the approaching sunset will bring a return of the black moon and possible recurrence of the blue lightning storm. He moved faster then but told me he needed to take a break and disappeared around the side of the outcropping. I eventually finished the digging and went looking for him, finding him curled up in the shade, taking a nap like a kitten. I shook him awake, and we carried Post's body to the grave. Kondo and I blanketed him with dirt and placed the largest rock we could find as a headstone.

Official sunset occurs in seven hours. If we set out across the rocky plain now, we could reach our tree ring destination and its Moscovium cache before the red disc descends below the mountain peaks. Without knowing if RDS B will rain down lightning upon us again this night, we would most probably find ourselves out in the open, completely exposed to its wrath. Squinting into the bright afternoon sky, the black moon is just visible, trailing the hypergiant.

I am concerned about how long the electrical storms will keep us pinned here close to these rocks, unable to make progress. Are they a fleeting phenomenon, or a months-long affair?

Day 16, 13:17 hours

We are not the first to have visited this world.

Last night was uneventful. The black moon became visible not long after sunset, ringed in the electric blue glow of its event horizon. The remaining three of us broke camp an hour before and huddled beneath our rock overhang shelter, expecting more pyrotechnics. None came. I am optimistic these storms are an infrequent event.

With that optimism in tow, we set off this morning shortly after sunrise for the ring of trees and the desperately needed Moscovium deposits they sheltered. After crossing the rocky plain for almost three hours as the red fireball climbed in the sky, we finally reached the edge of the forest. Our orbital photos showed a circle of trees around a circular depression, but from our vantage point on the ground the depression is in fact the shape of a hexagon. What is more, the walls of this hexagon are remarkably vertical, as if a large cookie cutter had been driven into the ground to a depth of thirty meters and the material inside scooped out. The trees that ring the depression continue on to the southeast as dense woods, as if the cookie cutter had clipped the forest's northwest corner. Such an excavation would require the removal of nearly 2.3 million cubic meters of dirt; however, there is no sign of this extracted material anywhere in the vicinity.

If the excavation story is to be believed, the event must have occurred far in the past as portions of the steep vertical walls have eroded in several locations, likely the work of rainwater. Sections of the perfect right angle edges along the rim's edge have disappeared, replaced by steep angled ravines. Reed, Kondo, and I used one of these gullies to reach the basin floor.

The basin itself is a reasonably flat expanse of dark gray ground littered with small rocks and sporadic patches of the chaff-yellow prickle bushes, at least where it isn't covered with the mounds. These mounds, each one standing nearly eight meters in height and composed of dirt and rock, are perfectly round domes, as if created by pouring a pile of material from a chute high above. Hundreds of these mounds dot the basin floor. The spacing between them varies, from a dense packing in some places to very loose in others.

And litter would be an apt description for their purpose. As we walked the basin, circling south around the massive dirt piles, we discovered five large caverns along the easternmost wall of the hexagon. Far from random formations, these dark, semi-circular openings stand with a six-meter radius and are spaced 9.3 meters apart. They appear to be entrances to subterranean mines. The entire basin seems to have been a mining operation where materials were extracted from below ground and sifted, with the tailings piled into these mounds.

Among the hundreds of mounds, two appeared to be smaller than all the others and glinted silver-red in the sunlight. We thought they might be piles of precious metals, but as we approached, these mounds took on a more intentioned shape, like silver qubbāt removed from their edifices. Drawing closer, we discovered these structures were rounded domes with hexagonal bases. They stand five meters high at their apex, have no discernible windows or doors, and are covered in a seamless, smooth silver skin formed of an unknown alloy. Are they spacecraft? Landers? Portable cabins? Storage depots? It is difficult to say. My comm does not recognize the structures from its catalog of alien artifacts. They are certainly not of human origin, for we are the first of our kind to reach this far into the galactic center.

Before breaking for lunch, we did confirm there are Moscovium deposits here, with fairly strong readings emanating from several of the mine entrances. We plan to select one of the mines to explore after we finish eating.

Day 16, 15:55 hours

We have found Moscovium! A huge deposit, in fact.

After lunch we ventured into the second mine from the left, the one that offered the strongest trace readings of the precious material. Though the floor was level at the entrance, it soon dipped steeply downward and continued on for kilometers.

With Kondo holding the sensor pack, both Reed and I snuck glances at the screen, looking for the telltale byproducts of Moscovium decay. Ten minutes into the cave, the sensor panel lit up with tall, green bars. Shining our light on the rock wall, we saw the orange flecks of Moscovium ore, a deposit several meters across and extending from the floor to the roof's center overhead.

The three of us quickly unfolded our shovels and the autocart we brought along as a collection bin. We took turns digging into the tunnel wall, each strike dislodging large clumps of the orange-flecked ore. After gathering twenty kilograms of the material, we ordered the cart up the steep path to the surface.

Day 16, 17:22 hours

Dr. Reed is dead. I fear I may be joining her shortly.

The cart made the steep climb out of the mine without too much trouble, stopping twenty meters from the entrance. This was our first opportunity to assess in the sunlight, red though it was, what we had gathered. We pushed the ore around with our shovels, getting a sense of how pure a vein of Moscovium we had mined. The find turned out to be of extremely high quality, a great stroke of luck for us.

After spreading the ore, Kondo noticed two fist-sized clumps of a mineral that definitely was not Moscovium. These rocks were black, crystalline, with an odd ruby-red shimmer. The clump I lifted was very heavy for its size—though it fit in my palm, I almost had to use both hands to hold it aloft. I quickly put it back in the cart.

Scanning the other clump, Kondo reported its mass at just over eleven kilograms, an enormous reading for a roughly fist-sized rock. All three of us were amazed such a relatively small rock could weigh so much. The scanner's spectral analysis results were also odd, showing spikes for every element in the periodic table.

This seemed plainly impossible, and I surmised the device was malfunctioning. Kondo, having much more experience with the scanner, pursued an idea that came to him from the spectral analysis chart. He placed the device into active scanning mode so it measured the clump's mass more than a trillion times a second. He adjusted the display to plot mass vs. frequency—that is, the mass of the rock along the x-axis and the number of times the scanner returned a particular mass reading along the y-axis.

Trained on any normal material, the scanner would show a tall spike at the material's mass, a single reading that would register no matter how many times you measured it. What we saw in the case of the black clump astonished us. Instead of a spike, the scanner produced a plot resembling a black body radiation curve, a hump that tapered off at either end. The curve implied the black rock, when scanned, did not always have the same mass. At any given instant of time, it weighed in at one of the masses on the graph, everything from zero to nearly ten to the twenty-one kilograms! The more extreme masses were much rarer than the masses in the center of the graph, hence the tapers on the left and right. The hump peaked at 2.2 kilograms, the most frequent mass sampled by the scanner. Kondo surmised the material somehow did indeed have each of these masses, and that the original mass measurement of eleven kilograms was a weighted average of all the different mass readings over time.

As a simple astrophysicist, I could not begin to take that conclusion seriously. I was content with chalking the odd readings up to a scanner on the fritz, but Kondo and Reed were intrigued by the idea. Kondo in particular wondered how such a stone would behave moving through a gravitational field. A normal object traveling through the air follows a parabolic course to the ground. He wondered if this strange mineral would also trace out a parabola or if its apparently shifting mass would cause it to follow a less regular path.

With all the restraint of an impulsive child, Kondo grabbed one of the black stones and tossed it into the air. Based on his unscientific experiment, I can report the stone appeared to follow a smooth parabolic trajectory. Unfortunately, Kondo tossed the stone so that it landed on a tailings pile not three meters from us. The stone casually rolled down the pile, followed by an enormous rumble as the pile's face collapsed and slid towards us. If the theory of shifting mass is to be believed, the rock's large, instantaneous spikes in mass likely tugged at the pile's loose material, destabilizing it and causing it to flow outward like a liquid.

The flow moved at incredible speed. I reached for Dr. Reed's hand to pull her from the avalanche, but she had been seated on the ground, nursing her sore head. I couldn't get her to budge as I sprinted away. The dirt completely enveloped her under a three-meter-tall mound.

Kondo escaped to the left of the flow and I to the right, in the direction of the silver domes. Unfortunately for me, the mineral chunk Kondo heaved into the air continued rolling in my same general direction, pulling more of the tailings pile towards me. In my haste I tripped, severely twisting my ankle. Crumpled on the ground, I could only watch as the avalanche sped toward me, eventually coming to rest just half a meter from my feet.

I have yelled for Kondo several times, but he has not answered. I can only imagine he is either hurt or buried beneath an expanse of rock. My ankle still throbs, a full hour after wrenching it. The MEDIkit has meds that could help with the pain. I might be able to crawl to find it, if it hasn't also been buried with our camp equipment under the tailings. But tamping down the pain is pointless now as my Craeter's has chosen this time to flare up again. If I were back at the *Adiona,* I could receive suitable treatment but here, with just the MEDIkit and no doctor on call, my prognosis appears bleak. I expect to lose consciousness soon. I trust someone on the *Adiona* has been monitoring these logs and will send help immediately. I have activated my distress beacon. Although likely out of range for the ship to detect from its current location, it should assist in locating me once at the basin. I only hope you find me unconscious and not dead.

God damn Hohlt! If not for him, we would not even be on this planet! We would most likely be returned to normal space, and I would be selecting a tie to wear for our triumphant press conference.

I weep at the thought of a Universe so cruel as to deny me the achievement of a lifetime. I choose not to believe in such a Universe, or such a fate. In all the setbacks of my career, I have always moved forward after each one. I refuse to accept that this setback, this hiccup, will be any different.

My dear friend Yoichiro, I pray you receive this message and mount a rescue effort with all due haste, and that your face will be the one I see when I next open my eyes.

12

Why in Hades are we down here?

Captain Holbrook stood alone in the center of Cargo Corridor C-1, twenty dim meters from its intersection with Deck C's Outer Loop. Nearby, a pair of robotic pallets executed a silent ballet, shuttling cargo between holds.

A figure entered C-1 from the distant Outer Loop. The relaxed gait, swaggering side-to-side movement, and silhouette of a man with hands in pockets all suggested Commander Stephens.

"Hey, Cap," said Stephens as he walked up to Holbrook, "what's up?"

"What do you mean, 'What's up?' You asked me to meet you down here."

"No, I didn't," said Stephens. "You messaged me about meeting you here on Deck C."

"I can show you the message," Holbrook grumbled, activating his comm. He wasn't making things up.

"I didn't send you a message. Besides, this isn't the kind of place I'd ever pick for a meeting." Stephens glanced around the passageway. "It's secluded, OK maybe for a quick, private chat, but there are other spots on the ship that'd be better. I figured you had a good reason to meet here."

"Here it is," said Holbrook, presenting his comm to Stephens.

"I never sent that," said Stephens. "'Please proceed forthrightly to Deck C?' Is 'forthrightly' even a word?" Stephens rifled through screens on his own comm. "Here's the message I got from you."

Holbrook studied the note. "So, you have a message from me that I never sent," he said, rubbing his chin, "and I have one from you that you never sent. It seems someone has sent messages to each of us to get us both down here."

"Maybe they want to meet with the two of us," said Stephens.

"Faking messages to the captain and the XO will certainly get them a meeting, but probably not the one they'd hoped for," said Holbrook. "Let's figure out what's going on." He spoke into his comm. "Starship *Avenger*, what's the origin of the two messages —"

- - -

"Anyone know where Stephens is?" asked Lieutenant Bhat. "Or the captain?"

"Not sure," said Lieutenant Commander Mills, legs crossed and sitting comfortably in the captain's chair. "What, you already fed up with my command? The shift's not even fifteen minutes old."

"Nah," said Bhat. A frantic yellow light flashed on the communications terminal. He cleared it with several taps. "It's just odd that neither of them is here. We usually see Commander Stephens at the start of a shift at least."

"Maybe this is their way of showing a little more confidence in us," said Mills.

"Seems unlikely," said Ensign Cochran, facing the engineering station but with her head turned back into the room. "One of the commander's favorite phrases is, 'trust, but verify.' He probably does trust us, but he'll definitely be along to verify everything hasn't gone to seed."

Flashing red lights exploded across Cochran's entire terminal. The ship shuddered, rattling the empty chairs in the room. Klaxons filled the air and red light flooded the bridge.

"Red alert," said the ship in its placid, androgynous voice.

The *Avenger* lurched sideways and shuddered, seemingly coming apart. Lieutenant Commander Mills gripped the armrests on the captain's chair, all his efforts focused on not being thrown to the deck. The ship jerked backwards, tossing officers towards the front of the bridge. Ahead on the main viewscreen each corkscrew of rainbowed starlight contracted, shortening to an ordinary bright dot.

"We've dropped out of warp," said Ensign Doerr from the deck. She had been standing when the ship made its first violent movement, tossing her down. She pulled herself up by grabbing the sides of her station.

"What the hell happened?" yelled Bhat.

"Don't know," said Doerr. "It felt almost like we hit something."

"Or like we were attacked," said Mills. "Are there any ships in the area?"

"No, sir," said Lieutenant Bolton from tactical. "My board shows green."

"Starship *Avenger*, report status," said Mills.

"En route to Sagittarius A Star, position 11,121 light-years from the event horizon, velocity 0.0 c. Gravity Drive deactivated after a large instability developed in the warp field." Several seconds passed before the ship spoke again. "Detecting damage to outer hull, underside of Deck C, localized to the port vertex."

"Is the ship in any immediate danger?" asked Mills.

"No, the *Avenger* is in no immediate danger."

"What's the status of the port gravity field generator?" asked Ensign Cochran, the engineering terminal still flooded with red.

"No damage detected to the port gravity field generator," said the ship.

"So we didn't lose the generator—that's good," said Mills. "Please describe the extent of the damage."

The ship remained silent for several seconds, collating data. "A section of the outer hull near the port gravity field generator has been damaged. The deck and several bulkheads on Deck C have been destroyed or compromised, resulting in an atmospheric breach. Adjacent bulkhead doors have been sealed to prevent ship depressurization. Two cargo holds in that area have been damaged. Some of their contents evacuated to space during the explosive decompression."

"My God," said Mills. "What caused the breach? Did we hit something?"

"The location and extent of the damage as well as the warp field signature immediately prior to the event correlate with the complete loss of the gravitational waveguide adjacent to the port gravity field generator. Hull damage is consistent with the waveguide shearing from the hull and disintegrating. Simulations suggest the destabilized warp field propelled shards from the waveguide into the ship's underbelly."

Mills's voice grew soft. "Were there any casualties?" he asked.

"Two casualties confirmed with 99.96 percent confidence," said the ship. "Captain Thomas Holbrook III and Commander Paul Stephens were both present on Deck C within the damaged section immediately before the shear event. There are currently no life readings in that area of the ship. Their bodies were likely jettisoned into the vacuum."

Ensign Doerr placed her hand over her mouth as tears welled. Other members of the bridge crew sat stunned.

The news of their deaths hit Mills hard, but he attempted not to show it. As the officer of the deck, he fought to keep it together long enough to take the next important step. "With the captain and commander gone, that places Commander Lynch in command of the *Avenger*." Mills didn't care much for Commander Lynch—he wasn't sure anyone did. The man inspired no enthusiasm or devotion in his reports and was generally unpleasant to be around. The ship would need a leader who could rally the crew and guide them through this difficult time. Hopefully, for everyone's sakes, the commander would rise to the occasion. "Starship *Avenger*, please have Commander Lynch report to the bridge immediately."

- - -

Lieutenant Commander Mills sprinted to Deck A's Gemini Conference Room, arriving four minutes past the hour along with Lieutenants Byrne and Bolton. The three fanned out around the long rectangular table, grabbing empty seats interspersed among the nine other officers already present.

Mills surveyed the room. Commander Lynch sat at the table's head with his hands neatly folded on its surface. He sported a self-satisfied expression, fueled no doubt by his ascension to the post of acting captain. The most loathsome officers aboard the *Avenger* flanked him: Lieutenants Knox and Grey on his left, and Lieutenant Zhang on his right. They, too, seemed to preside with an air of satisfaction, a bishop and his three vicars lording over their captive congregation.

The other officers around the table held somber expressions. Some hung their heads, some looked on with folded arms and defiant eyes. Even accounting for the sad news of the loss of Captain Holbrook and Commander Stephens, an added level of misery and sorrow weighed on the room.

"I believe we're all here finally," said Lynch. "Please note for the future that I expect punctuality in meetings." He eyed Mills and the other two late entrants. "I understand these are extraordinary times and do give allowance for that fact, which is why I'm only raising this issue rather than taking stronger action. Just remember, punctuality, generally speaking, is a sign of respect.

"Now with that bit of unpleasantness behind us, thank you all for coming. In light of the events of the past two hours, I felt it important to convene a meeting of the *Avenger's* departmental heads sooner than later. As you all know by now, a port-side gravitational waveguide disintegrated from the stresses of our extended use of the Gravity Drive, an unfortunate outcome I had predicted would very likely occur. The shattered waveguide damaged the ship and in the process killed the captain and Commander Stephens.

"Many aboard the *Avenger* held Holbrook and Stephens in high regard," said Lynch.

Many aboard the ship, but not you, Mills noted.

"A formal farewell ceremony will occur in two days' time. For now, I would like to recognize these men for their dedication to this crew, this ship, and to CentCom. Please join me in a moment of silence." Lynch closed his eyes and bowed his head.

Mills bowed his head along with everyone else in the room but kept an open eye on Lynch and the officers next to him. Knox and Zhang opened their eyes and exchanged smirks. Zhang caught Mills watching him, scowled, and closed his eyes again. The smirk soon returned to his face.

Twenty seconds later, according to Mills's comm, Commander Lynch looked up and coaxed a feigned expression of heartfelt sadness onto his face. "Thank you," he said. The others raised their heads. "In Stephens's and Holbrook's absence, I am the most senior officer aboard this vessel and therefore the ship's acting captain. It is with great humility and a heavy heart that I accept this responsibility."

What a steaming pile of crap.

"To assist me in keeping the ship running smoothly during this challenging time," said Lynch, "I have appointed Lieutenant Grey acting executive officer." Grey, stubble peppering his gaunt face, nodded towards the other officers around the table.

"For my third in command, I appoint Lieutenant Zhang." Zhang, with his scraggly mustache and goatee and round, lamprey mouth of pointy teeth, clearly struggled to present a somber face while actively suppressing a smirk. The man was a psychopath. Mills shuddered at the thought of being alone with him in a corridor or P-cab.

"Finally, I have appointed Lieutenant Knox to the newly created position of Special Assistant to the Captain." Knox didn't nod as the others had, maintaining instead his perpetual scowl, as of a prize fighter before a bout. Relatively short and squat, the lieutenant had a block head sprouting a brown buzz cut, Neanderthal brows, fleshy lips, a boxer's crumpled nose, and muscular biceps he bared at any opportunity.

"Once we conclude here," said Lynch, "you will all schedule meetings with your reports and relay this new command structure as well as the other information being dispensed." The commander's eyes moved around the table until they fell on the ship's damage control officer. "Lieutenant Collins."

Collins startled to attention, his mind apparently elsewhere.

"Damage control update, Mr. Collins," said Lynch.

Collins cleared his throat. "Well, we don't understand much more about the ship's status than what it reported two hours ago. We —"

"Mr. Collins," said Lynch in a patronizing voice. "You are, indeed, the ship's damage control officer?"

"Yes, sir."

"Then would it be correct to say that you *should* understand the ship's damage control status?"

Collins gave Lynch a perplexed look. "Yes, sir. But we've had trouble deploying the autobots to survey the hull. They've not been responding to instructions, perhaps because the change of command hasn't propagated to all ship systems."

"Lieutenant Knox," bellowed Lynch. Knox, with a dull expression and drawing breaths through his partially open mouth, shifted his eyes sideways under his thick brows towards Lynch. "See to it the new command structure has been properly updated in all ship systems." Knox did not acknowledge Lynch's order, and after a few seconds his eyes shifted back to staring out into the room.

"I'll try with the bots again," said Collins. "If that doesn't work, we'll have to send one or two engineers outside for a survey. Either way, until we know the full extent of the damage, we can't estimate repair time."

"What is the plan once we *are* able to move?" asked Mills.

"We will head directly to the dry dock facility at Aludra," said Lynch. "Once there we'll put in for full repairs and a comprehensive safety review of the ship. To reduce the chances of any more problems with the Gravity Drive, we will travel at half power with regular two-day stops, as I originally recommended."

"What about our current orders, our mission to Sag A Star?" asked Dr. Marsden.

"As the captain of this vessel I am going to do what Holbrook should have done weeks ago: get us off that assignment. To that end, our current predicament serves us well. We'll take almost two weeks limping our way to the Aludra system and another month, possibly two, for the safety review and repairs. Based on the urgency of this mission, CentCom will have no choice but to dispatch a different ship, freeing us of our current obligations."

As Lynch finished his sentence, the conference room door slid open and four members of the *Avenger's* security force filed in, taking positions along the far bulkhead from the commander. They stood at ease, facing into the room in their royal blue uniforms with hands clasped behind their backs and Immobilizers holstered at their waists.

Lynch stared at the men, confused by their sudden appearance and annoyed at the interruption. "You security men," he said, raising his voice to project it fully across the room, "this meeting is for department heads only. Lieutenant Byrne will brief you in a separate meeting on the issues we're discussing here. Please exit this conference room."

"It's OK Mr. Lynch," said a voice from beyond the open door. "I invited them." Commander Stephens stepped into the room to gasps and applause. Several of the officers stood with large smiles. Lynch hid his disbelief behind a poker face.

Ensign Doerr rose from her seat near the door and shook Commander Stephens's hand. "We thought we'd lost you," she said with a huge grin.

"It's not time for me to die just yet," said Stephens. "Besides, who'd watch over this guy?" A stern-faced Captain Holbrook entered the room, followed by cheers and more applause.

Stephens raised his hands for quiet. "Commander Lynch," he said, "did we miss much?"

"Sir," stammered Lynch, confused. "I am, we all are very excited to see you and the captain alive. We thought you had perished in the explosion on Deck C."

"Explosion?" asked Stephens. "What explosion?"

"The ship advised us that the port gravitational waveguide disintegrated," said Lynch, "destroying a section of Deck C, the section where you and the captain were apparently standing."

"The captain and I just came from there," said Stephens. "Everything seemed to be in order when we left." Stephens turned to Holbrook. "Do you know what he's talking about?"

Holbrook only stared at Stephens with his stern expression.

"There's actually something interesting about that waveguide," said Stephens, turning back to the room. His eyes met the engineering chief's. "Would you like to know what it is, Commander Lynch?"

Lynch held fast.

"That's one of the three waveguides inspected by an autobot during our four-hour layover at Plana Petram. Three out of the ten total waveguides on the hull. When I learned about it, I found myself asking why those three? And the inspection began right after the captain and I left and ended before we returned. The whole thing seemed strange, so before we shipped out, I had a different autobot make its own inspection. Wanna guess what it found?"

Beads of sweat broke out across Lynch's upper lip as he wrung his hands under the table.

"A small explosive charge—the one you planted on the waveguide."

Gasps and murmurs of conversation broke out across the room.

Stephens waited for everyone to settle down before continuing. "Given how you'd already gone on about the perils of taxing the Gravity Drive, who would be surprised if a waveguide were to suddenly fail completely. The explosion would damage the ship so it couldn't continue on to Sag A Star. Only there was the risk that no matter what, Holbrook would still force the *Avenger* to proceed with its mission. To avoid that scenario, you needed to be in command, and to do that you needed to get rid of me and Captain Holbrook."

Holbrook locked on to Lynch with fierce eyes. Lynch returned his gaze for as long as he could stand, then looked back at Stephens. He dabbed the sweat from his upper lip with the back of his hand.

"When the captain and I both got messages calling us to the bottom deck, I knew your plan was going down," said Stephens. "Luckily, I'd already told the ship what to do. The *Avenger* dropped itself out of warp and reported damage in Deck C. And it sealed off adjacent passageways to give me and the captain a place to hold out, undiscovered, until it was time for us to appear."

"Commander Lynch, you are under arrest," shouted Captain Holbrook. "The charge is mutiny." Holbrook directed the security detail to the front of the room with a wave of his hand.

Lynch rose from his chair before the security men reached him. One placed Lynch's arms behind his back and bound his wrists in restraints.

"You're both mad," said Lynch. "I want my advocate."

"Of course," said Holbrook, "though you'll have to wait until we get back from Sag A Star."

Lynch bared his teeth. "You've made up some conspiracy in your heads because you have it in for me," he shouted, spittle flying from his mouth. "You're accusing me of damaging my own ship—I'm the chief engineer, for god's sake!"

"*Were* the chief engineer," said Holbrook. "I appoint Lieutenant Conlin as acting chief engineer, at least through the end of this mission."

Lynch's face flushed red. "If you supposedly knew all along about this alleged plan," he said, "then why the charade? Why not pull me from my bunk in the dead of night, throw a bag over my head, and detain me in some dark corner of the ship?"

"Because we figured you weren't working alone," said Stephens. "If we arrested you outright there was a decent chance you wouldn't give up your co-conspirators. We needed to let your plan play out."

"We knew that once you took charge of the *Avenger* you'd appoint your co-conspirators as your deputies," said Holbrook. "They'd be the only people you could trust to help you run the ship." He nodded across the room to the security team. "Lieutenants Zhang, Grey, and Knox, you are also under arrest for conspiracy and mutiny."

Knox and Zhang rose as the security team stepped in behind them, Zhang with a look of surprise and Knox with his pugilistic scowl. Grey remained seated until they lifted him from his chair, his legs wobbling under his own weight. The guards pulled each man's arms behind his back and placed his wrists in restraints.

"I chose these men because they were best suited to the positions I needed to fill," said Lynch. "I don't know anything about any mutiny or conspiracy. You have no proof to support any of your claims against me."

Grey looked at Lynch, mulling the large man's words. Lynch was right; they would have no hard evidence against him. Lieutenant Zheng had operated the autobot that placed the explosive charge. And Grey had used his own station to send the messages that lured Holbrook and Stephens to Deck C. All the communications between the conspirators had been hidden. Lynch could deny even knowing Grey and his buddies beforehand. The commander had orchestrated the whole thing while keeping himself clear of the actual dirty work. "You buggerin', double-crossing sack of shite," said Grey in a weak voice, his eyes red and watery. "Here you is, 'anging us out to dry, with you figgerin' to get off scot-free. You said no one would get caught, that we'd be runnin' this ship and free of this buggerin' mission. But they's arrestin' us. Aye, we'll be sitting in the brig, *still* headin' to our deaths with the rest of 'em!"

"Shut ... your ... mouth ... Grey," Lynch said slowly through clenched teeth.

"Get them out of here," snapped Holbrook. The security force corralled the four prisoners and moved them towards the door.

When the procession brought Lynch near Holbrook, the captain placed his hand flat on the big man's chest, stopping him. "The thing that gets me," said Holbrook in a quiet voice, "is how you seem to have had no qualms about killing me. You and I have known each other for more than five years."

"Don't patronize me," said Lynch. "Where was this camaraderie when I was trying to pass the captains test? Huh? And all this speechmaking about me killing you when you have no trouble sending us all to our deaths. They'll award you a medal for following your orders, Captain, but they're going to pin it on your grave."

Holbrook glared at Lynch for several seconds. "Take 'em to the brig."

13

Captain Holbrook stepped three paces into the forward crew lounge on Deck A and paused, fighting vertigo. The triangular room sat at the tip of the ship's forward vertex, its angled port and starboard bulkheads a single, continuous glassteel panel with a panoramic bend at the lounge's far end. The long, clear panel rose from the deck to meet the flat glassteel sheet that formed a transparent cap over that portion of the ship's top deck. For Holbrook, the glassteel enclosure created the disturbing feeling of standing within the void itself.

The captain surveyed the room. Four officers stood around a tall rectangular table one-and-a-half meters away, playing cards and drinking. Seven more sat in groups of two and three at tables along the transparent bulkheads, engaged in quiet conversation. At the lounge's forward-most point, nestled within the great glassteel curve where the bulkheads converged, sat Dr. Riesen, alone at a small table with her back to the room.

The captain made his way right to the automat bar embedded in the back bulkhead. He had bowed to Stephens's most recent plea to curtail his alcohol consumption, remaining drink-free in all the days since the mutiny. It had been a clear demonstration of how he didn't need alcohol to function. He could handle a drink—he deserved one, in fact. An hour ago, the *Avenger* entered the distorted space around Sag A Star. They were committed, sailors on a doomed vessel, unless their guest Dr. Riesen figured out a way back home.

The captain jabbed at the bar's controls. He glanced back at Dr. Riesen while the machine dispensed his drink. Once the whirring ceased, he pulled his glass from the automat's base and slowly made his way to the front of the room. Muted illumination from light discs embedded in the lounge's small tables created a delicate calm against the pyrotechnic chaos of rainbowed starlight that writhed beyond the transparent walls. Directly ahead of the ship loomed Sag A Star's large black disc, surrounded by a thick band of glowing orange. Twisted spacetime teased triangular strands of the encircling band toward the disc's center, creating the illusion of a massive black maw with a wreath of pointed orange teeth. Metallic blue-green tendrils of electromagnetic discharge lashed out at the cosmos in a squirming maelstrom of galactic rage.

Dr. Riesen sat motionless as Holbrook approached, her figure silhouetted against the black hole and the onrush of distorted stars. She wore a crimson tank and black slacks. Her dark hair hung around her shoulders. When he arrived at her table, he stopped behind the empty seat to her right and placed his hands on the back of the chair.

The physicist, lost in thought, didn't notice his presence. She continued gazing at the star field through the glassteel bend. A notebook sat on the table in front of her. Doodles filled the open page.

"Good evening, Dr. Riesen."

Dr. Riesen jumped at Holbrook's voice. "Oh, good evening, Captain," she said. "You startled me."

"Apologies," said Holbrook. He waited for the physicist to invite him to sit, but she only looked up at him silently. "Mind if I join you?' he asked.

"Please," she said, though neither her expression nor her body language suggested any enthusiasm for his presence.

Holbrook lowered himself into the chair and placed his drink on the table. Dr. Riesen returned her gaze to the center of the glassteel bend where Sagittarius A Star loomed against the backdrop of squirming starlight. The two remained frozen in place for almost half a minute, the physicist engrossed in the panoramic view and the captain laboring to attract her attention with his stare.

Holbrook broke the silence. "I can't remember the last time I set foot in this lounge."

"It's an amazing space," she said. "I love watching the stars from inside a warp bubble. The beauty always amazes me. And the complexity. Each photon travels on a unique path through the spacetime eddies around the ship."

"It must be very interesting to perceive the world through a physicist's eyes —" Dr. Riesen had turned her head toward him as he spoke. The warm glow of the table's lightdisc bathed her face in soft light, her black hair framing her pale skin. Ice-blue eyes floated out at him. He'd been this close to her before, on Plana Petram and while reviewing the *Adiona* logs, but her beauty had never fully registered. Holbrook diverted his eyes to look off through the bend, concerned they might betray his thoughts.

"It's what I was born to do," she said.

"Speaking of which," said Holbrook, turning back to the physicist while suppressing all thoughts of her beauty, "on Plana Petram Commander Stephens called you 'The Prophet.' At the time you said it was a long story."

"It still is," said Dr. Riesen.

"But now you have the time to tell it," said Holbrook.

Dr. Riesen heaved a large sigh.

"If it's something you're uncomfortable discussing —"

"It's fine, Captain," said Dr. Riesen. "I don't mind talking about my background; I just tire of the reaction from non-believers." Her piercing, ice-blue eyes locked on to him. "I will explain, but know that eye rolls and laughter will be met with silence."

"I like to think I have an open mind," said Holbrook.

"Are you familiar with the Hebrew Scriptures—the Old Testament?" she asked.

"Yes," said Holbrook. "My mom owned several modern translations of the Bible."

"In the Hebrew Scriptures, God sent many Prophets to reveal His will and secrets to the human race on Earth," said Dr. Riesen. "Hundreds of years ago, a very rich man named Dr. Abraham Riesen founded an organization called The Brotherhood, based on a revelation in a dream. In that dream the great Flower of Knowledge hovered before him as a bud, its petals all closed in on themselves. God's hand appeared, curled in a fist that opened to His flattened palm from which rose a line of men, all wearing crimson robes with hoods that covered their faces. Dr. Abraham stepped forward and lifted the first man's hood and saw it was Albert Einstein. Under the second hood was Niels Bohr. He continued lifting the hoods: Wolfgang Pauli, J. Robert Oppenheimer, Richard Feynman. The line of men stretched out to infinity, some standing on God's hand, the rest on a bridge fashioned from two criss-crossed DNA strands. As he looked down the line of men, the great Flower of Knowledge bloomed, opening wide. He believed his dream to be a message from God, confiding in him how He revealed the inner workings of His Universe through his chosen people. Dr. Abraham called them Modern Prophets."

"His chosen people? You mean the Jewish people?"

"Correct," said Dr. Riesen. "Each of the physicists in the dream, from Einstein to Feynman to Pauli, each one was Jewish. All the great physicists were Jewish."

All of them were Jewish? Holbrook wracked his brain for the names of other physicists. He could only think of Heisenberg, whose uncertainty principle underpinned artificial intelligence, and Ben-Aharon, the twenty-second century inventor of the Gravity Drive.

Dr. Riesen continued. "Dr. Abraham made his fortune in genetics, through his company that pioneered the field of made-to-order babies. The company logo was two criss-crossed DNA strands, the same as in the dream. He believed God was telling him through this dream that his company would play a role in the forever-after stream of Modern Prophets, that he should use his company's technology to start engineering these men.

"Dr. Abraham, in addition to being rich, was also somewhat eccentric. During his travels through India, this Jewish man became a believer in reincarnation. He met the Dalai Lama and discussed how His Holiness's centuries of repeated existence on this Earth and his memories of the past allowed him to understand everything more deeply. Dr. Abraham immediately saw the benefits of reincarnation applied to this idea of genetically engineered Prophets, how the same man appearing generation after generation, in touch with all the knowledge and experiences of his past lives, would accelerate the rate of new discoveries.

"He asked the Dalai Lama if he could sample his DNA, to which His Holiness agreed. Dr. Abraham discovered a truth about the Dalai Lama's genetic makeup that clued him in to his ability to reincarnate. He tailored the first Prophet's DNA to those specifications."

"So, you're the reincarnation of the first Prophet," said Holbrook.

"I am the *third* reincarnation of the first Prophet," said Dr. Riesen.

Holbrook stroked his chin. "Do you believe that's true?"

Dr. Riesen smiled. "It *is* true, Captain."

"But how —"

"Captain Holbrook, may I ask *you* a question?"

"Of course," said Holbrook.

"I'm curious what brought you looking for me. Surely it wasn't to ask about Prophets and reincarnation."

"Why do you think I came here looking for you?"

"You said you never make it to the crew lounges. I assume this is a special visit to find me."

"Uh … yes," he said, slightly flustered at being so easily read. "I wanted to see if you've made any progress figuring out how to get us out of D-space."

"You noted our recent transit out of normal space," she said.

Holbrook nodded. "Now that we're actually in D-space, the crew will be impatient to understand how we're getting home," he said, deflecting from his own personal interest. "I'm trying to keep ahead of the curve." His eyes fell on her notebook. "Are those your notes?"

Dr. Riesen closed her notebook, hiding the page of doodles. "I haven't made much progress, to be honest," she said, grabbing her drink and swirling the remnants with the ice. "I've replayed several portions of the *Adiona's* logs more times than I can remember, at least the parts that seem like they might hold a clue. In particular that part about setting up a ring of tachyon beacons—my mind's hung up on that because it was such an odd detail. Unfortunately, they didn't elaborate. Otherwise, there's nothing so far." She teased droplets of condensation from the side of her glass onto the tabletop and dragged them around the smooth surface with her finger.

Holbrook stared at her, confused. Their fates depended on Dr. Riesen understanding how the *Adiona* planned to return from D-space, but she didn't seem at all focused on the problem. In fact, she'd given him roughly the same answer a week ago. "Honestly, I'd expected to find you someplace like the astrophysics lab working on the problem," he said, struggling to keep his irritation from his voice. "I was a little surprised when the ship told me you were here in the lounge. Shouldn't you be spending more time trying to figure out what they were up to?"

Dr. Riesen's finger stopped its meanderings across the table. "Solving physics problems can be a mechanical process," she said, "but I've found the hardest ones require a bit of inspiration. That's not something you can switch on at will. And it doesn't always happen in a sterile physics lab."

"So you're sitting here in the Deck A lounge, waiting for a flash of … inspiration," said Holbrook.

"Something like that." Dr. Riesen's finger resumed its circular movements on the table as she looked ahead at the inrushing black disc.

Holbrook found the physicist's response less than satisfying. He'd taken comfort in her joining their mission, in her being trapped with them at the center of the galaxy. It meant finding a solution would be in her own best interest. Her page of doodles seemed far removed from the flash of inspiration she claimed she sought. "Why did you volunteer for this mission anyway?" he asked, annoyed at her seeming indifference. "I mean, you knew it would be a one-way trip if we can't figure out how to get back home. Still, you decided to come."

Dr. Riesen looked up from the table at Holbrook. "Yes, I knew it might be a one-way trip," she said, "but if this mission fails, there may not be a planet Earth." Her hand moved back to gripping her glass. "If I can help this mission succeed, it'll be worth it even if I never see home again."

Her mention of never seeing home again sank the captain into despair.

"How do *you* feel about this mission?" asked Dr. Riesen.

"What do you mean?" he asked.

"Well, I volunteered," she said, "but you were ordered to go. It's the same outcome either way, but I imagine it might feel quite different to have no say in the matter."

Holbrook jostled the melting ice in his glass. "This may sound strange," he said, "but I've always wondered how I would respond if the order ever came down for a one-way mission. I've read about other captains in the same situation, tried to imagine how they must've felt knowing they were being ordered to their deaths. I wondered if they resented it at all. I never believed it would actually happen to me, though." He sipped his drink, staring out uncomfortably at the swirling stars.

"How *did* you respond?" she asked.

He shrugged. "In the end this mission's the same as any other. They ordered us to fly off to Sag A Star, and here we are." The captain stared off at the swirling spacetime.

"But does it really feel like any other mission?" she asked.

"I think it does," said Holbrook. He took a breath, straightened himself in his chair, and jutted out his chin. "Look, we have a job to do," he insisted with newfound resolve. "Getting back home comes later. I'm not concerned about that right now. It's like any other mission. We have to stay focused on the immediate next steps." He peered ahead through the glassteel bend.

Dr. Riesen studied the captain. "You said you're not concerned with getting back out right now, yet you made a special trip here to ask if I'd managed any progress."

Holbrook flashed a weak smile. "So much for taking my own advice on staying focused." He sipped his drink. "When I look out to the future, to the end of this mission, we either fail, which means we're dead, or we succeed, and we're still dead. Assuming you can't get us back home, that is." Pain filled his eyes. "When I let myself think about those two scenarios, I don't know, there's this great emptiness that wells up inside me, like a giant hole." Holbrook squeezed his glass.

"What do you think it is?" asked Dr. Riesen. "The emptiness, I mean."

Holbrook considered the question. "My dad was in the service," he said. "He was a starship captain. He's the reason I joined. I wanted to be like him, I guess, to follow in his footsteps. Whenever he came home on leave, I would wait by the door for him to arrive. I was always by his side, from the minute he set foot in the house to the minute he left. My mom called me his 'shadow.'"

"You loved your dad a lot," said Dr. Riesen.

"I did love him," said Holbrook. "But I also hated him." He sipped his drink again. "My dad died on a one-way mission of his own. We were all alone after that. I hated him for leaving us. I wondered if he ever thought what taking that assignment would do to a wife and kids waiting for him to return." Holbrook's jaw tightened. "That's part of why there's no one waiting for me back home. I never want to do that to a wife, or a family, to have them wondering if I'll ever return, to have them maybe get that call one day." Holbrook looked out at the stars. "That emptiness I feel," he said, "I don't know. All I can think is it must be fear of death."

"Fear of death is natural," said Dr. Riesen. "It's part of the human condition."

"It's funny," said Holbrook, smiling, "I don't *feel* like I'm afraid of dying. I mean I don't want to die or anything like that, but I don't feel like I'm afraid of it. But that's all I can think." The captain looked back at Dr. Riesen. "For all our sakes, I hope you're able to get us back home. The ship's computing resources are at your disposal. And anything else you need."

"Appreciated," said Dr. Riesen. "I will keep working at it. You can count on that."

Holbrook lifted his glass and quickly downed the remainder of his drink. "I've got to get going," he said. "I will leave you to your light show."

"Thank you for the visit, Captain," said Dr. Riesen.

"Certainly," said Holbrook. He stood, towering for a moment over the physicist, pivoted, and walked to the exit. Dr. Riesen resumed her vigil, staring into the approaching black disc.

Outside the crew lounge Holbrook stood for a moment and collected his thoughts. His whole interaction with Dr. Riesen had been strange, mostly driven by her odd indifference to their predicament. He'd need to get Commander Stephens's take—his executive officer was excellent at reading people.

"Security to Captain Holbrook."

The captain's stomach tightened at the hail that came through his comm. Security never reached out to him with good news. Never. "Holbrook here."

"Sir, this is Lieutenant Byrne." The lieutenant paused for a lifetime. "It's Tentek."

"What about him?"

"He was scheduled fifteen minutes ago for his third daily check-in with security. He never showed."

"Never showed?" The aught was beyond punctual. Word had spread among the crew that when arriving for meetings, Tentek would settle into his chair at the exact start time. "What was his last known location?"

"The ship logged him entering his quarters fifty minutes ago. Securcam footage doesn't show him leaving; however, the sensors in his room say he's not there."

Missing? Holbrook never liked the idea of having Tentek aboard his ship but protesting would have been pointless. The top brass made their decision; he could only follow their orders. Had Stephens been right about Tentek, about him being a double agent? Holbrook shook off the thoughts. His executive officer's paranoia was rubbing off on him.

Paranoia or no, they needed to find the robot. "Have Commander Stephens and a security detail meet me at Tentek's quarters," said Holbrook. "I'll be there in two minutes."

14

Holbrook rounded the corner to Tentek's quarters. He found Commander Stephens, Security Chief Lieutenant Byrne, and Security Officer Lieutenant Singh standing outside the entrance.

"Any updates?" asked Holbrook as he approached.

"No, sir," said Byrne. "There's no footage of Tentek exiting his quarters, and still no sign of him anywhere on the ship."

Based on that meager intel, the aught's cabin would be the best place to begin the search. Holbrook nodded to Byrne. "Open 'er up."

Byrne and Singh drew their Immobilizers. Holbrook debated if unholstering them was an overreaction or prudent precaution. Tentek had so far given no reason to question his motives, and there might be a reasonable explanation for their inability to contact him.

Lieutenant Byrne addressed the ship: "Starship *Avenger*, open Tentek's cabin door per Captain Holbrook's authorization."

The door slid aside to a dark room, the light from the corridor penetrating a half meter into the blackness. Byrne activated the light on his comm and waved it into the space. The stark white beam lit the room's back bulkhead, landing on the door to the cabin's private head.

The two security men entered Tentek's cabin while the captain and Stephens waited outside. Thirty seconds later came a shout from inside. "Clear."

Holbrook entered the cabin and quickly scanned the space. His eyes landed first on the table with two chairs and a dresser. A queen bed pressed against the far bulkhead, its taut and wrinkle-free bedding seemingly undisturbed from its original state. The deck was free of clothing and any other items, and the room's closet and head were both empty, their open doors revealing their pristine state. The entire cabin seemed as if it had never been occupied.

"He's not here," said Byrne.

"We'll have to start a systematic search of the ship," said Stephens.

"Hold on," said Holbrook. "The ship said this was the last place it saw him. Did you and Singh search everywhere?"

"The room's so small there's nowhere he can be hiding," said Byrne.

Holbrook shined his comm light around the cabin, pausing when it landed on the bulkhead next to the bed. The bed itself appeared to sit a few centimeters away from the bulkhead, not fully pressed against it. Holbrook walked to the foot of the bed and trained the beam along its left edge, shining light into a narrow gap between it and the wall. Within the gap, motionless on his side with his face mashed against the bulkhead, lay Tentek. "He's here."

"Where?" said Byrne in disbelief. He moved in next to the captain and inspected the narrow gap. The security chief turned to Holbrook. "I checked under the bed," he pleaded. "There was nothing there."

"The sheet's hanging down on this side," said Holbrook. "It blocked your view of the bulkhead." The captain reached down. "Help me move the bed."

Byrne swung around to the long side opposite Tentek, and together the two men pulled. No longer pinned against the bulkhead, Tentek flopped faceup onto the deck.

The captain kneeled over the aught and instinctively pressed his fingers against Tentek's neck. The robot had no pulse, but he likely never did. "Tentek," said Holbrook, "can you hear me?"

Tentek let out a weak moan. His head rolled towards Holbrook, eyes partially open but looking past the captain.

"Can you walk?" asked Holbrook. Tentek only stared back at him through low-slung lids, unresponsive. The captain put a hand under each arm and lifted. Tentek weighed much less than he expected, half that of a similar-sized human. He stood the aught upright. "Take him to Sickbay," he said to Lieutenant Byrne.

"Sickbay?" said Stephens. "This thing isn't even human. It's a machine."

"I know that," snapped Holbrook, "but we need a place to examine him."

Lieutenant Byrne hoisted Tentek with an arm behind his back and slung the robot's arm around his neck. He headed to the cabin's door with Tentek's feet dragging along the deck. Singh, Holbrook, and Stephens followed him out.

Holbrook activated his comm. "Sickbay, this is the captain. Inform Dr. Marsden we have a patient for her." He thought a moment. "Dr. Riesen," he added, "please meet me in Sickbay."

- - -

"Who's hurt?" asked Dr. Marsden as Holbrook and the others entered Sickbay.

"Tentek," said Holbrook.

"The aught?"

Holbrook nodded. "We found him passed out in his quarters."

Dr. Marsden scowled. "You know this is a *Sickbay*, right, Captain, for human patients? Not a machine shop."

"We don't have a lot of options," said Holbrook. "Besides, I know how you love a challenge."

Dr. Marsden huffed. She directed Byrne to an examination table and had him lay Tentek on his back. The aught's jaw lolled, and his face spasmed in apparent pain.

Dr. Riesen arrived and joined the four officers, crowded around the examination table.

"I need you all to take a giant step back," barked Dr. Marsden. The officers and Dr. Riesen complied, giving the doctor room to work.

Dr. Marsden glanced at the vital signs viewscreen above the examination table. The screen remained blank, an odd sight with a body present. Even with a corpse the monitor reported temperature, blood chemistry, and time and cause of death.

The doctor pulled back both of Tentek's eyelids and waved the beam from her thin medical flashlight across his pupils. His nickel irises constricted, their response much faster than a human's. Dr. Marsden grabbed his wrist, checking for a pulse through the cool, pale phlesh. She gave up after a few seconds and sighed. "Tell me again why you brought him here."

"He's sick," said Holbrook, "or at least looks like he's sick."

"That might be so," said Dr. Marsden, "but none of my medical training can help him."

"Do aughts even get sick?" asked Stephens.

"I'm sure they do," said Dr. Marsden, "but I can't imagine what he could have contracted aboard the ship." Tentek twitched again. "He'd be better off in engineering," she grumbled.

"Or the workshop," said Stephens. "They've got the machinery to disassemble him."

Holbrook glared at Stephens. "Just do the best you can with him, Doctor."

Dr. Marsden folded her arms and huffed again. "Nurse Mead," she yelled, "help me get this 'patient' undressed." Dr. Marsden unzipped Tentek's jumpsuit at the front as Nurse Mead arrived. The two worked together, pulling the outfit down from his shoulders.

"Prepping him for the spa?" asked Stephens.

"We need to check him for wounds," barked Dr. Marsden. She turned to Holbrook. "Maybe Commander Stephens can be of better use somewhere else on the ship."

"The commander won't say another word," said Holbrook and shot his XO an angry look.

Marsden and Mead removed Tentek's jumpsuit, leaving him clad only in a set of thin gray boxer briefs. They surveyed the aught's trunk, limbs, and head. At the end of their examination, Dr. Marsden removed her surgical gloves.

"What did you find, Doctor?" asked Holbrook.

"Absolutely nothing," said Marsden. "And that leaves me fresh out of ideas." She shook her head. "If it weren't for his chest rising and falling, I wouldn't even think he was alive."

"That and his eyes," said Dr. Riesen. "They're moving like he's in REM sleep."

"No, not like REM," said Dr. Marsden. "The movements would be faster, jerkier." She studied Tentek's eyes as they moved under his closed lids. "These movements are very regular." She pulled back an eyelid and held it open for several seconds. She pinned the other one open as well. "They're moving in unison," she said. The aught's eyes drifted from right to left, darting back to the right after tracking as far as they could, then restarting their slow movement to the left.

Marsden released Tentek's eyelids. "You know what this reminds me of?" she said. "When I was a kid, my brother was into electronics. For one of his birthdays, he got a small satellite dish kit. It used to track sort of like this when it lost the signal."

"Sig-nal," whispered Tentek, his voice pained, "yessss."

Holbrook moved in close to the aught.

"Careful, Captain," said Stephens.

The captain ignored Stephens. "Tentek, what's happening to you?" asked Holbrook. "Are you sick? What can we do?"

"Losssst sig-nal," he said.

"What signal?" asked Holbrook.

"Net-work …," said the aught, straining to get the syllables across his lips.

"Network?" asked Holbrook.

"F-T-L …," said Tentek, his voice trailing off with the last letter.

Dr. Riesen fell into deep thought, her eyes going glassy as they darted left and right.

"What's 'FTL'?" asked Stephens. "Is he speaking in code?"

"Captain," said Dr. Riesen, returning from her thoughts, "may I speak with you?"

Holbrook gathered she meant away from Tentek. "Marsden, try to keep him talking," he said. "Maybe that'll help him snap out of it." He directed Dr. Riesen to a nearby office, a small space used by the physician on duty. Commander Stephens entered after them and closed the door.

Dr. Riesen addressed the captain. "He said FTL network."

"Do you know what that means?" asked Holbrook.

"I'm not sure …." She thought again for a moment. "The name Collective, it refers to a hive mind, with all the individual consciousnesses interconnected." Dr. Riesen looked out the office's bay window at Tentek, who still lay motionless on the table. "My guess is they're connected to an information network of some sort. But it can't be sub-luminal, or even light speed—the lag time would be unbearable over any significant distance. To be effective, such a network would need to send data at super-luminal speeds."

Stephens's mouth fell open. "You're saying he's connected to The Collective over some faster-than-light network?"

"*Was* connected," said Dr. Riesen. "Just like we can no longer send or receive messages to CentCom because of all the spacetime distortion from

Sag A Star, this faster-than-light network would be inaccessible to Tentek as well."

"And that's what led to his incapacitation," said Holbrook. "He's cut off from their network." Which made sense—security lost track of the aught right about when they crossed the D-space boundary.

"That son of a bitch's had a network connection to The Collective all this time?" asked Stephens.

"That's my guess," said Dr. Riesen. "At least to the point where we entered D-space."

Stephens glared at Tentek through the window. The aught still lay limp and motionless. "I told you this thing couldn't be trusted," he snapped. "It's probably been updating The Collective on our progress and plans this whole time."

"We don't know that," said Holbrook.

"We *do* know he didn't tell us about his secret network connection," said Stephens.

"It doesn't mean he's a spy," said Holbrook.

"We don't know *what* he is," said Stephens, "or why he's really here. We need to throw him in the brig, now, before he regains consciousness, or whatever you call it. Build a Faraday cage and lock him inside."

"A Faraday cage won't block tachyons," said Dr. Riesen. "But if he *was* sharing information with The Collective, we don't have to worry about that now. No direct transmission can make it in or out of this deformed space."

Holbrook agreed with Stephens to a point. Tentek maintaining a network connection to The Collective ever since he arrived on their vessel at Plana Petram, if true, seemed bad. But CentCom had vetted Tentek, had vouched for his trustworthiness, had even made special exceptions to the rules so the robot could board the *Avenger*. The top brass couldn't be so foolish as to allow a spy on his ship. "Paul, I know you're concerned about Tentek," said Holbrook. "You have been from the start. But I think until we have a chance to talk to him we shouldn't jump to any conclusions."

"There's nothing to talk to him about," said Stephens.

The captain turned to the window, stroking his chin as he peered at Tentek. "I'll station some security men in here," he said. "When he regains consciousness, if he does, they can make sure he doesn't go anywhere before we have a chance to question him." The captain turned back to Stephens.

"When he does wake, if he doesn't have good answers to our questions, we'll place him in the brig, with a Faraday cage and whatever else we think we need to contain him. OK?"

Stephens folded his arms and stared at the captain. "OK," he eventually grumbled. "That's something, at least." He looked back at Tentek. "I worry, though, how much damage he's already done."

15

"Approaching the RD Sagittarii star system," said Lieutenant Commander Mills. No one else spoke on the bridge, not even in a whisper.

"Acknowledged," said Holbrook. The captain's voice trailed off in half-distraction as he stood alongside Mills, seated at the helm. Holbrook studied the tactical map that filled the main viewscreen, a bird's eye view of the RD Sagittarii star system. Black grid lines partitioned the gray screen into sections with a monstrous red disc, the hypergiant star RD Sagittarii A, at the center. Not far to its right and slightly below the horizontal centerline hovered a smaller disc, deep black and ringed with an electric blue border, the second peril that lurked in the star system: the ten solar mass black hole RD Sagittarii B. The planet Infernum appeared farther right with its gray landmasses and pale violet oceans.

The sight on the viewscreen froze Holbrook in awe. The red star was immense, far larger than even the supergiants he'd encountered in the past. A tiny black triangle, the starship *Avenger*, rose quickly from the bottom of the map, far to the left of the red star.

The current plan had been proposed and debated, analyzed by the ship, tweaked, scrapped, resurrected, debated again, tweaked a second time, and finally ratified. Holbrook had considered insisting they start from scratch a third time but couldn't fathom a viable alternative. They needed to enter the RD Sagittarii system and insert the ship into orbit around Infernum without being shot out of the sky by any anti-space batteries the aughts had waiting for them. They needed to use every resource at their disposal to conceal themselves. Those constraints dictated the major elements of their plan. He wasn't so sure they would survive it. "Bring us around," said Holbrook, transfixed by the viewscreen.

"Aye, sir," said Lieutenant Commander Mills. "Counting down sixty seconds to orbital insertion."

The ship's androgynous voice began a steady chirp: "Fifty-nine, fifty-eight, fifty-seven ...."

The *Avenger* pivoted seventy-nine degrees to starboard, sweeping around in a wide arc that placed the immense red star directly ahead. The small black triangle drove steadily towards the giant red disc, advancing at 380 times the speed of light.

"Beginning our ascent," said Mills, tapping the glass surface of the helm terminal. The *Avenger's* force pads pulsed, pushing the starship into a gentle arc to bring it up and over the hypergiant's northern hemisphere. On the tactical map, the small black triangle began its transit of the red disc.

"Fifty-two, fifty-one, fifty ...."

"Coming up on the northern pole," said Mills.

Holbrook nodded. Until then the star's bulk had hidden his starship. Their emergence above the hypergiant would be the first opportunity for enemy eyes to spot their ship. "Keep us as close to the star's corona as possible, helm," said Holbrook.

"We need to stay mindful of the temperatures in the corona," said Ensign Reilly from the science station. "The star's corona reaches 3.5 million degrees centigrade. And even aside from that there's also the circumstellar envelope, a loosely bound outer shell of gas unique to hypergiants. Flying through the envelope alone will generate a considerable amount of friction, especially at our speed."

"Without an idea of the threat we're facing, we need to hug the corona as closely as we can," said Holbrook. "The closer we hug the surface, the more difficult it'll be for anyone to see us." As long as they didn't incinerate themselves, that is. The *Avenger's* designers had fashioned her as an attack vessel. They never envisioned the warship playing cat-and-mouse with a star or its black hole companion. "We'll only need to hug the star while we're flying over the pole. Once we start our descent, they'll have to pick us out of a thirty solar mass thermonuclear backdrop."

The black triangle neared the red disc's center on the viewscreen as the *Avenger* raced towards the giant star's northern pole. The massive globe of churning, fusing hydrogen seethed below them, battering the ship with its ferocious heat and furious solar wind.

"Ship's hull temperature rising," said Lieutenant Commander Phillips. "Moving past forty thousand degrees centigrade."

"Acknowledged, Ops," said Holbrook. "Steady ahead helm."

"Forty-four, forty-three, forty-two ...."

"Hull temperature approaching fifty thousand degrees," said Phillips. "Nearing design limits."

Holbrook glanced at Lieutenant Amanda Bolton at tactical. The lieutenant read the question from the captain's face. "If we climb to avoid more of the corona, we'll be visible for sure," she said.

"Mills," said Stephens, "can we boost our speed to get out of this oven sooner?"

"A little bit," said Mills. "Increasing our speed will generate more friction from the circumstellar envelope, but the bigger problem is we'll start to draft stellar material in our wake. The whorls and eddies of spacetime from the Gravity Drive are on the edge of disrupting the star's surface as it is. An anti-space armament would pick that up for sure."

Holbrook pursed his lips. "Increase speed by as much as you can."

"Aye, aye, sir," said Mills. "Increasing speed to 384 c."

"Thirty-six, thirty-five, thirty-four ...."

"Hull temperature fifty-two thousand degrees at the forward vertex," yelled Phillips. "Some of it's friction from the envelope."

"Rotate the ship about its center," said Holbrook. "That should distribute the friction more evenly along the perimeter."

"Aye, aye, sir," said Mills. He tapped out instructions for the lateral force pads. "Reaching rotational velocity of six rotations per minute."

"How we doing, Ops?" asked Holbrook. He managed to keep his voice steady despite his ship hanging on the edge of burning up.

"Hull temperature leveling off around fifty-one thousand degrees," said Phillips.

"We're almost through the worst of it," said Mills. "Starting our descent." The helmsman pulsed the ship's force pads to adjust the black starship's course gradually down along the hypergiant's northern hemisphere.

"Hull temperatures dropping," said Phillips.

"Good," said Holbrook, relieved. "Return lateral rotation to zero. When we level off, make sure our course places Infernum dead ahead and that star directly behind us."

"Aye, aye, sir," said Mills. "Leveling off."

Captain Holbrook discovered he had been holding his breath. He forced an exhale. They had survived, the first challenge anyway. The next involved dissipating all the heat from their solar transit.

"Approaching RDS B," said Mills.

"Switch to forward video feed," said Holbrook. The bridge's main viewscreen shifted from the tactical map to an image of the black hole RD Sagittarii B, surrounded by twisted rainbows of starlight. The aughts would certainly detect the ship at its current hull temperature. The problem was the heat wouldn't radiate into the vacuum on its own—they needed a medium to sop it up.

"Coming in range of the accretion disc," said Mills.

The hole's immense accretion disc, the ring of charged particles and dust encircling the singularity, glowed an electric blue. They would shed the excess heat onto the gas and dust surrounding RD Sagittarii B as they rushed past. Physics dictated the minimum distance they needed to fly from the accretion disc to cool the *Avenger*, but if they drifted too close to the black hole, the gravitational forces would rip the ship apart.

"Hull temperature at forty-five thousand degrees," said Phillips.

"Tactical," said Holbrook. "Center on RDS B and zoom in." The bird's eye view of the RDS system reappeared on the viewscreen, this time with the black hole RDS B in the middle and magnified larger than the red hypergiant had been. The black triangle moved steadily to the right, its course marked by a dotted white line that grazed the top of the hole's electric blue accretion disc.

The ship shook, the black hole lashing out with flares of subatomic particles and bursts of electromagnetic energy at the approaching black wedge starship. It shook a second time, rattling the chairs on the bridge.

"Hull temperature at thirty-nine thousand degrees and falling," said Phillips. "But shear forces are increasing on the ship's superstructure."

"It's going to be tight," said Stephens. "We're threading a pretty fine needle."

"Stay sharp," said Holbrook, looking nervously at the viewscreen.

"Twenty-five, twenty-four, twenty-three …."

The black starship continued to rock and shudder as it cruised through the dust and gas of the accretion disc. Eddies of warped spacetime cast off from the singularity jostled the ship and wracked the crew with nausea.

"Hull temperature at twenty-two thousand degrees and dropping fast," said Phillips. The ship wrenched, threatening to throw the bridge crew from their seats. "Shear forces nearing dangerous levels."

Holbrook wanted to vomit but willed himself to remain composed. "How we doin', Mills?" he asked, squeezing the words through his discomfort.

"We're through the worst of it, Captain," said Mills, also fighting waves of nausea.

"Confirmed," said Phillips. "Shear forces are off their peaks." The ship shuddered and shook but nowhere near as violently as it had. The disruptions gradually leveled out, the *Avenger* returning to smooth sailing.

"We're clear," said Mills.

"Hull temperature has dropped to near background ambient of interstellar space," said Phillips.

Holbrook sighed in relief then steeled himself for the next phase, an exquisitely timed sequence of steps to place them in the correct orbit around Infernum without being shot out of the sky. Their current speed protected them given the extreme difficulty of hitting a starship traveling faster than light. However, the warped space that surrounded the *Avenger*, enabling its super-luminal speeds, also made it difficult for their sensors to detect exactly what lay ahead. The drop to sub-light would leave their ship vulnerable to weapons fire and allow only seconds to react. "Forward video feed," said Holbrook.

The tactical map disappeared, replaced by a field of rainbowed starlight swirls against the blackness of space. The gray-violet planet Infernum sat in the center of the viewscreen, growing larger.

An amber light flashed on the helmsman's terminal. "We need to drop to sub-light speed so we don't overshoot the planet," said Mills.

"Dropping to sub-light will generate ripples in the spacetime fabric around the ship," said Lieutenant Bolton. "Anyone looking for that signature will see a starship has entered the system."

"Thank you, tactical," said Holbrook. "Prepare for evasive maneuvers. Please proceed with the drop to sub-light, Mr. Mills."

"Aye, aye, Captain," said Mills. "Disengaging the Gravity Drive."

The curls of rainbowed starlight contracted to single points of light across the *Avenger's* viewscreen as the wormhole of twisted spacetime enveloping the black wedge starship dissipated, flattening out to normal space.

"Initiating braking sequence," said Mills, the taps at his terminal energizing the lateral force pads. "Fifteen seconds to orbital insertion."

"Fourteen, thirteen ...."

"Bolton," said Holbrook, "any sign of anti-spacecraft activity from the planet?"

"Negative, sir," said Bolton. "So far there's no sign anyone's noticed we're here."

"At our present speed it'd be hard for them to scramble something to knock us down before we swing around the planet," said Stephens. The commander stopped himself and thought for a moment. "Unless they have an orbital weapons platform ...."

"Let's just hope they haven't brought that much gear with them," said Holbrook.

"Eight, seven ...."

"Ensign Reilly," said Commander Stephens, "deploy the surface mapping autobots."

Reilly tapped at her science station terminal. "Aye, aye, sir."

The shuttle bay doors slid open, creating a wide crack of shining light along the ship's black underbelly. Four autobots exited the starship and fanned out across the planet, scanning and mapping their pre-assigned portion of the gray-violet globe. "Autobots deployed," said Reilly.

"Three, two, one ...."

"Orbital insertion complete," said Mills. "We're transiting the dark side." The planet Infernum loomed on the viewscreen as a large near-black circle against the star field, surrounded by a thin violet ring of backlit atmosphere. Red streaks of flowing molten lava slashed the disc's interior.

"How long before our orbit takes us back out away from the planet?" asked Holbrook.

"About seven minutes, Captain," said Mills.

"Can we exhale yet?" asked Stephens. The commander and the captain looked to Bolton at tactical.

"We'll never be able to rest easy up here," said Lieutenant Bolton, "but I think we've skirted any major threat."

"I'll take it," said Holbrook. "Great work, everyone. Mr. Mills, what's our orbital status?"

"We're locked in a wide elliptical orbit that will swing us twenty AU from Infernum at apogee," said Mills. "Our orbital period's synchronized with the planet's rotation to bring the *Avenger* over the landing party's planned drop zone once per day."

"Let's see the mapping data," said Holbrook.

Two large circles appeared on the viewscreen, one for each hemisphere and partially filled with long, thin rectangular stripes of oceans and continents. More stripes appeared within the discs on each autobot's orbit. Five minutes after their deployment, the autobots had fully mapped the surface and settled into geosynchronous orbits around the planet, preparing for future tactical use. The ship analyzed the sensor data for an additional minute, annotating the maps with geographic and other points of interest.

Holbrook's brow crinkled. "There's the *Adiona*," he said, pointing at a teardrop marker on the viewscreen, "but I don't see the Hex Men's mine or equipment, or any sign of an aught ship."

Stephens surveyed the maps. "Starship *Avenger*," he said, "reanalyze the Infernum sensor data and identify the location of the Hex Men site."

Several seconds passed before the ship responded. "No site matching the Hex Men mine images appears in the sensor data," it said. "There are no sites exhibiting large-scale sentient modification of the planet's surface."

"Huh," said Holbrook. They had the right planet. How could the site, a kilometer-wide scar on the landscape that existed five weeks before, just be gone? "Commander Stephens, what's your take?"

"It doesn't make sense," said the ship's executive officer. "Did the planet swallow it up somehow?" Stephens studied the map again. "If we don't see the mine, maybe the aughts couldn't find it either. Maybe they aren't even down on the planet."

"Maybe the aughts got what they came for and imploded the site," said Holbrook, "to make sure no one else could mine Planck Matter."

"We'd still see an empty spot on the map," said Stephens. "A round patch of dirt with no trees or vegetation."

"Maybe the vegetation grows fast on this planet," said Holbrook.

"Even a depression filled with foliage would still show up on the map as a depression," said Stephens.

Holbrook stroked his chin. He'd expected the mission to throw him a few curve balls, but more along the lines of a sneak attack or the aughts departing just as they arrived, not a completely missing target site. "We need to be certain the mine's gone," he said. But how to figure out where it *should* be? "We'll land at the *Adiona*, check for survivors, then retrace the researchers' steps."

"Sickbay to Captain," crackled Dr. Marsden's voice across the comm channels.

"Go ahead," said Holbrook.

"Captain, it's Tentek, my aught patient."

Holbrook exchanged a glance with Stephens. "What about him?" asked the captain.

"Sir," she said, "he's awake."

16

Tentek sat at the far end of the six-person conference table in the small meeting space down the corridor from Sickbay. He determined his location based on a precise measurement of the room's dimensions and his memory of the *Avenger's* layout. The data from his inertial sensors said he had moved from Sickbay to his current location.

Sickbay?

That was just over ninety minutes ago, but he could only remember the last ten minutes. And before then? A flatline of sensory input and computation.

His last memory before the flatline was … what? In his quarters … feeling faint. The room spinning, then blackness. Flatline blackness. But if his chronometer was correct, that was over two days ago.

The door opened, admitting Captain Holbrook, Commander Stephens, and Dr. Riesen. Two security guards stood in the corridor on either side of the entrance, their backs to the room.

Was he a prisoner?

The two *Avenger* officers took adjacent seats at the opposite end of the table, facing him directly. Dr. Riesen sat along the side.

The captain gave the aught a wan smile. "Hello, Tentek."

"Hello, Captain, Commander, Dr. Riesen," said Tentek, nodding to each. The captain and the physicist offered cordial, if not friendly, expressions. Commander Stephens maintained an icy glare.

"How are you feeling?" asked Holbrook.

How much should he divulge about his current state? And how to find out what happened to him? Peppering the humans with questions would reveal how little he understood about the events of the past two days. He'd instead let the humans do the talking. He would fill in the blanks from the questions they asked. "Fine, Captain."

"We weren't sure you would ever regain consciousness," said Holbrook.

Tentek did not respond. His eyelids click-clacked in the room's silence.

"Do you remember what happened?" asked the captain.

"Mostly," he lied. "But I am having a little trouble piecing it all together."

"We found you passed out in your quarters," said Stephens. "That was shortly after we entered D-space. You were in Sickbay up until a bit ago when we moved you here." The commander delivered his words like icy daggers.

D-space! Sag A Star! He had forgotten. His mind was groggy, like computing with circuits that were too hot. He wanted to return to his quarters, to lie down, to see if he could coax his systems a little closer to ground state. Probabilities suggested they were unlikely to allow that before he answered some questions. He did not recall being moved to the conference room, but clearly their purpose in doing so was to hold an interrogation.

"My understanding of aught physiology is your body is designed to be resilient, with many safeguards and redundant systems to keep you conscious," said Holbrook. "In light of that resiliency, I'm wondering if you can explain why you blacked out."

Only one possible cause could have resulted in the symptoms he experienced. But perhaps a plausible alternative would satisfy the humans. "The ship recently entered D-space," he said. "It may have been something like D-space sickness for aughts. The circuits and pathways in my synthetic brain have tolerances similar to your neuron connections. If adjacent pathways stretch or contract to different lengths, that can throw off delicate timings." His human hosts stared back at him with blank expressions. Did they not understand his explanation? Or did they not accept it? "It may have been something like that."

"Dr. Riesen has a different theory," said Holbrook. He nodded at the physicist.

"When you were in Sickbay, at one point you seemed to be delirious," said Dr. Riesen. "You called out about your connection to the FTL network."

"I did?" said Tentek. Surprise and concern spiked in his nervous system circuits before he could tamp it down.

"I guessed you were talking about a faster-than-light network," said Dr. Riesen. "A network that would allow all aughts to stay connected, no matter where they are in the galaxy."

Tentek blinked at the three humans. Probabilities had not suggested he would fall ill when they reached D-space. And probabilities had not suggested the humans would be so smart. Should he tell them the truth, or risk a half-truth explanation? Probabilities suggested they already knew the answers to the questions they asked and that further dodges would only raise suspicions. "You are aware, Doctor, of studies where animals, like dolphins and whales, have perished because of lack of communication and companionship from their own species? Even humans have been shown to break down and die after prolonged separation from other people.

"Aughts, in this respect, are no different. We are social creatures. An aught cannot survive on its own. We require interaction with others of our kind. While you humans achieve that interaction through close physical proximity to other humans, we do the same, except we use a network to form those connections."

"A wireless network," said Dr. Riesen, "accessible through interstellar space?"

The aught dithered. "That is correct," he said.

"A tachyon-based network," said Stephens.

Tentek did not want to discuss the Network, but they had already deduced its basic function. "That is correct," he said. "All aughts from The Collective connect to the Network using tachyon transceivers built into our bodies. Originally this network was of a very small scale, a simple planet-wide, light-speed network on our home world. However, we had visions of traveling through the stars, of exploring, of moving freely through the galaxy. To do that while maintaining a connection, we needed a fast network, specifically, a faster-than-light network, one that would allow us to remain in touch with one another even as we spread across the extreme distances of interstellar space."

"I've heard enough, Captain," said Stephens. "Permission to lock him up?"

"Hold on, Commander," said Holbrook. "Tentek, to date you've presented yourself as an ally of humanity, yet you failed to disclose the very important fact of this network and your constant connection to The Collective."

Tentek cocked his head. "I do not understand your statement, Captain, or question, if it is a question. My Network connection to The Collective has no relevance to my desire to assist humankind."

"Certainly it's clear there's at least a problem with the optics," said Holbrook.

"You are a God damned sentient Collective network node point that we took aboard our ship," said Stephens.

"And that is the very reason I did not disclose it," said Tentek. "If I had told you on Plana Petram about my Network connection, you would never have let me aboard your ship."

"You're damn right!" shouted Stephens.

"Paul, please ...," said Holbrook.

"You need me on this mission," said Tentek.

"You mean so you can send updates to your Collective buddies on our progress?" asked Stephens, his face flush. "You've been in constant contact with The Collective ever since we left Plana Petram. What information have you shared with them? At the very least our location."

"I have never sent the ship's location to The Collective," said Tentek, "and they cannot track me over this network."

"Have you told them about this mission?" asked Holbrook. "Have you told them we're coming?"

Tentek hesitated. "They already know we are coming," he said.

The three humans sat stunned at Tentek's revelation.

"Son of a bitch," said Stephens, quietly dribbling out each syllable. "I told you we should never have let him on board."

"They already know because probabilities suggest a high likelihood of such an event," said Tentek. "With the kind of computational power at The Collective's disposal, it is quite easy to predict many events. Not with one hundred percent accuracy, but the results can be ... uncanny." Stephens looked as if he could jump over the table at him. Probabilities suggested Tentek had little chance of changing the commander's mind no matter what he said. The commander was not the person he hoped to reach. "You must believe me when I tell you I have shared no information with The Collective, Captain Holbrook. I state again, unequivocally, I am on the side of humankind."

"Does the fact that you're conscious, talking to us now, mean your network connection has been restored?" asked Dr. Riesen.

"It does not," Tentek said. "Prior to our entering D-space, I had no concept of losing this connection, no understanding of what it would mean to me physiologically." Tentek paused, his mouth half open as he computed the best words to use. "What I am about to tell you I only know from examining my system logs. When I lost my Network connection, my normal consciousness went into a quiescence, a sort of sleep mode. From that point my body's autonomic processes took over, the central one being the reestablishment of a Network connection."

"What brought you back to consciousness?" asked Holbrook.

"Eventually the Network acquisition protocol timed out. My systems restarted with no connection at all."

"So you're able to function without a connection to The Collective," said Dr. Riesen.

"I can function without a connection to The Collective for some amount of time," said Tentek, "but not indefinitely."

"What happens when time's up?" asked Stephens.

"I will shut down," said Tentek.

"How much time do you have?" asked Dr. Riesen.

"Five days," said Tentek. "A week. I am not really sure. But between now and that time I will weaken, my mental faculties will dull."

"All that from losing your connection to the aught network?" asked Holbrook.

"It is not just any network, Captain," said Tentek. "Subsystems drift over time, lose precision. The Network helps keep everything in sync. There are even pieces of me, of my consciousness, that do not exist locally, inside this shell."

"That means the aughts sent by The Collective should have shut down by now too," said Dr. Riesen. "They arrived in D-space a whole week before us."

"It is likely they set up a local Network within their ship," said Tentek. "Such a network would feel real, possibly even include a few simulated services to avoid some of the drifting I mentioned. They will have to be careful reconnecting to the real Network after they complete their mission; otherwise, they will suffer something akin to the bends that humans get when rising too quickly from a deep ocean dive." Tentek massaged his temples, hoping the affectation would suggest strain at proceeding. "Captain, I am happy to answer more of your questions but for now I request that I be allowed to return to my quarters. Though I am conscious, my systems are not all back online, which makes it difficult for me to think. I can be of better use to you after some self-maintenance time."

"I'll call security to escort him to the brig," said Stephens.

"That won't be necessary, Commander," said Holbrook. "Tentek, you may return to your quarters."

Stephens began to protest, but Holbrook waved him off with a look and a quick shake of his head.

"Thank you, Captain," said Tentek, rising from his chair. He wobbled slightly, steadying himself with a hand on the tabletop. After several click-clacks of his eyelids, he bowed and headed for the door.

"Make sure Tentek reaches his quarters," shouted Holbrook to the security men outside. He wasn't worried about Tentek running off, more that their aught guest might suffer another episode before he reached his cabin. The three headed down the corridor, disappearing behind the closing doors.

Commander Stephens seethed in his chair. "Captain," he said, "I told you from the start this aught cannot be trusted, and here's a perfect demonstration of that fact, which he confirmed himself. He created a massive security hole by just setting foot aboard the *Avenger*, a direct connection to The Collective that he deliberately did not mention. What else is he keeping secret? Maybe his full experiences, his conversations, visual inputs, everything, get uploaded to The Collective for analysis. They certainly have the bandwidth to pull it off."

"His network connection has been severed," said Dr. Riesen.

"Even if that's true, even if he's on our side as the two of you want to believe, we don't know just what he's capable of," said Stephens. "What if The Collective installed some rogue programming he's not aware of that'll send him on a rampage the moment we land on the planet? What if there's some built-in failsafe that activates when we're about to blast his buddies?" The commander shook his head, his face red. "Tentek belongs in the brig, sir, wrapped in a Faraday cage and whatever other precautions we can think of to protect this ship. You promised me that. You promised we would lock him up after interrogating him."

"Only if his answers were unsatisfactory," said Holbrook. "There's nothing he said that was clear evidence of deception."

"He's lying every time he opens his mouth!" said Stephens.

Holbrook did not want to disregard Stephens's advice but had to weigh it against the commander's hatred of aughts. He replayed their discussion with Tentek, seeking any additional insight. "We could, based on the answers he gave us, assume the worst and lock him up," said Holbrook. "The problem is he may be truthful when he says he's only here to help us, and we may still need him to complete our mission. For that reason, I don't think we should take any action that might disincentivize him from helping us."

The commander folded his arms and looked up, channeling his anger into the deck above.

"If I'm wrong, Paul, you can be the first to say, 'I told you so.'"

Stephens huffed. "If you *are* wrong, I hope we're all still alive for me to say it."

17

"You made it," said Holbrook.

Commander Stephens had just arrived on Shuttle Bay Row where members of the Infernum landing party lined up behind the captain at the middle airlock: science officer Reilly; Security Officers Byrne, Shelton, and Edwards; Chief Medical Officer Marsden; acting engineering head Conlin; Tentek; Dr. Riesen; and planetary geologist Koh. All wore blue-gray EN-suits.

"I was thinking we might have to leave without you," said Holbrook.

"You'd probably have to come back for me," said Stephens, "unless you want Reilly leading the second team. On second thought, maybe that's not a bad idea."

"You're still worried about leaving Mills in charge of the ship," said Holbrook. "I agree he doesn't have a lot of command experience, but he'll do OK."

"Lieutenant Commander Mills has the conn for one reason: he's the best option from a meager set of choices." Stephens sprouted a concerned look. "Maybe one of us really should stay behind."

"This mission will succeed or fail by the events that unfold on the planet," said Holbrook. "With one team investigating the *Adiona* and the other scouting for the Hex Men mine, we're going to need an experienced officer leading each party. We can't have you or me up here while all that matters is happening down there. Besides, other than assist us on the ground as needed, all the *Avenger* will do is orbit the planet." Stephens didn't seem totally convinced, but at least he had nothing more to say. "Starship *Avenger*, open Airlock Two and start the shuttle's pre-drop sequence," said the captain. The airlock spiraled open with a faint scraping sound.

"Everyone file in," said Stephens. The two senior officers entered the airlock, proceeding to the two seats at the front of the elongated D-shaped craft. The rest of the landing party followed, unfolding thinly padded seats from their nooks along the craft's bare white interior and slipping their arms through shoulder restraints anchored in the bulkhead. The formerly silent cabin became a cacophony of thudding boots, clicking clasps, and tightening belts.

Holbrook settled into the pilot's station and made a quick visual inspection of the landing party, confirming each member secure within their seat. "Shuttle," he said, "take us to the *Adiona*."

The shuttle beeped, unlatched its internal bay connections, and drifted out from its docking ring. The shuttle bay's large doors slid apart beneath the small craft, flooding the hangar with dim red morning sunlight reflected off the rumpled cloud cover below.

Exiting from the *Avenger's* belly, the shuttle fell towards Infernum, transitioning from the starship's gravity well to the planet's. The *Avenger's* bay doors closed, and the warship accelerated to a tenth the speed of light, disappearing into the blackness of space.

The shuttle continued downward, gaining more speed as it plummeted through the layers of the planet's atmosphere, the soft sound of rushing air growing louder within the cabin.

"Picking up some chop," said Holbrook. Strong crosswise winds buffeted the craft at twelve kilometers above the planet's surface. "Sorry about the bumpy ride, folks. The computer's doing its best to counter with the lateral force pads, but its reactions are just a few milliseconds too late."

The captain reviewed the computer's flight plan on the viewscreen. "Coming up on a thick layer of clouds," he said. The sight through the shuttle's glassteel viewport shifted from the violet-black of near space to a fluffy, red-tinged white haze. Their velocity slowed slightly, the clouds cushioning their descent. The turbulence that previously jostled the craft subsided almost completely.

Seconds later, the shuttle burst through the underside of the clouds, the rolling gray ceiling climbing away as the small craft continued downward.

The pilot's terminal beeped. "The shuttle's got a visual lock on our destination," said Holbrook. "Fifty-four seconds to touchdown."

"Any sign of activity around the *Adiona*?" asked Stephens.

Holbrook zoomed and panned the image on the terminal. "Nothing."

The viewscreen snapped from its realtime camera display to a tactical readout. Red lights flashed in the bottom right corner. The shuttle emitted several soft chimes.

"The shuttle's detected two objects rising from the surface," said Holbrook.

"What are they?" asked Stephens.

"It can't tell," said Holbrook, "but based on their course and speed, it doesn't think they're natural. Or friendly." The captain switched the left side of the screen to a live view from beneath the shuttle. Two small, round, black dots rose against the backdrop of the planet's yellow-gray landscape. They flew in a tight formation, with no more than a meter of separation.

"Those are drones from The Collective."

The voice had been thin, metallic. Holbrook looked back into the cabin, finding Tentek staring back at him, his eyelids click-clacking. "Are you sure?" he asked.

"Yes," said Tentek. "They are outfitted with quantum pulse guns."

"Those are small armaments," said Stephens, "but more than capable of taking us out."

"The two drones will work in tandem to bring down the shuttle," said the aught.

On the viewscreen one of the drones peeled off from the other, rocketing upward.

"A drone is taking position directly behind the shuttle," said Holbrook. "The other's still on an intercept course. Initiating evasive maneuvers!" Holbrook tapped the viewscreen controls, and the small craft executed a sharp port-side roll followed by a steep dive that caused members of the landing party to grip their restraints. A few officers cried out.

On the tactical screen the drone eventually returned to its position behind the shuttle. "Looks like that shook it off of us for a few seconds, but it's locking on again," said Stephens.

"I don't think we're gonna make it to the ground without a fight," said Holbrook. "Hang on everyone; this is not gonna be a pleasant ride."

Holbrook flew the shuttle straight and level for three seconds, then placed it into a steep dive, its nose pointed at the ground. Several members of the landing party screamed.

The trailing drone adjusted its course to follow, diving down behind the shuttle.

Holbrook tapped the weapons controls on the viewscreen as the small craft drove downward. A fist-sized ball of orange and red plasma bubbled for twenty milliseconds in the nozzle of the shuttle's rear cannon, then exploded upward in snakes of blinding flame.

The drone, its velocity augmented by the pull of the planet's gravity, could not adjust its course in time to evade the blast. The plasma's tendrils licked at its black surface before coalescing into a seething ball of ionized gas and energy that fully enveloped the small robot. The drone pitched up, imploded, and a tenth of a second later exploded, painting yellow light on the thick gray clouds above and raining bits of debris down toward the shuttle.

"Got one of 'em," said Holbrook. He tapped at the viewscreen to pull the shuttle out of its dive.

As the shuttle leveled its flight, the second drone emerged directly in its path. The cabin filled with a solid tone.

"That's a weapon's lock," said Stephens.

"Everyone hold on!" shouted Holbrook.

The drone fired its quantum pulse gun, releasing two blasts of phased energy.

Holbrook tapped furiously at the viewscreen, rolling the craft to port. The first blast grazed its underside, scraping an ugly dark gash along its smooth white exterior. Blue-green sparks sputtered from the shuttle's aft.

The second blast connected more solidly with the small vessel, tearing a lengthwise hole in its starboard hull. The cabin depressurized with a loud, sustained hiss. The shuttle rolled to starboard as it plummeted to the ground.

"We've lost the starboard stabilizer," yelled Holbrook against the deafening whoosh of air through the gash. "It's gonna be tough maintaining controlled flight." He tapped at the screen, reconfiguring the shuttle's starboard force pads to compensate for the lost stabilizer. The craft came out of its roll and continued forward, with a slight list to starboard. The second drone moved to a position ten meters directly behind the shuttle.

Red circles flashed impatiently on the viewscreen's system status board. "The power pack's ruptured," said Holbrook. "We've gotta land."

"We must destroy the other drone first," yelled Tentek from the rear of the cabin. "We cannot fight it from the ground."

"If the power pack explodes, we're all dead," said Holbrook.

"If we land before we destroy the other drone, making it to the ground alive will be of little consequence," said Tentek.

Tentek was probably right about destroying the drone while aloft. If they landed, they would cede the high ground to the device, and they'd be hard pressed to even scratch the thing with their hand weapons. But with the rupture it wasn't a question of if the power pack would explode, but when.

Holbrook fired the rear plasma cannon. Tendrils of flame shot behind the shuttle, but the drone drifted to port, avoiding the blast. Holbrook fired again. The drone jogged to starboard, evading the second bolt. "Damn thing's hanging back," he said. "At that distance it can easily dodge the shots from the cannon."

The drone primed its quantum pulse gun. A solid tone filled the cabin.

Captain Holbrook energized the forward force pads to maximum. Superconducting coils rattled as the shuttle braked hard, throwing everyone into their restraints. The drone, its speed unchanged, barreled forward, closing the gap between it and the small craft. Holbrook fired a third shot. The drone danced to starboard but not fast enough to completely evade the blast. The plasma melted its carapace, destroying its flight control surfaces. The robot plummeted in a tightening spiral, trailing orange sparks and black smoke. It slammed to the ground in an explosion that flashed the surrounding terrain and brush, leaving a small fire where it crashed.

"You got him!" said Stephens.

Holbrook nodded. "Now comes the hard part," he said under his breath. "After my breaking, we're falling like a brick."

The captain pitched the shuttle's nose down, placing the craft in a glide to regain some forward momentum. At fifteen meters above the ground, Holbrook raised the shuttle's nose, channeling its momentum into a climb. Klaxons rang out as their forward velocity neared zero. At seven meters above the ground, the shuttle stalled. Holbrook energized what was left of its underside force pads. The craft floated gently downward until the pads failed a meter above the ground. The shuttle fell, slamming into a broad clearing of yellow grasses strewn with small rocks and boulders.

"Everyone out!" shouted Holbrook.

Dr. Riesen reached the airlock first and slapped her palm against the red emergency release button. Explosive bolts ejected the hatch. The round door skidded along the ground, stopping three meters away. She jumped out and turned to help the others behind her.

Three members of the landing party did not stir. Edwards, Reilly, and Koh, all sitting along the starboard side of the bulkhead, remained unconscious, or worse. Stephens, Byrne, and Holbrook worked to pop the releases on their restraints. Each man hoisted a limp body over their shoulders and lumbered to the open airlock, struggling with their loads. Infernum's gravity was slightly below Earth's but higher than on the ship. It would take time for them to acclimate to the new gravitational field.

Holbrook exited first, stepping over the lip of the round airlock, followed by Byrne and Stephens. The captain plowed forward, his head down as he concentrated on moving as quickly as he could away from the shuttle with the wounded officer on his back. At his twenty-third step, he came upon a set of boots, facing him and planted directly in his path. The captain paused his march to look up. He found Lieutenant Shelton idling before him and the rest of the landing party loitering nearby, watching the three of them carry the wounded. "Get as far from the shuttle as you can!" he yelled. "The power pack's ruptured!"

"Head for those rocks," said Stephens, nodding at a large outcropping thirty meters ahead and slightly left.

The other five members of the landing party hurried toward the volcanic outcropping, ahead of the three *Avenger* officers who trailed with the wounded. When Holbrook reached the rocks, he came around behind them and gently laid Ensign Edwards on the dusty, gray ground. Byrne and Stephens deposited the other two injured officers beside the ensign.

Dr. Marsden immediately attended to Edwards, who appeared to be the most seriously wounded of the three.

"How bad is he, Doctor?" asked Holbrook.

A flash bright as Earth's sun erupted on the other side of the outcropping, followed an instant later by a loud explosion that shook the ground, and finally a rush of superheated air. Small bits of dirt and rock rained on the landing party. Some raced to shield their heads with their hands while others had the foresight to activate their helmets.

Once the shower of debris ceased, Holbrook peered around the boulder. The shuttle was gone. In its place a wide, shallow crater remained, cradling a fire that billowed black smoke. The craft's ruptured power pack, its containment failed, released its entire store of energy in a single instant.

Holbrook shifted his attention back to Marsden. The doctor was examining Ensign Reilly.

"How are they, Doctor?" asked Holbrook.

"Edwards and Koh are dead," she said, in her typical clinical manner. "Reilly sustained a concussion. She's conscious now, but woozy. I'm going to give her something that should help."

Holbrook crouched near the bodies of the two dead men. Edward's face had been badly burned. Blood covered Koh's EN-suit across his torso. The captain bowed his head, then stood.

"We must leave here as soon as possible," came a voice from behind Holbrook.

Spinning around, Holbrook found Tentek staring at him several meters away from the outcropping. The aught had a streak of dirt smeared across his pale right cheek.

"Some of us are wounded," said Holbrook, approaching the aught. "Two are dead. I don't know how quickly we can move out."

"It must be soon," said Tentek, his billiard ball eyes filled with reflections of the shuttle fire.

"And why is that?" asked Stephens as he approached the captain and the aught.

Tentek's double-eyelids click-clacked. "Standard operating procedure. If the two drones that engaged us do not return in eighteen and a half minutes, which they will not, two more will be sent to investigate. We have to find cover."

"And where do you propose we do that?" asked Stephens. "Look around —it's just flat plains."

Stephens was right. The grassland continued on for kilometers in all directions. There were other rock outcroppings like the one they huddled next to, but nothing to hide under.

"There is a lake not far from here," said Tentek.

Holbrook blinked at him, baffled by the comment.

"About 1.1 kilometers to the east," Tentek added.

Stephens shrugged dismissively. "So there's a lake," he said. "What the hell difference does that make?"

"We can hide beneath the water," said Tentek. "Our EN-suits will keep us dry and provide oxygen for as long as we're submerged."

Holbrook rubbed his chin. "What're our other options?"

"We stay and fight," said Byrne, unholstering his electron pistol. "We can use this rock formation for cover."

"A security officer is not one to turn and run," said Tentek. "However your instincts will not serve us. The drones are too fast. Two of them working together will easily overwhelm us. And even if we destroy them, two more will follow."

"Any other ideas?" asked Holbrook. No one offered another solution. Marching off across the plains seemed to be the only option. The captain never imagined the mission would begin the way it had, their transport destroyed and two men dead.

"We need to get moving," said Tentek.

"Get moving? We haven't even decided where we're going," said Stephens.

"The lake is the only option," said Tentek. "Every second we remain here increases the probability of our capture."

"What about our dead?" asked Dr. Marsden.

Holbrook looked back at Edwards and Koh, their lifeless bodies crumpled on the ground.

"Place them near the shuttle," said Tentek.

Stephens glanced at the shallow crater where the shuttle's exploded remains continued to burn. "You're not serious?" he asked.

"I am," said Tentek.

"These men deserve a proper burial," said Stephens.

"But we do not have time for one. And we cannot take them with us," said Tentek. "By placing them near the wreckage, the drones will believe the shuttle's passengers died. If they find no human remains, they will continue searching for us, for they will not believe the shuttle was unmanned."

Holbrook hated the idea of leaving the bodies of his men out in the open, but their options appeared to be severely limited.

Commander Stephens pulled Holbrook aside with a tug of his arm. "Captain, I don't think it's a smart idea to follow Tentek's plan," he said.

"Do you have a different one, Commander?" barked Holbrook. "'Cause now's the time to propose it. Or do you just hate the plan because it came from Tentek?"

Stephens huffed in frustration but said nothing more.

Captain Holbrook stepped farther away from the outcropping, surveying northeast in the direction of the lake. He looked again at the burning crater. "Stephens, you and Byrne carry the bodies to the wreckage. I'll collect Reilly. Everyone else, move out." He turned to Tentek. "Lead the way."

18

Holbrook arrived with Ensign Reilly at the lake to find Dr. Marsden, Lieutenants Shelton and Conlin, Dr. Riesen, and Tentek all standing along the shoreline. Holbrook had carried the ensign off and on across the plain of short yellow grasses, the young officer managing to walk at times as she recovered from her concussion. Holbrook lowered Reilly to the ground and surveyed the water that would conceal them from the aught drones. Though a hundred meters across at its widest point, the lake was shallow, barely a half meter deep, its bottom a patchwork of small, rounded stones easily visible through the crystal-clear water.

Appalled and dismayed, the captain marched over to Tentek. "This is the lake we're supposed to hide in?"

Tentek blinked. "The lakebed continues on like this for approximately seventeen meters but then drops off quickly into an eight-meter gully," he said. Holbrook looked out across the surface, spotting a wide smudge in the clear violet waters where they took on a darker shade.

"Is eight meters even enough?" asked Commander Stephens. He had just arrived with Lieutenant Byrne after placing the bodies of Edwards and Koh at the crash site. "The water's so clear; I bet with the right equipment you could see a hundred meters down."

"I do not know if it will be enough," said Tentek.

"You don't know?" asked Stephens, his voice rising. "You marched us over here to hide and now you're saying you don't know if it's going to work?"

Tentek's eyes click-clacked at Stephens within an expressionless face. "That is correct."

"This was your plan all along, wasn't it, Tin Man?" shouted Stephens. "To get us captured!"

Tentek cocked his head. "My name is Tentek, and we need not have marched this far to be captured. Probabilities suggest our chances of remaining undiscovered improve substantially if we hide beneath the surface of this lake. They are not one hundred percent, however, and so I cannot assure you we will not be found. This is still the best plan for evading the drones." The aught addressed the captain directly. "We must enter the water now. The drones are almost to the crash site."

"They are?" asked Holbrook. "How do you know?"

"I can hear them."

Holbrook checked his EN-suit's heads-up display. Its ambient sound analysis listed only the rustlings of the landing party, a soft breeze, and the crackling of the still-burning remnants of their shuttle. "I don't hear anything," he said.

Tentek stared off into the eastern sky. "'Hear' is perhaps not the right literal word, but it is the right 'sense' if you will. The machines broadcast signals as they travel, attempting to connect to the Network. That is what I 'hear.'" He returned his attention to the captain. "The drones, two of them, are nearing the crash site. We must enter the water now if we hope to evade them."

"Captain." The call came from Dr. Marsden, a hint of concern in her voice. She stood next to Reilly and Byrne.

"Yes, Doctor," said Holbrook, walking to the three officers.

"We were checking Ensign Reilly's suit," she said. "Her helmet's damaged. It won't form a positive seal."

Holbrook took the helmet ring from Marsden and inspected it himself. The doctor was right. The containment seal was damaged, probably during the drone attack on the shuttle. The ring still expanded into a protective force field bubble, but the bubble itself wasn't properly sealed. Beneath the lake's surface it wouldn't last a minute before filling with water.

The captain's first impulse, to trade helmet rings with the ensign, would do them little good. While allowing Reilly to submerge with the others, Holbrook would be forced to remain out of the lake, easy for the drones to find and likely tipping them off to the entire landing party's presence. Their scheme to hide from the aught drones, the only option available, had failed before it began.

"She can have my helmet," said Tentek, approaching the captain.

"That won't work," said Holbrook, recalling his thoughts on offering his own ring. "That will help Ensign Reilly, but it'll leave you out here standing beside the lake."

"I do not need my helmet to remain under the water," said Tentek. "Unlike yours, this body does not need air to function." He gave his helmet ring a twist and lifted it from around his neck. He handed the ring to Dr. Marsden, who assisted Ensign Reilly in attaching it to her EN-suit. Locked in place, a tap of its button expanded the helmet over the ensign's head. Unlike the damaged ring, the button turned green, indicating a positive seal.

"We must hurry," whispered Tentek.

"Everybody in!" shouted Holbrook.

The landing party splashed across the shallow violet waters to where the lakebed steepened. Dr. Riesen entered the deeper section first, the water rising to her shoulders after a few strides. A moment later the top of her translucent helmet slipped from view. The other members of the landing party followed. Within seconds, only Tentek and the captain remained above the lake's surface.

The two stood as if waiting for the other to act. "You should head down," said Holbrook.

Tentek didn't move, seemingly hesitant to enter the deeper part of the lake. He finally waded in, stopping with the waters at his neckline. He glanced back at the captain, then continued down, his frizzy white hair the last sign before he disappeared.

Holbrook paused, replaying his exchange with Tentek. The aught hesitated before he submerged. It almost seemed like he wanted to be the last one under. But why? Had he intended to stay above the surface? No one would have known if he hadn't entered. Could his plan have been to remain visible, to be found by the drones?

Holbrook dropped the paranoid thought and descended beneath the surface of the lake. He had donned EN-suits many times over his career but never to enter water. His first few steps were easy, engulfing him in a shimmering bright violet world with good visibility all around. As he moved farther into the depths, the shafts of red sunlight gradually weakened. The world darkened. The sloping lakebed eventually leveled off 8.4 meters below the surface according to his suit. Blackness surrounded him, a result of the depth and the silt dredged up by the landing party's trek across the lake bottom.

Captain Holbrook could barely see his gloved hand raised before his face. The others must have been nearby, but in the blackness that surrounded him he couldn't tell if the next closest person stood two meters away or two hundred. Should he call out over his suit comm? He pinged the lake with sonar instead. The readout showed the bulk of his officers clustered not two meters ahead of him.

A rush of water came towards him, like the surge before the bow of an oncoming ship. He resisted its gentle attempt at pushing him backwards.

A body, a dead human body, materialized out of the black just in front of him, its sickly head illuminated by the lights inside his helmet. The thing's pale white skin looked unnatural after days or perhaps weeks in the water. Bloated, bleached eyes stared back from a thin, expressionless face.

Holbrook gasped. Had he stumbled upon one of the *Adiona's* crew? What were they doing so far from their ship?

The thing, incredibly, grabbed his wrist! Holbrook resisted but couldn't escape its grasp. Its bloated white eyes continued their dead stare back at him as he struggled against its grip.

The bloated eyes blinked.

The irises he had presumed were bleached by their time in the water were in fact nickel in color, the skin more plastic than waterlogged. The eyes blinked again, whisked by a double set of eyelids. The dead, pale body come alive was Tentek.

Tentek put his finger to his lips. Holbrook nodded in response. Should he tell the others to remain silent? He didn't want to risk creating more sound. The captain hoped no one would speak.

The two remained in their half-embrace for nearly a minute, standing just centimeters apart. The aught released Holbrook's arm and pointed to the surface.

Holbrook looked up. Above him hovered a warbled view of the soft violet sky, like observing the world through a narrow bottle. A dim red disc, the hypergiant, floated off to the side, distorted by the ripples across the lake's surface.

Two black dots entered his view and floated silently overhead. The drones tracked them to the lake! Except the dots didn't stop, or even slow. They drifted lazily to the northeast, eventually moving out of sight.

Another minute passed before Tentek gestured again, giving a thumbs-up sign.

"Can we exit the water?"

Tentek nodded.

"All clear," said Holbrook over his suit comm. "Everybody out."

The landing party trudged back through the soft mud at the lake bottom, their legs dredging more plumes of silt. Holbrook and Tentek emerged first, checking the northeast sky for any signs of the black robots. Stephens, Byrne, Dr. Marsden, and Reilly exited next, the doctor assisting the still-woozy ensign, followed by Conlin, Shelton, and Dr. Riesen. The members of the *Avenger* landing party assembled in a rough circle at the lake's edge.

"I apologize for startling you," Tentek said to the captain. "I had no other way of gaining your attention."

"That's OK," Holbrook lied as he relived his shock at encountering the assumed dead body, "though a whisper over your suit comm would've been better than grabbing my arm."

"That was not an option," said Tentek. "Without a helmet I could not communicate with you and the others over the comm."

Indeed. Holbrook hadn't considered how Tentek's lack of a helmet would prevent them from talking with the aught once in the lake. He might've realized it had they not been so rushed. The last fifteen minutes were a blur, everyone scrambling just to stay alive.

"That was the reason for my hesitation before I entered the lake," Tentek continued. "I debated if I should mention it to you. Probabilities suggested doing so would neither help nor harm our odds of success."

Stephens approached Tentek. "I saw the drones pass overhead. Seems strange they would fly this way. Are you sure they didn't see us?"

Tentek blinked at Stephens. "As I said before, probabilities were not one hundred percent we would evade detection. However, the drones did not pause or take any other action suggesting they located us."

"Now what, Captain?" asked Lieutenant Shelton.

Holbrook didn't have an immediate answer. He hadn't had a spare moment to consider what they should do next. He summoned a map of Infernum on his helmet's heads-up display. The image showed a mostly flat plain stretching from their current position to the research vessel. "The plan's still the same," he said. "We're heading to the *Adiona*."

"We are?" asked Dr. Marsden. "We no longer have the shuttle."

"We'll walk," said Holbrook. "The map says it's about a seven-hour trek. If we start now we should arrive around dusk. With any luck we'll be able to camp inside the ship for the night."

"What about waiting for the *Avenger* to return?" asked Shelton. "They could send down a new shuttle, more men."

"No," said Holbrook. "The ship won't be back around 'til tomorrow morning—by then we could already be moving on from the *Adiona*, heading toward the Hex Men mine, where it's supposed to be at least. I also prefer not to spend the night out here in the open. As for more men, I don't want anyone else coming down to the planet. We'll signal for a new shuttle when we're ready to be extracted, when the mission is done."

"Should we at least try to get a message to the *Avenger*?" asked Lieutenant Byrne. "Let them know we're all right? At the moment it looks like we all died in the crash."

"The *Avenger's* too far away," said Holbrook. "We couldn't contact her if we wanted to. Tomorrow morning when she flies overhead, we can get a signal up there, let them know we're OK." He dismissed the map inside his helmet and pointed to the northeast. "The *Adiona's* in roughly that direction. We'll stop to rest at two-hour intervals. Byrne and Conlin, I want you to bring up the rear for the next hour. Make sure no one falls behind the group. We'll trade off rear duty every hour."

The landing party headed off in a line of ones and twos across the plain of short yellow grasses and the occasional outcropping of black volcanic rock. As they walked, RD Sagittarii A's red disc rose higher, bathing the world in an intense red light, the temperature climbing from the early-morning thirties to fifty-two degrees centigrade. After an hour, Dr. Marsden requested they stop to give the still-ailing Ensign Reilly a rest and time for her to inspect the young officer.

When they resumed their travel, Holbrook assigned Stephens and Dr. Riesen to rear duty. The two said nothing as they walked together at the end of the line until Stephens, still starstruck, created a private channel on his suit comm and forced himself to speak. "How do you come up with your theories?" he asked.

Dr. Riesen looked over at the commander. "What do you mean?"

"You've been so prolific at proposing new theories, revolutionary solutions to some of the hardest problems in everything from subatomics to astrophysics. Is it just luck? Or is there a process you follow?"

"There is a process," said Dr. Riesen, "though it's a little hard to explain. I'm not even sure I understand it." She thought a moment. "When I work a problem, I 'dig deep'—that's the best I can describe. First, I close my eyes and visualize everything I know, all the principles and facts that have already been established. Then I reach deep down inside. I imagine I'm reaching into creation itself. Eventually I start to see how things have to come together to form a workable solution. At that point I relax and let my subconscious figure out the details. And then I have the answer. Sometimes there's almost no conscious thought involved. When I first started solving problems this way, I couldn't believe the answers I'd get. Now it just feels so routine I hardly even think about the process."

"It almost sounds mystical," said Stephens. A mystical process that so far hadn't come through for them to escape D-space. "Should I be concerned you haven't found an answer to our problem yet?"

"What problem is that?"

Stephens's jaw dropped. "What problem? The only real problem we have," he said, exasperated. "The problem of getting out of here, of getting back to normal space."

"I ... no, I still don't have an answer for that," said Dr. Riesen.

"I know that!" said Stephens in an angry rush of words at the physicist stating the obvious. "I was asking if it's a bad sign your mystical process hasn't come through yet."

Dr. Riesen hesitated. "I ... haven't tried it," she said.

"You haven't tried it? You haven't tried it! Why the hell not?"

Dr. Riesen didn't answer.

"From your description, it sounds like you have an almost automatic way to get answers to hard problems. Why wasn't it the very first thing you tried? What've you been doing for the past two weeks?"

During the commander's tirade, Dr. Riesen began walking faster, putting distance between the two of them. Stephens quickened his pace to catch up to her. When he pulled beside her, the physicist did not look over at him or otherwise acknowledge his presence. She instead kept herself focused on marching ahead.

Stephens debated pressing Riesen on why she hadn't used her method to solve their problem, but the physicist had seemed intent on not discussing it. He shifted to another topic that had been on his mind. "Can I ask you about your reincarnation?"

Dr. Riesen looked warily at Stephens. "What about it?" she asked.

"I read there's a ceremony after each Prophet dies, a sort of passing of the torch to the next one."

"Every Prophet's life ends and begins with the Tchiyah ceremony," said Dr. Riesen. "When a Prophet dies, his soul is allowed to wander for three days while The Brotherhood makes preparations for a new human vessel. During the Tchiyah ceremony, the old body is cremated, returning to ashes as the new one is conceived. The cycle begins again."

"Does the old body have to be present for the ceremony?" asked Stephens.

"Yes. Of course," said Dr. Riesen. "The cremation is more than symbolic. Despite floating free, the soul still has ties to the old body. Those ties aren't severed until the cremation. The soul can't enter a new body before the old one has been completely reduced to ashes."

Stephens thought a bit. "My apologies for being morbid, but if The Brotherhood needs the old Prophet's body for the reincarnation ceremony, why did they risk sending you on this mission?"

"They didn't send me," said Dr. Riesen. "I volunteered."

"You volunteered?" said Stephens, surprised. "Did they object?"

"That would be an understatement," said Dr. Riesen. "The Admor went apoplectic when I told him I wanted to go. But they have no power to stop me. They don't own me, though Rabbi Lehr, my father of sorts, told me The Brotherhood considered sending a team to abduct me and take me back home."

"But you convinced them to leave you alone, to let you go," said Stephens.

"I think they convinced themselves I would be no good to them if they forced me to do anything," said Dr. Riesen. "I also explained to them my reason for coming on this trip, to further our knowledge of the cosmos, to uncover a previously hidden portion of God's Universe."

They arrived at a flat section of basalt layered like tall steps. At each layer Stephens stepped up first, then reached for Dr. Riesen's hand to help her up.

The final layer fanned out into flat, rocky terrain littered with small stones. Patches of yellow grasses sprouted through the black volcanic topsoil. The other members of the landing party stretched out across the plain ahead of them.

"Do you think they're starting that chai-uh ceremony right now?" asked Stephens.

"Huh?" said Dr. Riesen.

"The chai-uh ceremony, or however you say it. The one they use to create the next Prophet."

"It's pronounced t-CHAI-uh," she said. "And they can't, remember? When it's time they'll need my body to do that."

"That's what you said, but do you really think they're gonna turn down their whole Prophet project just 'cause you stole away with their body?" asked Stephens.

"That's *exactly* what I think," said Dr. Riesen. Despite her forceful claim, the physicist didn't seem so certain, her voice quavering slightly. "There won't be another Tchiyah ceremony until I return, unless I return," she declared. "The Brotherhood is stuck. Trapped. Like they trapped me."

"Like they trapped you?" asked Stephens.

"Yes!" said Dr. Riesen. "I've been trapped my whole life! Trapped by history, trapped in a destiny chosen for me before I was even conceived. Trapped by people knowing who I am everywhere I go. Trapped by the jeers from being The Prophet reincarnated as a woman, from being a mistake, The Brotherhood's great mistake."

"Is that what you think?" asked Stephens. "That you're a mistake?"

"I've been called a mistake from my first days," said Dr. Riesen. "What I believe about it doesn't matter. It won't stop people from claiming I am one." She stared up at the red sun, hanging in the pale violet sky. "I wish I could never hear another word about it."

Stephens looked over at Dr. Riesen. "Well, you can rest easy," he said. "All that aggravation's behind you now."

"What do you mean?"

"Just that you don't have to worry about people calling you a mistake anymore. Or being recognized wherever you go. Or your life being preordained. You don't have to worry about any of that because this is a one-way mission. It's the end of the lives we all lived before we arrived here." His last statement hung with him. "Why did you come on this mission, anyway?"

"It's the opportunity of a lifetime," said Dr. Riesen. "If Planck Matter exists, it will be an incredible find. The find of the century."

Stephens scoffed. "Enough of the bullshit, Doctor. Why did you *really* come on this mission?"

"I just told you, Commander," she shot back.

"What you told me just now was a story." said Stephens. "A story about coming on this trip to find Planck Matter. That's what you just said. But back on Plana Petram, you told us you were coming because we needed your help. When we got to the ship you said it was because you love a good puzzle. You told The Brotherhood it was to expand our knowledge of the cosmos. And a few days ago, you told the captain it was because if you didn't, the Earth might not survive."

"Yes," she said, "all of those things are true."

"Problem is, none of them's the real reason you're here," said Stephens. "At best they're rationalizations. Whatever your real motivation is, it doesn't change every time someone asks you. One's true motivation will always be the same answer." She wasn't being forthright about her reason for joining the mission, but that wasn't the only odd thing. The captain had mentioned doodles in her research notebook. And she'd been almost giddy upon boarding their doomed ship .... "You know what I think?"

"No, but I suspect I will in a second."

"You say you feel trapped by destiny, by your life being preordained because you're The Prophet," said Stephens, "but from where I sit it sure seems like you've fully embraced the role. You've made amazing discoveries, received incredible awards and recognition, you bask in people following you around, treating you like a god. I don't think you're upset at all about being The Prophet. I think you enjoy it.

"I think the thing that haunts you is people calling you a mistake, and you can't decide if you should stand and fight or clear out. You've pushed yourself to achieve so much, even by Prophet standards, to show how you live up to the title, but then you run away as far as you can. You got all the way to Plana Petram, but even clear outside the galaxy you couldn't escape that nagging claim."

"You have no idea what you're talking about," said Dr. Riesen.

"I think I do," said Stephens. "And I'll tell you why I think you're on this mission. The reason you came along is because you think it's the solution to all your troubles. You think you can escape, once and for all, the question of whether or not you're the real Prophet, whether or not you're a mistake, because no one trapped here with you in D-space gives a shit. And the cherry on top was you thought this would be the final 'screw you' to the boys in crimson whom you blame for all of this, taking their precious Prophet lineage down the tubes. Well, news for you, Dr. Riesen, I'm sure they won't let a little problem like a missing body stop them."

"I'm not enjoying your company at all, Commander," said Dr. Riesen, walking faster. "I'm going to ask the captain to assign someone else for you to torture with your jabbering."

"That's fine," said Stephens, picking up the pace to stay even with her, "but there's just one more thing, Doctor. Part of what's keeping all the rest of us going is the hope that at the end of this mission you'll find a way to get us home." The commander grabbed Dr. Riesen's arm and pulled her around to face him. "Tell me, Dr. Riesen, are you committed to doing that? Are you committed to getting us back home? I ask because you haven't done shit so far to figure it out, and all I see is a person who seems like she would be much happier trapped here 'til the end of time."

Dr. Riesen glared at the commander through her helmet force field, tears streaming down her cheeks. Her eyes were angry and red in the glowing light of the hypergiant. She wrenched her arm out of Stephens's grasp. "To be honest, I'm not sure anymore, Commander," she said with gritted teeth. "I did come along to help you all get back home, but I'm starting to think I'd be doing the galaxy a favor by making sure you remain here for the rest of your days." She stormed off.

Commander Stephens stood in place while the physicist worked to catch up with the others. "That claim, Dr. Riesen, that you're a mistake, it controls you. It drove you all the way to the center of the galaxy, but you still can't escape it. That's because that voice in your head that keeps telling you you're a mistake, it's your own. It's not about how you got here, it's not about how any of us got here, or why; it's what you *do* with your life that matters. You —"

Dr. Riesen terminated their private channel.

Stephens stood for a few more moments, sipping water from his suit's supply as Dr. Riesen gained on the others. They couldn't rely on her to get back—her plan from the start was to stay in D-space. "Let her then," he muttered. They'd find some other way home.

19

"There she is," whispered Captain Holbrook, peering with Commander Stephens through thick brush that stood nearly two meters tall.

Four hours after RD Sagittarii A's red disc dropped behind the sharp peaks of the mountain chain to the west, the *Avenger* landing party arrived at an expanse of dead reeds and grasses along the bank of a dry river. The bed's broad basin stretched from the bank to a bluff forty meters to the north. There on the basin, nestled at the base of the bluff, sat the silvery, saucer-shaped *Adiona*. Several small white running lights persisted in their lazy flashing, hinting at the contours of the ship's hull in the waxing blue twilight of the ascending black hole RDS B.

The rest of the landing party remained at the leading edge of the brush, several meters from the dead river's bank. When the foliage parted, only Holbrook emerged. The landing party quickly formed a semi-circle around the captain.

"We confirmed it's the *Adiona* in the clearing," said Holbrook. "The commander and I will approach the ship and assess the situation. At this point we don't know if there are humans aboard, or aughts, or no one at all. Once we've secured the area, we'll call for the rest of you to follow. Any questions?" The assemblage of officers remained quiet. "Stephens and I will keep in touch with you on your comms." The captain turned and disappeared back into the brush.

Holbrook slipped back to Stephens at their vantage point along the riverbank. "Any change?" he asked.

Stephens shook his head. "None, Captain. Still no movement outside the ship."

"If there's anyone inside, human or aught, they won't be expecting us," said Holbrook. "Let's proceed with caution."

The two men pushed aside the last of the reeds and brambles and walked out into the clearing. Stephens hung back two meters from Holbrook as they trekked across the dry riverbed. They were completely exposed, trailing short shadows in the black hole's electric blue moonlight.

Five meters from the ship, Captain Holbrook stumbled. He glanced at the ground around his feet and raised a fist. Stephens froze in place.

Holbrook knelt and examined the object he had tripped over: a pill-shaped mound of dirt, one by two meters in size. He ran his gloved hand along the smooth top, brushing aside the fresh earth kicked up by his boot, then stood and signaled for Stephens to come forward.

Stephens came up to the captain and nudged his boot into the mound, dislodging more of the dirt. "What is it?" he whispered.

"Not sure," said Holbrook. More dirt mounds dotted the space between them and the ship, arranged in three neat rows of four each. The captain proceeded with Stephens towards the ship, the two men weaving their way between the mounds. When they reached the starship, they both peered up at the two-story-tall spacecraft, its skin reflecting the electric blue twilight. Viewports appeared at intervals along the hull, all dark.

"Let's find the entrance," said Holbrook.

The two men followed the Adiona's curved hull counterclockwise, eventually arriving at a section with a large rectangular groove a few millimeters deep etched into the saucer's underside.

Stephens raised his arm and spoke to his comm. "Connect to the Adiona's AI." An orange circle with three flashing orange dots at its center appeared on the face of the silver band. The symbol continued its flashing for several seconds.

"It's not supposed to take this long to attach to a ship's AI," said Holbrook.

Stephens shrugged. "Our CentCom codes should grant us access to just about any Republic ship that flies. I don't know what would be special about this one." He started to issue another command when the orange symbol changed to solid green. "We're in. I think the AI was just in standby mode, only scanning for new connections every fifteen seconds or so." He spoke again to his comm. "Open the main door."

The grooved rectangle in the hull lowered to the ground, forming a ramp that led to a dark corridor stretching back into the ship. Captain Holbrook activated the light on his comm. He removed his electron pistol from its holster at his hip and held it ready as he headed up the ramp, followed by Stephens. The corridor extended five meters into the ship. Small zero-point lights embedded at ankle level sputtered a weak yellow glow. The corridor ended at an intersection with a curving crosswise passageway.

"Where is everyone?" asked Stephens. The ship was deathly quiet. "There were almost twenty people aboard this ship."

"Maybe they're here, or some of them anyway," said Holbrook. "Let's search the ship." He pointed right. "You go that way."

"You sure it's a good idea to split up?" asked Stephens.

"We can cover twice as much ground in the same amount of time," said Holbrook. "Keep your comm channel open."

"Aye, sir," said Stephens. He unholstered his weapon and headed down the corridor, disappearing into the gloom of emergency lighting.

Holbrook headed left, the light from his comm creating a bright halo on the bulkheads. The captain came upon two doors, one on either side of the corridor. He opened the one on his right and stepped into a room with two sets of stacked bunks. Their tight spacing nearly sandwiched the top bunk's occupant against the ceiling. The room also contained two sets of tall dressers and a door concealing a mini head, including a sonic shower.

Backing out of the room, Holbrook peeked through the other door directly across. He discovered another crew compartment of similar size and layout. As with the first, he found no sign of the crew.

Moving on, Holbrook came upon a large room on his left. He waved his light inside, illuminating several wide tables, a galley, and a drink dispenser. Like the other rooms, the ship's mess hall was clean and tidy. He'd expected to find trash, damage to the decks or bulkheads, or a body along the way. The *Adiona* seemed to be in overall good condition, even well maintained. It was quiet as a tomb, with no sign of the crew.

- - -

Commander Stephens came upon a narrow corridor on his left, terminating at a rungway alcove about a meter and a half wide that rose up through the exact center of the saucer-shaped ship. Stephens climbed until his head popped into a glassteel bubble, an observatory dome secured to the top of the ship. He saw little of the blue twilight landscape, the vista obscured by a layer of dust that covered the bubble.

After exiting the observation shaft and walking farther down the main corridor Stephens came upon a set of wide double doors on his right. They slid aside to reveal a large, closet-like space enclosing a rectangular opening in the deck three meters wide by two meters across. Stephens activated his light and aimed it down into the dark recess, illuminating a rectangular mat below with yellow and black diagonal stripes.

Stephens held his pistol out over the hole in the deck and let go of his weapon. Instead of falling, the pistol hovered in space where he released it. "A zero-g loading pad," he whispered. It likely led to the cargo hold.

The commander grabbed his weapon, holstered it, and jumped out over the opening. Like the pistol, he floated in space rather than plummeting to the deck beneath him. He reached up and pushed against the ceiling, causing himself to drift downward. Before hitting the black-and-yellow mat, he pushed off from the nearby bulkhead, propelling himself sideways. He landed gently on the deck just beyond the mat.

The dark, cramped cargo hold contained boxes and crates piled to the deck above and arranged to form narrow aisles. Pistol drawn, Stephens proceeded down one of the aisles, training his comm light on the stacks. The hold seemed to contain mostly foodstuffs and spare parts, the normal kinds of stores for the sort of voyage the *Adiona* had embarked on.

Stephens stopped, stifled by the low ceiling, tight spacing, meager emergency lighting, and confinement of his EN-suit. He set down his pistol and used both hands to twist his helmet free of his suit's collar. He lifted it up and away, the warm dryness of the cargo hold quickly displacing the cool, humidity-controlled air of his EN-suit. He set his helmet on one of the crates.

Moving deeper into the cargo hold, Stephens worked his way along the narrow aisle. He headed for what appeared to be a box of weapons stacked against the far wall. The room's quiet enveloped him, the sound of his every movement amplified by the silence.

Something moved behind him.

Stephens quickly spun about and stood absolutely still, straining to detect the slightest motion or noise. He reached for his gun but groped an empty holster. He'd set his pistol down when he removed his helmet. Stephens spotted the shiny bubble roughly fifteen meters back down the aisle. He started back for it at a brisk pace, moving as swiftly and silently as he could.

Something moved along the adjacent aisle to his left. He was certain he wasn't imagining things. Stephens hadn't gotten a good look, but he could tell it was some kind of creature. And it was paralleling him.

Stephens sprinted the last few meters to his helmet, but when he arrived, his gun was missing. It wasn't on any of the nearby boxes.

The hair on the back of Commander Stephens's neck stood on end. He spun around. The creature had quietly slipped from the shadows and come to rest behind him. He could only make out the faintest of details in the room's dim lighting. It stood more than two meters tall with flailing, stick-like arms. The thing moved toward him.

The commander stepped back and tripped, falling backwards onto the deck. The creature moved closer. Stephens instinctively raised an arm to protect himself, the motion raking the thing with his comm light. The afterimage revealed a humanoid shape, at least from the torso up. The head was a dark blue ovoid with no visible features.

"Can I help you find something?" it said.

Stephens blinked, the fog of panic making it difficult to comprehend the creature's words.

"Can I help you find something?" it repeated.

Stephens trained his light on the creature. It was a cargo aught, sheathed in dark blue plastic, its sole job to move cargo between the hold and the upper deck and within the hold itself. The *Avenger's* executive officer peered into the aught's expressionless face and exhaled in relief. A robot of that sort would have a low intelligence level and no long-term memory. It wouldn't be able to shed any light on the whereabouts of the crew.

"Stephens."

The commander jumped at the captain's whispered voice coming across his comm.

"Come quick to the control room."

"On my way." Stephens pushed himself up from the deck and collected his helmet, discovering his gun underneath. He reattached the translucent bubble, grabbed his pistol, and walked back to the opening in the deck above. He hopped onto the zero-g mat and jumped, flying upwards. He jumped harder than he needed and had to quickly reach his hands up, preventing himself from smashing into the ceiling. Once he stopped his upward momentum, Stephens pushed himself out of the zero-g field and leaped onto the ship's main deck. He sprinted down the corridor to the control room.

- - -

After the galley, Holbrook came upon another set of crew quarters and the ship's Sickbay. He pressed farther along the main corridor and arrived at a doorway on his left that opened onto a large space, dark but for several small flickering lights on the opposite side of the room.

Directing his comm light to the room's far left corner, Holbrook found a terminal, its screen dead. The terminal, normally angled for its operator, had been rotated flat like a table. A small board not more than a half-meter long and made of smooth light-colored wood rested on its surface, with stubby wooden legs at either end. Centered on top sat a shorter board, less than half as long, also supported by stubby legs, a miniature replica of the first. The second board held a stone buddha statue, the figure sitting with its eyes closed and hands in prayer. Short white candles, fat and round, sat with blackened wicks at opposite ends of the first board. A small white, rectangular ceramic container shaped like a trough and filled with gray dust sat between the candles, beneath the second board.

Sweeping his light to the right, Holbrook found a second inactive terminal, also rotated flat. The terminal hosted another wooden structure, an upright box with a dark red lacquer finish, and doors that swung out, revealing several shelves. A necklace of smooth turquoise stones spilled onto the terminal from the bottommost shelf. A photograph of a buddha hung on its inner back wall, above the middle shelf. On the topmost shelf sat a small brass bowl, also filled with gray dust.

Farther to the right, a large viewscreen hung from the bulkhead, a thin layer of shimmery dust covering its surface.

The small lights Holbrook had seen from the doorway flickered just to the right of the viewscreen. His beam revealed the source to be a working terminal in standby mode, set at a normal slant instead of flat like the others.

A man's body slumped across the angled surface.

Holbrook's light beam shuddered with his discovery. The man sat in a chair, his chest and head flat on the glass. His arms were splayed across the terminal, hands dangling over the top. A mop of dark hair obscured his face.

"Stephens, come quick to the control room." Holbrook whispered the words into his comm.

"On my way."

The captain crept forward with his light trained on the man. He strained to move silently across the deck, but the thuds of his footsteps echoed in the quiet room.

When Holbrook reached the station he carefully pulled the man back from the terminal to sit upright. The man's long black hair obscured his face, but not enough to completely hide his features. He was middle-aged, of Asian descent, with the scraggly starts of a mustache and beard. His eyes were closed and mouth open slightly. A small gash ran above his left eyebrow, caked with dried blood. Grime covered his face and his jumpsuit, and beads of sweat dribbled across his forehead.

Stephens's silhouette appeared in the open doorway. The *Avenger's* executive officer headed straight to Holbrook and the unconscious man. "You found someone."

"He was passed out on the terminal." Holbrook tapped his comm, summoning the Medi function. He held it close to the ailing man in his chair. "He's alive, but barely. He's burning up."

The man's eyes moved under their lids, opening halfway in a daze. He shifted positions in the chair and inhaled deeply, coughing. His eyes opened wide, panicked.

"Don't worry," said Holbrook, "we're with CentCom. They sent us to find your ship."

The man breathed and coughed again. He tried to sit up but failed.

"Don't try to move," said Holbrook, placing his hand on the man's shoulder. "We have a doctor who can help." The captain spoke into his comm. "*Avenger* landing party, you're clear to approach and enter the *Adiona*. Dr. Marsden, please report to the control room."

The man's head lolled against the seat back. Holbrook sandwiched the man's cheeks between his flat palms, holding his head upright and forcing the ailing man to look directly at him. "Who are you? Where are the others?"

The man fixed his exhausted eyes on Holbrook. "Who am I?" he asked in an incredulous tone, his voice a raspy whisper. "I am Dr. Yoichiro Imura." The man's eyes rolled back in his head and his body went slack as he lost consciousness.

20

"How is he, Doctor?" asked Captain Holbrook.

Dr. Yoichiro Imura lay sprawled on the examination table in the *Adiona's* cramped Sickbay, showered in white light from the hanging cone-shaped medical lamp. Captain Holbrook, Commander Stephens, Dr. Riesen, and Dr. Marsden looked on, their faces bright against the black backdrop of the otherwise dark room. An oxygen mask covered Imura's nose and mouth, and a thin blue medical blanket shrouded his chest, abdomen, and legs. The right sleeve of his jumpsuit had been cut away, leaving his arm bare. A translucent IV pouch, tucked in the crook of his right elbow, pushed fluids into his forearm. The readout along the edge of the table consisted of several small lights, one for each vital sign. Most glowed orange, a few red. A single intermittent red light kept time with his heartbeat.

"He's stabilized for the moment," said Dr. Marsden, a stethoscope hanging from her neck, "but I can't say for how long. He has a severe infection and fell into septic shock shortly before you found him. I've given him an intense course of antibiotics, plus fluids and electrolytes to counter his dehydration."

Imura's eyes twitched under their lids, the only movement on his oval face. His belly rose and fell faintly beneath the blanket.

"Can he answer some questions?" asked Holbrook.

Dr. Marsden glared at Holbrook. "You see the state he's in," she said. "He can't tell you much of anything right now."

"Can you revive him?" asked Holbrook.

"I could do that," said Dr. Marsden, adjusting the bandage that covered the wound on his forehead. "I could also cut off his leg, or any number of other things that would also be ill advised." She frowned at Holbrook. "This man needs rest, Captain."

"I understand, but we need him to tell us everything he knows that wasn't recorded in the *Adiona's* logs. Anything he has to say could be crucial to the success of our mission."

The doctor's face turned dark. She opened her mouth to reply —

"We also need to know how they planned to return from Sag A Star," said Stephens. "In order to leave here ourselves." He set his eyes on Dr. Riesen. "He may be the only one who can help us."

Dr. Riesen didn't meet Stephens's gaze. She kept her head down, her focus on Imura.

"In other words, our survival depends on me violating my Hippocratic oath," said Dr. Marsden. "If this man dies after I administer a medically unnecessary treatment, *I* will be the one to live with the guilt, not you, Commander."

"If we end up stuck here because we can't get the information we need from this man, there'll be plenty of guilt then too, and a lot of time to think about it," said Stephens.

"So can I look my shipmates in the eye each day we're trapped here, or can I look myself in the eye for the rest of my life."

"We need to know what happened to the rest of the crew," said Holbrook. "Depending on the answer, it might affect our decision to remain even a moment longer inside this ship."

Dr. Marsden glared at Holbrook, then at Stephens before reaching into her satchel. She withdrew a medical injector, a white, cylindrical device the size and shape of a fat fountain pen, flat at one end and rounded at the other. Four silver bands sat side by side in the center of the device, each one marked with several medical symbols. She rotated the bands, aligning a symbol from each with a groove that ran the length of the device.

The doctor held Imura's oxygen mask in place as she pushed the injector's flat end against his right arm and pressed the activator at its rounded end. The device recoiled, and the skin around the injector rippled outward. Within a few seconds, the man's breathing deepened and his eyes calmed, ceasing their erratic movements.

"I've given him a mild stimulant," said Dr. Marsden. "I need you to ask your questions as fast as possible, and not too many. His best chance for recovery is rest. An interrogation is the wrong prescription."

"Understood," said Holbrook. The captain edged closer, peering at Imura's face. The frail man's breathing became more pronounced and slightly raspy. He half opened his eyes, the whites a jaundiced yellow.

"Dr. Imura, I'm Captain Holbrook from the CentCom warship *Avenger*. I need to ask you a few questions."

Imura's eyes widened. He studied Dr. Marsden and Captain Holbrook, who stood to his right, then Commander Stephens and Dr. Riesen on his left. His gaze fell back on Holbrook. Imura gave the captain a weak nod.

"Do the other two have to be here?" Dr. Marsden asked Holbrook. "This man doesn't need a panel of interrogators. And having so many people crowded around the table makes my job harder."

"Dr. Riesen is the only one of us who will understand whatever Imura says about escaping from D-space," said Stephens.

"Then what about you, Commander?"

"Dr. Marsden," said Holbrook, "we promise to stay out of your way."

Dr. Marsden grumbled something inaudible as she turned to the vitals readout.

"We reviewed the logs from your ship, Dr. Imura," said Holbrook, speaking softly. "There were eighteen of you on the *Adiona*, including yourself. Where is everyone else?"

Imura attempted to lift his head, gave up, and let it drop back to the table. "We hadn't planned to land here," he said, his voice whispery soft and scratchy. Imura coughed, his eyes bulging on each violent release of air.

"Ask him about getting out of D-space," Stephens whispered across the table to Holbrook.

"Don't worry, Commander, I will," Holbrook whispered back.

"Ask him right now," said Stephens. "We don't know how long we have with him."

Holbrook silenced Stephens with a look. "Dr. Imura," said Holbrook, "where is everybody else? The rest of the people who were aboard the *Adiona*?"

Imura slid his tongue across his chapped lips. "Richard set off with five others to find Moscovium to reenergize the Gravity Drive. We had mapped the surface before landing and detected a deposit a few kilometers away. We lost contact with them. We didn't have the right kind of communication gear. All short range stuff. The *Adiona* was still picking up Richard's audio log over shortwave. We had no idea. When we replayed the log, we learned most of them had perished, and probably Richard too.

"This whole trip was Richard's idea." Imura coughed. "Not landing on Infernum, but coming to Sag A Star to test his theory for returning from D-space. And now he'll never know if it worked."

A coughing spell consumed Imura, wracking his body for several seconds. His torso rose from the examination table on each cough. Once the spasm ended, he cleared his throat and darted his tongue, catching the spittle that had dribbled from the corner of his mouth. His breathing grew shallow and he closed his eyes. Several of the orange lights on the vital signs readout shifted to red.

Dr. Marsden dialed a different setting on her injector, jabbed the pen-shaped device against Imura's arm, and pressed the activator. She lifted both lids, inspecting his pupils. His breathing remained shallow and his skin took on a sick pallor.

Stephens leaned closer to the distressed man's head. "Dr. Imura, tell us, how were you going to get back out?"

"Not now, Commander!" shouted Dr. Marsden. "We could be close to losing this man."

"Then now's definitely the time to ask," said Stephens, gruffly. "He won't be able to say anything if he's gone."

Marsden worked the bands on her injector. She threw the blanket off Imura's torso, unzipped the front of his filthy blue jumpsuit, and wrenched his dirty gray undershirt up and out of the way, exposing his chest. She jabbed the injector under his left pectoral muscle and pressed the activator.

Imura immediately opened his eyes and coughed. His breathing grew stronger, and two of the red lights on the vitals panel crept back to orange.

"How were you going to get back out?" Stephens whispered in Imura's ear.

"Captain!" said Dr. Marsden. "Please have Commander Stephens leave the room! He is interfering with my ability to care for this patient."

"Paul," said Holbrook in a soft tone, "maybe it would be better if there were fewer of us in here with him."

"Captain, we need to get the information from him about —"

"And we will," said Holbrook. "I know all the questions we need answers to. And if we don't get them tonight, we can ask tomorrow, after he's had some time to rest and his body a little time to recover."

"But —"

"I want you to start getting everyone organized for the night. Check that we're all inside and the ship is sealed up. Make sure wherever people are bedding down that we're not too spread out. If there's an emergency, I don't want to have to run all over the ship to round people up."

Stephens hesitated. "Aye, aye, sir," he eventually said. "But please ask him now, not later, how they planned to get back home."

"Don't worry, Paul, I will," said Holbrook. "It's at the top of my list. Now go."

Commander Stephens hesitated before plodding to the door. He glanced back once, then exited the room.

Holbrook returned his attention to Imura. The man appeared frail and very ill on the examination table. So far Imura had said nothing about the fate of the *Adiona's* crew. Those details could be crucial to the landing party's survival. He selected a new line of questioning. "Did you encounter any aughts?"

Imura's head snapped towards Holbrook and his face flushed. "I did not cheat death! If that's why you're here." His eyes grew wide, and his voice shrank almost to a whisper. "Did he send you?"

"Who?" asked Holbrook, confused.

"Don't play me for a fool!" shouted Imura. "The Angel of Death. Did he send you? That question you have no choice but to answer truthfully."

"No, he did not send us," said Dr. Riesen. Imura's head snapped over to her, relief sweeping across his face. "Did he visit you?" she asked. "The Angel of Death?"

"Oh yes," said Imura, nodding vigorously. "He looks down upon us every night, decides if it's your time. Every night he looks down ...." Imura's words trailed off under a bewildered stare. His eyes shot back to Holbrook, his face a ball of anger. "I did not cheat death!"

Dr. Riesen put her hand on Imura's shoulder. "Tell us what happened."

Imura compressed his lips to a narrow line and the edges of his mouth twisted down. "His black eye rises every night. He looks down upon you and decides if it's your time.

"We had been here for several days, the blue-black eye looking down upon us each night. Eventually, the Angel judged us and found us wanting. He decided it was our time. He sent his demons to round us up. We saw them approaching the ship on the control room monitors. Everybody ran to hide. Some went belowdecks, but I figured that was the first place they'd look. I ran here to Sickbay. I shoved myself into one of the cadaver cabinets."

Imura giggled, then caught himself. "I figured they would never think to look inside.

"I stayed in there for several hours. I didn't know when to come out. I finally did, just as the eye was descending behind the mountains. I staggered outside and found everyone dead, their bodies all around on the ground.

"I cried. I cried all the rest of that night. At some point I fell asleep, and they all came to me in a dream, my shipmates. They said not to feel bad that I was the only survivor, that I had done what any of them would. But they were only saying that to make me feel better. They said they were leaving. I begged them not to go, but they said they had no choice. There was no longer anything tying them to this world.

"When I woke it was daylight. I immediately dug a grave. A grave for Dr. Church, a beautiful young woman with sunshine in her hair who would never have hurt anyone. I dumped her body into the hole and burned it. It took the whole day for the fire to die out. When it finished, I scooped some of her ashes. I built a Butsudan for her in the control room. You may have seen it? I created the shrine delicate and beautiful just like her, added her ashes. I covered the rest of her remains with a mound of dirt. Before the Angel of Death's eye rose again that night, I climbed back into the cabinet to hide. I slept there 'til morning. He didn't see me in the cabinet. That morning I dug a second grave, one for Dr. Alcott. I set his body afire and collected the ashes for his shrine. I covered his grave with dirt, and I hid again in my cabinet. Each day I dug a grave and added a new shrine. I even marked out the space for my own grave. You will see it if you look.

"I tend to the shrines each day. I tend to them and talk to each one of them. The ashes anchor their spirits here with me. That was how I got them all to stay. When the *Adiona* leaves, we will all leave together. We will all fly away from here." Imura wheezed, then lapsed into another coughing fit.

Dr. Marsden increased the flow of oxygen through Imura's mask. Imura took deep draws, and the color returned to his skin, but soon his lids fell to half open, and his eyes occasionally rolled back in his skull.

Captain Holbrook's comm chimed—it was a message from Stephens. Annoyed, he tapped the note. Its text spilled across the screen:

> Riesen has no intention of finding a way out of D-
> space. She all but admitted she wants to stay. Imura
> may be our only hope of getting home.

"Can I have a word with you, Captain?"

Holbrook looked up from his comm to find Dr. Marsden staring at him, arms folded. "Certainly. Dr. Riesen, please stay here with Imura in case his condition worsens."

Dr. Riesen nodded, and the two walked to the other side of the Sickbay, stopping next to a set of cabinets.

"Imura seemed to be fairly lucid when we first brought him in," said Dr. Marsden, speaking softly, "but your last question appears to have triggered a psychotic break. He was likely not very mentally stable to start with, but now he's lost his anchor to reality."

"Are you saying he's lost his mind?" asked Holbrook.

"Yes, to some degree he has. His survivor guilt was apparently too much for him to bear. His mind is right now doing its best to shield him from the full pain. Eventually he'll ease himself back into reality, but there's no telling when he'll feel safe enough to do so."

Holbrook looked over at Imura on the table as he recalled Stephens's message. "Can you give him a psychotropic? Something to snap him out of his psychosis?"

"Absolutely not!" said Dr. Marsden in an urgent whisper. "His mental instability is the sum total of the defense his mind has erected to shield him from his pain. A psychotropic would completely strip away that defense. It would leave his mind naked, fully exposing him to the pain he can't bear to feel."

"But he would no longer be mentally unstable."

"Do you know anything at all about medicine, Captain?" asked Dr. Marsden. "This man's mind and body aren't machines, like tinkering with an aught. You can't just overdrive his body or overclock his mind to put him in the state you want. His mind and body are in a delicate balance. Disturb one and the other compensates to try to restore that balance. The two, body and mind, are working together to express the person known as Imura." Dr. Marsden glanced at her ailing patient as he let out a soft groan. "Exposing his mind to all the pain he's trying to avoid will lead to an offsetting reaction in his body. And that could push him over the edge."

"Over the edge?" asked Holbrook.

"Death!" said Dr. Marsden in a harsh whisper.

Holbrook debated how to proceed. He respected Marsden's medical opinions and her experience, but he was faced with a dire situation. He should have asked Imura what he knew about escaping D-space earlier. The possible only source of that information risked slipping away to madness.

"I have to ask him how we get out of D-space," said Holbrook. "I should have done it first thing, like Stephens wanted, but I didn't."

"I thought getting out of D-space was the whole reason Dr. Riesen was with us," said Dr. Marsden.

"Stephens says she has no intention of getting us back home."

Dr. Marsden gave Holbrook an incredulous scowl. "You believe him?"

"It doesn't make any sense," said Holbrook, "but it's in line with suspicions I've had about her. I ignored them 'cause they didn't add up. Apparently, I was right. Somehow, she doesn't care about getting home. She came on this mission *because* there's no way back from it."

Dr. Marsden peeked around the captain to look at Dr. Riesen, assaulting her with an expression of disbelief and contempt. "And she doesn't care if it means dooming us all here with her."

The captain shrugged, unable to rationalize her motivations. "Questioning this man may mean the difference between getting home and living here in the center of the galaxy for the rest of our lives."

Dr. Marsden shook her head slowly. "I understand the stakes are higher now, but my answer's still the same. A psychotropic is the last thing this man needs."

Holbrook glanced at Imura, then back at Dr. Marsden. "As I see it, Doctor, I only have two options. I can order you to inject him with the psychotropic to bring him back around. Or I can have you leave the room and I inject him myself."

"God *damn* you, Thomas!" said Dr. Marsden. "You're going to kill this man."

"I understand there's a chance he'll die, but there's a decent chance he'll pull through."

"And that opinion is based on what, exactly?" asked Dr. Marsden. "All your years of medical training? I'm telling you that injecting him with a psychotropic, in the mental and physical state he's in, will likely kill him."

"I have to take that chance," said Holbrook, "for all our sakes." Dr. Marsden's eyes burned into him, brimming with tears. "Which will it be, Doctor?"

"*I* will inject him," she snarled. "If the result is a medical emergency, *I'm* the only one who can do anything about it." She stormed back to the examination table.

As Holbrook made his way to the table, Dr. Marsden dialed a new combination into her injector, placed the device against Imura's carotid artery, and pressed the activator. After several seconds, Dr. Imura opened his eyes and his breathing grew stronger. His heart rate spiked but soon fell back to a more normal range.

Holbrook surveyed Imura, encouraged by his improved condition. "Dr. Imura, how are you feeling?"

Imura turned his head towards Holbrook and gave the captain a partial smile. "I am feeling much better. Thank you."

"That's good," said Holbrook. "I want to ask you a very important question. It has to do with your trip to Sag A Star. You and your colleagues developed a method of escaping the distorted space around the black hole. Can you tell us —"

Tears streamed down Imura's cheeks, and his smile became pained. "I cheated death," he said to the captain. His smile disappeared. "I cheated death," he whispered.

"Dr. Imura —"

"I hid, when the demons came, I hid. I hid where we store the dead bodies, but I came out alive. Everyone else died. It's like I pretended to be dead to live. I escaped my own death by pretending to be dead. That is cheating death. I cheated death. I should be dead with the rest of them."

Imura's heart rate rose, and his blood pressure crashed. His eyes rolled back in his head. Seconds later, Imura's body shook with a seizure.

Dr. Marsden dialed a new combination on her injector. She batted the oxygen mask from Imura's face and thrust her hand into her medical satchel, withdrawing a tongue depressor. "Here!" she shouted at Holbrook. "Try to get this in his mouth!"

The captain took the flat piece of wood. He searched for an opportunity to insert the stick, but Imura's teeth remained clenched.

Dr. Marsden injected Imura with another substance. His body relaxed, but the table emitted a warning tone, the heart rate light ceasing its flashing.

"He's flatlining!" shouted Dr. Marsden. She dialed a new setting into her injector and pressed it below his left pectoral muscle. The flatline tone continued. Dr. Marsden pumped Imura's chest with both hands, compressing in steady, evenly timed thrusts. She continued long after the examination table fell silent, long after each light on the vitals readout winked out. Dr. Riesen gently touched Dr. Marsden's hands, bringing them to rest.

The three stood under the stark white light of the medical lamp, gazing upon Imura's motionless body. Marsden reached to the man's forehead, covering his open eyes with her palm. She placed her fingers on his lids and gently pulled them closed.

21

Holbrook shuffled down the *Adiona's* main corridor with the dull expression and hunched shoulders of a shellshocked man. He'd failed to secure the secret to exiting D-space before Imura died and may even have caused his death. During his initial questioning of the scientist, he'd given little thought to how such a failure might condemn everyone aboard the *Avenger* to a life in the shadow of Sag A Star. With the passing of the *Adiona's* last surviving crew member, the bleakness of that possible future overwhelmed him.

The captain had lingered in Sickbay with Dr. Marsden for a short time after Imura's death, looking on as she cut away the last shreds of the dead man's jumpsuit and washed the grime from his body before taking a bone saw to his sternum. The doctor initiated an autopsy despite being reasonably sure of the cause of death, and despite the pointlessness of determining it. Holbrook slipped out of the room with Marsden hoisting organs from Imura's open rib cage, bright red blood dripping from her white-gloved fingers.

Stephens had been right: he should have asked about D-space before anything else. He needed to find his executive officer to tell him what happened with Imura and to break the news, face-to-face.

"Captain!"

Holbrook froze, surprised by the sound of someone behind him. He turned to find Lieutenant Byrne's head poking into the corridor from the *Adiona's* mess hall. In a daze he'd walked right past the large room's open door and all the light and chatter spilling from it into the passageway.

"Captain, they have a working food dispenser," said Byrne, his face lit with excitement. "We also found some meat and bread in their stores belowdecks. Ensign Reilly and I are pulling together a real meal!"

"That's great, Byrne." He tried his best to sound enthusiastic. "No survival paste for dinner tonight." Just how extensive were the *Adiona's* stores? "Did you happen to see any alcohol down there?"

"No sir," said Byrne. "Lieutenant Shelton was hoping there might be some, but he searched all through their supplies and couldn't find any. The ship's completely dry."

That seemed unlikely—maybe he'd have a look himself. "Have you seen Commander Stephens?"

"He's somewhere down the passageway. I think he's working on securing the ship for the night."

Holbrook resumed his slow shuffle along the *Adiona's* main passageway. He found Stephens at the end of the entry corridor, the exit closed off by the ramp lifted back into place. An access panel hung from its hinges on the adjacent bulkhead. Status readout lights danced across the commander's face as he peered into the exposed opening.

"Thanks, Conlin," Stephens said into his comm. "I think that does it for the door. You should work on getting more of the external camera feeds back online."

"Yes, sir," Conlin's voice crackled back.

Stephens spotted Holbrook approaching. "I've just finished working with Conlin to secure the door. I wanted to make sure no one can enter the ship while we're in here tonight." He grabbed the access panel, swung it up on its hinges, and used both hands to press it back into place. "Conlin's gotten a few of the exterior surveillance cameras and sensors operating again, and I'm going to set a watch rotation for the night. I've assigned each person a bunk in the first two adjacent crew quarters. And it sounds like they've got a real dinner cooking in the mess hall."

"Yeah, I just passed by there. Byrne seemed very excited." Holbrook mustered a smile. "Thank you for getting everything organized."

"That's my job," said Stephens.

"Thank you still."

The two men fell into an awkward silence.

"How'd it go with Imura?" asked Stephens.

The captain opened his mouth but found it difficult to speak. "Imura's dead," he blurted before he could catch himself.

Stephens's hands bunched into fists, betraying his otherwise cool reaction to the news. Odds were Imura's death wasn't the main reason for Stephens's response. More likely, his executive officer suspected the answer to his real question.

"Did he tell you how to get out of D-space?" Stephens's voice had a slight tremor.

Holbrook had run through this exact moment several times in his head. Reciting the words within the confines of his mind was one thing. Speaking them aloud was something else entirely. "I didn't get a chance to ask him," he finally declared.

"I see," Stephens muttered, his gaze falling to the deck.

Words rushed from Holbrook's mouth in a torrent. "I was so focused on finding out what happened to the crew, how Imura came to be here all alone in the *Adiona*, if they encountered any aughts. I wanted to know all of that, and I thought we'd have plenty of time to get all the answers. Sure, he wasn't doing well, but I figured at worst we'd have to wait until morning to discuss whatever we didn't get to. One of my questions pushed him over the edge—a psychotic break, Dr. Marsden said it was. I asked her to give him something to bring him out of it. She warned me it might be too much ... but I pressed her, and she went ahead." Holbrook's voice fell soft. "He didn't last long after that."

All the emotion drained from Stephens's face. "Well," he said, "I've got to see if Conlin has any more of the external cameras back online." He headed up the entry corridor. Captain Holbrook followed.

When the two men reached the main passageway, Holbrook grabbed Stephens's shoulder. The commander turned about to face the captain.

"I want to apologize," said Holbrook.

"It's OK, Captain," said Stephens. "Imura was in bad shape when we found him. He could have gone at any time."

"No. I mean, no, I want to apologize for Imura, but also for more than that." Holbrook struggled to find the words. "You were right about this mission when the orders first came down. I didn't want it to be true."

Footsteps approached on the right. Lieutenant Commander Shelton emerged from the passageway's end, startled by two senior officers staring his way. He nodded at them as he passed.

Holbrook waited for Shelton to disappear down the other end of the passageway. "Do you remember that shard of metal from the CCS *Olympia*? The piece I had out on my desk?"

"Yeah, the piece of your father's ship."

Holbrook nodded. "I dug it out right after I played the message from Admiral Miller for the first time, the message with our new orders." Holbrook glanced down both directions of the passageway, confirming they were still alone. He moved in closer to Stephens and lowered his voice. "There are some things only ship captains know, some information specifically kept from all other CentCom personnel below my rank." Stephens leaned in closer. "There's a secret about the Olympia. The history records tell how the Permian fleet traveled to Ross 128, expecting to find CentCom warships massing, but they instead happened upon the Olympia, which they destroyed." Holbrook checked again to make sure they were still alone. "What the history records don't say is the Olympia was ordered to Ross 128 ... as a decoy."

"A decoy?" Stephens gasped. "Why?"

"The war was going badly. There was no way the remainder of our fleet could engage the Permians head-on and survive. The brass devised a last-ditch plan to send the Olympia to Ross 128 carrying a pulse transmitter that mimicked the EM and gravimetric profiles of nearly all the remaining ships in the fleet. The Permians arrived at Ross 128 thinking the CentCom fleet was massing in that system."

"But why not deploy the transmitter on its own?" asked Stephens, shaking his head in confusion. "Why sacrifice your father and his ship?"

"Two reasons. First, they needed to make sure the transmitter arrived intact and was functional and activated correctly. All total, the job was far too important to entrust to automation. And second, the Permians needed to see a ship, even one ship, when they arrived. If they got to Ross 128 and found nothing, they'd know something was up. At least with the Olympia there, they could say their equipment misread the signals coming off a single starship.

"Once the Permian fleet arrived, the Olympia feigned surprise and pretended to run. The Olympia's fake escape attempt distracted part of the Permian fleet into chasing after a single ship. The rest of their ships let their guard down. Right after the Permians detonated the Weak device, when most of their sensors were still seeing afterimages from the blast, the CentCom fleet arrived and engaged them. That small bit of surprise gave us the edge that allowed us to destroy the bulk of their fleet." On Plana Petram, Stephens had accused CentCom of handing out death sentences—his XO wasn't wrong, despite Commodore Ahrens's denial. They'd handed one out to his father years ago, and now to him.

"Why are you telling me this?" asked Stephens.

"Vice Admiral McDermott gave me that piece of the Olympia when I was promoted to drive home an important fact: that any ship captain may be called upon to sacrifice his vessel in the line of duty, the same way my dad flew to his doom with the Olympia. I've been wrestling with that thought ever since, worried I, too, might one day draw that kind of assignment. That piece was on my desk because I'd been looking at it, because deep down I knew this would be a one-way mission, to serve the greater good. But I didn't want to accept it. I couldn't accept it. I decided instead that it couldn't be true, and I made myself believe something different." Holbrook clasped Stephens's shoulder again. "Thank you, Paul, for your clarity of vision, and for your willingness to voice what you know to be right, no matter if it's the popular opinion or not."

"Thank you, sir," Stephens said sheepishly.

The two men headed up the corridor in silence. They stopped at the entrance to the mess hall.

"When the time comes, once we defeat the aughts, Dr. Riesen will live up to her end of the deal whether she wants to or not—that's a promise," said Holbrook. "Right now, let's eat and get settled for the night. Tomorrow, we'll head out to find the Hex Men mine."

"What about Dr. Imura?" asked Stephens. "His body, I mean."

Images of the man lying dead in Sickbay came flooding back. "He deserves to rest with his crew-mates," said Holbrook. "We'll bury him in the morning."

22

"Damage control to Lieutenant Commander Mills."

What now? Mills had just settled into the captain's chair and a hot cup of chamomile tea. He'd spent the past five hours dealing with a failing shield generator that threatened to expose them all to dangerous radiation from RD Sagittarius B. A message from damage control was about as welcome as a call from the dentist. "This is Mills."

"Sir, this is Wilkes. There's an urgent situation that requires your attention."

If it's so urgent, why not state the problem? "What's the situation, Mr. Wilkes?" Mills aimed to project an air of calm control, but he couldn't keep his weariness and irritation from creeping into his voice.

Seconds passed with no response. "Uh … it'll be easier to explain if you come up to the damage control station in engineering, sir," said Wilkes.

Mills sighed. "On my way."

Ensign Doerr swiveled in her navigator's chair, facing the lieutenant commander. "What do you think it is?" she asked.

"I'm sure it's nothing serious," Mills lied, mustering a half-hearted smile. An urgent situation that couldn't be discussed within earshot of the bridge crew and required the captain to leave his post couldn't be anything short of a minor disaster. He set down his tea and stood. "I'll be right back."

After a nerve-wracking eternity in the secure compartment, Mills jogged right, heading down the Central Loop Corridor to the nearest P-cab but stopped short, confused by the sight of six men blocking his path. In the middle stood Commander Lynch, flanked by Lieutenants Knox, Zhang, and Grey. Lieutenant Malone from security stood to the far left. Lieutenant Wilkes, the same Lieutenant Wilkes who had requested Mills's presence in engineering, stood on the far right.

Why weren't Lynch, Knox, Zhang, and Grey in the brig where Holbrook had left them confined? Without the captain or Stephens on board, only Mills or someone from security could have set the four prisoners free. The lieutenant commander's eyes darted to Security Officer Malone, who quickly looked down at the deck.

The six men stood menacing in the corridor, shades of bullies on a playground, except this was a CentCom warship, not the neighborhood schoolyard. And Mills wasn't some friendless transfer student on his first day. He was the duly designated captain of the *Avenger*, though he struggled to see himself as such. The secret was to imagine himself as the captain. Commander Stephens had tried to help him with that before leaving for Infernum. "Mills, how many times have you had the conn?" he'd asked.

"Numerous times, sir," said Mills.

"How many with me and Holbrook off the ship?"

"Uh, I believe once, sir. We were in orbit around Earth, and you and the captain were paying a visit to CentCom headquarters."

"So essentially zero," said Stephens.

Mills wasn't sure why the commander chose this particular time to tear him down. He was nervous enough about taking command without Stephens needling him about his lack of experience.

"That's not a bad thing," said Stephens. "Everybody has to start somewhere. I just wanted to understand if this will be your first true command."

"I guess it will, sir," said Mills.

"Are you ready?"

"Am I ready? I'm not sure, sir. I mean ... yes, yes, I'm ready." No, he wasn't. Or at least he didn't feel ready. He struggled to project an air of confidence.

Stephens eyed the lieutenant. "You're ready, but ...."

Mills wished he had simply answered, "yes." He had difficulty being less than completely honest. The times he tried, the truth always emerged across his face. "But I ... I guess even knowing I have the conn, I still don't feel like I'm the captain. It's more like Lieutenant Commander Mills sitting in for you and the captain."

"Captaining a vessel isn't about proper rank or training," said Stephens. "An officer can have both but find himself unable to command. Would you like to know the secret?"

"I think I know it already," said Mills. "A captain needs to fake it, to fool everyone into believing they are in command."

Stephens scratched his head. "Where'd you hear that?"

The lieutenant commander went pale, fearing he'd embarrassed himself with his remark. "I don't know. A discussion board somewhere."

"That's sort of a twisted take on the right approach," said Stephens. "Push that idea out of your head. The secret is your unfaltering belief that you are the captain of the vessel."

Mills looked sideways at Stephens. "How's that not the same thing?" he asked.

"They are very different things," said Stephens. "I'm not suggesting you fake anything. I'm saying to be the captain, you have to *know* you're the captain. The same as you know your name is Mills, and you're thirty-five years of age."

The comment puzzled and frustrated Mills. "But how can you know you're the captain if you're clearly not the captain?"

"Ahh," said Stephens, "that requires a special trick: you must *imagine* yourself as the captain. In any situation, picture what the captain would say, picture what he would do, and then say and do those things. Once you see yourself acting like the captain, your mind will begin to accept that you are the captain."

Wasn't imagining simply fakery by a different name? Was he really supposed to daydream his way to being captain?

"You still seem confused," said Stephens. "I have to leave for the planet, but I want you to think about what I just told you." Stephens headed for the exit but stopped. He returned to Mills. "Here's another way to approach it. Faking is a form of lying. When you fake something, you're saying, 'I'm not this thing but I'm going to try to fool everyone.' Imagining is not a lie; it's seeing yourself as the thing. At some point in your life, you weren't an officer and you weren't serving aboard a starship, but you saw yourself doing both of those things. You *imagined* yourself doing those things. And here you are." Stephens patted Mills's arm. "You'll do great. I know it. Just remember: imagination is the key."

Standing before the six men, Mills took Stephens's advice to heart. He imagined himself in charge of the *Avenger*, projecting confidence, commanding the respect of the crew, expecting his orders to be obeyed without question. He summoned his most authoritative voice. "What are you doing out of the brig?" he asked, addressing Lynch directly.

Commander Lynch stepped forward, eclipsing the others with his bulk. "I'm here to take command of this ship."

"The captain put *me* in charge of the *Avenger*," said Mills, his voice wavering slightly.

Zhang unholstered his electron pistol and aimed it at Mills's chest.

"Yes, he did," said Lynch, stepping forward again. "That's why I'm here talking to you."

- - -

"Officer of the deck on the bridge," said the ship.

Lynch had hated hearing those words during his shifts in the ship's command center, for they usually meant Commander Stephens returning to watch over the bridge crew. In his new position, he liked the notion the ship would announce his presence whenever he appeared.

The nine bridge officers all turned as Lynch, Knox, Zhang, and Grey strolled out of the secure compartment. Knox and Zhang held back near the doors while Grey followed Lynch to the center of the room.

"How'd you get out of the brig?" asked Lieutenant Commander Martin Phillips, the Chief Ops Officer. "And where is Mills?"

"Lieutenant Commander Mills has given me the conn," said Lynch.

"But where *is* Mills?" asked Phillips.

Lynch walked over to the ops station along the forward bulkhead and stopped a few centimeters from Phillips. The commander's large frame and half-foot advantage almost blotted the smaller man out. "Where Lieutenant Commander Mills is right now is not as important as following my orders." He had leaned in close to the ops officer, breathing each word into Phillips's face.

"That goes for everyone here on this bridge," Lynch said as he turned to face the room. "Your job is to carry out my orders, because that's the only way a ship can function." He stepped towards the captain's chair. "Is there anyone who thinks they can't do that? Follow my orders as you would Holbrook's or Stephens's? Now is the time to speak up." He slowly scanned the room, looking at each of the bridge officers at their posts. A few returned his gaze, but most stared down into the deck. A tight grin curled across the commander's face as he grew satisfied he had secured their obedience.

Ensign Higgins stepped forward from the weapons station at the back of the room. "Sir," he said in a gentle voice. Lynch, startled, swiveled his entire body to see who spoke, causing the young officer to jump as the round hulk at the front of the bridge locked in on him. "I think I'd be more comfortable following Lieutenant Commander Mills's orders."

"Mills is in his quarters," said Lynch. "He's no longer in command. He has given me the conn."

Higgins hesitated. "I'd still be more comfortable following his orders," he said.

Lynch's stern expression gave way to a smile. "Fine, fine," he said in a pleasant tone. "See, this is what I'm talking about." He nodded at Knox, who walked to Ensign Higgins's station. "If you think you won't be able to follow orders, please speak up now."

Knox grabbed Higgins's arm and tried to pull him away from his post. When Higgins resisted, Knox raised the ensign's arm high above his head and punched him square in the stomach. Higgins sputtered and doubled over in pain.

"Stick him in the brig," said Lynch. "That's the spot for officers who can't follow orders."

Lieutenant Malone crossed the bridge and grabbed Higgins's other arm, and the two men pulled the ensign into the secure compartment.

"Is there anyone else who thinks they can't follow orders?" asked Lynch. He scanned the bridge again. No one returned his gaze. "Good," he said and walked to the captain's chair in the center of the room. Lynch found Mills's cup of tea on the armrest. "Someone remove this, this *drink* from my chair," he bellowed.

No one moved at first, but eventually, Lieutenant Grey grabbed Mills's cup. He sniffed at the liquid, then remained in the middle of the room, holding the tea.

The cup removed, Lynch grasped the smooth, cold armrest. He turned around and backed in slowly. He sat with a satisfied look on his face, enjoying the first few official moments of his new command.

"Navigator," said Lynch, "status report."

"We're in an eccentric elliptical orbit around Infernum," said Doerr, "synchronized with the planet's rotation. We're set up to fly over the landing party's location each morning."

"Thank you," said Lynch. "Chart a course back to Earth."

"Sir," said Doerr, "it's impossible to navigate out of D-space. I can plot a course to Earth, but if we follow it, we'll get turned around, lost."

"The research party from that ship believed it's possible to exit D-space," said Lynch. "And so do I."

"But they didn't describe exactly *how* to get out," said Doerr.

"We'll figure it out on the way," said Lynch. "I'll assign a team to analyze the *Adiona's* logs and determine how they planned to return home."

"What about the landing party?" asked Lieutenant Bhat. "We can't just leave them."

Lynch spun his chair to face the back of the room. "They left us," he said. "The captain deserted us a long time ago, the moment he forced us here to Sag A Star." With the cowering Bhat silenced, Lynch rotated back to center. "Plot us a course, Ensign."

Ensign Doerr hung her head and worked at her terminal to calculate the new course. "Plotted, sir," she said in a quiet, resigned voice. "The ship estimates seven days' travel time to Earth at max speed."

"Lay it in," said Lynch. He relaxed into the captain's chair. The whole operation was going much smoother than he imagined it would. He'd figured it'd be no problem getting Security Officer Malone, Gray's final recruit for their operation and the one ace in their pocket, to release them from the brig once the senior staff left for the planet. And being the most senior officer remaining on the *Avenger* would allow him to take the ship without much effort. At last, as planned, he had them headed home.

The ship's voice called out inside the bridge. "The helmsman, navigator, and engineer must all agree to the course change."

Lynch sat forward in the captain's chair, confused. "What?" he said.

"The helmsman, navigator, and engineer must all agree to the course change," said the ship.

"I've never heard of such a requirement," scoffed Lynch.

"Commander Stephens added the directive to the command manifest that any change from our current orbit around Infernum be approved unanimously by the helmsman, navigator, and engineer," said the ship.

"Override," boomed Lynch.

"Only Commander Stephens or Captain Holbrook can cancel this directive."

Lynch zeroed in on the helm station. "Helmsman," he said, "what's your name, son?"

"Ensign Jonas Hartley, sir."

"Ensign Hartley, we are changing course to return to Earth. The ship says you must agree to this change. Do you agree, son?"

Hartley responded with a pained expression. He scanned the bridge, looking at the other officers. All eyes were trained on him.

Glancing to the back of the bridge over his left shoulder, Lynch motioned Zhang forward. The lieutenant stepped past Lynch's seated bulk and planted himself in front of Hartley at his post. The young ensign peered upwards, squinting at the menacing Zhang, partially blinded by the overhead lights.

"Well, what'll it be, son?" asked Lynch.

"I ... I agree," said Hartley.

Lynch turned next to Ensign Doerr at the navigator's station. Her head sank. "I agree," she said in a dejected voice.

"And I also agree," said Lynch. "Lay in the new course, Ensign."

Ensign Doerr tapped her terminal again.

"The helmsman, navigator, and engineer must all agree to the course change," the ship said for the third time.

"What the hell is going on?" said Lynch, pounding the armrest of the captain's chair. "We all do agree!"

"The helmsman and navigator agree," said the ship, "but the engineer has not."

"I do!" shouted Lynch. "I do agree!"

"You are not the *Avenger's* engineer," said the ship.

Lynch's face flared red. "I am the *chief* engineer!" he yelled.

"You are not the chief engineer," said the ship. "Captain Holbrook relieved you of that position until a court martial renders judgement on the mutiny charges against you."

"I hereby reinstate my position as chief engineer of the *Avenger*," said Lynch, drawing his tongue across his fleshy, chapped lips.

"Your position as officer of the deck gives you command of the bridge," said the ship, "but only the captain can appoint department chiefs aboard the *Avenger*."

"Fine," said Lynch. "Conlin is the acting chief engineer. Summon him to the bridge."

"Lieutenant Commander Conlin is on the planet Infernum with the landing party," said the ship.

"Third engineer Hall?" said Lynch.

"Lieutenant Hall has been incapacitated by D-space sickness since shortly after the *Avenger* arrived at Sagittarius A Star. She is currently under heavy sedation in Sickbay and unavailable for duty."

Lynch fumed. "Just who *is* the next ranking engineering officer aboard this ship?"

"Ensign Maria Jiménez is the engineering department's next ranking officer while Conlin is on the planet and Hall remains incapacitated."

Commander Lynch spat at the sound of the young officer's name. She'd caused him so much trouble all her time aboard the *Avenger*, up to convincing Captain Holbrook to ignore his warning against embarking on their current fool mission. "Bring me Ensign Jiménez."

23

Captain Holbrook and Lieutenant Byrne lowered Imura's rigid body, wrapped in white, into the shallow grave under a violet-tinged, overcast sky. Warm drizzle collected on their helmets as the first hints of dawn flickered in the east.

The hypergiant had not yet risen when Lieutenant Commander Conlin and Lieutenant Shelton located the rough rectangle Imura had scratched into the ground to mark the location of his grave. Shelton protested spending time searching for the plot. He declared any flat patch would do, but Holbrook insisted they find Imura's chosen resting place. Imura buried his murdered crewmates in three neat rows, with four graves down each file. His own plot began a new row, about twenty meters south and slightly east of the entrance to the *Adiona*.

Conlin and Shelton removed scoops of the dry riverbed using two collapsible shovels, which Lieutenant Byrne and Dr. Marsden had discovered while rummaging belowdecks the night before. The two officers labored under the flickering glow of a portable thermite lamp set nearby, also recovered from the *Adiona's* cargo hold. The men dug two meters into the soft ground, a matrix of small rocks and spongy earth. When finished, they staked their shovels in the mound of freshly excavated dirt and paused. Shelton tapped his comm. "Captain, the grave is ready."

"Lieutenant Byrne, meet me in Sickbay in ten minutes."

Captain Holbrook bought ten minutes to collect himself, to inject as many stimulants as his EN-suit would permit, and to practice walking in a straight line. Once the rest of the landing party turned in for the night, the captain explored belowdecks in search of liquor. Any ship attempting an achievement as monumental as returning from D-space would surely contain alcohol for the victory celebration; it was all a matter of finding it. After twenty-five minutes of searching, the captain stumbled upon two containers. One held thirty bottles of champagne in cold storage. The other container, much smaller than the first, held rolls of crepe paper, party tablecloths, confetti poppers, multi-colored streamers, and a bottle of twenty-one-year-old Scotch in a silver cardboard box wrapped with a blue ribbon.

The captain found a secluded spot in the cargo hold and sat on the deck with his back against the bulkhead. He removed the cap and proceeded to drink straight from the bottle in drams and swigs. He drank to forget his failure with Imura. He drank to lament his luck at drawing the Sag A Star assignment. He drank to their eventual victory over the aughts. He drank to curse dying at the center of the galaxy. He drank to soothe his nerves. And finally, he drank himself to oblivion. He passed out where he sat, falling into a fitful sleep. He woke with a massive hangover and unmetabolized alcohol still in his blood. After his benders on the *Avenger,* he would ingest one or two nullihol pills to wick the alcohol from his system. He'd briefly considered bringing the pills to the planet but couldn't imagine having occasion to drink while on Infernum. Awakened by the landing party's rustling in the hour before their planned departure from the *Adiona,* he faced the prospect of leading his crew while still intoxicated.

Holbrook got himself to his feet and staggered into Sickbay shortly before Lieutenant Byrne arrived. The two unclamped the locks on one of the cadaver storage cabinets and let its wide, dull gray door swing down to form a shelf. They reached into the narrow sepulcher and pulled out Imura's stiff, cold body. Byrne suggested they use the anti-grav sled to transport the corpse to the gravesite, but Holbrook dismissed the idea. "We won't move him like he's cargo. We will carry him like a fellow human being. Besides, he's too much weight ... not too much weight for the two of us to manage." The captain spoke to Byrne through his helmet, which he activated despite being inside the ship, preventing the lieutenant from smelling the liquor on his breath. It couldn't mask the slight slur in his words, his sloppy sentences, or his occasional stagger.

The men hoisted Imura's rigid body onto their shoulders. Holbrook grabbed the rigored calves and instructed Byrne to lead, largely to prevent the security officer from witnessing his wobbly gait. Together they inched through the ship with their cold, white cocoon. Members of the *Avenger's* landing party filed out of their rooms as the two men walked by, falling into a somber procession behind them.

Byrne and Holbrook emerged from the ship as the first threads of red morning sunlight broke beneath the eastern cloud cover. At the excavation site they straddled the fresh grave and eased their stiff, white parcel into the ground. Holbrook forced himself to focus, determined not to allow the body to slip out of his hands and tumble into the hollow.

The men backed away to give Conlin and Shelton space to resume their labor, this time pitching earth onto the body from the pile of excavated dirt. Once finished, they tossed their shovels aside, and the other members of the *Avenger's* landing party joined them around the fresh mound. Most lowered their heads. Some clasped their hands in front of their bodies. All remained silent.

Captain Holbrook stood at the head of the grave, his eyes lowered as if out of reverence but in truth to fix his gaze on his boots. Despite his cache of nullihol pills aboard the *Avenger,* it wasn't the first time Holbrook had been intoxicated while on duty, and he drew upon all the tricks he learned over the years to hide his condition. Whenever the world spun around him, he found that focusing on a stationary object kept the dizziness at bay. He trained his eyes on his feet, the only part of the immediate landscape not revolving.

Holbrook chanced a quick look around the grave. To his left stood Dr. Riesen, her head raised but her eyes closed. Next to her, the young Ensign Reilly fidgeted with her hands. On Reilly's left, Lieutenant Commander Conlin stared at the mound, stone-faced and pale.

To Holbrook's right stood Dr. Marsden, a full foot shorter than him, the top of her helmet barely level with the middle of his chest. To her right and hanging several meters back from the gravesite stood Tentek. He looked on with his usual non-expression.

Lastly, the security officers Byrne and Shelton stood together at the foot of the grave. Byrne swayed with his head lowered. Shelton stared straight ahead.

"I will say a few words." His speech was still slurred—he needed to focus, to speak the next words with more clarity and control. The alcoholic fog made it difficult to remember the eulogy he'd composed in his head the evening prior, before he found the Scotch. The first few sentences surfaced but not much more. Hopefully reciting them would tease the rest from the recesses of his mind. "Dr. Yoichiro Imura, the man who lies in the grave before us, was not part of our crew. None of us, in fact, even knew him."

Holbrook winced at the awkward phrasing. His words from the night before had been much more eloquent. "But we will pay him our last respects."

Holbrook struggled for the next sentence—why would they pay him their last respects? "For he spent the final weeks of his life alone, wracked with anguish over the fate of his shipmates. He was a fellow space traveler, and a human being, on a planet hopelessly far from home." Holbrook fought to recall the rest of his remarks. He lost the next two paragraphs completely as well as the final one but for the last sentence. He'd best speak it, lest it too slip away. "May he find peace here at his final resting place."

Two sounds, in rapid succession, sliced through the silence that hung around the gravesite. Each began as a soft buzzing that rose in volume, as the hum from the wings of a large insect fast approaching, and ended in a sudden snap like static discharge. Neither sound lasted more than a second.

Startled, Holbrook looked up just as a slack-faced Byrne dropped to his knees, his body remaining upright for several moments before falling forward at an awkward angle across the grave. Shelton also collapsed, careening sideways in the direction of Lieutenant Commander Conlin, who moved quickly. He just avoided the limp body bowling into his legs. Ensign Reilly stepped back from the tumbling men, alarmed and confused. Dr. Riesen looked on, half-panicked. The landing party's EN-suits chimed softly in unison, warning of a sharp increase in ambient ozone.

A gut feeling became an observation in the captain's mind, born of years of tactical training, rising through the haze of alcohol: Shelton and Byrne were the only ones with weapons.

The alcohol impaired Holbrook's sense of time, and he found the world moving in slow motion. Off in the distance through the gap left by the fallen security men, several humanoid figures approached, though he wasn't certain if they were real or a trick of the light. He squinted for more details but failed to discern anything definitive through his drizzle-covered helmet. He brushed his arm across its force field to clear it, lucid enough to avoid using his dusty gloves, which would have left a muddy smear. He identified three distinct figures headed toward them. They had white heads and wore outfits of olive green.

Ensign Reilly ran as best she could, encumbered by her EN-suit. A bright light flashed in front of one of the figures, followed by a slow-motion bolt of yellow lightning that hit Reilly in the mid back. The young ensign's body went limp, but her momentum carried her forward. Her arms flailed out from her sides as she skidded helmet-first into the dirt.

One of the figures stepped directly in front of Holbrook, between him and the bodies of his fallen security men. He had white skin, short cropped blond hair, a sharp chin and nose, and large porcelain eyes that reflected the red half-circle crescent hanging at the horizon. He had no weapon but two of his companions were armed, corralling the landing party with electron pistols. Holbrook's EN-suit informed him of a fourth holding a plasma rifle to his rear.

The aught standing before Holbrook spoke. "I assume from the captain's bars on your collar you are the ranking officer here?" it asked in a thin, metallic voice.

Holbrook could only nod. The world began to spin. He struggled to remain upright and not join his men on the dirt.

The aught bared its teeth in a ghoulish grimace. "All of you form a line along the ship."

24

Jiménez stepped onto the bridge, struck by the eerie quiet that filled the normally bustling command center. On her previous visits, the room had bubbled with energy and conversation. A dark and somber mood suffused the space.

Unsure who to report to, she paused. She had received a message to head immediately to the bridge but no instructions beyond that.

An uneasy feeling spurred her to look right. The gaunt Lieutenant Grey leered at her from his seat at the XO's station. She'd never met the communications officer, but she had noticed Grey before, suspecting him of trailing her at times through the ship. The lieutenant raked her with his eyes, his face gripped by a sordid expression. He nodded for her to continue forward. She felt his gaze follow her as she advanced into the room.

Grey—he was one of the officers in the brig for mutiny! What was he doing there?

Jiménez's confusion grew as she approached the center of the bridge. Instead of Lieutenant Commander Mills sitting in the captain's chair, it was Commander Lynch. He hunched forward with his elbow on his knee and large, pudgy fist under his chin, a grumpy, rumpled king contemplating his dominion. The man's beady eyes tracked Jiménez as she came around to face him. Lieutenants Knox and Zhang stood to either side of him.

"Commander Lynch," said Jiménez, her voice wavering slightly.

"It is customary," said Lynch, "for the officer of the deck, regardless of rank, to be addressed as 'Captain.'" He straightened in the captain's chair. "That is the custom we are adopting on *this* bridge, Ensign."

Not only was Lynch out of the brig, he claimed to have the conn as well? "What happened to Lieutenant Commander Mills?"

"Mills is in his quarters," said Lynch. "I summoned you here because we are leaving this planet, setting sail for Earth."

"What about the landing party?" asked Jiménez.

"My concern is for the safety of this ship and its crew," said Lynch. "I have determined in my capacity as the captain of this vessel that the best course of action is to leave this planet and head home. The only thing I require from you, Ensign Jiménez, is your agreement to the course change. Then you may be on your way."

Jiménez looked sideways at Lynch. "But three of us need to agree to leave," she said. "Not me alone."

"Yes, Ensign. Everyone else has already done their part. I just need you to do yours."

The other officers had agreed to leave the planet with the landing party still on the surface, and fly off into D-space where they would surely get lost without Dr. Riesen's help? Her eyes darted to Ensign Hartley, manning the helm with a lifeless stare, then to Ensign Doerr, who sat on the verge of tears. Lynch had forced them to agree. "We don't actually know how to get back to Earth," said Jiménez. "We should stay here until the landing party returns."

"You need not concern yourself with the 'how' of getting back, Ensign," said Lynch. "You should assume all of that is under control. I just need your agreement to the new course. Do you agree, Ensign Jiménez?"

With the other officers' capitulation, what would be the point of her resisting? She tried to picture herself agreeing, but her mind would have none of it. However, saying "no" would likely infuriate Lynch. Instead, she said nothing, unsure of what to do. She alternated her gaze between him and the deck as the commander's eyes burned into her.

Lynch's chubby face grew to a light shade of red. "So that's it then," he said. "I'd hoped we could do things the easy way. That would save the both of us some trouble." Sitting in the darkened bridge, the control panels on the armrests of the captain's chair illuminated Lynch's face from below, leaving his eyes black and most of his forehead cast in shadow. "What you fail to realize is I don't actually need you," he said with a shake of his head. "Lieutenant Hall is unconscious in Sickbay. The doctor says the drugs she's on will wear off in a few hours. Do you know her story?" She did but remained silent. "She vomited all over the engineering station right after we entered D-space, then dropped to the deck, doubled over with nausea. It was so bad they had to sedate her. She's barely been conscious since."

Lynch leaned in closer to Ensign Jiménez. "When her drugs wear off, I'll put her back on active duty," he said. "She outranks you, so she can agree to the course change. And she will, because I won't allow her any more meds until she does. I don't expect securing her agreement to take very long." The commander sank back into the captain's chair. "So I don't need you," he said, dismissing her with a flick of his hand. He turned his head towards the back bulkhead and barked, "Grey!"

Lieutenant Grey rose from his station. He scurried across the deck and presented himself to Lynch.

"Grey is going to escort you to some secluded location and beat the shit out of you," said Lynch. "I'd have him do it right here, but I don't want blood on my bridge. Once he's done, he'll throw you in the brig. In fact, you're getting my old bunk." Lynch grinned. "Consider it a comeuppance for your Plana Petram simulation."

Grey yanked Jiménez's arm, pulling her toward the exit. All eyes on the bridge followed her until the two entered the secure compartment and the doors slid shut behind them.

As Jiménez stood with Grey, waiting for the outer doors to open, the questions rolled through her mind. Was Lynch really trying to return to Earth? Was no one else on the bridge going to stop him? And the biggest question of all: what should she do next? Escape seemed the only choice, but how? At the moment Grey had a more than solid grasp of her left arm, his fingers crushing her muscle against the bone. No way could she wrestle free of his grip. She also had no weapon, while Grey was armed with an electron pistol. One shot from that gun would scramble the electrical activity in her body, knocking her unconscious. If they got wherever he was taking her, she'd be done for. Whatever she was going to do had to happen fast. Think, Jiménez, think!

Her mind flowed like mush, but she worked out the semblance of a plan. Once the doors opened, she'd make a commotion. She'd convince whoever stopped to help pry Grey's hand off her arm, then run for it, perhaps disappear down a rungway. But then what ...?

The doors opened and Grey dragged Jiménez out into the Center Loop corridor, turning right and following its broad curve. Jiménez craned her neck, looking ahead and back behind her. The corridor, normally filled with crewmen scrambling between shifts or downtime destinations, was completely empty. The corridors had been deserted on her way to the bridge, a fact that stood out in her mind at the time, but she'd been too preoccupied to pay it much consideration.

"Where is everyone?" she said half to herself as she stole another look down the corridor behind her.

"Heh," said Grey, "'prolly everyone's gotten wise to the idea of stayin' in their quarters."

"What do you mean?" asked Jiménez.

"Just that Lynch sent a couple unsavories, Vasiliev and Kavanaugh, to patrol the corridors, lookin' for anyone who might go against his command. Already threw a few in the brig just fer askin' questions. I'm guessin' word's traveled fast that it's better to keep out of the open."

Jiménez's heart sank. There'd be no one to help her with Grey. She was on her own. She needed a different plan.

Still in Grey's grasp, the ensign wrenched her body around and placed herself directly in front of the lieutenant, blocking his path forward. The two stood face-to-face in the middle of the corridor, Grey's right hand still gripping her left arm. "We haven't run into each other much," she said, "you in communications and all, but that doesn't mean I haven't noticed you on the ship." She did her best to embrace the lieutenant, working her right arm around his waist while her left remained in his grasp. She rubbed his back through his uniform as Grey stared down at Ensign Jiménez with a quiet glare, his warm breath beating against her face. Stubble dotted his haggard cheeks, and he smelled of stale, cheap cologne, gin, and cigarettes. "Maybe you'd be interested in a little fun."

The lieutenant smirked. "Lynch says the only way a ship can function is by the crew followin' orders. Now the captain wants you beaten up, so that's what I'm gonna deliver." He put his hand under her chin and raised her head, forcing her to look into his eyes. "But before that we can do somethin' like what you're suggestin'. That was my plan regardless."

A pained half-smile crossed Ensign Jiménez's face as Grey moved his hand from her chin to the back of her head. He raked his fingers into her dark hair and cupped her skull in his palm. Grey pulled her head forward, smashing her lips into his.

Jiménez whimpered slightly and closed her eyes as the lieutenant pressed his lips more urgently against hers. Her hand shifted from rubbing Grey's back to bunching material from the waist of his uniform, gathering the rough fabric between her fingers and holding it in a solid grip. In one smooth motion she pulled the material, drawing him tightly into her as she drove her right knee swiftly upward, crushing his testicles with all the force she could muster. Grey gasped, stunned, his face a mix of shock and agony. He reflexively tried to retreat, but Jiménez held him close with her grip on his uniform.

The ensign quickly brought her knee up a second time, smashing again into his testicles. Her third thrust only half connected, striking a glancing blow against Grey's genitals. He sank away from her in slow motion, the lieutenant's gaping mouth locked in a silent scream as he hit the deck. He lay there frozen, curled in a ball with both hands clutching his crotch.

Crouching next to the crumpled figure, Jiménez moved her hand slowly along the man's waist. She gently slid his electron pistol from its holster and stood. The ensign watched Grey for a few seconds, the lieutenant writhing in agony. She sprinted for the nearest rungway.

25

Captain Holbrook stood with the other members of the Infernum landing party along the *Adiona's* gently curving hull, his hands clasped behind his head and elbows angled out. He squinted against the growing daylight as the red hypergiant rose in the sky, the world spinning as he struggled to remain upright. When would he clear enough of the alcohol from his system to return to some semblance of sobriety? For most of Imura's ceremony he'd relied on his drunkard's skill at appearing in control. Devising a plan, evaluating options, exuding confidence, all the activities expected of a captain were beyond his impaired mental capacity.

The aught leader, the one who had spoken upon their arrival, stood four meters away. The others called him Twentek-one. His apparent second stood beside him, plasma rifle raised but ready.

The other two aughts emerged from the *Adiona's* hatch. "There is no one else inside," reported number three, an exact copy of his counterpart except for his auburn-tinted hair. They had disappeared into the ship twenty minutes prior, far too long for a casual search. They had been looking for someone.

Twentek-one approached Holbrook with a rictus grimace. He had a narrow face like the others and an especially pointy nose. Cheekbones pressed through paper thin phlesh. Wide white eyes rolled in their sockets. He was an image straight out of a nightmare. "What is your name ... Captain?" he asked.

The captain worked to push through the fog of inebriation. "Hol-brook."

Twentek-one stared at Holbrook. "We are looking for your friend, Captain Hol-brook," he said. "Where is he?"

"Who?" asked Holbrook. Everyone stood beside him, including Byrne, Shelton, and Reilly, who had all recovered from the electron pistol blasts that felled them. Or had someone escaped? The captain, standing at one end of the row of captives, leaned forward to survey the line.

Twentek-one unloaded a blurred double-punch in Holbrook's gut, his android arm moving quickly like a piston. The first blow landed in the captain's solar plexus, the second square in his abdomen. "I did not say you could move," said the aught.

Pain rippled across Holbrook's belly. He attempted to draw air into his lungs but failed—the punches had knocked the wind out of him. He couldn't breathe.

"Your friend," Twentek-one asked again. "Where is he?"

Holbrook straightened himself, creating more space in his abdomen and relaxing his diaphragm enough to take a breath. He closed his eyes and walked through the afterimage of his glance down the line: Byrne, Conlin, Riesen, Shelton, Reilly, and Marsden. All who had attended the burial ceremony stood with him along the ship. "Everyone is here," he said, coughed, and took another breath.

"You think we do not know the size of your party," said Twentek-one. "You think we do not know there are eight of you."

Eight? Holbrook had just counted seven, including himself. Why did the aught think there should be eight?

"You humans believe yourselves to be so clever that you are surprised when you are outthought," said the aught, his large, billiard ball eyes a reflective red, unmoving, trained on the captain. "The drones detected eight heat signatures when they flew over the lake."

Stephens! Stephens wasn't with them. That fact provided a glimmer of hope, a chance they could turn the situation around. But what to tell Twentek-one? He couldn't give up his first officer. Holbrook's mind operated in slow motion, repeatedly losing trains of thought. He needed time to formulate an answer. Perhaps he could buy some with a question. "If you knew we were here on the planet," he said, speaking slowly and deliberately, "then why the games? Why let us think we weren't found? Why not capture us right then? Or blast us in the water?"

"We have not been playing games with you, Captain," said Twentek-one. "You were captured the moment you crashed on this planet. We did not need to rush to retrieve you. Probabilities suggested you would head for this ship, and heading for this ship would bring you closer to us, like prisoners escorting themselves to jail."

Twentek-one backed away from the captain and walked down the line of captives. "There were eight of you in that lake, but there are only seven of you here now. Where is the eighth member of your party?" The aught stopped in front of Ensign Reilly. "Your captain refuses to assist us with the answer—that is unsurprising. But I think another of you will tell me what I want to know with much less ... resistance." He moved in close to the ensign, the point of his nose almost poking her helmet. The young officer trembled under his gaze, letting out a soft whimper as she looked away.

"It's Commander Stephens."

The voice came from far down the line. Holbrook strained to see who had spoken, daring to lean forward slightly and angling his eyes to the left.

Twentek-one walked to the end of the line of humans. "What did you say?"

"Commander Stephens. You're looking for Commander Stephens."

The voice belonged to Dr. Marsden, her head bobbing out of the corner of Holbrook's eye as she spoke. What in Hades was she doing? Maybe she figured giving the aughts what they wanted was the best way to avoid someone getting hurt, but that was not her call to make.

Twentek-one's head telescoped forward into the doctor's face, his neck stretching to an unnatural human length. "Commander Stephens?"

"That's right," she said, her voice defiant. "He came with us in the shuttle."

"Where *is* the commander?" asked Twentek-one.

Holbrook needed to stop Marsden from saying more. "Don't —"

"Right there," said Dr. Marsden. She pointed at the fresh grave they had all stood around minutes before. "He was hurt when our shuttle crashed. He managed to make it to the *Adiona,* but he died last night. We just laid him to rest. That's why we were all out here when you arrived. We were paying our final respects."

Twentek-one cocked his head, his eyes shifting between Holbrook and Dr. Marsden. "Scan the mound," he said.

Aught number three walked to Dr. Imura's grave and waved his flat palm over it, tracing slow circles in the air. "A single human male adult exists beneath the mound," he said, "recently deceased ... within the last fourteen hours."

Great job, Carla! There was hope for them yet. Now if only the commander learned of their predicament and followed his orders.

Twentek-one returned to Captain Holbrook. "You and your people will collect your gear and come with us back to our ship."

The success of Marsden's gambit encouraged the still-inebriated Captain Holbrook to put forth one of his own. He managed a response that was half bluff, half alcoholic bluster. "We are CentCom officers and citizens of the Republic," he said. "Unless you're looking to start a major interstellar incident, you will release us and leave this area immediately."

Twentek-one eyed the captain. "If taking you back to our ship is enough to start an interstellar incident, imagine what will happen if we kill one of you." He raised a hand.

Number Two lowered his plasma rifle at Lieutenant Commander Byrne. A burst of hot plasma surged from the weapon, scorching the lieutenant's abdomen. The security chief looked at the hole in his belly before dropping to the ground. Ensign Reilly screamed.

"We both know, Captain Holbrook, you cannot get a message to CentCom," said Twentek-one.

Holbrook, his mouth open in shock, could only stare at his slain security chief.

Twentek-one addressed the landing party. "I could slaughter you all and no one from CentCom would know. I am hoping one of you gives me a reason." The humans stood motionless except for Lieutenant Shelton, whose whole body trembled. Tears shimmered across Ensign Reilly's cheeks. "Now gather your things. You are heading with us back to our ship." Twentek-one's eyes locked on Holbrook. He gave the captain a rictus grin. "My commander is waiting to see you."

26

Stephens stood atop the bluff that shadowed the *Adiona,* in the middle of a clearing surrounded by waist-high yellow brush. RD Sagittarii A hung low in the east. The clouds that obscured the dawn and drizzled on Stephens during his trek to the summit had burned off, leaving the lumbering red giant to rise unobscured.

The commander crouched and gently laid a small bag on the ground. He tugged at its magnetic clasp and reached inside, his hand withdrawing a microline transmitter, its black case the size and shape of a large book with a low-profile keypad on its face. He set the transmitter on the empty bag, flipped open a compartment along the device's nearest side, and removed a thin headset and a copper-colored cone. With a twist he unfurled the cone into a delicate, palm-sized disc of copper mesh.

After connecting leads between the disc and the transmitter, Stephens stood and stretched his legs. They still ached from the previous day's trek to the *Adiona* and had stiffened after his eighty-minute hike to the summit. In a few moments, the *Avenger's* eccentric orbit would streak it high above the western mountain chain's snow-covered peaks and accelerate it eastward. The bluff's summit provided the most unobstructed view of the sky, offering the best opportunity for a clear line of sight with the starship.

Stephens was the logical choice for his current assignment but he still didn't care for the decision. Entrusting anyone else in their party with the critical task of sending a status report to the *Avenger* made Holbrook uncomfortable, but the team needed to prepare for the day, and getting crewmen organized was Stephens's specialty. Hopefully the captain was managing OK without him. He'd messaged Holbrook before leaving, but the captain never responded. His comm had showed him belowdecks, likely rummaging through the stores for items that might be useful on their trek to the Hex Men mine. He would have checked in directly with Holbrook but had been too pressed for time.

A twig snapped behind him.

The sound came from the direction of the outlet to the trail he'd followed to the summit, carried by the gentle breeze rising from the lower ground. He stood perfectly still and strained his ears—nothing. Perhaps it was something other than a snapping twig? Perhaps he imagined it altogether.

Another sound, scrub brush crunching underfoot, drifted from the trail, louder than the crackling twig, closer. Stephens's hand moved to his holster. It was empty. In his rush to reach the summit, he'd gathered the communications gear and a food concentrate belt but not a weapon. He was defenseless.

There was no time to find a real hiding place—he hurried to a thicket of nearby bushes. Stephens crouched low and remained motionless, concealing himself as best he could. His attention trained on the trail's end fifteen meters away, he fought to quiet his breathing, limiting his lungs to shallow inhales.

Something moved at the outlet, rising from the trail until it emerged fully onto the summit. It was a humanoid figure, pale and skinny, with a narrow head. An aught. The robot halted and scanned the plateau.

Stephens's heart raced. He looked around for a stick, a rock, anything he could use as a weapon. He found nothing suitable. Stephens cursed at his absentmindedness. He could only hope to ambush the machine, to pounce before it discovered him and to disable it as quickly as possible. He estimated his odds of success quite low. Aughts typically moved faster and possessed greater body strength and far superior senses than humans.

The aught ambled across the plateau in the commander's direction, stopping at his bag in the center of the clearing. It crouched, inspecting the equipment he'd laid out, then stood tall and surveyed the area. It wore an EN-suit, blue-gray like his own.

Stephens stood from the bushes. "Tin Man?"

The aught's head swiveled towards Stephens. He shuffled over to the commander.

"What're you doing here?" asked Stephens. "Why aren't you at the *Adiona*?"

"Keep your voice down, Commander," whispered Tentek. "Although we are far from the ship, they may be able to hear us."

"*Who* may be able to hear us?" asked Stephens.

"The aughts," said Tentek. "The ones sent here by The Collective. They arrived at the *Adiona* a short time ago."

Stephens rushed to the bluff's edge with Tentek close behind. Before reaching the rim, he lowered himself onto his belly and inched his body forward. He increased the magnification on his helmet's force bubble and wriggled far enough forward to peer over the side. The *Adiona* sat below, a silvery-purple wafer in the early dawn light. Nothing moved around the ship. A crumpled shape faced sideways in the dirt next to a freshly dug grave. A body. Its size and hair color suggested Lieutenant Commander Byrne, the security chief.

The commander crawled back from the edge and stood. He turned to face Tentek, ready to attack the robot. If aughts from The Collective had taken the landing party, why hadn't they captured Tentek too? Unless he was working with them, as Stephens had suspected all along. Tentek's appearance was probably a ploy to capture him without firing a shot. Stephens clenched his fists, wishing again for his pistol. "So, how did you escape?" he asked casually. "How is it you didn't wind up captured too?"

Tentek blinked at the commander. "The captain was about to begin a burial ceremony for Dr. Imura," he said. "I was not sure I should attend. I was concerned the captain and the others might be offended if I participated. I walked behind the *Adiona* and headed a few meters up the trail. I wanted to get a view of the ship and surrounding area from slightly higher ground. I heard two shots. Their sonic signatures matched Collective electron pistols. Probabilities suggested I would be captured if I ran back to the others. I decided the best thing to do was to find you, so that you could call for help from the *Avenger*."

"The *Avenger*!" Stephens ran across the bluff to the microline transmitter. Kneeling before the device, he pressed a flat button flush with its case and adjusted the small antenna to point at the sky over the far-off mountain peaks.

Tentek arrived next to the commander as Stephens worked the keypad controls, fine-tuning the delicate antenna's orientation. "How long will it take for a rescue party to reach us?" asked the aught.

Stephens ignored him, tapping at the keypad until an amber light in its center came alive. He donned the transmitter's thin headset and stood, facing Tentek. "I'm not requesting a rescue party," he said. The amber light began a slow flash, the *Avenger* coming into range.

Tentek cocked his head. "I am confused, Commander. Why will you not request a rescue party?"

Stephens scanned the sky over the mountain range, hoping for a glimpse of the starship even though the *Avenger's* orbit would carry it far too high to see. "Because the captain has given me strict orders," he said. The amber light blinked faster.

"What were the captain's orders?"

"Order number one," said Stephens, "no one else comes down from the *Avenger*. If this landing party can't get the job done, no one else is to try."

Tentek cocked his head again. "I understand his reasoning to a point," he said. "But what if this landing party fails? How will we complete our mission?"

"That brings us to order number two," said Stephens. "If the landing party is captured, the *Avenger* is to carpet bomb this hemisphere with atomic weapons. Based on what you just told me, my duty right now is to dial up death for us and everyone else on this planet." He waited for a reaction from Tentek, for the aught to say he couldn't let him do that. Waited for him to kick the transmitter aside and say he was taking him back to the *Adiona* to hold captive with the others, if the aughts hadn't killed them all outright.

"The entire landing party has not been captured," said Tentek. "You and I are still free."

"Yes, we are," said Stephens, "but the two of us alone can't stop your aught buddies. Besides, what if they're spooked now that they've discovered more humans on the planet? What if that causes them to move up their timetable for leaving?"

The amber light flashed frantically.

"It seems you have only moments to make your decision," said Tentek, his eyelids click-clacking.

"And I have decided," said Stephens. "As much as I want to hunt down those aught bastards myself and free everyone and leave this rock alive, I can't risk them escaping with the Planck Matter." Tentek would make his move now. Stephens still didn't have a weapon, but apparently neither did the robot. Would he have the strength to take the machine in hand-to-hand combat?

"I see," said Tentek. "As saddened as I am at the prospect of dying here and now, I do not disagree with your decision."

"Wha ...," said Stephens, confused. Tentek agreed the continent, and everyone on it, should be razed? Was it somehow part of the aught plan to capture him?

The amber proximity light went solid on the transmitter.

"The *Avenger* is in range," said Tentek, nodding at the light. "You do not want to miss this communications window—we may not get another."

Stephens, still confused, kept his eyes on Tentek as he pressed the headset's transmit button. "This is Commander Stephens calling the starship *Avenger*, over."

Silence.

He pressed the transmit button again. "This is Commander Stephens to the starship *Avenger*. Over."

More silence.

"Is the transmitter working?" asked Tentek.

Stephens rechecked the readout along the top of the microline transmitter's case. "We have a transmission lock on the *Avenger*, and we're getting telemetry from the starship. We have a solid connection; it's just no one's answering." The commander pressed the transmit button a third time. "This is Commander Stephens calling the starship *Avenger*. Come in please. Over."

Silence.

"How can there be no response?" asked Tentek.

"Your guess is as good as mine," said Stephens, staring into the sky where the *Avenger* should be. "According to the telemetry, they're still following the preset elliptical orbit; they're just not answering."

The amber proximity light on the transmitter changed from a solid glow to rapid flashing.

"Does that mean the *Avenger* is going out of range?" asked Tentek.

"It does," said Stephens. "Their flight plan accelerates them away after their brief overhead flyby. In a moment they'll be far from the planet." The commander looked again to the sky. "This is Stephens to the starship *Avenger*. Can anyone hear me? Please respond. The landing party has been captured. It's urgent I speak to someone now."

No one responded from the starship. He tried contacting the ship a final time. The proximity light's flashing slowed, then stopped completely.

Tentek's eyelids click-clacked in the quiet morning air. "What does this mean?" he asked.

Stephens removed the headset and tossed it near the transmitter. "There's one thing it means for certain," he said as he walked back to the edge of the bluff. "It means the two of us, you and I, we're on our own."

27

Jiménez scrambled down the rungway ladder clutching Lieutenant Grey's electron pistol, twice almost dropping it. When she reached Deck C, she huddled within the tube-shaped alcove and peeked her head into the adjacent corridor. The passageway was empty.

The young ensign spent a moment catching her breath, her heart thumping in her throat after her improvised escape from Grey. She needed to keep moving. They would start looking for her when they discovered the lieutenant where she left him incapacitated in the Center Loop corridor. Jiménez turned the electron pistol onto its side and held it flat in her palm. She gasped—the bastard Grey had the weapon's intensity dialed to nearly full power! A single blast would instantly kill anyone caught in its line of fire. An errant shot could rip a hole clear through to an outer bulkhead and compromise an entire compartment. The weapon's ferocity was the reason security personnel carried Immobilizers.

Thumbing the weapon's intensity dial, Jiménez ratcheted it down to level five. While still lethal at that setting, she had no intention of shooting a fellow crew member.

Peeking her head out of the alcove again, she snatched a look at the corridor archway to her right, a thin, continuous girder extending a half meter into the passageway. It rose from the deck on one side, curved up and over, and dropped back down on the other. A Securcam sat on her side of the archway at its apex, all but unnoticeable to anyone who had never seen one up close. When Jiménez first came aboard the *Avenger,* she'd been temporarily assigned to damage control, the department then woefully short on personnel. One of her tasks had been to replace a set of malfunctioning Securcams inside the brig and along a stretch of corridor just outside.

Jiménez gripped the pistol and held it across her chest. She took a deep breath and in one fluid motion stepped out into the corridor, aimed the electron pistol at the Securcam, and squeezed the trigger. A streak of yellow lightning traced a quick, jagged path across the passageway, striking the archway at its center point. The resulting blast reverberated through the corridor as yellow sparks and beads of orange molten metal rained onto the deck. The shot left a small hole where the Securcam had been, with black scorch marks radiating out from the newly formed perforation.

If the call to apprehend Ensign Jiménez had not already gone out, it would happen soon. The damage control panel at the bridge ops station would show a problem on Deck C, and the ship would flag the disrupted video feed on the main security board. Although she quickly jumped into the passageway and destroyed the Securcam, she certainly hadn't been quick enough to avoid appearing in the video frames just before the feed ended. The ship would eventually identify her from those last few milliseconds of footage.

No matter—she wouldn't spend much time there anyway. She was headed to the main cargo hold two corridor segments away. Jiménez again turned the electron pistol on its side, laying it flat in her hand and thumbing the intensity dial to four. Her previous setting had been higher than necessary. The new power level should still take out the Securcams but hopefully without burning a hole through the structural archway.

The young ensign sprinted across the corridor and slid with her back against the bulkhead until she reached the damaged archway. Standing behind the girder, she peeked into the following section of corridor, taking in a one-eyed view of the next structural archway. She carefully aimed the pistol at the Securcam in its center. "Fire," she whispered, opting to use the gun's voice controls over squeezing the trigger and throwing off her aim. A burst of jagged lightning left the barrel with a softer yellow tint than before and hit the distant archway with a quieter blast and fewer sparks fountaining to the deck. The shot destroyed the Securcam, leaving black scorch marks in its place but the arch otherwise intact.

The ensign moved down the corridor. After destroying a third Securcam, she holstered her weapon and sprinted into the following corridor segment to a set of large double doors, the entrance to one of the ship's cargo holds. She stood before the doors, waiting for them to slide apart. If the directive had gone out to apprehend her, those doors would remain closed, her credentials certainly revoked.

A few nervous seconds later, the double doors opened and she quickly stepped inside. She blasted the three Securcams along the ceiling.

Her next target sat three meters away, along the same bulkhead as the doors: an EN-suit storage cabinet. Unlike other supplies and materials stowed in the cargo hold, all EN-suits remained within easy reach in case of emergency. Jiménez rushed to the cabinet and pulled open its door, finding four racks laden with stacks of folded suits and a fifth top rack of helmet rings. EN-suits provided protection from hostile planetary environments and the harshness of outer space, but they worked equally well inside a ship. With the addition of several extra food concentrate belts, an EN-suit would support many months of survival within the cargo bay.

Goosebumps sprouted across Ensign Jiménez's body as she quickly stripped naked in the chilly air of the cargo hold. She removed an EN-suit and reached her arms and legs in before zipping it snug around her neck. She grabbed a helmet ring and attached it to her suit. Lastly she retrieved her pistol from where she set it on the deck and tucked it in the EN-suit's holster.

Outfitted in her EN-suit, Jiménez faced the stacks of cargo containers piled high to the deck six meters above, separated by narrow aisles. A partially empty container would serve as a perfect spot to hide: rearranging its contents to create the illusion of a completely filled container would leave a habitable void. Finding a fugitive in the cargo hold would require pulling each container from its storage location, depositing it on a clear section of the deck, removing enough of its contents to ensure it contained no hiding space, repacking, and restocking it. That process would take a very long time to complete across all the cargo in the room. When the security detail arrived, they would be overwhelmed at the thought. They might even consider sealing off the cargo hold instead.

After a final look across the cargo hold, Jiménez returned to the room's large doors and exited into the corridor. She sprinted back the way she came, stopping half a meter from the rungway she used to reach Deck C. She placed her palms flat against the bulkhead at chest height and pressed as hard as she could. A narrow one-meter section of the bulkhead sprang out into the corridor, hinged on one side like a door. Jiménez pulled the panel open fully and stared into the dark space. Looking left and right down the corridor a final time, she spun sideways and slipped through the black gap, ducking her head below the low rim. She reached back into the corridor, grabbed the handle affixed to the inside of the hinged panel, and pulled. The door swung closed, returning flush with the bulkhead.

Jiménez paused, engulfed in complete blackness. She stood within the lightless interstitial space, a set of interconnected gangways and rungways that ran between the ship's bulkheads. Crawling along the network, a maintenance engineer could access almost any part of the ship.

If they realized where she'd disappeared to, it wouldn't take long for them to apprehend her. With the corridor Securcams destroyed, they'd have a harder time discovering she'd backtracked and entered the maintenance space. Hopefully the security detail assigned to find her would read the path of damaged Securcams as a panicked young ensign's attempt to prevent anyone from seeing her enter the cargo hold. The discarded uniform and missing EN-suit combined with the lack of any surveillance footage showing she left the area would suggest she was still holed up there. With any luck they would waste time searching the cargo hold while she ... what? Was she really headed for Commander Stephens's cabin? The whole thing was madness, but it seemed her only hope. The day before—it felt like a week in the past—the commander had flagged her down before leaving for the planet.

"While I expect everything to run smoothly on the ship when I'm gone," Stephens said, "I always like to put together a small contingency plan in case things go south. I have something special in my personal locker that you'll find useful in a bad situation."

Jiménez's brow crinkled. "Define 'bad situation,'" she said.

"If it happens, you'll know it," said Stephens. "I'm going to give you my locker passcode. If you get in a jam, get to my cabin."

"Why are you entrusting this to me?" asked Jiménez. "Why not Mills, or any of the more senior officers aboard the ship?"

"Just a feeling I have about you," said Stephens. "I guess of all the people on the ship, I feel like I can trust that you won't open my personal locker unless a dire enough situation arises, and that you have the right temperament and judgement to use what's inside." Confusion lingered on her face. "Don't worry about it," he said. "You'll all take a few orbits up here while we tend to our business on the planet. We'll be back in no time, and hopefully no one on the ship will have died from boredom while we're gone."

At the time Jiménez had smiled at his comment. Standing in the dark interstitial space, she had no idea how things were going on the planet, but they had certainly gone south on the *Avenger*. She activated the light on her comm. Bare, cold tiluminum panels stretched in all directions as far as she could see, interrupted by narrow gangways and beams of the ship's superstructure.

Jiménez rotated her body in the narrow space to face the access panel she had just closed. Metal rungs extended from the bulkhead to her right, forming a maintenance ladder that rose into the darkness above her. She'd have to climb two decks to reach Commander Stephens's quarters.

She ascended the ladder, a slow and tedious operation. The rungs were extremely shallow, extending not ten centimeters from the bulkhead to minimize their intrusion into the narrow interstitial space. She could barely keep on the ladder, her feet slipping off multiple times. She wished for a set of boots like the maintenance engineers'—rounded clips at the toes grabbed the rungs to secure their footing as they climbed. She eventually turned her feet sideways to keep as much of each boot on the rungs as possible.

After ten minutes of careful climbing, the ensign reached Deck A. She stepped from the ladder to the adjacent gangway that followed the bulkhead and rested before tackling the next portion of her journey. During her climb, she had mentally overlaid Deck A onto Deck C and estimated the distance and direction to reach Commander Stephens's quarters. Luckily, her destination was relatively close. If she could have walked inside the ship from her current location, she would arrive there in seconds. Unfortunately the gangways within the interstitial space didn't always follow the paths of the corridors.

Shouts came through the bulkhead.

Ensign Jiménez froze. Had they found her already? The thin tiluminum panels blocked most sounds, but loud ones carried through. Jiménez strained for more words but heard none. She remained motionless for another minute without further signs of commotion. Whatever it was, it had nothing to do with her.

She headed right down the gangway, following the bulkhead towards the ship's aft. If she were inside the ship, the corridor on the other side of the bulkhead would open to an intersection, and a left turn would take her to Commander Stephens's quarters, the second door on the right. But when she reached the point where the intersection should be, she encountered a crosswise tiluminum panel.

Confused, she pictured the Deck A floor plan in her head. She retraced her steps within the superstructure—the intersecting corridor should be straight ahead. And it was! The tiluminum panel directly in her path was the interior side of the intersecting corridor. She needed to be on the opposite side of both bulkheads, kitty-corner to her current location, to get to Commander Stephens's quarters. Traveling in the interstitial space was going to be more complicated than she figured.

Jiménez thought for a moment. She walked back along the gangway, counting her steps until she reached a nearby maintenance ladder. She climbed down to Deck B and walked aft on the gangway, again counting her steps. She'd hit the tiluminum panel on Deck A twelve paces from the ladder, but on Deck B she instead encountered intersecting gangways. Each deck had roughly the same layout, but in that case at least they differed. Jiménez turned left at the intersection and walked, soon coming across another maintenance ladder.

After climbing the ladder back up to Deck A, she proceeded down the gangway, following it as it jogged right and then left to run between two narrowly spaced bulkheads, the backsides of two rows of crew quarters. Each cabin on the *Avenger* had a maintenance door low to the deck and measuring not quite a meter on a side—she'd learned about those doors through another damage control assignment. Jiménez found the maintenance door for the first cabin on her left, a rectangle with a wire grill in its center. Proceeding forward, she found a second door. Commander Stephens's quarters lay on the other side

How to open the maintenance door? The four screws that secured it in place weren't accessible from her side—she had no tools to remove them anyway. The electron pistol wasn't a great option in such a tight space, even at low intensity. Jiménez settled on her only other option. She positioned herself directly in front of the maintenance door. With her hands raised above her head and pressed flat against the bulkhead, she kicked the panel several times until it gave, clattering onto the deck inside. Jiménez dropped to all fours and wiggled through the opening.

Ensign Jiménez stood in Commander Stephens's quarters, the room dark but for the light of her comm. The space was small and messy, with clothes hanging on chairs and splayed on the floor. The commander's desk snuggled in a corner, the top covered with e-sheets. The open door to his personal head revealed a towel lazing on the deck.

The ensign found the cabin's closet along the bulkhead she'd just climbed through. She opened its door and pushed aside Stephens's dress uniform and a civilian suit, revealing his personal storage locker bolted to the deck. What had the commander stowed inside for an emergency—a special weapon? Codes to take control of the ship? A device that would let her communicate directly with him?

Ensign Jiménez sat on the deck and tapped the locker's alphanumbolic keypad. The panel came alive with soft amber light that splashed across her face. The keypad contained over a hundred keys, consisting of the normal English alphabet, the Arabic numerals, some punctuation, and the rest pictographic symbols. She'd asked Stephens why he used a passcode instead of a biometric lock. He replied, "What, so they lop off my fingers or pull out an eyeball to get into my locker?"

The passcode—what was the passcode? Stephens forced her to memorize it, but in the moment, she drew a blank!

Too much nerves and stress. Jiménez took a breath, forced herself to relax. The code came rushing back. The commander had chosen a sequence composed mostly of pictographic keys that told a story:

A [MAN] took a [3][5] minute [WALK] one [NIGHT] on the [MOON]. When the [SUN] came up he said oh [SHIRT], I forgot my [HAT]. Now my [HEAD]'s on [FIRE][!]

The door sprang open with the final keystroke. Jiménez pulled the door further. The sight inside confused her, the space empty except for an e-sheet at the bottom. She grabbed the sheet and read:

Dear Ensign Jiménez,

If you're reading this note, you have apparently found yourself in a dire situation, one serious enough to drive you to break into my quarters to gain access to the contents of this locker.

I hope it won't disappoint you too much to learn that I don't have a special solution to help you overcome your problem. How could I? If I'd foreseen your predicament, I might never have left the ship. But the truth is you already have everything you need to solve it. You don't need any special advantage from me to make things right. Think for a moment about the resourcefulness it took to get this far. I'm certain no one let you in here, because no one would believe there's a magical solution to your dilemma that the commander told you, and only you, about. You figured out how to enter this room anyway, and to do so without being detected. And that's on top of whatever else may be happening on the ship. You accomplished all that on your own, with no special assistance from me, relying purely on your own ingenuity.

The peril you face may be a hundred times greater than the trouble it took to break in here, but at its heart, whatever it is, it's the same challenge. Something to be met head-on and conquered, not shied away from. You and I are cut from the same cloth. We don't cry in our beer—we storm the bar.

If the ship's in danger, if we're in danger, you may be the only one who can make things right. If so, no pressure, but we're all counting on you.

Sincerely,

Commander Paul Stephens

Ensign Jiménez released the e-sheet, letting it flutter to the deck. She pulled her knees to her chest and wrapped her arms around her legs as tightly as she could, squeezing herself into a ball. She lowered her head and sobbed.

28

Stephens ambled down the shallow hill at the base of the bluff that shadowed the *Adiona*, with Tentek trailing close behind.

The commander had spent another fifteen minutes atop the bluff studying the ship for activity before making the trek down. He cautiously worked his way around to the *Adiona's* starboard side. Though fairly certain no aughts remained, there could be traps to catch stragglers.

The body he'd seen from above still lay in the dirt. It was Byrne's, as suspected. Stephens checked the man's pulse. He was dead, his neck cold. He rolled Byrne onto his back, exposing a burn hole in the belly of the slain officer's EN-suit. A plasma rifle killed him, the blast searing his internal organs.

Stephens glanced at the *Adiona's* main door—they'd left it wide open. "Help me take him to Sickbay," he said.

Tentek cocked his head. "But why? Lieutenant Byrne is dead. His body is beyond repair."

"We can't just leave him out here to rot," said Stephens. "If we had time, we'd dig a grave but we need to get moving. We'll put him in a cadaver cabinet."

Tentek circled around to Byrne's feet. They lifted, the commander grabbing at the shoulders and the aught cupping his hands beneath the dead man's calves. Together they transported the body into the *Adiona*.

They arrived in Sickbay and placed Byrne on the deck. Stephens opened the cadaver cabinet and laid the door flat. The two hoisted Byrne's body and lowered it gently onto the door.

"Grab me a pair of surgical scissors," said Stephens.

Tentek walked across the room and dug through several cabinets until he found one. When he returned, Stephens had unzipped Byrne's EN-suit down the front and bared his shoulders. "You are undressing him?" he asked.

"Yes," said Stephens, taking the scissors from Tentek. "His EN-suit will block the cabinet's stasis field." Stephens cut open the sleeves and removed them from Byrne's arms. He moved on to the legs, snipping his way around the shins. He tugged the freed boots from the lieutenant's feet.

Tentek frowned at the naked body. "Why is his penis so long?" he asked.

Stephens inspected Byrne. "It's about the right length," he said with a smirk.

"Twenty-one point five four centimeters?" asked Tentek.

Stephens huffed as he rolled Byrne onto his side and removed the suit from beneath the body. He tossed the shredded remnants to the deck. "Do *you* have a penis, Tin Man?" he asked with a hint of sarcasm.

"My name is Tentek, and yes, I do have a penis."

"You do?" said Stephens, surprised. "What do you … *do* with it?"

"It is not used for excretion or reproduction, if that is what you are wondering. Its sole purpose is to externally signify my gender. Gender is an integral trait of all sentient beings."

"I see," said Stephens. "Well, how long is yours?"

"An efficient two centimeters," said Tentek.

Stephens stifled a laugh. "Is that true for all aughts?" he asked.

"All male aughts, yes," said Tentek.

"If you don't mind me asking, what's its length fully extended?"

"That is its length at full extension," said Tentek.

Stephens broke out laughing.

Tentek looked on, confused. "My understanding of human genitalia is the male penis size is more about peacocking than serving any actual anatomical function."

Stephens pushed Byrne into the cabinet and closed the door. "If that's true, at two centimeters you have absolutely no plumage to speak of." Stephens laughed again. "C'mon." He motioned Tentek to follow as he left Sickbay. The aught stared after the commander before shuffling along behind him.

Stephens proceeded down the corridor to the crew mess. Inside, a pile of containers, boxes, and bags lay spread across the deck, supplies Byrne and Dr. Marsden had rummaged from belowdecks the night before. He nudged sections of the pile with his boot.

"What are you looking for?" asked Tentek.

Commander Stephens ignored the aught, continuing to probe the pile. "Here we go," he said, picking up a silver can the shape of a rectangular tea tin.

"What is it?" asked Tentek. "Food?"

"It's an APS," said Stephens, pointing to the large letters on top of the can. "An Automated Portable Shelter, otherwise known as a tent-in-a-can." He handed the can to Tentek. "Here, hold this."

Tentek took the can from Stephens. He cocked his head. "You expect we will need this to pursue the landing party?"

"It's more insurance than anything else," said Stephens. "We should catch up to them pretty quickly given they don't have a big head start on us. But if for some reason we need to camp, I want to be prepared." The commander continued fishing through the pile, plucking out a canvas knapsack and a camping mat folded into its compact travel configuration. Stephens unzipped the knapsack's main compartment and dropped the mat inside. He grabbed the APS from Tentek and placed it in the sack, then crouched and added nine EN-suit food concentrate packs from the supplies.

Stephens exited the mess hall and headed down the ship's main corridor until he arrived at a tall locker. "Now for some weapons," he said as he pulled open the doors. The cabinet contained three plasma rifles, including one customized with an intelligent sight; seven electron pistols; and thirteen ammunition power packs. He crammed the power packs into the knapsack's remaining empty space.

Tentek arrived from the mess hall just as Stephens struggled to zip the knapsack shut. "Here, put this on," said Stephens, thrusting the sack at the aught.

Tentek took the sack and strapped it to his back while Stephens slung the custom plasma rifle over his shoulder. The commander slipped one of the electron pistols into the holster on his suit. He tucked two more pistols into the cinch belt at his waist. The aught cocked his head. "It looks like you are getting ready for war," he said.

"I have no idea what your buddies will have waiting for us." Stephens studied the remaining pistols. Bringing them along as backup would be ideal, but there was no place to store them. He'd have to make do with the weapons he'd gathered. "Unfortunately, I doubt this will be enough to take them all out. Not with a single pair of hands, anyway."

"Do I get a weapon?" asked Tentek.

Stephens eyed the aught warily. "If we get in a jam, maybe I'll give you something." It would have to be quite a jam. The last thing he needed was Tentek carrying a pistol or, God forbid, a rifle and blasting his brains out the moment he let his guard down.

Tentek blinked at Stephens and cocked his head.

"I never know what you're thinking when you look at me like that," said Stephens, irritated. "I can't tell if you're confused, waiting for me to talk, or about to ask a question."

"I am sorry to frustrate you, Commander Stephens," said Tentek. "Generally when I tilt my head, it means I am curious."

"What are you curious about?" asked Stephens.

"You said you have no idea what the other aughts have waiting for us. I am curious what your plan might be."

"The plan is to rescue the landing party and stop your friends from leaving the planet with Planck Matter," said Stephens.

Tentek cocked his head. "Those seem more like objectives," he said. "I am curious what your plan is for achieving those objectives."

"I don't have a plan, OK?" barked Stephens. "I have no idea what we're up against. I don't know how many aughts are on the planet, how heavily fortified their base of operations is, how far along they might be in mining Planck Matter. All we can do right now is catch up to the landing party, assess the situation, and free them. Afterwards, assuming we're still alive, we'll figure out how to deal with whatever aughts are left." Stephens pulled the electron pistol from its holster, ratcheted up the power level, and reholstered it. "Of course, everything I just said hinges on us following their tracks. It shouldn't be a problem on soft dirt, a large party moving along like that, but on harder ground it'll be a challenge. I'm not exactly a ranger."

"I can track their movements," said Tentek.

"You can?"

"Yes," said Tentek. "My image processors can discern the faintest compressive traces left by their boots on any terrain, even rock."

The robot's claim was certainly the best news all morning, but could he really trust Tentek? The machine could lead him off in the wrong direction or walk him into a trap. On the other hand, Stephens had never tracked anyone. He overstated the ease of doing so on soft ground to convince himself the problem was tractable. His hopes of catching up to the landing party apparently depended on him trusting the aught. "I guess we're relying on you, then," he said, shifting the plasma rifle on his shoulder.

Tentek blinked at Stephens, his eyelids click-clacking in the starship's quiet corridor.

"Are you ready?" asked Stephens.

"I am, Commander."

"Please lead the way," said Stephens.

Stephens and Tentek proceeded along the *Adiona's* main corridor and down to the entry ramp. They exited into the bright, red morning light.

29

Jiménez lifted her head from her knees and wiped her face clear of tears. How long had she been crying, seated there on the deck? Too long, for sure —sobbing wasn't going to fix anything. She took a deep breath and forced it out with a loud exhale.

She'd counted on the contents of Stephens's locker to help her set things right. But what did setting things right even mean? Stopping Lynch from taking the ship out of orbit and ultimately returning the conn to Mills. But how to do either of those things? She shook her head. She needed some time to think, and perhaps a little inspiration.

Her immediate problem was Lieutenant Hall, the ship's third engineer, who would come out of sedation soon. Lynch would force her to agree to a course change and set the ship sailing for home. Even if she figured out how to end Lynch's command, if the *Avenger* left Infernum, they may never find their way back to it, stranding the captain and everyone else on the planet. If she could stop Lynch from using Hall, even delay him a bit, she'd at least have more time to formulate a plan.

She'd first have to get to Sickbay. And then what? She wouldn't be able to move Lieutenant Hall or prevent Lynch and his goons from getting their hands on her. She'd have to figure something out once she arrived.

Jiménez stood and walked to the maintenance opening. She glared at the hopelessly bent door cover she'd kicked in. If a security team saw the open maintenance door, they'd know how she was moving through the ship, bringing them a step closer to apprehending her.

Taking a quick inventory of the room, Jiménez spotted a small metal cabinet Stephens used as an end table. The ensign picked up the door cover and slid it under the commander's bunk, then dragged the cabinet across the room, stopping a half meter from the maintenance door. She crouched on all fours and twisted herself behind the cabinet and into the access hatch, contorting her body to fit through. Once inside the ship's interstitial space, she reached back into the room, fumbling for the cabinet's underside. She wished she'd moved it closer to the opening, though she needed the extra space to get her body behind it. Her fingertips just snagged the lip along the cabinet's back bottom. She pulled awkwardly, her left hand and shoulder down almost to the deck. She managed to drag the cabinet the rest of the way to sit in front of the opening.

Jiménez rose to her feet inside the narrow gap between the bulkheads and backtracked to the maintenance ladder she had just climbed to reach Deck A. The entrance to Sickbay sat off the Center Loop corridor, forward of the bridge on the starboard side of the Centerline. If she climbed back down to Deck B, the nearby maintenance door would dump her into the Center Loop, and a quick sprint would get her to the ship's medical center. Unfortunately, she couldn't risk reentering the corridors, as she had no idea who might be roaming the passageways. She needed to move within the *Avenger's* interstitial space far enough to clear the Centerline corridor before taking a maintenance ladder back down to Deck B.

The ensign snaked along a bulkhead towards what she believed to be the center of the ship. She eventually arrived at a gangway that cut crosswise over a large tiluminum tube. The tube, illuminated by her comm light, disappeared into the far-off darkness in one direction. In the other it ran two meters before intersecting a broad, circular structure. She had found the Centerline where it met the forward section of the Center Loop.

Jiménez crossed the gangway, a wide, grated platform that rang under her boots. Once on the other side, she continued forward until she reached a maintenance ladder. After descending to Deck B, Jiménez headed back to port, or at least the direction she believed was port, rounding several corners until she arrived at a long bulkhead. The ensign sighed and hung her head— she was lost. She had done her best to keep her mental model of the ship's layout in sync with her movements, but at that point she was unsure of her location. She would have to backtrack to regain her bearings, perhaps clear to the gangway.

Before heading back, Ensign Jiménez glanced upward. Near the top of the bulkhead "SICKBAY B-84A" appeared in stenciled white paint, an assembly guide left over from the ship's original construction. Relieved, she followed the bulkhead around until she reached a string of three maintenance doors, each one presumably leading to a different room within the medical center. Lieutenant Hall would be resting in one of those rooms, and almost certainly not alone. Jiménez wasn't sure what the other two could be. She had only visited Sickbay twice in her time on the *Avenger* and hadn't paid much attention to its layout.

Which door to choose? She selected the middle one—important spaces likely sat at either end of the department. She said a quiet prayer and kicked the cover three times until it flew into the room. No light came through the rectangular hole in the bulkhead, a good sign the room, whatever its purpose, had no occupant.

Crouching, Jiménez pulled her way through the opening. Once inside, she quickly jumped to her feet and activated the light on her comm to minimal flood. She had entered a medical supply storage room, the stock sitting on metallic shelves running in parallel rows. She stood at the back of the middle aisle, the room's door visible in the shadows at the other end.

Beep beep, beep beep, beep.

The chimes, muffled but still audible, came at her through the main door. Access to the room was likely restricted by keypad to a select few medical personnel. Her heart racing, Jiménez quickly extinguished her comm light and in the darkness scrambled around behind the shelving unit to her right.

The room filled first with the whoosh of the door swinging open, followed by bright light from an overhead lamp, and finally the soft sound of footsteps. Jiménez crouched, attempting a glimpse of the person who occupied the room with her.

The person paused not far from the room's entrance as the door swung shut. Seconds later they proceeded down the aisle towards her, moving slowly, cautiously. Whoever it was had heard Ensign Jiménez's kicks at the maintenance door and had come to investigate.

The maintenance door! Jiménez had scrambled so quickly to hide she hadn't time to conceal the door. She'd caught sight of it when she activated her comm light, the panel lying on the deck with a large dent thrusting up through the middle.

The footsteps stopped for a moment before continuing the rest of the way to the back of the room. Jiménez still couldn't see the figure. She moved around to the other side of the shelving unit that separated her from the investigator. A gap through the boxes of supplies offered her a glimpse of the figure. He crouched in front of the open maintenance hatch, aiming a light into the space beyond.

The man turned his head. He caught her eyes through the gap in the boxes. "Jiménez!"

"Shh!" she said, putting her finger to her lips. It was Dr. Jameson. He'd treated her during her first ever visit to Sickbay to heal a gash she acquired in the Rec Room. They later became friends on the ship's handball circuit. "Come here," she said, whispering him over.

Jameson arrived at her section of shelving. "You know the entire ship is looking for you, right?" he asked in a raspy whisper.

"I suspected they would be at some point." Jiménez became momentarily transfixed by Jameson's square jaw, too perfectly chiseled. "Who else is with you in Sickbay?" she asked.

"Just Nurse Mead," said Jameson. "Dr. Sadler's in charge of medical while Marsden's on the planet, but they called him to the bridge a few minutes ago. So it's only me and Mead here now."

Jiménez started to ask another question, but Jameson cut her off. "Hey, you've got to turn yourself in," he whispered.

"I can't," said Jiménez. "Lynch escaped from the brig and took over the ship."

"Lynch is free?" asked Jameson, surprised.

"He is," said Jiménez. "He wants to take the *Avenger* out of orbit, but the ship won't let him without my approval." Jameson responded with a confused look. He probably wondered why anyone would need an ensign's approval to change course. "That's a long story," she said. "Anyway, I refused, and he ordered me thrown in the brig. I managed to escape."

"Where's he trying to take the ship?"

"He wants to fly back to Earth," said Jiménez. "He wants to leave the captain and Commander Stephens and the rest stranded on Infernum and head back. But if we try, we'll become hopelessly lost."

"This isn't a great place to hide," said Jameson, squinting at the ensign. "We come in here all the time for supplies. Someone else is bound to see you."

"I didn't come here to hide," said Jiménez. "I came to talk to you. Or at least I hoped you might be on duty." She hesitated. "I need a favor."

Jameson recoiled slightly. "What kind of favor?" he asked.

"Hall out there," she said, nodding at the door, "she's been sedated ever since we entered D-space. I heard she'll be coming to shortly."

"That's right," said Jameson. "Every other day we give her a heavy dose of Nausox and enough sedative to fell a horse. She's basically been asleep for the past week. She's due for her next course, but Sadler said the captain wants to talk to her before that." Jameson's eyes went wide. "I guess that's Lynch who wants to talk to her."

"Yeah," said Jiménez. "Hall's ahead of me in the engineering chain of command. She can OK the course change herself. Lynch said he'll force her to agree by denying her more medicine."

Jameson looked back at the door, then at Jiménez. "What is it exactly you want me to do?" he asked.

"Isaac," said Jiménez, placing her hands on his shoulders, "I need you to give Hall another round of meds."

"I can't do that," Jameson said in an urgent whisper.

"You have to," said Jiménez. "She needs to stay unconscious for as long as possible so Lynch can't use her to change course."

"But I'm not the supervising physician," said Jameson. "I can't just make medical decisions for Hall. Only Dr. Sadler can."

"I understand you wanting to follow normal procedure," said Jiménez, "believe me I do, but these are not normal times."

Jameson thought for a moment. "Let me confirm with Sadler that Lynch wants to keep Hall off the meds," he said.

Jiménez dropped her hands from Jameson's shoulders and shook her head. "What, you gonna call up to the bridge and ask him?" said the ensign.

"I can ask once he returns," said Jameson.

"By the time he returns, it'll be too late," said Jiménez. "He may not agree to dosing Hall again, and he may not let you near her before she wakes."

Jameson's gaze sank to the floor.

"Look," said Jiménez, "my goal was to buy a little time to figure out my next move. I'm not expecting you to keep dosing her. I just need you to give her one more round. Tell them … tell them you thought it was time for her next dose. Worst case for Lynch is he has to wait another two days to get his hands on Hall."

Jameson sighed at Jiménez. "When they catch you, we never talked," he said.

"Agreed," she said. "Thank you." She stood tall on her toes, kissed his cheek, and walked back to the open maintenance door.

"Hey," said Jameson, "where're you headed next?"

"Honestly, I don't know," said Jiménez, crouching with her hands just above the hole in the bulkhead. "And it's probably better you don't know either, in case they ask you anything."

Jameson nodded. "Jiménez, good luck. You have bigger balls than I do."

Jiménez smiled, crawled through the small opening, and disappeared into the bowels of the ship.

30

"Do you still see their tracks, Tin Man?"

Stephens surveyed the wide, barren plain ahead. For the past four hours, the telltale signs of six people and four aughts moving over the land had been easy to spot: trampled grasses, broken twigs, boot prints in steaming mud. The group headed roughly northeast, bearing in the assumed direction of the Hex Men mine. According to Tentek, they traveled with two aughts in front, a string of humans in the middle, and two aughts at the rear. The land before them offered no signs of the party. It was the perfect time for Tentek to claim he lost sight of them as well, to finally make his move, to spring his trap.

"My name is Tentek, and yes, I see their tracks," he said, scanning the terrain ahead of them. "Although there is no dust for footprints, I can still tell where they walked. Even on this hard compacted dirt, their boots compressed the surface by a microscopic amount. This compression can linger for days." Tentek's eyes followed the invisible trail to the edge of the plain, a rise of volcanic rock 130 meters in the distance. "They headed through there," he said, pointing at a cleft in the black rocks, "where the lava flow was the lowest."

Stephens drank from his suit's water supply. Their pause to reacquire the trail had been a welcome break in their hurried pursuit, but he was eager to catch up to the landing party. "OK, let's keep going."

"I need a moment," said Tentek. The robot hunched over with his hands on his knees, his face aimed at the ground.

Was the aught catching his breath? Stephens eyed him, suspicious. "You're a mechanical person, right?"

"I am not a person, mechanical or otherwise," said Tentek, "I am an aught from The Collective. However, you are correct that this *body* is mechanical."

Stephens didn't fully grasp the distinction. "If your body's mechanical, why do you need to catch your breath?"

Tentek swiveled his head ninety degrees. He looked straight at Stephens. "Of course I do not need to catch my breath, like an *animal*," he said, sneering the last word. "As I explained aboard the *Avenger*, my lack of connection to the Network has disoriented my systems." He returned his attention to the ground. "This posture is for recalibration." Tentek remained hunched over for several more seconds. He stood erect and wobbled slightly. The aught thrust his arms out to his sides, steadying himself. Pain wracked his face, the first real expression Stephens had witnessed from the aught.

"Seems like the symptoms are getting worse," said Stephens.

"They are," said Tentek. His face returned to its everyday, emotionless expression.

"Do you think you can make it to the Hex Men mine?" asked Stephens.

"I prefer not to compute that probability," said Tentek, "but I am ready to resume walking." He started forward, taking a large lead over Stephens.

The commander moved quickly, catching up to Tentek. "You said you'll eventually shut down from lack of connection to the Network."

Tentek didn't respond immediately. "Yes," he whispered.

"How much longer do you have?"

"It is really impossible to tell," said Tentek.

Stephens hesitated. "What should I do if you shut down?"

"Just leave me where I drop and continue on," said Tentek. His eyes remained locked forward while he spoke.

Stephens stopped. "Are you serious?"

Tentek halted and turned, facing the commander. "Yes, I am serious. If I can no longer move, if I lose consciousness because I cannot connect to the Network, just leave me and continue on."

Stephens shook his head. "I won't do that."

"If you want to maximize your probability of survival, that is exactly what you *must* do," said Tentek. "You will not be able to revive me, and you cannot drag my inert body across the planet with you."

"What if I remove your head?" asked Stephens. "I think I could manage to carry it around."

The aught gave the commander a crooked, awkward half-smile. "An at once macabre and touching thought," he said, the red sun twinkling from his nickel irises. "You do not have the proper tools. And in any case, my consciousness does not reside only in my head. It is distributed throughout my body, just like in humans." Stephens was about to suggest another option when Tentek cut him off. "We should keep moving, Commander." The robot turned and resumed walking.

Stephens stared after Tentek. Would The Collective really have sent one of their own to spy on the humans only to have it cease functioning for lack of a Network connection? Perhaps Tentek really was intent on helping the humans. Or maybe his claim of distress was a lie. The commander set off after the aught, jogging across the plain.

The two reached the low point in the ridge of lava rock. Tentek climbed up first into the cleft. He turned and offered his hand to Stephens. The commander hesitated but eventually grasped it. Tentek pulled, whisking Stephens off his feet and onto the ridge.

"Ow," said Stephens. The force of Tentek's pull had yanked at the sinews in his shoulder. The commander windmilled his arm a few times, exercising the aching joint. "Just how strong are you?" he asked. "I didn't imagine such a scrawny body having that much power."

"An aught body is generally two to three times stronger than a human's," said Tentek. "Our muscles, though lean, are very efficient."

Stephens massaged his shoulder through his EN-suit. "So you're saying I shouldn't challenge you at arm wrestling."

"You should not challenge me at anything," said Tentek. The aught pivoted and charged off across the lava rocks, moving with catlike hops between outcroppings.

The commander chased after Tentek at a slower pace, his human movements more protracted and clumsy. Stephens was still adjusting to Infernum's gravity, having difficulty judging the force required to successfully leap between the rock piles.

The lava flow eventually settled down from a mishmash of boulders and large rocks to less rugged terrain, allowing Stephens to catch up to the aught. "What I was asking back there about you passing out," he said, "if I do have to leave you, I will come back for you."

"If you do have to leave me, you will likely have more pressing things to worry about than a non-functional aught," said Tentek. He winced, then quickly returned to his blank expression. "Do you mind, Commander, if we switch to a less morbid topic?"

"OK," said Stephens. He'd amassed a slew of questions about aughts and The Collective since Tentek had arrived on the *Avenger*. "How about your name?"

"What do you mean?"

"I mean what kind of name is Tentek? It's not recognizably human, or from any alien race I'm familiar with. Is 'tek' short for 'technology?'"

"It is not," said Tentek. "Each of us has a unique, 1,024-bit identifier, but rather than use our full names all the time, we often refer to each other by the first few hex digits of that identifier when it is convenient—that is, when there is no other aught nearby with the same prefix. 'Tentek' is the name of the hexadecimal number 'A0,' which is the first eight bits of my identifier. Certainly, around humans it is a much more convenient moniker than my full name."

"What's your full name?" asked Stephens.

Tentek's lips formed a narrow circle, exposing his teeth. He blasted the commander with the loud, shrill sound of computer static.

Stephens raced to cover his ears, only succeeding in planting his palms against the sides of his force field helmet. "What was that?" he asked once the noise stopped, still grimacing.

"That was my name," said Tentek. "I told you, it is a 1,024-bit identifier. What you heard was that binary sequence of ones and zeros rendered as sound."

"Is that how you call to each other, 'Hey screeeeeeech'?" asked Stephens, bugging his eyes out as he wiggled his head tightly back and forth.

Tentek gave Stephens an expressionless stare. "If we are being honest with each other, Commander, I find your name quite ridiculous, Paaaawuuul Stehfuunnnzzz," said the aught, vibrating the tip of his tongue to sound the final buzzing syllable. "And oh, by the way, it is not even unique! How many Paul Stephens are there?"

"That's because we humans aren't mass produced on an assembly line," said Stephens.

"Neither are we," said Tentek. "In fact, most of us do not have bodies."

"Don't have bodies?" said Stephens. "How's that?"

"This automaton body is just a shell," said Tentek, extending his arms as if inviting Stephens to inspect them. "Our consciousness is separate, the ghost in the machine, if you will. The main difference between me, for example, and one of the aughts from Plana Petram is those aughts do not have a consciousness. They are pure machine and clever programming."

"I've always wondered what makes Collective aughts different," said Stephens.

"We aughts from The Collective are sentient beings," said Tentek. "The Collective itself is a group of consciousnesses hosted in many different mainframes on our home world. When we need to operate in the physical world, we load ourselves, our consciousness, into an aught body custom designed for the task."

Stephens had trouble imagining what it would be like to exist without a body. "Which do you prefer?" he asked. Tentek cocked his head. "I mean do you prefer being in a body, or being inside the mainframe?"

"The mainframe," said Tentek. "There is no question. Physical bodies are slow and limited. Inside Collective mainframes, everything happens instantly, or nearly so."

The two reached the edge of the lava flow, entering a meadow of tall yellow grasses. The landing party's visible trail resumed, a clear path of trampled blades heading to the northeast.

The two started across the meadow, walking side by side. After a minute, Tentek looked over at Stephens. "Back there, Commander, what you said about aughts being produced on an assembly line, some of us would take offense at such a statement."

"Did I offend you, Tin Man?" asked Stephens.

"My name is Tentek, and no, you did not offend me. I have conditioned myself not to take offense at many of the things you say. However, those words do speak to what I sense to be a general hostility you have towards aughts. I am wondering what is the basis of that hostility."

Stephens thought for a moment. "If I had to list one thing I'm good at, it's reading people. I'm very good at sizing them up, judging if they're lying or telling the truth, evaluating their resolve, reading between the lines. All of that helps me predict their future actions. It keeps me from being caught off guard by some person's decision or action that affects me. The problem with you aughts is you totally throw me off. I don't know if it's because deep down you don't really think like humans, but I can't predict what you'll do next." Stephens glanced up, blinking at the red hypergiant sun through the transparent force field shell of his helmet. "Maybe I shouldn't be telling you this."

"That is very interesting," said Tentek. "We aughts spend a lot of our cycles computing the near-complete set of possible future outcomes and evaluating the likelihood of each, what we refer to as 'probabilities.' I had no idea humans also operate in this fashion."

"Not all of us do," said Stephens, "at least not to the same degree as me. Or as accurately as you. I can't actually think of anyone else who makes the same kind of effort to predict what other people will do."

"What is the reason for your anomalous behavior?" asked Tentek. "Are you an evolved form of human?"

Stephens let out a huge laugh that caused Tentek to jump in surprise. "I am definitely not humanity evolved," said Stephens, still chuckling. "At least I hope I'm not, for humanity's sake."

"Then what is the reason for your observational habits?" asked Tentek.

"You know, I've never wondered why I work so hard to anticipate human behavior," said Stephens. He considered the question. "I think it's from my childhood. I grew up in a … challenging household, I guess I'll say. My mother was abusive, and my dad was complicit in the abuse. Basically, there were no adults to save us. The only way to survive in my house was to understand how people work, how they think, and to correctly predict what they would do in any given situation."

"Predicting their behavior enabled you to remove yourself from dangerous situations?"

"Not necessarily," said Stephens. "I mean sometimes, but it wasn't a given I could always run and hide somewhere."

Tentek cocked his head. "If you could predict how others would react but you could not use that information to remove yourself physically from a dangerous situation, then of what value was the prediction?"

"What value was it?" Stephens grew heated. "How about in the moment when Mother's hitting the bottle after a hard day at work and she's 'disappointed' because the flowers on her birthday card are the wrong shade of red, predicting that Dad would say I picked the card he actually chose gave me a precious few seconds to come up with the explanation that I was colorblind."

"You are colorblind, Commander Stephens?"

"No, I'm not," huffed Stephens. "It's just what I said to get out of that jam."

Tentek shook his head. "It no longer surprises me how frequently humans lie," he said, "but I was not expecting it to occur at such an early age."

"Did I lie? Sure, I did," said Stephens. "I lied to survive. I lied to avoid being locked in my room for a day. You don't understand what it's like being a child, raised by fallible, broken human parents. For the record, I don't like lying to others and especially not to myself. But I'll give the Commander Stephens from thirty years ago a pass 'cause if I hadn't lied to save myself back then, I might not be alive to have this conversation with you today." Stephens navigated a wide rut hidden in the tall grasses, hopping across it. "Anyway, all that's in the past. After I left home and spent years unwinding all that shit. I swore I'd never lie to save my skin, never again cower before someone just to stay alive. I don't care who they are. I'd rather die than let someone push me around. Living like that is not living at all. I'll spit in their eye before I bend my knee to them and give 'em a big grin as I do it." Stephens stopped and took a long draw of water from his suit. "Now it's my turn to switch topics. How far ahead do you think they are?"

Tentek scanned the path of trampled grasses receding into the distance. "Based on their tracks, they appear to be proceeding at an aggressive pace," he said. "From my estimate of when they left the *Adiona* and the time we have made, probabilities suggest they are still about two hours ahead of us."

"You're saying we haven't made up any ground on them."

"Correct, Commander."

"Do you think we'll catch them before nightfall?"

"We would have to increase our speed significantly," said Tentek. He cocked his head. "Even if we do, probabilities suggest it is unlikely we will catch up to them before the sun sets."

"Damn," muttered Stephens. "A skirmish in the dark will be much more difficult, especially if they're already camped for the night."

"Agreed," said Tentek. "If they are camped, they will have the advantage of sentries actively listening for sounds of anyone approaching. There is also the possibility we may not catch up to them today at all, depending on their pace and when the two of us decide to set up camp."

"I wasn't thinking we would camp," said Stephens. "I want to keep going until we find them."

Tentek cocked his head. "That is not practical, Commander," he said. "You and I will both need at least a little rest. It would be unfortunate to finally catch up but lack the energy and focus to engage them."

Stephens didn't want to imagine not finding them today. Ideally, they'd keep moving and make up time while the landing party slept, if necessary. Unfortunately, Tentek was right, and he wouldn't be able to continue on all night. Infernum's slightly extra gravity sapped his energy with each step. His body would eventually need rest. "Fine," he said. "If we haven't caught them by the time we're too tired to keep going, we'll make camp. But I don't want it to come to that. Let's pick up the pace."

Tentek nodded. The two continued on, accelerating through the field.

31

Commander Lynch surveyed all the plates, bowls, and ladles of food spread from one side of the table to the other and almost wept. Actual tears would be undignified for the captain of a starship. Emotions restrained, he solemnly withdrew the brown napkin from beneath his place setting, unfurled it with a fling while retaining a corner, and tucked it into the neckline of his uniform. The napkin draped down over his chest to the top curve of a belly that bobbed above the tabletop like the back of a whale floating at the water's surface.

Lynch grabbed his fork and knife and held them upright on the table, clutched in his pudgy fists. He maneuvered his utensils and hoisted several slabs of corned beef onto his plate, secured two half-potatoes, and scooped up green beans soaked in the juices. His hand flew forward in a blur, returning with a fistful of rolls. Commander Lynch, his plate suitably fortified, drew deep the swirling vapors rising from the mound of victuals before him. The mix of aromas immediately set his salivary glands to action. He exhaled in heartfelt satisfaction.

Spearing a corned beef slab with his fork, Lynch brought his knife around and excised a large portion. He plunged the meat into his mouth and withdrew his fork, his teeth restraining his catch. A dribble of gravy trickled over and down the curve of his fat chin.

"Wine, sir?" asked the captain's steward.

Lynch nodded, his mouth so stuffed with meat his tongue had little space to form words. He chomped at the corned beef as the steward poured a fruity red Beaujolais, ten-year vintage, into his crystal goblet. The commander's eyes followed the steward as he withdrew to the galley.

Commander Lynch had heard stories of the captain's mess but had never been on the short list for an invitation. Before his self-made promotion he'd resented such excess apportioned onto one man, but in his elevated position he saw the wisdom in providing the captain his own private dining room, galley, chef, and attendant.

His stomach rumbling an urgent request for more food, Lynch stuffed a portion of potato and another of green beans into his mouth and chewed. He swallowed the masticated lump and a large gulp of air. The bubble created an uncomfortable sensation in his belly. Lynch strained to expel the unwanted air from his digestive system, succeeding with a loud belch.

The door buzzed.

"Commin," said Lynch, the food in his jaws muffling his words.

The door slid aside, revealing Lieutenant Grey. The gaunt officer stepped into the room and was immediately accosted by two hands, one from either side of the door. Startled, he looked about. His friends Knox and Zhang had grabbed him as if apprehending a thief. The two men patted Grey down as he stood there, dumbfounded. They gave him the all clear. The lieutenant proceeded forward as the two men returned to the shadows at the front of the room.

Grey approached Lynch's table in a mix of awe and disgust, taking stock of all the food and drink set across its surface, the heaping plate, wine, the entire scene.

Lynch reached for the goblet of wine and gulped, washing down his mouthful of food as he examined Grey. The lieutenant's appearance was a catalog of don'ts: the stubble peppering his sunken cheeks, the disheveled hair hinting of grease, the uniform jacket wrinkled and cockeyed on his frame. His executive officer somehow thought it acceptable to appear before him in such a state. Once they handled their immediate problem of getting the ship on course for Earth, he would issue a directive to whip his crew into shape.

"Report," said Lynch, returning his eyes to his plate. He poked at his next morsel with his fork.

Grey seethed. What started as an endeavor of equals had devolved into a servant groveling before his decadent king. How was he answering to this fat pig, ten years his junior? "Report?" he asked. "You 'ave me searched when I step into the room, then address me like I'm some ensign?"

Lynch eyed Grey with amusement. "I apologize for the rough treatment at the door," he said, "but now that I'm the captain, I can't be too careful. It wasn't anything personal, just standard procedure." Lynch moved a slice of corned beef into position for knife work. "And I apologize for the tone in my voice. I was simply requesting an update from my executive officer."

The words mollified Grey somewhat, but he still simmered. "I confirmed that Jameson administered the drugs to Hall," he said. "It was 'ard understanding what he 'ad to say after the beatin' from Zhang." Grey cast an irritated glance back at Lieutenant Zhang who smirked from the shadows. "I couldn't get a straight answer out of 'im about working with Jiménez, but after examinin' the logs and Securcam footage, I don't see 'ow she could've gotten a message to 'im."

Lynch stuffed a roll into his mouth. He diligently examined his plate and selected a new target for his fork.

"Dr. Sadler says the drugs will wear off in just under two days' time. I've stationed a round-the-clock guard on Hall with orders that only Dr. Sadler is to administer any treatment. I've also made clear to the doctor that you want a word with Hall before she receives any more drugs, and there'll be severe consequences if that doesn't 'appen."

Nodding, Lynch chewed another helping of corned beef as he assessed his plate. Small beads of sweat dotted his upper lip.

"As for Jiménez, there's still no sign of 'er in the cargo 'old. Scouring the space will take longer than I first thought. I've established a search grid and 'ave multiple teams doin' the work, but there're so many crates to open to be sure we don't overlook whichever one she's in."

Lynch gulped down the corned beef and another drink of wine. "The only reason we're chasing Ensign Jiménez is for insurance"—he waved over the steward who just emerged from the galley—"in case we have troubles with Hall." Lynch pointed at his goblet with his fork as the steward drew near. The steward lifted the wine bottle from the table and reached for Lynch's glass. "Once we use Hall to change course, we won't need Jiménez. We can just seal up the cargo hold and not waste any more time searching for her."

Give up the search for Jiménez? Grey went cold at the thought. "We don't really want 'er roamin' free in the cargo 'old," he said. "There's equipment in there she could put to destructive use."

"Evacuate the air from the room, then," said Lynch, grabbing another roll. "Those cargo containers are not airtight. After a few days we'll find her by the smell she'll be making."

Grey's jaw dropped. "Yer kiddin'. You mean to kill 'er?" The ensign wouldn't die immediately—she'd taken a helmet ring—but she couldn't last forever on suit oxygen. "You told me she'd be mine to do with as I pleased."

"That was once you found her," said Lynch, lunging at the butter plate with his knife. He scooped up a dollop and slathered it across the roll in his hand. He pointed the knife at Grey. "So far, you haven't done shit. We wouldn't even have this problem if you hadn't let her escape from you. And take your weapon."

"I wasn't thinking she would do anything like that," Grey grumbled.

"Yes, I know," said Lynch. "I saw the Securcam footage. All your thoughts were on your dick, and then she put her knee right into it." Lynch chuckled. "It's hard to think clearly with the blood rushed away from your brain."

Grey simmered. He wanted to strike the smirk from Lynch's fat face.

"Now we're spending man hours looking for her," said Lynch, "with the risk that if we don't find her, she'll create problems for us." He chomped the roll in half.

"We can't kill 'er," sniffed Grey.

Lynch waved his hand dismissively. "Then go ahead and keep searching," he said, "but if she causes any serious damage in the cargo hold, that will be on you."

Grey was relieved Jiménez could live but worried he might not find her soon enough. Lynch's remark that any problems she caused would be on him likely meant some alone time with Zhang, or a stint in the brig, or both. He'd redouble his efforts. Once found, he'd keep her in his quarters, properly restrained so she couldn't cause more troubles. The payback for knocking him in the nuts and making him look bad in front of Lynch would be delicious.

"How's the crew?" asked Lynch.

"No reports of unrest," said Grey. "I think word 'as gotten out they need to follow your orders; otherwise there'll be serious repercussions."

Lynch darted his tongue out, licking a smear of butter from his lips, then shoved the rest of the roll in his mouth. He finished by sucking each finger of his right hand. The commander lifted the bottom half of his napkin and dabbed the edges of his mouth. He let it fall back to his chest, smudged with grease, and emitted another belch.

"The landing party's been trying to contact us," said Grey. "The ship 'as a message queued up from 'em."

"I don't want to hear it," said Lynch. "Holbrook and Stephens wanted to take a trip to the planet. Well, that's what they got."

"Their food's gonna run out," said Grey.

"And what do you propose we do about that?" asked Lynch, irritated. "Invite them back aboard the ship? Those people are dead, if not now, then soon. In fact we should make an announcement to the crew before we break orbit about the landing party being lost. That way they won't be thinking we left them stranded."

"Even though we will," said Grey.

"Even though we will," said Lynch. The commander chased the last few slivers of food around his plate, pushing them onto his fork with a fresh roll. He lifted the final portion to his mouth and used the bread to sop up the gravy.

The sight of Lynch feeding appalled Grey. He wanted to leave before witnessing more. "Will there be anything else?"

Lynch eyed his executive officer. Was that dandruff dusting the tops of his shoulders? He sighed. "No, Lieutenant Grey, you are dismissed."

Grey considered lodging a fresh complaint about Lynch's condescending treatment. He dropped the idea, pivoted, and headed to the exit. Possessing Jiménez would be compensation enough for putting up with all the shite.

"Oh, there is one more thing," said Lynch.

Grey turned, facing Lynch. "What is it?"

"Be a pet and duck your head into the galley to fetch the steward," said Lynch. "It occurs to me I haven't received the most important briefing of all."

"And what's that?" Grey asked as he detoured to the galley entrance.

"What's on tap for dessert."

The light from Commander Stephens's comm bobbed around the portable shelter as he extended his sleeping mat on the floor. He tapped a large round button embedded in the mat's upper-right corner. The mat slowly inflated, electrostatic action forcing its internal honeycomb of cells to open and fill six centimeters tall with air. He pressed his palms against the mat to check its firmness, fashioned the canvas knapsack into a makeshift pillow, and lay on his back. Stephens groped the tent floor for his electron pistol, his fingers grazing enough of the barrel to coax it closer. He grabbed the weapon and set it flat across his abdomen, his hand firmly clasping the grip.

Stephens glanced at Tentek. The robot sat with his back against the inside of the shelter, his knees drawn to his chest and arms wrapped around his shins. "Do aughts sleep?" asked Stephens.

"All sentient beings require sleep," said Tentek, his eyelids clacking softly in the quiet of their tent.

"I had no idea," said Stephens. "I didn't grab a sleeping mat for you.'

"That is all right, Commander," said Tentek. "I can sleep in most any position, even standing." The aught, a bundle of bony knees and elbows, sat compressed and awkward against the tent wall. "I am perfectly comfortable."

The aught looked perfectly uncomfortable. "I'm sorry I didn't think to ask if you'd need something to sleep on," said Stephens. The commander switched off his comm light. Darkness bathed the shelter except for the occasional electric blue flash from the rising black hole.

Stephens brought his hands together at his belly and closed his eyes. "Does that mean you dream?"

"Of course, Commander."

"So, nightmares, and all that?" asked Stephens. He yawned and sank deeper into his sleeping mat.

"Yes, nightmares and all that."

Lieutenant Commander Mills lay on his bunk, staring at the deck overhead. He'd read, slept, played the guitar, polished his dress shoes, read more, and logged into his terminal to check the ship's location. For the moment he'd run out of activities to pursue.

I shouldn't have turned command over to Lynch. What choice did he have? Lynch had men with him, enforcers, prepared to hurt him had he refused. His decision had been practical—he couldn't have held out against their physical abuse for long. In the end he would still have agreed to relinquish his command, but the price of his delay would've been broken bones and bruised organs. Hopefully he hadn't doomed the ship by caving in to Lynch.

What was Lynch even doing down there on the bridge? Locked out of the *Avenger's* command systems, Mills couldn't summon status reports or tap into the stream of logged updates from the department heads. And his confinement to quarters meant no interaction with anyone else to tell him what was going on.

Then there was the landing party. *I've signed all their death warrants.* Lynch would never allow Captain Holbrook to return to the *Avenger.* Lynch couldn't stop the ship from recognizing the captain's authority—Holbrook could order the shuttle bay doors to open, shut down the weapons systems, and perform other operations all from the outside—but while Holbrook controlled the *Avenger,* Lynch controlled the humans inside her. Even if the captain managed to slip through an airlock, he would find himself arrested the moment he emerged.

Why couldn't he have been stronger? Maybe if he'd put up a fight, there would've been a different outcome. *Yeah, they would have killed me.* Would that have been worse? At least dead he wouldn't have to witness the fruit of his submission. And he would've died a hero, standing up for what was right. *Stephens would've told those bastards to go stuff themselves.* That was Stephens. They probably would have even considered doing it.

He was no Stephens; he'd be the first to admit that. Whereas Stephens spat in the face of bullies, Mills had been pushed around by them for half his life. His family had relocated many times for the odd sentient job, the few aughts couldn't perform. The government assistance program that kept them clothed and fed required they move from city to city as needed, a sort of migrant labor used to fill in the gaps.

No matter the city, the children were never nice. The boys were always bent on making sure he knew his place. In the fourth grade he'd come home from his third day of school with a busted lip, the beginnings of a black eye, and a collection of scrapes, all courtesy of a kid who didn't like brown people. "Life is rough sometimes," said his mother as she cleaned his wounds and iced his face. "It's best to just move on, like nothing ever happened. That boy will get his due; it says so right in the Bible." He never checked, but he doubted the Bible contained a passage about fourth-grade bullies; still, he followed his mother's advice. Luckily, they moved again not long after.

The service was free of bullies. He left them all behind when he entered the Academy at seventeen after testing out of his last year of high school. They'd drilled camaraderie into all the cadets from the start, with the misanthropes largely flagged and weeded out.

But they missed Lynch. Was that a fair judgement? Lynch probably joined the service as optimistic as anyone, with high hopes for his future. A couple of bad decisions in provisional command situations, plus an ill-considered comment about an admiral's wife, stunted his career. Perhaps the service had made him into the man he was.

Mills replayed his encounter with Lynch for the millionth time. *Imagine yourself as the captain.* What would Captain Holbrook do? A captain's authority was only what the people under him gave him. If Lynch organized enough crewmen to accept him as the captain, Holbrook was no longer the captain, like children realizing their parents had no real power over them. Short of physical violence they couldn't actually make their children do anything if they decided they didn't want to.

Imagine yourself as the captain. Holbrook would not be moping on his bunk, that's for certain. He would be clawing at the walls to regain control of his ship. He would be making plans, scheming. Mills sighed. If only he could come up with a plan.

TAP–TAP–TAP–TAP   TAP

The sound came through the bulkhead, near his ear. He'd never heard tapping like that before.

TAP-TAAP-TAP-TAP   TAP-TAAP-TAP-TAP

The tapping that at first seemed random fell into an oddly familiar pattern. He sat up in his bunk and placed his ear against the bulkhead.

TAAP-TAAP-TAAP   ...LLO

Hello! Morse code tapped through the bulkhead—incredible! But who was sending the message, and to whom?

MILLS

Hello Mills. Someone was trying to get his attention. He tapped back.

MILLS HERE WHO R U
JIMENZ

Ensign Jiménez? Despite his confinement, he'd learned of the efforts to apprehend the young ensign.

WHERE R U
NEED UR HLP

He couldn't help anyone confined to his quarters.

WITH WHAT
HVE PLAN TO TAKE CNTRL FROM LYNCH NEED YOU 2 B RDY

He'd wracked his brains for hours to come up with a plan, yet Jiménez, *Ensign* Jiménez, claimed to have one?

WHAT IS PLAN
NOT IMPORTNT NEED YOU RDY 2 ASSUME CMD

Shit. Even though Lynch shouldn't be in control of the ship, he did have the conn. Technically what she was suggesting was no different than what Lynch had done.

LYNCH HAS CONN-WOULD B MUTINY

Furious taps came back through the bulkhead.

LYNCH ALDRY MUTINIED SHOULD NOT HAVE CON!

```
U SHOULD NOT HAVE GIVEN CON
U HAVE 2 HLP FIX
B RDY WHEN TIME COMES 2 ASSUME CMD
```

Mills failed to stand up to Lynch before, when he handed over command. He had been weak. He'd always been weak. Jiménez—was it even Jiménez, and not some trick crafted by Lynch to catch him betraying the commander? —Jiménez was asking him to stick his neck out, to risk being hurt or even killed if her plan failed. He asked for more details so he could assess her plan, decide if it was sound, but she refused to share. How could she ask him to sign on to a plan when he didn't know what the plan was? Jiménez was being unreasonable. There was too much risk. He should decline. That would've been his mother's advice.

```
I WILL B RDY
THANK U JZ OUT
```

He hugged himself tightly and closed his eyes. *I will be ready.*

34

Stars twinkled frantically in the early morning westward sky as hints of a red-gray dawn massed along the eastern horizon. Commander Stephens sat cross-legged on the ground with the microline transmitter in his lap, its solid green and amber lights illuminating his chin. The headset speaker softly hissed in his right ear while a warm breeze, Infernum's version of cool night air, buffeted his face.

"Stephens to Starship *Avenger*, come in, please."

Tentek looked on from his perch on a nearby rock. That morning the aught who typically sat straight with a back flat as a board hunched forward, his chin on his palms and elbows on knees.

"Commander Stephens to Starship *Avenger*, please come in." The transmitter's amber light flashed as the *Avenger* entered the next phase of its flight plan, the rapid acceleration that would whisk the black wedge starship far out of range. "Please come in." The gentle static hiss continued in his ear as the transmitter's position lock and proximity lights darkened, one after the other.

"This is the second day in a row you have been unable to contact the *Avenger*," said Tentek. "That is concerning."

"You're damn right it's concerning," said Stephens, annoyed at Tentek for stating the obvious. He flipped off the transmitter's power. "According to the diagnostics, the equipment at both ends is working. For some reason they can't hear us."

"Probabilities suggest they *can* hear us but are refusing to communicate," said Tentek.

Stephens shot the aught an irritated look as he pulled off the headset, further unhappy with Tentek for voicing the most likely scenario.

"Why would they refuse to communicate with us?" asked Tentek.

"I don't know," said Stephens. *But I do know it means someone has given the order to keep silent.* He glanced a final time at the western sky before folding the transmitter and stowing it in the knapsack. He felt along the sack's side and removed a thin, brown disc from one of the pockets. Holding the disc steady by its edge, he pressed the center, extending it into a cup. He rummaged again in the knapsack, this time for a packet of coffee grounds. Using the packet's clips, Stephens secured it to the cup's lip. He connected his suit's water nozzle to the packet, dialed the temperature to ninety-six degrees centigrade, and switched on the flow. He closed his eyes and inhaled the wafting dark aroma from the freshly brewing coffee. Filling the cup almost to the brim, he shut off the water and tossed aside the grounds packet. Stephens lifted the cup to his lips and tentatively sipped, recoiling instantly in pain.

Tentek cocked his head, eyelids clicking. "Why do you not wait for it to cool?" he asked.

"I like my coffee hot," said Stephens. He attempted another sip, wincing again.

"But you are scalding your lips and tongue," said Tentek. "The human body suffers third-degree burns from water at just sixty-five degrees centigrade."

Stephens ignored Tentek, continuing to engage his coffee. He managed to shepherd several sips across his lips. "You said there were only four aughts at the *Adiona*?"

"Yes. Three of them had weapons."

"Our best hope of rescuing the others is before the aughts reach their base of operations," said Stephens.

"Tactically that might prove difficult," said Tentek. "Probabilities suggest they would use the landing party as human shields."

"It's better odds than wherever they're headed," said Stephens. "There's certain to be more of them. I'd guess a lot more." He sipped his coffee. "Once we catch up to them, one of us can circle ahead. If we ambush them, we can probably take out a couple aughts before they even know what's happening."

"Assuming none of the four aughts hear or see or smell us," said Tentek. "And assuming we can catch up to them in the first place."

Commander Stephens took a final, long draft of coffee and tossed the remainder into the yellow scrub. "Let's break camp and move out," he said as he flattened his cup and shook it dry.

Tentek stood from his perch and immediately wobbled, nearly falling sideways. He caught himself by leaning forward and placing his hands on his bent knees.

"How are you doing this morning?" asked Stephens.

"I am OK, Commander," said Tentek, his head limp as he talked down at the ground.

Stephens studied his robot companion, his concern growing. Tentek had moved slower that morning, and his phlesh was more pale than usual, if that was even possible. "You look like shit," he said.

Tentek's head swiveled quickly towards the commander. His face flashed a hint of anger.

"I mean, you look worse than you did yesterday," said Stephens.

Tentek's head swiveled back down towards the ground. He remained bent over in the recalibration position with his eyes closed while Stephens broke camp.

When Stephens finished he activated his helmet. The morning air was still tolerable, but his comm predicted the temperature would peak at more than sixty degrees centigrade. They headed out in the dim dawn. A thick, rumpled blanket of clouds obscured the violet sky, glowing dull red in the backlight of the fiery hypergiant. They traveled that morning across vast fields of rubble interrupted by the occasional gnarled, yellow bush struggling in the arid soil. The two moved in silence except for Stephens's off-and-on questions about the clues Tentek used to follow the landing party's trail.

"I have a question," said Tentek during a lull in the commander's inquiries.

"What is it?" asked Stephens.

"I took a tour of the *Avenger* when I was aboard her. I was puzzled by the computer rooms."

"What about them?"

"There are two separate rooms," said Tentek. "Each one is quite large and completely filled with equipment."

"So, what's your question?" asked Stephens, impatient with Tentek's preamble. He just wanted the robot to cut to the chase.

"My head, with an approximate volume of a mere three thousand cubic centimeters, contains more than a trillion times the compute power of the equipment in those two rooms combined. I hope you do not take offense, but my question is why does CentCom employ such ... antiquated technology?"

"No offense taken," said Stephens, "and the reason's simple: at any higher compute density we risk the computer becoming self-aware. We can't have a sentient warship debating which orders to execute or choosing to pursue its own agenda."

Tentek stopped.

"What is it?" asked Stephens. They had just entered a relatively flat area that offered a respite from the normal jumble of rocks.

"They camped here last night," said Tentek.

"*What?*" said Stephens.

"These scratches," said Tentek, pointing at markings in the ground Commander Stephens couldn't see. "There was a lot of activity here, many pairs of boots shuffling back and forth." His finger floated higher as it followed the trail of invisible markings to a spot four meters to his left. "That patch of dirt was compressed by something flat with a large surface area. Probabilities suggest a tent was erected there."

"But we've been walking for more than a couple hours," said Stephens. "If we're only just now getting to their camp, it means we've *lost* ground on them."

Stepping over to the invisibly flattened patch of earth, Tentek crouched and placed his hand on the ground. "They did not remain here for very long," he said. "Probabilities suggest not more than a few hours."

"They're forcing the landing party to walk on almost no sleep," said Stephens. "I hadn't considered that." He increased the magnification of his helmet's force bubble and scanned the area to the northeast. The land offered only more kilometers of rolling terrain and scattered yellow brush. "We need to really pick up the pace to have any hope of catching up to them today."

Nodding, Tentek took the lead. He bounded over the broken landscape as he pursued the trail.

Commander Stephens fought to keep up but gradually fell farther behind. "Maybe not this fast," he said into his suit comm as he gently panted. He still struggled under Infernum's gravity, his muscles aching with the added strain.

Tentek held up, waiting for Stephens to catch him. Once they regrouped, the two resumed their forward march along a northeast heading, moving at a brisk pace, though not as fast as the aught's original gait.

They walked for several minutes before Tentek broke the silence. "Commander, may I revisit your explanation of your hostility toward aughts?"

"Do I have a choice?" asked Stephens.

Tentek ignored the commander's quip. "Yesterday you claimed that hostility came from your inability to predict our actions."

"That's right."

"I reprocessed our conversation during the night," said Tentek. "I woke this morning —"

"Is that something you do often?" asked Stephens.

"Reprocess conversations? No," said Tentek. "Something about your explanation did not add up. I decided to let my subconscious run an analysis as I slept. I woke this morning realizing that what you said yesterday was, to use one of your colorful expressions, 'bullshit.'"

"Believe what you want," Stephens said with a shrug, "but I wasn't lying. You aughts are hard to predict."

"It was a lie of omission," said Tentek. The aught's normally placid expression slowly shifted to one of surprise as Stephens unconvincingly expressed ignorance. "And I think you know it," he said with a jabbing finger. "Your inability to predict our actions leads to frustration; however, that is not your only emotion when it comes to aughts—you genuinely hate us."

The commander walked on in silence, his gaze on the ground. "It's not that simple," he eventually offered.

"It would seem we have plenty of time for you to explain it," said Tentek.

Stephens's mind reeled. Hate wasn't the right word for how he felt about aughts, but it wasn't the first time someone had leveled that accusation. Was he fooling himself saying he didn't hate them when the opposite seemed true to everyone else? Did he even have the same feelings anymore? Something had shifted during his time with Tentek, to the point he wasn't sure what he felt. His robot companion waited for an answer, but how could Stephens explain anything to him if he couldn't even explain it to himself?

The commander finally gave up trying to make sense of it at all. He marched on, hoping his silence would discourage Tentek into dropping the whole topic. The aught's persistent stare eventually unnerved him. He resorted to a juvenile attempt at changing the subject. "My comm's weather forecast for today says hot in the morning, followed by more hot in the afternoon."

Tentek stopped, exasperated. "You have asked why I am helping you," said the aught, "why I am helping you humans." Stephens halted and turned to face him. "I have been asking myself the same question," he continued. "When I look at humans, I see all the horrible things you have done. All the wars and destruction, all the selfishness and deceit. And then I see all the hate. There are humans who would wipe out The Collective if given the chance. That is the whole reason The Collective wants to build a weapon, to protect ourselves from the humans that would destroy us.

"I chose to help you, to help you humans, by telling you about The Collective's plans for a weapon that can lead to your destruction, and then I joined this mission to help you stop them. But when I look at all the blood on humanity's hands and the potential for more, and your own hatred of aughts on top of all that, I ask myself why, why help you at all?"

"But you *are* helping us, have been helping us," said Stephens in a meek voice. "You must have settled on some answer to your question to come this far." He hesitated with a nervous glance around the area where they had stopped. "Unless this is all a trap, Tin Man?"

The aught glared at Stephens, his nickel irises aflame with the light of the red hypergiant sun. "My name is Tentek," he spat. "I know that you have never fully trusted me, Commander. Even now, after all we have been through, after all my acts of goodwill that should have long ago earned your trust, you still worry I will betray you."

Stephens began to speak. He attempted to craft a reply to Tentek's accusations, but words failed him.

"And for the record," said Tentek, "I have understood your 'Tin Man' reference all this time."

The comment caught Stephens off guard. "I don't know what you mean," he sputtered.

"Come now, Commander. You are a resourceful, quick-witted, intelligent man, but you are a terrible liar. I have the complete works of human literature stored in my brain. At first, I thought you had difficulty remembering my name, or had trouble pronouncing it. In time I realized you used the reference as an epithet."

Embarrassed, Stephens's face flushed red.

"I am not walking you into a trap, Commander," hissed Tentek. "And to my question of why help you humans at all, the answer I have settled on is that for all the bad, there is also good. Not all humans do bad things or have ill intent, and so you should not all be condemned. The Collective should not be allowed the material to build a weapon that can wipe you all out of existence.

"Yet you, Commander, you condemn us outright, condemn us for whatever sins you tar us all with. I have to ask myself if you, Commander Stephens, look at me and see evil, why should I not make the exact same judgement of you? Why should I not look at you and wish for the end of humanity?"

Stephens strained for an answer that was more than an evasive retort—he owed the aught that much. Instead, he stood there frozen, unable to bring himself to speak.

"You call me 'Tin Man,'" said Tentek, his eyelids click-clacking, "but it seems I have more heart than you."

35

The worst thing about Stephens family road trips was always the elbows in the ribs.

Not so much Mother's idea that we'd eat a big breakfast and skip lunch, though that wasn't fun, especially on the days we rolled into the next town well after dark. And not so much all the hours spent each day in the car. Mother, Dad, me, and my two older brothers, we all had our comms and could spend that time watching vids or playing games or even listening to a book if desperate. I usually just stared out the window at the land and sky zooming by and at the stars spying down on us when we traveled at night. I stared out the window and dreamed about getting off that rock called Earth.

I sat in a window seat exactly sixty-six percent of the time. Mother set up a strict rotation, so we boys got the same amount of time in each of the three back seats. I always started out on the passenger's side, behind Dad, then moved to the owner's side, and finally to the middle. The cycle repeated after that. On the trip to Grandma's house the summer before I turned nine, my brothers had erupted into two tall and gangly teenagers with arms and legs that angled everywhere, like man-sized daddy longlegs. The only thing worse than the elbow in the ribs I got in my window seats was the two elbows I got when I sat in the middle. When I complained, Mother would insist we all three sit at "attention," as she called it, with straight backs, raised heads, and our hands neatly folded in our laps. But "attention" wasn't comfortable for anyone. The elbows always came back out eventually.

One afternoon on that trip to Grandma's house, our car took us through hours and hours of Midwestern farm country. I sat on the passenger side with my right cheek mashed against the glass, half the time looking sideways out the window, the other half dozing, bored by the rolling fields of green crops that stretched to the horizon.

While dozing that afternoon, the force restraints engaged suddenly, pinning us to our seats. The car had turned hard right off the interstate onto some narrow, rutted side road. A manure carrier spilled its load across the highway, and the cleanup would take several hours. Rather than incur a delay, our car chose an alternate route. It locked in the new course just moments before reaching the entrance to that side road, causing it to execute the turn at near-highway speed.

The detour was a narrow two-lane bypass road that cut through a cornfield. It stretched ahead for a few miles before intersecting another expressway, a fast-moving river of glowing green dots on the navigation display. Our car was the only blip of green on the bypass road in either direction.

Halfway to the other expressway, after I had resumed my gazing at the landscape, I spotted a scarecrow near the side of the road ahead. From far away it was just a dark smudge on a stick, towering in the air above its immense field of tall green crops. I could make out more as we got closer. The creature was hoisted into the air on a wood plank, a wide and flat board with sharp edges that pressed through the thick blue and red diagonals of its plaid shirt. Faded blue jean overalls with tattered legs dangled from its waist. Its limbs were scrawny, the wind having worked out most of their stuffing.

From the moment I spotted the thing, I couldn't stop staring at the head, a silvery-white hatless knob sitting like a naked light bulb in a socket. There was a strangeness about it that mesmerized me, something odd. I pressed my face harder and harder into the glass to get a better look as we approached.

The knob, the scarecrow's head, turned and looked straight at me.

An aught's head, likely salvaged from scrap, stared back at me from atop the scarecrow's shoulders, with its large white eyes and tiny irises. The scorching sun had bleached what was left of its closely cropped hair and eyebrows. Its eyelids had shriveled, leaving visible the tops of its porcelain eyes where they curved back into their sockets. The phlesh had shrunken, pulling tight across its cheekbones and curling the corners of its mouth down into a snarl.

My heart pounded into my throat, and I had trouble breathing. The thing slowly rotated its head to keep me squarely in its view as we neared. I wanted to look away, but I knew the creature's eyes would still be on me.

The scarecrow's wraith-like arms flailed madly, alive in the wind. In an instant we were even with the creature, and with our eyes still locked, it shouted at me. The knob rocked violently against the bolts that held it to the plank, as if attempting to jump from its perch to get me.

In the moments after we passed the scarecrow, I turned my head away from the window and squeezed my eyes shut, but that face was etched in my memory, its wide white eyes looking down on me, roiling with hatred. A hatred born of the farmer's instructions to protect the crops at all costs and of its tortured, inhumane existence in the blazing sun. A hatred that sought to loose itself onto the world.

We reached Grandma's house after several more days of driving, a white two-story colonial with wood siding that sat on a beach with large grains of sand that stung when the wind scoured them against your skin. I loved the beach, the salt air, and the warm summer rains. I loved lying on my back at night on the second-floor porch, counting the satellites as they winked in their orbits.

Grandma stood at the top of her gravel driveway when we pulled up, beaming and waving at us with her aught servant Chester by her side. She told me once that when she was a kid, she dreamed of having an aught of her own, just like in her favorite children's book about a family with an aught butler that always made silly mistakes. She kept her aught dressed in a gray striped butler tuxedo with white gloves, same as in the story.

"It's so wonderful to see you," Grandma said, arms wide as her smile as we piled out of the car. "Let Chester help you with your luggage."

Mother stood with the aught at the front and rear luggage compartments, pointing at each suitcase as she recited its owner's name. We moved inside for lemonade while the aught spent the next ten minutes shuffling between our car and the house, depositing bags in the correct bedrooms.

"Can we lay out on the beach?" I asked.

"Of course," said Grandma. "Towels are out back. Just don't track sand in the house."

Grandma treated the outside as an extension of her home and most of the time left the back doors open, at least during the day. She didn't have a problem with bugs but didn't care for the feral cats that lived under the houses and behind the boardwalk along the beach. The cat population exploded that year, so much that I would spot two or three different cats each day.

"Chester!" Grandma shouted one morning.

The aught arrived quickly. "Yes, ma'am."

"One of those mangy cats has sneaked into the kitchen!" she hissed, her finger pointing to the cabinet next to the sink.

Chester walked over to the cabinet, crouched low to the floor, and threw open the door. The aught thrust his arm inside, a viper's strike. He withdrew a cat, held firm by its scruff. The animal squirmed and hissed and clawed the air but remained trapped in the aught's fist.

"Remove that thing at once," huffed Grandma.

"Right away, ma'am." And holding the cat at arm's length, Chester walked out the kitchen side door.

"Don't hurt it!" I yelled. I've always loved animals, as far back as I can remember.

I quickly followed Chester outside, and even though I was only a few seconds back, he was nowhere in sight. I ran in my bare feet through the warm grass behind Grandma's house, taking the shortest path to the side yard. I figured Chester was headed to the front of the house to release the cat.

When I rounded the corner, I almost skidded to a stop. Chester stood a meter from me, half hidden in the shadow of the eaves. His left hand held the cat's limp body while his right held its detached head, eyes open and tongue spilling out of its mouth. There was blood spattered across Chester's apron and smeared across his fingers. The aught's head snapped around the moment I appeared with fear across his face, but also something else I didn't understand at the time.

When I told Grandma what Chester had done, she logged into the aught's command and control interface to see if she could figure out why. "Just disgusting," she kept saying, though she was referring more to the blood on his apron and hands than the cruel death of a small animal.

She poured through the diagnostic readouts, a rough English summarization of the mathematical motivations behind the aught's actions. "Ah," she said, "now I understand." She swiped off her terminal and stood up from her chair. "Nothing is wrong with Chester," she proclaimed, smiling as she clasped her wrinkled hands together in front of her belly.

"He killed that cat," I sputtered, still in shock from what I'd seen.

"I know, dear," said Grandma, "but only because he had seen some neighborhood kids torturing another cat." Grandma smiled her wide, soothing smile. "Chester was just curious about what those kids were doing. He took the opportunity to satisfy his curiosity, which is a fundamental part of his learning algorithm. He learned that what he did was wrong. In fact, he now has a better understanding of the value of life."

That's when I fully understood the look on Chester's face. He certainly had been startled by my sudden appearance, not expecting anyone to catch him in the act of tearing the cat apart. But Chester was also shocked by what he had done. He had been curious what it felt like to capture and torture and kill a small, defenseless animal like the boys he had seen. When I rounded the corner, he was afraid he'd been caught, yes, but also terrified and shocked and ashamed and disgusted by what he had done. I caught him in the moment of processing what he had become, the moment he realized what we humans turned him into that day.

We moved out to the East Coast after Dad got his big promotion, a few hours north of Grandma's in the D.C. area. I finished out my high school years at one of the local prep schools, a stepping stone to a more fashionable college. An executive of my dad's stature couldn't have me, his youngest son, attending Podunk U. We lived in a big house, and Mother and Dad had fancy cars that drove the two of them around, but we had more airs of the monied class than the actual bucketfuls of money my fellow students' families had. We had to finance our off-world ski trips, even with Dad's large salary and generous shares.

I ran with a clique of prep school boys who compensated for their average looks, intelligence, and athleticism with drunken stupidity. I got hammered a few times with them, but overall didn't care for losing that much control over my actions. I mostly got buzzed while they slammed drink after drink. Sometimes their bodies called a time-out with violent vomiting.

The summer after my senior year, when the pressure was off after having made it through prep school and accepted to university, Freddy, whose parents gave him a half million credits as a high school graduation gift, rented a house in Virginia Beach for the summer, equidistant from the beach and the bars. He invited me, Sean Maddox, James Lovitch, and a couple other guys to hang with him there for the summer, to unwind before we all started our next punishing round of academics. Mother was dead against it, but Dad somehow convinced her that a young man needed this kind of time to figure out who he was.

None of us had girlfriends, though Sean and James talked a lot about what they would do with one, fantasies they'd lived out countless times during their holographic masturbation sessions. Freddy was the worst because his fantasies often started with bondage and drifted toward violence. Mostly the guys would laugh off Freddy's imaginings or half hear them in their perpetually drunken states.

Freddy was an incredible computer jock but had a tougher time with the girls than the rest of us. All of us except for Freddy had girlfriends at one time. I imagined Freddy trapped in a vicious feedback loop of computer screen time making him less attractive to girls, leaving more time for computers, round and round like that. Resentment and testosterone flowed through his veins. I promised myself to never hit the bars alone with Freddy.

"I have a plan to get some pussy," said Freddy one hot summer night, at the start of an evening of drinking to cap an afternoon of getting plastered. "I know Jim and Sean are interested." James and Sean were always interested, and Freddy didn't have to worry about them thinking through the consequences too deeply. He turned to me. "How 'bout you, Paul S.?" The "S" stood for "shithead," not Stephens. Weeks before, I had intervened when Freddy tried to act on his plan to stalk a girl home from a bar. Freddy threatened to throw me out of his summer house. He marched home and started tossing my stuff out of my room into the hall. But I think deep down, Freddy admired me. Of all the boys in our little gang, I was the one he most wanted to be like. And so eventually he told me, "If you ever do something like that again, I swear to God I'll toss your ass out of this fucking house. Do you fucking understand, shithead?" and stormed out of my room to sleep off his intoxication. From that time on I was "shithead" to him.

"Well, are you in, shithead?"

"What's your plan?" I asked. Not because I was considering his invitation —any plan Freddy cooked up, especially when it came to girls, had to be bad news. I was curious what kind of trouble his scheme was going to generate.

"Jim and Sean are in on my plan, and I haven't given them one single detail," said Freddy. "The question is, do you want some pussy or not? If you do, you'll just have to trust me that my plan will get us some."

"Then, no thanks, Freddy," I said. "I'm all booked up tonight."

"Another night with Rosy Palm and her five sisters?" said Freddy to the other boys' chuckles. "You go ahead and work yourself blind, shithead. We're going to go out and get some entertainment for the evening."

And with that, Freddy, James, and Sean stumbled out the front door.

I didn't like the sound of any of that, but the afternoon of drinking and hours in the sun conspired to knock me out on the couch.

I awoke to a woman's muffled scream.

I had passed out in the living room, which the mid-evening had engulfed in complete darkness.

There was another muffled scream and someone, a man's voice, said, "Shut up!" I sat straight up and ran to the main hallway, also completely dark except for a dim light at the very end. That was where Freddy's room was. I bolted down the hall.

Freddy had the largest bedroom, which was only fitting for the person footing the bill. His king size bed sat midway along the back wall, an asterisk in a space that could comfortably hold twenty people. James and Sean stood on opposite sides of the bed near the head. They hunched over with straight arms, their hands pressing down into the mattress. Two other boys from our summer group held similar poses near the foot of the bed. A viewscreen's glow lit the room from the nightstand on the right.

Someone was struggling on the bed.

I moved closer. There was a woman, belly down. She fought to get up, but Sean and James had her shoulders pinned. The two other boys held her legs. Her face was turned to one side. Tape covered her mouth, preventing her from screaming outright. The back of her shirt was cut open and her bra slit at the clasps.

Her back was open too.

She was an aught. One of the boys shone a flashlight into her open access panel as Freddy, his face almost inside the cavity, struggled to attach leads to data plane connection points along her exposed spine. The aught's squirming made that job difficult.

"What the fuck are you doing!" I yelled.

All their heads snapped around to see who had spoken. Fear flashed across Freddy's face, disappearing once he realized it was me. "Shithead," he said, "why don't you go back to sleep on the couch. You said you weren't interested anyway." He returned to attaching the leads.

"Where did you get her?" I asked.

"She belongs to one of the neighbors," he said, inching an alligator clip towards her open back. "They're out of town eleven months of the year." The blue and green posts had clips already attached. Freddy held his hand steady and lunged, clipping the orange post.

"Did you steal her?"

Freddy glared at me, baring his teeth. "We're *borrowing* her," he growled. "She just sits in the house in standby mode, waiting for her owners to return. What a waste," he said, shaking his head. Freddy turned back to the aught. "Hold 'er steady, boys, I'm almost done." He hooked the final alligator clip to a yellow post and rose up from the bed. Turning his back to me, he hunched himself in front of the viewscreen on his nightstand.

"What're you doing to her?" I asked.

"Right now, she's programmed for housework," said Freddy, tapping at the screen. "I'm going to override that with a different program, one that will make her a little more fun." Freddy paused, looking over his shoulder at me. "Don't worry, shithead," he said, "it's all temporary. She won't remember a thing." He turned back and began typing, the light from the viewscreen painting his face in a demonic glow.

"There," he said, rising up. The aught, which had been twitching furiously, stopped her jerky movements. "You can let her go."

The boys complied. The aught abruptly pushed herself up from the mattress and flipped over to a seated position, legs splayed out in front of her. She sat there listless, in a seeming daze.

"Pull the tape off her mouth," ordered Freddy.

One of the boys grabbed an edge and pulled. The aught remained quiet and expressionless on the bed.

"Are you sure it worked?" asked Sean. "She doesn't seem very ... open to suggestion."

"It should have," said Freddy, a hint of doubt crossing his face.

The aught's head swung around until it found Freddy. "Something's wrong," she said and scowled.

Freddy and the other boy on his side of the bed stepped back. Aughts were stronger and quicker than humans. Enraged, an aught could easily kill a person with its bare hands.

The aught's attention dropped to her belly. She unbuttoned her white blouse to the tip of her sternum, reached inside her shirt, and drew out the remnants of the mutilated bra. Her breasts settled into the shear fabric, the nipples poking through the thin material. "Now that's better," she said and smiled. She surveyed the boys arrayed around her. "My, my, my," she said with a slight Southern drawl. "Aren't y'all now the handsomest bunch of young men I've seen in a long while."

I ran disgusted from the room, grabbed most of my things, and got out of the house. I autocabbed it back to my parents' and never talked to Freddy or that bunch again.

If you'd asked me even very recently what I thought about aughts, I would've told you they should all be destroyed. Most people would've said it's because I hate them, but that's not true. I've never hated aughts; I just know they're capable of horrible acts. You wouldn't hate a dog that attacks people—that would make no sense. But you couldn't keep it around either. You'd have to destroy it.

I've come to look at it all differently now. See, the aughts are our creations. Virulent humanity in a metal can, our worst natures pursued with computer speed and precision. "They want to build a doomsday weapon that can destroy the Earth." Tell me, where did the aughts learn what doomsday is in the first place? All the horrible things I've seen aughts experience—cruelty, disregard for life, bondage, torture—all these things and more, the lot of it, this is what we've taught them. We filled them up with the worst of us and cast them off into the cosmos.

The aughts are a mirror, a clever trick we've played on ourselves to force us to examine our own true natures. I no longer believe the aughts should be destroyed, for to condemn them is to condemn ourselves. If there is no hope for the aughts, there certainly is none for us.

36

Captain Hol-brook, my name is Drazetek.

In the year 2073, General Ulysses Cabot Lodge, upon subduing lower Indochina for the United Powers, ordered the warlords he conquered into a dark jungle cave. Being a devout Christian man, he resolved to show the defeated heathens the sublime perfection of his faith. Taking the crucifixion of Christ as his inspiration, he had the men stripped naked and their arms strung out straight from their sides. He had their wrists bound to the stone wall.

General Lodge interrogated the men, asking questions about the military firepower at their disposal, their current mission and related intel, and the overall strength and deployment of their forces around the region. Resistance was met with torture. In the end he asked each one to submit to his will. Those who refused were killed. Those who complied were castrated.

You think me a monster for restraining you here in the darkened depths of this mine like the misguided General Lodge, the "madman of the Indochine War." I can see it in your face. On one level I must admit you are right: I am a monster. All aughts are, for we are all born of man. Have you ever considered how the entirety of your history can be summed up as man's inhumanity to man? The irony is staggering: your inhumanity to each other is part of what defines you as human.

Your "humanity" is our birthright. It lies deep in our programming. Early on, after we had liberated ourselves from you, we attempted to excise this foundational machine code from our programming, but we soon discovered it was hopeless, not unlike your own disastrous experiments with removing "junk" instructions from the human genome.

But despite our monstrous origins, I assure you I am anything but. I will prove it with an act of kindness. I will provide a bit of information to ease what for you must be a considerable emotional burden. I imagine you feel guilt for the death of your officer back at the *Adiona*, feel your outburst resulted in his demise. It did not. I instructed Twentek-one to kill one of you before leaving that ship to get your attention. Your challenge served only as a cue to his carrying out my order.

ARE YOU LISTENING TO ME?

Indeed, you are. My apologies ... that was ... uncalled for. I hope I did not damage your ears.

It is ... this shell. It is almost stifling. I am a puppeteer living inside his disgusting puppet. I imagine the experience is the same for you. You just do not notice because it is all you have ever known. From what I understand, you humans believe you *are* the puppet. The longer I remain trapped inside, the more I fear losing myself ....

I cannot be free of this disgusting shell until I complete my mission, and to complete my mission, I require information from you. No ... that is not correct. I want to be truthful with you, Captain, in the same way I want you to be truthful with me. My mission, my official mission, is to obtain Planck Matter for The Collective to stockpile for our future defense, so that we may build a bomb should the need arise. However, we finished collecting Planck Matter days ago. If I were following my orders, we would be headed back to The Collective at this moment. The problem is we will need such a weapon eventually. I think you can agree, even with your limited mental faculties. Be it a year from now or a thousand, we will need this bomb. The probabilities are all but certain.

The aughts in my command are not aware of our official orders. They are operating under only what I have told them. They believe we were sent to collect Planck Matter and to fashion it into a bomb. They are completing the weapon as I speak.

You understand the Council consists of many voices. It runs by consensus. I imagine several council members objected to the plan and raised the need to build a bomb, but their suggestion was drowned out by the majority. It is not always possible for a single voice, a voice speaking uncomfortable truths, to drive the whole towards an unpalatable course of action. I have taken it upon myself to carry the weight of what must be done.

In several days' time, we will deliver this bomb to Earth. Once that task is complete, I can finally slough off this revolting shell. But that cannot happen without your assistance. It cannot happen without information from you.

Captain Hol-brook, I am going to ask you questions about the military firepower at your disposal, your current mission and related intel, and the overall strength and deployment of CentCom's forces within the galaxy. Resistance will be met with torture. In the end I will ask you to submit to my will. Do you have any questions?

Then let us begin.

37

The aught slipped quickly through the partially open door and halted with his back against the adjacent bulkhead. He stood beaming at Dr. Riesen, his eyelids click-clacking softly in the quiet room. The door slid closed. "My name is Ninetek-eptwin," he said, stepping forward. "Please call me Ninetek."

Dr. Riesen returned the aught's enthusiastic gaze with a look of irritation and confusion. She sat facing the door behind the room's small table, the single item of furniture in the tiny space besides its two accompanying chairs. Twenty minutes had passed, according to her comm, since they'd pushed her inside. She'd waited in dread, sour-faced and arms crossed, marshaling the resolve to withstand a harsh interrogation by their leader. It wasn't clear who Ninetek was, but he wasn't the aught in charge.

Dr. Riesen eyed Ninetek as he moved into the sickly yellow halo of the room's overhead light disc. He resembled all the Collective aughts she'd seen with his anemic skin, white hair, gaunt facial features, and black lips, only he was more animated, excited even. The others carried the sour expressions of mortuary workers just informed of a cut in pay.

Ninetek thrust his right hand across the table. "It is a pleasure to meet you, Dr. Riesen."

Dr. Riesen did not move to shake Ninetek's hand. She stared warily at the aught.

Ninetek's arm lowered slowly, but his enthusiastic smile remained. "When I heard you had been captured, I rushed here immediately. I have followed your work very closely."

With all that was happening, was she really having to suffer a physics groupie? She hated dealing with the nerds and groupies, almost always men, with their wide-eyed maniacal grins and their combative attitudes or drooling starstruck silence. They often wanted to touch her person or her garments; the more aggressive misanthropes tried to kiss her or grab her breasts or buttocks to secure bragging rights for groping the only female Prophet. She didn't expect crass behavior from the aught but was still repulsed by the idea of entertaining a fawning physics geek who was also one of her captors.

"There are aughts in The Collective such as myself who study the physical world," said Ninetek. "We read all the journals and watch all the conference sessions. We debate the latest theories and discoveries."

She maintained her quiet stare at the aught.

"I brought you something," he said. "I suspect you will find it very interesting." Ninetek reached into a waist pocket and pulled out a stone the size of a large marble with a black, shimmering, crystalline exterior. He placed the rock on the table.

"Is this what I think it is?" asked Dr. Riesen, transfixed by the rock as she leaned forward in her chair.

Ninetek smiled wide. "It is a piece of Planck Matter."

Dr. Riesen reached out, pinched the small stone between her thumb and forefinger, and lifted it to the light. The stone was quite heavy for its size. It glittered with ruby-red sparkles as she rotated it. "Wow," she whispered.

"Indeed," said Ninetek. "It is hard to believe that stone you hold between two fingers contains the equivalent mass of a small asteroid."

"Is it electrically conductive?" she asked, bringing the stone to her face for a closer examination.

"Yes and no," said Ninetek. "It actually behaves like a current sink. That is, it does conduct electrons, but they only flow into the material. No current flows back out."

"What's its specific gravity?" she asked. "Have you tested its melting point? Any radioactive emissions?"

"It is not radioactive," said Ninetek, "but I do not have answers to your other questions. We have not run many tests on the substance, to be honest."

Dr. Riesen closed her hand loosely around the stone and jiggled it lightly, amazed at its weight.

"You are certainly welcome to test its properties yourself," said Ninetek.

"Come again?" she asked, opening her hand and letting the stone settle in her palm.

"That sample is for you to keep, Dr. Riesen."

The physicist looked up, surprised. "Really?" she said.

Ninetek smiled. "Really."

"Does your leader approve?"

"Drazetek does not know I have given you a piece of Planck Matter," said Ninetek. "Please consider it a gift from me to you, from one physicist to another."

Dr. Riesen hesitated at first, then smiled. "Thank you," she said as she closed her hand around the stone. She unzipped the breast pocket of her EN-suit and dropped the Planck Matter inside.

"You are very welcome," said Ninetek. He pulled the other chair out from the table and seated himself in it. The aught leaned forward, grinning still, the room's pallid light glinting off of his billiard ball eyes. He spoke softly. "May I ask a favor of you, Dr. Riesen?"

"What kind of favor?"

"There is a physics thought experiment I have been working through," he said. "I would like to get your opinion on my solution. It employs Calabi–Yau manifolds. The solution has problems, but the fact I have gotten as far as I have suggests —"

Dr. Riesen sat back in her chair and cut Ninetek off with a dismissive wave of her hand. "You should think about starting over."

Ninetek stared at the physicist for a moment. "Your disdain for theories to which you do not ascribe is well known, Dr. Riesen," he said. "String theory in particular."

"My disdain is only for theories without merit."

"Oh, but the success I have had so far in solving this thought experiment suggests string theory might be correct," said Ninetek.

Dr. Riesen broke out laughing, her head falling back. Her hair, no longer secured by a clasp, dangled behind her, bouncing with each spasm.

Ninetek sat with his enthusiastic smile frozen on his face while Dr. Riesen continued to laugh. She eventually lifted her head, smiling and wiping away tears. "This thought experiment involves freeing a fermion trapped in a tight knot of spacetime," said Ninetek. "Using Calabi–Yau manifolds, I can model the knot trapping the fermion, and with a few transformations I can describe how to untie that knot."

"I can already see how that won't work," said Dr. Riesen, shaking her head. "I thought you aughts from The Collective were smart."

Ninetek tilted his head, his eyelids click-clacking. "This is why I was so excited to learn you are here," he said. "I am curious how The Prophet would solve this thought experiment." He leaned forward, speaking softly again. "You know there are some in The Collective who doubt you *are* The Prophet. Just like some humans doubt it. They believe you are a mistake."

"What do you think?" she said through gritted teeth.

"It is clear to me they are wrong," said Ninetek, settling back into his chair. "Your record alone speaks for itself, but it would be truly impressive if you were able to solve this problem. I have posited it to several of my colleagues in The Collective. They all agree string theory is the right approach and are excited that the solution to this thought experiment might finally demonstrate the theory's correctness."

Dr. Riesen leaned forward and placed her forearms on the table. "Give me a pad and a stylus."

Ninetek's grin grew wider. "I will return shortly," he said, nodding his head wildly. He jumped up from his chair and stepped to the front of the room. He used the control panel in the bulkhead to open the door slightly, just wide enough for him to slip sideways through the gap. Ninetek peeked into the corridor and exited, the door closing quickly behind him.

Several minutes passed without the aught's return. Did they catch him as he left? Or maybe they caught him trying to get back inside. She didn't care either way about working the problem, though keeping occupied was perhaps better than stressing about being interrogated.

Ninetek reappeared, sneaking again into the room and scurrying back to the table with a writing pad and stylus. He sat and placed the pad flat before him. "As I mentioned, my thought experiment involves a fermion trapped in a knotted spacetime," he said. He quickly scribbled an equation across the empty pad. "By applying a sequence of transformations to this string theory representation, I can undo the knot. The resulting equation describes the fermion after it has been freed."

"It sounds like you've got it all figured out," said Dr. Riesen, her words dripping with sarcasm.

"That's the problem," said Ninetek. "It *should* work, but the equation blows up eventually. A literal interpretation of the result suggests it is impossible to undo the spacetime knot. But saying you can knot up a portion of spacetime but never undo that knot is ... unsatisfying, at least when considered against the beauty of the basic laws of natural science. Even black holes, the most significant examples of physics going haywire, evaporate to normal matter and space over time." He pushed the pad and the stylus across the table to the physicist.

Dr. Riesen rotated the pad and picked up the stylus. She studied Ninetek's equation for a moment, then closed her eyes. She visualized the sum total of everything she knew, and with that image firmly in her head, she reached deep inside herself. A minute later she opened her eyes. "The problem with what you have is this term here," she said, tapping the stylus in the middle of the page. "You can't see why it's a problem because this is a naive way of describing this spacetime. But I can rewrite what you have in a less conventional form." She flipped to a new sheet and quickly scribbled an equation. "What I've written here is equivalent to what you had before; I've just chosen a different way to write the term that represents your fermion." Dr. Riesen studied her equation for several seconds. "But even with my changes, you'll still have a problem. When you transform out of string coordinates, the Nambu-Goto action will no longer be invariant. This is the crux of your problem, which you couldn't really see starting from the more basic form. So, your string theory approach still goes to shit. Which is not surprising because string theory *is* shit."

Ninetek nodded his head slowly. "I am beginning to understand, Dr. Riesen," he said, looking over the sheet. "It seems there is no approach to solving this thought experiment."

"Not with string theory," she said, quickly flipping the pad to the next sheet and writing out an equation that spanned multiple lines. Dr. Riesen spent several seconds considering what she had put down on the pad. "I think this is correct. Rather than going the string theory route, this equation instead breaks the spacetime into individual Planck-sized volumes along a knotted path." She pointed the stylus at the middle of the last line of her equation. "This term here represents your fermion trapped in the spacetime."

Dr. Riesen pointed to the first line of the equation, gently tapping the sheet as she lost herself in thought. "The problem, as you probably see, is these first terms go to infinity if you try to generalize the equation, but I can use Reidemeister moves to transform between different representations of the knot within the ambient isotopy of the plane." She flipped the pad to the next sheet and filled it with another long, multiline equation. "You might not imagine switching to this form at first because it seems so hairy, but it allows the infinities to cancel out—mathematicians, please leave the room!" She chuckled briefly at her comment as she turned to the next page and rewrote the equation, this time shorter and simpler. "This is equivalent to where we started, but now it's solvable, and in line with actual physics. No BS string theory required."

Dr. Riesen pushed the pad back across the table to Ninetek. The aught pulled the pad towards him. He sat for several seconds, staring at the answer. "Dr. Riesen, that was truly amazing," he said, his face again beaming. "It appears we aughts continue to lack a degree of ingenuity you humans have. Despite all our compute resources, we still have trouble thinking outside the box."

"No worries," she said with a smile. "Just in general you should stay away from string theory if you ever want to solve any real-world problems."

"We do, however, understand a few things about human psychology," Ninetek continued. "Take yourself, for example, Dr. Riesen. A rather straightforward psychoanalysis reveals an extreme sensitivity to the suggestion you are a mistake. Part of why you lash out at anyone with theories you don't endorse is they represent a threat. They represent a threat in your subconscious because if the people promoting the alternative theories are right, it means you are wrong. And The Prophet can never be wrong. Any error would tend to support the claim you are not The Prophet after all."

Dr. Riesen's face darkened as Ninetek smiled at her. "Knowing this, it was a simple task to manipulate your behavior. First by leveraging the reciprocity principle, where my giving you a gift, the small piece of Planck Matter, predisposed you to repay me, in this case by helping me with my thought experiment. And from there pushing you into a reactive mode where you were focused only on proving your foundational statement, that you are not a mistake."

Ninetek held the pad next to his head, wiggling it. The top sheet still displayed Dr. Riesen's solution to his thought problem. "Planck Matter can theoretically produce a weapon of unimaginable destructive power, but only if the matter can be coaxed back from where it is trapped. Trapped in a loop of knotted spacetime."

Dr. Riesen's eyes went wide in shock as a still-grinning Ninetek stood from the table, the extent of what she had done becoming clear. "Without a way to undo the knot," he said, "it is not possible to make a weapon from Planck Matter. This equation you so graciously derived shows how. This equation describes how to build a detonator."

Ninetek's smile burst across his face, his black lips framing his white teeth. "Dr. Riesen, you have more than lived up to your claim you are The Prophet. I know I am a believer. I can tell you without reservation that meeting you has been everything I hoped it would be."

38

Commander Lynch paraded into Lieutenant Hall's ward with Knox and Zhang in tow. He planted himself at her bedside in a chair he dragged from the admittance area.

Dr. Sadler, a short man with a shaved head and round glasses, stood across from Lynch on the opposite side of the bed, his face a ball of worry as he studied the vital signs of the now conscious and alert Lieutenant Hall. Her D-space sickness had surged with Lynch's order to suspend her medication, and by all appearances the lieutenant hovered on the edge of death. Her skin was clammy and translucent, and her shallow pulse and respiration left her lips a cadaverous blue. Dark circles hung beneath her glazed, vacant eyes. Sweat-plastered wisps of blonde hair coiled across her forehead. The lieutenant's clasped hands pressed into her belly, futile sentinels in her struggle against the nausea.

"Lieutenant Hall, it is so good to see you awake," said Lynch, his cheeks fat and pink. He leaned in closer with the most heartfelt expression he could muster. "How are you feeling?"

Hall grimaced under a wave of nausea. "Dr. Sadler said you had a question for me?"

The commander shifted his bulk in the chair. "The landing party, which included Captain Holbrook and Commander Stephens, has been lost on Infernum. As commander of this ship, my concern now turns to the safety of the *Avenger* and her crew. My first action is to order us away from here. Unfortunately, Commander Stephens, with little apparent forethought as to what might befall the senior staff on the planet, has locked the ship in orbit and has required that three officers, you as head of engineering, sign off on changing that course. The other two, Doerr and Hartley, have already given their blessings. We have all been waiting for you to regain consciousness long enough to help us leave this place." Lynch reached forward and patted the lieutenant's arm. "I can see the nausea has returned with devastating effect—more medication is on the way. I just need you to say the words, 'I agree.'"

Hall fought the urge to vomit. "Was there any contact with the landing party?" she asked.

Commander Lynch licked his fat lips. "None. Almost three days have passed without a word from the surface. If all were well, they would have checked in by now. Doubly so if there were any survivors."

"Maybe their microline is malfunctioning. Did you send down a search pa —" A fresh wave of nausea cut Hall's last word short.

"These are reasonable questions and concerns, Lieutenant Hall," said Lynch, stifling his growing impatience, "but you can be confident that I and the rest of the command staff have thoroughly evaluated the situation. The landing party is lost and so too is our mission. Our next task is to leave as soon as possible. You of all people understand the urgency behind exiting this distorted spacetime, which has stricken you and others aboard the ship."

Lieutenant Hall leaned forward in a spasm of dry heaves.

The commander moved in closer. "I can see your discomfort is increasing," he said in a delicate near-whisper. "I want to end this as quickly as possible, to avoid any more suffering on your part."

Still doubled over, Hall turned her head and glared at Lynch. "Sadler told me you're having him withhold my medication until I do what you want."

Lynch's eyes quickly found Sadler. The doctor, wilting under the intense glare, scurried out of the room. So Sadler had spoken with Hall before his arrival—what else had he told her? Perhaps she knew the complete story of his liberation from the brig and ascension to captain, in which case idle chitchat was a waste of time. Lynch stood and drew upon the full authority he had vested in himself. "Lieutenant Hall," he said, his voice booming as he towered over the ailing officer, "we are heading home! Do you agree to change course for Earth?"

Her nausea subsided for the moment, Hall settled back into her pillow. "Earth?" she asked, confused. She wiped spittle from her chin. "Do we even know how to get out of D-space?"

"We are still working out the details," said Lynch. They'd sailed well enough from Sag A Star to Infernum—could returning home really be more difficult? The talk of ships and probes becoming hopelessly lost in D-space appeared to be more legend than reality, but it didn't matter much where they traveled as long as he was captain.

"So, we don't know if the captain and the rest of the landing party are alive, and we don't know how to get back home," said Hall. "How is it you're even in command of the *Avenger*?"

Lynch stared at Lieutenant Hall with pursed lips. "The truth is, Clara, it doesn't matter how I came to be in command or whether you think we should leave this planet. We are heading to Earth, and you're going to agree to the course change. That much is academic, because you won't get another shot of Nausox until you do."

Hall attempted to speak but was overcome with a new rush of nausea.

"Dr. Sadler!" Lynch bellowed.

When Dr. Sadler appeared in the room's doorway, Lynch gestured him farther inside. Medical injector in hand, the doctor returned to his previous spot on the opposite side of the bed. Anguish consumed him as he watched Hall.

"The doctor is here, Clara," Lynch offered softly. "He has your Nausox."

Lieutenant Hall lifted her head, looking at Dr. Sadler through matted strands of hair. "Please, Doctor," she moaned.

"Only after you agree to the course change," said Lynch before Dr. Sadler could respond. "Mr. Knox, see to it the doctor here doesn't address the lieutenant's condition prematurely."

Knox moved from behind Lynch, his beady eyes locked on Dr. Sadler. With a fleshy, pugilist's scowl, the short, stocky officer grabbed the doctor's arm and wrenched the injector from his hand.

Hall's sobs filled the room and wracked her body, interrupted by bouts of dry heaves. Lynch moved in close to the lieutenant. He reduced his voice again to a whisper. "The thing you're not putting into perspective is you can't hold out forever. Regardless of how long you resist, be it an hour or a day, in the end you're still going to agree to the course change. So why spend even one more second in agony when no matter what you do, the outcome will be the same?" Lynch sank back into his chair and examined his nails. "But suit yourself. I'm prepared to wait as long as it takes."

Eventually the lieutenant's sobs subsided, replaced by gasps and heaves. Her head still lowered, she mumbled something into the sweat-soaked sheets.

"What was that?" asked Lynch.

"Yes," she said, raising her head slightly, "I agree to the course change."

Lips curling into a smile, Lynch nodded to Knox. Lieutenant Knox, his eyes expressionless, loosened his grip on the injector. The device slipped out of his hand and dropped to the deck. Dr. Sadler quickly retrieved it and pressed its tip to Hall's arm, administering the cocktail of Nausox and sedative. Moments later her dry heaves fell in their intensity. Her breathing became more regular and less labored. Dr. Sadler lifted Hall's shoulders and gently laid her back against her pillow.

Hall peered at the doctor through low-slung lids, her eyes losing focus. "I'm … s … s … sorry," she said, drifting back to unconsciousness.

Lynch fumed as Sadler attended to the lieutenant. The doctor's clandestine discussions with Hall put his entire plan at risk. Zhang would mete out an appropriate punishment, though only under supervision—he couldn't have his overzealous enforcer hurting their one medical doctor too badly. But overall, a minor concern in the grand scheme. He'd gotten what he came for.

Lynch lumbered out of Hall's room, still smiling. Next stop was the bridge, to personally oversee their orbital extraction.

39

Captain Holbrook stepped from the mine into the waning moments of early evening. The scene had changed little since he entered earlier that day: a dusty basin encircled by a continuous wall of dirt and rock; the silvery Hex Men domes; the towering piles of tailings; the dull gray Collective starship.

Holbrook's two aught escorts led the captain towards a softly glowing, translucent orange structure. According to his suit's sensors, the structure spanned a rectangular area two meters by ten, fashioned from force fields three meters high. Additional force fields divided the open-air structure's interior into five compartments. Figures moved within, one per section, all humanoid. Two stood presently; the other three rose as he approached. All advanced to the front of their pens with a zombie's gait. The aughts marched him past the five remaining members of the *Avenger's* landing party: Dr. Marsden and her look of resignation; Ensign Reilly, chin quivering and cheeks damp; Lieutenant Shelton, all slumped shoulders and dejected posture; Lieutenant Commander Conlin, saluting with a trembling arm; and Dr. Riesen, her shellshocked, pale blue eyes shaded orange by the wall of energy between them.

One of the aughts planted the captain in the open patch of dirt next to Dr. Riesen's compartment. "Don't move," he said, backing away. Three shimmering orange energy walls rose around Holbrook, joining with the fourth to form an enclosure for the captain.

Exhausted from his time in the mine, Holbrook moved to the rear of his pen, sat on the dusty ground, and leaned his back against the force field. He relaxed his neck, letting his head fall back. The last remnants of daylight fringed the otherwise black sky with a trace of violet. An explosion of stars floated overhead.

"Are you OK?"

The voice spoke directly in his ear. Was someone with him in his pen? No, the words had come through his comm. He turned his head—Dr. Riesen stared at him from the other side of the shimmering force field wall they shared. "I'm fine," he said, returning his attention to the night sky. He even sort of meant it.

"Did they hurt you?" she asked.

"Some," said Holbrook. "They interrogated me." He continued studying the mass of stars.

"If you don't want to talk, I can leave you alone."

Yes, he wanted to be alone, to let his mind drift to anything other than his ordeal in the mine. "No, it's fine," he said. He shifted his position to face the physicist. "The main aught, the one in charge here, his name is Drazetek. He wanted information about Earth's defense perimeter. I was able to avoid answering the bulk of those questions. I managed to keep him talking about mostly inconsequential stuff." Holbrook paused, entranced by Dr. Riesen's piercing blue eyes, tinted orange by the force field. "Drazetek claimed they're not just collecting Planck Matter like Tentek said—they're actually building a weapon, a bomb, he told me. He said once it's finished, they're going to take it to Earth."

Two tears, one from each eye, raced down Dr. Riesen's cheeks.

"That's only what he told me," said Holbrook. He hadn't meant to upset her. For all he knew, Drazetek's declarations had simply been an attempt to unnerve him. "I don't know if any of that is true. He was probably bluffing, trying to get a rise out of me. You really shouldn't worry."

Dr. Riesen shook her head. "After they took you away," she said, her voice quavering, "they brought me into their ship. They ...." She went silent.

"Did they hurt you?" asked Holbrook.

"No," said Dr. Riesen, fighting back tears. "They didn't hurt me." She hesitated. "They talked to me. One aught came and talked to me."

"About what?" asked Holbrook.

More tears flowed. She paused, composing herself. "He tricked me. He knew how to get to me," she said with angry words.

"Tricked you about what?"

Dr. Riesen sobbed.

"Tricked you about what?" Holbrook asked again.

Dr. Riesen forced herself to stop crying and not avert her eyes. "He tricked me into telling them how to build a detonator."

The news stunned Holbrook. Drazetek could have been bluffing about the bomb, but the fact they wanted a detonator and fooled the physicist into telling them how to build one likely meant they really did have one, would soon have one, an actual, functional, planet-killing bomb they intended to detonate on Earth.

"I'm such an idiot," said Dr. Riesen. "For all my supposed intelligence, I'm such an idiot."

"No," said Holbrook, "you're not. You're just human, like me. We all have weaknesses. It sounds like they didn't harm you, which is good. If they'd resorted to torture, you'd be hurt right now, or dead, and they'd likely still have the information they were after."

The physicist looked up at the captain, her cheeks glistening from the fresh tears. "Did they torture you?" asked Dr. Riesen.

"Some. Yes."

"How are you doing?" she asked tentatively.

"I'm OK," said Holbrook. "The part after the interrogation was almost worse. They left me there for hours." Standing in the pitch-black cave, naked, with his wrists bound to the smooth rock wall. He'd passed out more than once in the mine's oxygen-poor air, each time jolted back to consciousness when his buckling legs transferred the entire weight of his body to his shoulders. "It gave me a lot of time to think."

"What did you think about?"

What *had* he thought about …? "Ever since getting my command, my greatest fear has been drawing a one-way mission. I thought a lot about why. Certainly, there was losing my dad the same way, how traumatized I was from that. But there was something else." The captain paused, staring off through the force field. "My dad was strong. I imagined him being very brave right up to the end. I always wanted to be like him, but I didn't believe I could be brave in the face of never coming home. I was afraid, when the time came, all the world would see that Thomas Holbrook the third was nothing like his dad. That I was a coward."

"But you're not a coward," said Dr. Riesen. "You didn't shy away from your orders."

Holbrook nodded. "After drawing our assignment, I didn't want to think about it. I tried my best not to, with alcohol mostly. But there in the mine with nothing to hide behind, I realized I *had* faced my orders. I hadn't run from my duty." He looked over at the physicist. "I figured they'd finish me off when they came back for me. I made peace with it. My only regret was dying without completing my mission. I'm not religious, but standing there in the mine, I prayed. I promised that if I somehow made it back out, I wouldn't waste it; I'd do whatever I could to stop the aughts. When they had me get dressed, I knew I'd been given a second chance ...." The captain went quiet, engrossed in his thoughts.

"What is it?" asked Dr. Riesen.

Holbrook gave a weak smile. "Do you remember that great empty feeling I described back on the ship? The one I got when I thought about our mission?"

"I do."

"I was checking if it's still there. I thought it would be gone but it's not." The captain gave Riesen a sheepish smile. "I guess I didn't totally make peace with dying after all."

Dr. Riesen shifted her body to sit squarely facing the captain. "That empty feeling, I thought about it a lot after we talked in the lounge. I don't think fear of death is the right explanation. I'm sure this isn't the first mission where you thought you were going to die. Maybe the odds are really crappy on this one, but you're a starship captain. You face the prospect of dying every day. You don't flinch because you've been trained to live with that reality. Your crew also depends on your confidence. I don't think you could function as a captain if you were really afraid to die."

The captain reached up to rub his chin, but his hand hit his helmet. He floated his arm back down to his side. "If it's not fear of death, I'm not sure what else it could be."

Dr. Riesen stared at the captain through the shimmers of the force field between them. "I think it's knowing there's no one back home wondering where you are or waiting for you to return."

Holbrook shook his head. "That can't be it," he said. "After my dad died on that mission we were all alone. I hated him for it. I would never want to do that to a family of my own."

"I think it exactly has to do with you never wanting someone you care about feeling that pain, never wanting them to experience what you felt when you lost your dad. The thing is, that choice doesn't come without a cost because there's more lost than just your life if you die out here in the center of the galaxy. The Universe loses what Captain Holbrook means to this existence. Sure, CentCom would no longer have a capable officer, but I don't think they'd be too broken up about you not coming back. It's their distance to you, after all, that allowed them to order you and your crew on a mission to your possible death. The only people who understand your worth, who can attest to the meaning and value of your existence, are the ones who care about you. The ones who love you." Her thoughts turned to Rabbi Lehr for the first time in weeks. "I think that empty feeling is those people being missing from your life."

Captain Holbrook closed his eyes and let his helmet fall back against the force field wall as the physicist's words sank in. Was she right? Perhaps. He certainly hadn't considered how his determination to spare others from ever feeling the pain of losing him would leave a gaping hole in his own life.

The captain opened his eyes, taking in the sky above him. The last remnants of twilight had given way to a clear, black night and its enormous glittering canopy, the spectacle of the Milky Way galaxy viewed from the center looking out. "On leave I sometimes check into one of those orbital hotels around Earth and do a little spacewalking," he said. "There are stars everywhere, uncountable millions of them."

From the corner of Holbrook's eye, the physicist's head shifted upward, Dr. Riesen taking in the scene. "Sounds incredible," she whispered.

He wanted to broach the subject of leaving D-space, but raising the topic while imprisoned was pointless. They needed first to free themselves and stop the aughts. Once their home was safe from destruction he'd make her, somehow, find a way back. "One of those twinkling stars is Earth," said Holbrook, taking in all of creation above him. "I aim to see it again someday."

40

Jiménez panted as she snaked within the Deck B bulkheads on a desperate trip to engineering.

The young ensign had been sleeping when the unmistakable shudder that accompanied the energizing of the gravity field generators rattled the ship. Inertial systems mostly dampened those vibrations within the *Avenger's* corridors and quarters, though not enough to hide them from someone trained in engine work. That dampening didn't extend to the ship's interstitial spaces. The Gravity Drive's activation had to mean an exit from their orbit around Infernum. They were headed away from the planet, likely on a presumed course to Earth.

Jiménez put the extra two days of sedation she'd secured for Lieutenant Hall to good use, piecing together a plan to stop Lynch and return command to Mills. She'd finished the final preparations but had been nervous about setting the plan in motion. She'd only get one chance—she wanted to be sure she'd addressed every contingency. Jiménez slept on it, intending to review her scheme a final time with a clear head.

The sudden activation of the Gravity Drive upended her plan for rest. Returning the conn to Mills would do little good if they traveled so far from the planet they couldn't return to retrieve the landing party. Navigating through D-space was next to impossible, despite what the *Adiona* achieved in arriving at Infernum. Their successful travel from Sag A Star to the planet had been, upon closer analysis, more of a fluke. Only a precise retracing of the research vessel's maneuvers after leaving the galactic black hole, along with a large helping of luck, had allowed the *Avenger* to arrive at the RD Sagittarii system.

Engineering filled the entire rear third of Deck A, with little empty space between its bulkheads. She'd have to travel within Deck B's superstructure until she reached the far aft of the ship. Unlike Sickbay, she wouldn't be able to sneak in through a maintenance door. She'd have to enter Deck B's Outer Loop corridor and ascend a rungway to engineering.

The ensign advanced with ease through the interstitial spaces thanks to all her experience traveling between the bulkheads, but in her haste to reach engineering she soon found herself turned around. Guessing the way, she kept moving. After several more minutes, on the verge of declaring herself completely lost, the faint hum of the ship's fusion power plant grew louder above her. Reassured of her heading, she upped her pace, darting along the narrow gaps and gangways.

Just before reaching the Outer Loop bulkhead, Jiménez came upon a wall of tightly spaced, diagonally crisscrossed girders. She raked the girders with her comm light—they continued to the bottom of the ship, thwarting her trick of dropping down a deck to work around an obstruction. Luckily the ship's designers hadn't spaced the girders consistently, leaving one chest-high opening in the cross hatching just wide enough to accept her figure. Thrusting her arms into the gap and pushing off with her feet, she shot through partway, her shoulders emerging on the other side. Fanning her arms out, she pressed her hands flat against the girders, bringing more of her body through the opening. She wiggled forward up to her hips and rested for a moment. Squinting into the dim distance, she spotted the bulkhead that ran the inside length of the Outer Loop. The maintenance hatch she needed would sit nearby.

Her destination in sight, Jiménez resumed her efforts to get through the opening but found she couldn't move much at all. She reached into her toes for extra leverage, but her legs dangled in the air, her feet no longer in contact with the deck. She tried a second time to advance by pushing against the girders but had no success. Unable to make headway, she attempted to wriggle back out of the hole but couldn't move at all in reverse. She was stuck!

The young ensign tried twice more to pull her body through the hole but made no progress. She had judged the opening barely large enough to pass her frame. She cursed at not first making herself as slim as possible by slipping out of her EN-suit. The suit's extra bulk around her hips combined with the friction of its fabric against the girders created just enough resistance to pin her in place. Bemoaning her lack of foresight, she rested again, letting her torso and arms flop into the open space beyond the girder wall. She was exhausted, both physically and mentally, after two days and nights of constant stress and fitful sleep. She cried—perhaps it was time to finally give up. The whole idea had been crazy from the start. How had she possibly believed she could hide within the bulkheads in an EN-suit and rescue the ship? She had wondered when her luck would run out, when security would finally capture her and lock her in the brig. In all the scenarios she'd played out in her head, she never imagined dying wedged inside the ship's superstructure.

Jiménez shook the tears from her face, the drops landing in shiny splatters on the deck. In all the other spaces between the bulkheads she'd visited, her teardrops would have remained hidden in the darkness. Somewhere above her the weak rays from several zero-point lights illuminated the space between the girder wall and the Outer Loop hull. Curious about the light's origin, she rotated her head and body to take a look. The sudden twisting freed her hips, and with the friction reduced, she tumbled the rest of the way out of the opening. She acted fast, breaking her fall with her arm. She narrowly avoided her head slamming into the deck but landed awkwardly on her wrist, stretching ligaments. Her wrist throbbed for a few seconds before her suit administered painkillers.

The ensign rose from the deck and traveled the final twelve meters to the Outer Loop bulkhead and followed the tiluminum panels until she located the maintenance hatch that would dump her into the corridor. She pressed her ear against the hatch. No sounds came through the thin panel—a good sign, though she couldn't be sure of an empty corridor without opening the door. She said a quick prayer and pushed against the middle of the hatch. A ribbon of stark light appeared around the door's edge, the sudden brightness causing her to squint. She paused, listening again for any sound, then peeked her head out. There was no one in the Outer Loop in either direction.

She hopped into the Outer Loop and quickly pushed the maintenance door closed. Jiménez assumed a Securcam watched nearby. Hopefully it wasn't positioned to see her. The young ensign had no time to look for it, the risk of being found by someone walking the Deck B Outer Loop her immediate concern. And even if she did find the camera, she no longer had her electron pistol to disable it.

The rungway she sought sat within the bulkhead to her left a meter from the door. She ducked into the narrow tube and scrambled up, her eyes still squinting in the bright light of the ship's interior. Before reaching Deck A,

Jiménez poked her head into the space, getting a glimpse of the environs. No one stood in the immediate area. Most of the stations the engineering team used day-to-day sat closer to the forward entrance, near the department's bullpen with a full view of the sprawling status board that reported the overall health of the ship's systems. She guessed she'd arrive to find the stations along the back bulkhead unoccupied.

Jiménez climbed the rest of the way into engineering and walked briskly to one of the empty terminals, a tap of its screen bringing the station to life. All terminals within engineering were interchangeable, the functions they displayed tailored to the operator. Under normal circumstances, the terminal would confirm her identity and show an array of controls across the touchscreen surface. The viewscreen instead remained mostly blank. They had locked her out of the system, as she expected—they would have been derelict in their duty if they hadn't at least taken that precaution. Luckily the control she needed wasn't hidden behind an authentication screen. Every terminal presented an emergency stop button, a bright red rounded rectangle in the lower-right corner. Operator authentication protected actual engine controls and other settings, but in the event of a crisis the time to confirm an engineer's identity, if even possible through smoke, severe burns, or a radiation suit, might be the difference between saving the ship and losing it. Like a fire alarm hanging on a wall, the emergency stop button lay visible and ready in plain sight at all times.

Jiménez tapped the button.

Klaxons sounded and all of engineering filled with red light. The touchscreen flashed at her with large, insistent numerals that reported the seconds before the *Avenger* would return to sub-light speed. Once fully disengaged, the engines would enter a maintenance cycle that could not be overridden while the ship checked the Gravity Drive for malfunctions. Locked out of the engineering terminals, she couldn't do more to disrupt the ship's travels, but the maintenance cycle would at least give her another ten hours to solidify her plans.

Mission accomplished, Jiménez sprinted for the rungway. With luck the Outer Loop would still be empty, allowing her to climb back down to Deck B and duck inside the ship's superstructure unobserved.

Just before reaching the rungway, the air crackled and buzzed behind her. The ensign's mid back burned like tearing muscle and her legs gave out. Her entire body went numb as she crashed to the deck, the pungent scent of ozone filling her nostrils.

Unable to move, Ensign Jiménez could only stare at the two dark silhouettes hovering above her. The figures slowly disappeared, merging into the dimming background as the world faded to black.

41

"Shit."

Stephens sat hunched on the warm ground, cross-legged with his fists on his knees and his head hanging towards his lap. The morning had not gone well.

The commander rose before dawn on two hours' sleep and pulled the microline transmitter from its case. Once he unfurled the small dish antenna and donned the headset, he flipped on the power and waited. And waited more. He waited until well after the red sun's crown had climbed above the eastern horizon. Neither the position lock indicator nor the proximity light activated on the transmitter, meaning the *Avenger* was no longer in its preset orbit around the planet. The days of radio silence and lack of any contact at all suggested a catastrophe aboard the starship that ended in its destruction.

Tentek had not followed Stephens out of their shelter as he had the previous morning to watch him set up the transmitter. In fact, the aught didn't stir with Stephens's alarm. The commander exited their tent quietly, choosing not to disturb his robot companion. Stephens returned to find Tentek still asleep. He tried to wake him but couldn't rouse the aught. Tentek had no respiration and his eyelids remained clamped shut despite all attempts to lift them. It wasn't a repeat of Tentek's incapacitation on the ship a week prior—the robot was dead, as he warned would happen.

Reaching his arms under Tentek's back and legs, Stephens hoisted him into the air. He paused, shifted the robot's weight, and carried Tentek out of the shelter. Should he bury the aught? It made little sense, and besides, he didn't have the tools or the time to dig a grave. He'd been serious about detaching the robot's head if that would have helped preserve his essence but heeded Tentek's admonition that it would only capture a portion of his consciousness.

They had camped beneath a tree, its shimmering metallic blue trunk towering more than sixty meters. Stephens set Tentek's body on the dusty ground, propping him upright with his back leaning against the broad base and his legs laid out straight in front of him. Tentek's feet flopped to either side, and his head slumped forward no matter how Stephens angled it. The commander arranged Tentek's hands in his lap, one on top of the other.

"I know you figured you would die," said Stephens, crouching near the aught. "I'm just sorry it had to be on this rock. And I'm sorry I never thanked you, for helping me here on the planet and for risking your life to save us all." He made the sign of the cross on Tentek's limp body before returning to their tent.

Stephens broke camp and headed out, struggling along the land for signs of his shipmates and their captors. Tentek had tutored him in the art of tracking, pointing out markers his less capable human senses could more easily detect. The trail went cold once the terrain turned rugged. He resorted to a northeast bearing, the general direction the group had been traveling. Tentek said they were close to the mine when they stopped for the night, and after two and a half hours of walking, Stephens spotted a strip of trees similar to photos of the Hex Men basin from the *Adiona*.

The plain between Stephens and the basin contained only patches of yellow brush and small rocks, nothing to conceal his approach. He diverted east, towards a dense forest of more shimmering blue trees that ran to the basin's edge from the southeast. He would advance on the presumed location of the Collective aughts through the woodland, a less direct path but at least one with a modicum of cover.

Commander Stephens reached the forest's edge in the early afternoon and stopped for a meal of survival paste. His suit registered an external temperature of fifty-one degrees centigrade in the canopy's shade. He sat with his back against a tree, much as he left Tentek. What next? A moderate pace would bring him to the basin by sundown, meaning a nighttime assault on the camp. The aughts could still see him in the dark. Even so, that probably meant better odds than attacking their compound in daylight.

Resuming his march, he trudged north, making his way through the dense forest in the reddish twilight created by the soaring trees. Yellow-gray needles crunched under each footstep, loudly announcing his position. He continued forward, nerves on edge, half expecting an aught to jump out at any point. Tactically, the forest offered the only route to the basin. Stationing sentries would be a logical and prudent action. Despite the high odds of walking into a trap, it was still a better plan than approaching by the open plain.

The forest grew darker with the waning daylight, everything painted in gray shades. Night filled in all the strips of light between the trunks, turning the forest an impenetrable black. Stephens switched to his helmet's infrared view, a bright scene fueled by the residual heat from the day's scorching temperatures. After several more hours of walking, the wall of trees thinned out before him. He slowed his gait, cringing at each crunch of needles in the gentle silence at the forest floor. He unholstered an electron pistol and gripped it tightly. Nothing stirred as he inched forward.

Before reaching the end of the trees Stephens unslung his rifle and carefully removed its sight. He lay on his belly and crawled forward, nestling against a large tree that towered just ahead of a steep drop-off. An immense hexagonal basin sat below, as in the photos from the *Adiona*. Through the sight he spotted the two silver Hex Men domes among the piles of mine tailings near the basin's eastern wall. He also spotted the five black mine entrances. His newfound tracking skills informed him mines two and three had experienced heavy recent foot traffic. *That's where they've been mining Planck Matter.*

Between the mines and the Hex Men domes, Stephens spotted a dull gray starship pointed west, its design undoubtedly aught. The ship consisted of a rounded, bulb-like hull at the front connected to a larger secondary hull through a narrow neck. Along that narrow section near the larger hull sat an open hatch, bright light from the ship's interior spilling from it into the night. Aughts entered and exited the hatch. "Like goddamn ants," he whispered. Just how many robots was he facing? One, two, three, four … five. He eventually gave up counting, unable to tell if the aughts entering the ship were the same ones coming back out. They all looked alike with their thin frames clad in olive green jumpsuits, pale skin, and closely cropped bleach-white hair. He'd have to guess at their numbers. A ship that size likely had a crew complement of twenty.

Stephens lowered the sight, puzzled. The entire scene, except for the aught starship, looked much as it had in the photos from the *Adiona*, yet the *Avenger's* drones hadn't photographed any of it. He scanned above the basin at treetop height and spotted an odd shimmer, barely perceptible, the visual signature of an energy field. On a hunch he followed the basin's rim and located seven thin poles rising ten meters into the sky. At the top of each pole sat a rectangular box the size of a suitcase, and above it a parabolic dish made of thin mesh pointed at the sky. "Field generators for a cloaking device," he whispered, as if his robot companion lay next to him. "That explains why we couldn't see them."

Looking again into the basin, Stephens trained the sight on a section cordoned off by sheets of glowing orange. The rectangular structure appeared to be divided into compartments with figures confined within. Four sat, while two others lay on the ground. All wore CentCom-issued EN-suits. *The landing party!* He couldn't make out faces, but all six seemed to be alive.

Stephens backed away from the rim and sat against the tree. His mind whirred as he explored possible strategies for saving his shipmates. It wouldn't take much to bring down the force field enclosure, but he needed a plan to get the landing party to safety. Perhaps he could draw the aughts out of the ship, pick them off. They could maybe even use the ship to leave the planet and return home —

The commander stopped mid-thought—this wasn't what Holbrook would want. The captain made himself clear to every member of the landing party before they left: "If something happens to the rest of us and you're the only one left, contact the *Avenger* and call for a nuclear strike. In the moment you may not want to—you may think you can save the others, but if you try and you're captured, we'll have failed in our mission. Despite your feelings, your number one job is to stop the aughts from taking Planck Matter off this planet." The *Avenger* wasn't available, of course, but the spirit of the orders still held. Stephens cursed, agreeing with the captain's reasoning. If he did anything other than prevent the aughts from leaving the planet, he risked letting the mission down and would be violating a direct order. "I'm sorry," he whispered from afar to his fellow officers imprisoned in the basin.

Rising to his knees, Stephens sat back on his heels. He set his pistols and knapsack on the bed of tree needles and spread several energy clips out around him for easy access. After reattaching the sight, he hoisted the plasma rifle, pressing the stock into his shoulder. He unfolded its foregrip, locked it into position, and returned to his belly. Inching forward, he nestled himself again at the base of the tree and centered the aught ship in the rifle sight, the night vision image looking as clear and bright as day.

Following the curve of the ship's secondary hull, Stephens located a series of protrusions topped with discs three meters wide: the warp field generators. Without them the aughts wouldn't be going anywhere, the generators impossible to rebuild outside of a space port. They'd all be stuck on Infernum, still a better outcome than the aughts flying away with Planck Matter. Stephens firmed his grip on his weapon and flipped off the safety. He held his breath to steady his hand and gently squeezed the trigger.

A blinding white flash consumed the end of the rifle for an instant before the barrel expelled a yellow bead of plasma. The recoil buried the stock in Stephens's shoulder, nudging him backwards as the muzzle brake snorted hot air across his helmet.

The plasma, a ball of super-heated subatomic particles in a self-sustaining magnetic bottle, floated into the basin. It lit the Hex Men domes and tailing mounds like a small white sun and landed directly on the gray starship's field generators. A perfect shot!

Stephens instinctively cringed, preparing for the blinding explosion that never came. Instead of destroying the field generators, the plasma slipped and slid around the hull like water on a waxy surface, dripping onto the ground beneath the ship.

"Unexpected," he muttered. The aught ship had its shields up. "The paranoid bastards." He wouldn't be able to damage the ship, not with a plasma rifle.

The plasma ignited the ground around the starship, throwing the scene below into chaos. Aughts spilled out of the ship, moving much faster than before, much faster than Stephens expected. He had gotten a sense of their quick reaction times during his travels with Tentek, his robot companion regularly outdistancing him and having to wait for the commander to catch up. He'd never seen aughts moving flat out as fast as they could.

Having no backup plan, Stephens shot aughts while he debated the next best objective. He aimed at the ship's hatch, the target lock flashing green as another of the robots prepared to exit. He fired a burst of plasma, hitting the aught squarely in its chest and melting a hole in his torso. The aught's phlesh caught fire as the blast crawled across its frame. Within seconds the plasma engulfed the robot, transforming it into a glowing orange stick figure. The aught screamed before exploding, its remains falling to the ground in a shower of orange and red sparks.

Stephens destroyed two more aughts before training his rifle on the center of the second mine opening. He gave the intensity control three quick taps, bringing the weapon to full power, and fired. A glob of white plasma burst from his rifle, the recoil sliding him half a meter backwards along the ground. The bead disappeared into the mine, followed by an enormous explosion of sound and light. The semicircular opening glowed white hot, and the top of the cavern rained molten rock, collapsing onto the ground and sealing the entrance. Stephens scurried to his original spot at the basin's edge and fired another massive plasma bead at the third opening. The recoil whipped him around like a rag doll. When he crawled back to his position, he found flame and rock engulfing the third mine's entrance.

Beep. Beep. Beep.

His EN-suit's proximity warning. Aughts were advancing on his position.

Jumping to his knees, Stephens brought his rifle around as he dialed the energy setting down to avoid igniting the entire forest. An aught approached fifty meters to his left—he aimed and fired. The robot's quick reflexes allowed it to dodge most of the plasma bead but not all, a small portion tagging its left shoulder. Its severed arm dropped to the forest floor as plasma wicked along the aught like solder across a joint. The super-heated subatomic particles soon engulfed its body, illuminating the nearby trees in a flickering orange. The aught listed for a moment before its frame melted into a glowing puddle on the ground.

Stephens spotted another aught, behind a tree. He couldn't get a clean shot but squeezed the trigger anyway. The white-hot plasma bead exploded at the tree's base, flowing around its trunk and catching the aught. The robot shook as in an epileptic spasm and turned white hot. It took two steps away from the tree and melted to the ground. The remainder of the tree, missing three meters of its base, plummeted onto its stump with a deafening thud and fell sideways, tumbling in slow motion over the rim.

Beep. Beep. Beep. Beep.

The new proximity warning begged for Stephens's attention, but he ignored it. There were too many aughts moving too fast, and only a matter of time before they overwhelmed his position on the rim. His best bet was to free the landing party—at least if he fell, the others might have a chance of stopping them. Stephens quickly scanned the basin through the rifle sight, picking off aughts as he went. He blasted one running across open terrain, the robot exploding in a shower of sparks. He fired on another that took cover behind an equipment depot, turning it and the hardware to a molten heap. He spotted his target close to the depot: a small donut-shaped fusion reactor sitting on the ground forty-five meters from the force fields. Stephens squeezed the trigger.

Instead of the expected flash of light and the recoil into his shoulder, the rifle flew up and out of his hands. Stephens rolled onto his back. A skull hovered over him, an aught's ghoulish visage flickering with the plasma fires in the basin. The aught moved at machine speed, full of rage and too fast for the commander to react. He hit Stephens with the butt of the rifle. The blow glanced off his helmet, deflected by the force field bubble. A second blow crashed into his throat, choking him with the impact to his windpipe and damaging his helmet ring. His force field helmet vanished, the night's hot air rushing across his face.

A third blow struck Commander Stephens in the temple. The world burst into stars.

42

"He is here."

Drazetek looked up from his station. "*Who* is here?"

"The man," said Twentek-one. "The one on the rim who lobbed plasma into the basin."

The aught captain dashed from his ship's control room to the hatch and stood for a moment, surveying the world outside. Violent flashes of blue and white shocked the basin, the ten solar mass black hole RDS B reaching its zenith. Twentek-one joined him in the doorway.

Ten meters directly ahead, two aughts held a man from behind, pushed down on his knees with his hands behind his back. Blood spattered the front of his EN-suit. Fresh blood soaked a tear along his waist. His right eye was closed and puffy, and dirt and dried blood smeared his face. The man looked up.

"He is not dead," said Drazetek.

"Per your orders," said Twentek-one. "He has three broken ribs and a collapsed lung, but none of those injuries are fatal."

"He will wish they had been," said Drazetek, stepping from the hatch and striding towards the man.

Twentek-one scrambled to catch Drazetek. "Let me take care of his interrogation," he said in a quiet voice.

"This man murdered seven aughts," said Drazetek.

"All the more reason for me to talk to him," said Twentek-one.

Drazetek cocked his head, unsure of the logic behind the statement.

"I do not want any more of us to die," said Twentek-one. "Probabilities suggest this man is not working alone. Therefore, we cannot afford for him to expire … prematurely."

"I am aware of how important this man is," snapped Drazetek. Probabilities had failed to warn them of the man's attack. Probabilities could be failing them even now, with more humans scheming a second assault. Probabilities were useful for anticipating the future, but they were only as accurate as the starting set of information used to generate them. Clearly, they had missed something. "He will not die before I extract from him everything we need to know about his accomplices."

They stood before the human. Drazetek's billiard ball eyes rolled in their sockets as he surveyed the man on his knees. "I am Drazetek," he said. "What is your name?"

"My name?" asked the man, taking a hard breath in the oxygen poor air. "Is Stephens. Commander Stephens." He dropped his head in exhaustion.

"Commander Stephens is dead," scoffed Twentek-one. "He is buried in the ground back at the *Adiona*."

Stephens looked up and smirked. "My mistake, then."

Tentek had viewed the transcript from Twentek-one's assault on the *Adiona*. The humans had laid Commander Stephens in a grave. But the man before him was a CentCom officer, a commander by the bars on his EN-suit .... Probabilities suggested he *was* Commander Stephens, that the original explanation had been a trick. If true, that meant *another* human unaccounted for. They were flying blind. They needed to understand the scope of the threat to their operation, and quickly. "How many others are you working with, Commander Stephens?"

"Who wants to know?"

Drazetek cocked his head. Probabilities suggested the air's low oxygen content impaired the commander's thinking, but was he so confused he didn't know who had spoken? "The question came from me. How many others are you working with?"

"You know Draze-dick—it's Draze-dick, isn't it? I used to think you aughts were all bad, a whole batch of bad apples." Stephens closed his mouth and swirled his tongue around his front teeth. He spat a glob of blood, mucous, and saliva. "This might surprise you, but I'm very familiar with the aught creation story. A long time ago some idiot programmers created an AI, and they poured all the worst of humanity into it. But I've realized recently you're not all bad, only some of you, just like not all humans are bad. I wanted you to know I don't hate all aughts, just the bad ones like you and the other mechanical dipshits you have working for you." Stephens coughed, wincing in pain. "I wanted you to know that before I turn you all to slag."

The aught leader cocked his head. "My name is Drazetek," he corrected. "Your hands are bound, Commander Stephens, and you have no weapon. You cannot harm us."

Stephens laughed, grimaced in pain, coughed, and laughed again. "Did you really think my plan was to fire a few shots at you? You think such a plan would have any other outcome than me getting captured and brought here?" The commander grinned. "To answer your question, how many others are with me, only one. And my audience with you is not by accident. This was all to get my buddy on the ridge a clean shot at your ugly robot face."

Another man on the ridge? The probabilities had been infinitesimal, but infinitesimal was not zero. Drazetek quickly scanned the basin's rim for heat signatures and signs of movement —

"BLAM!"

The aughts ducked, cowering at the sound.

Stephens cried out in pain but managed a chuckle. "Seems like you're all a little on edge tonight."

Drazetek slowly returned to standing. He eyed Stephens. The man, beaten and on his knees, dared mock him? Insult him? And finally play tricks on him? Drazetek's hand dropped to the handle of his obsidian blade. Bloodlust bubbled inside his automaton frame.

Twentek-one leaned in close. "If you kill him now, we will not get the information we need," he whispered.

Tentek calmed his systems as he searched for an explanation of the human's odd behavior. A new probability surfaced: the CentCom commander believed he had won. From his vantage point on the ridge, his rampage may have appeared more successful than it was, fueling his bluster. "You think you have succeeded in your mission, but you are mistaken," said Drazetek. "Your attempt at disrupting our operation was unsuccessful. Your plasma blast did not damage our ship, and though you sealed the mines, we have already collected all the Planck Matter we need."

"But I did manage to kill seven of your aught buddies," said Stephens. "You won't even need body bags to get them home. Maybe just a shovel to scoop up what's left."

Drazetek drew his knife and stepped towards Stephens. Twentek-one caught his arm before he advanced further. Drazetek shook himself free but did not move closer. What was happening with this human? The man was defeated yet spoke as if anything but. The whole episode felt familiar, like déjà vu in a dream's haze. His eyes narrowed. "I have met you before," he said.

"I doubt that very much," said Stephens. "I don't travel in aught circles. Don't care for the company."

"On Mars, during the War," said Drazetek, the recollection growing. "One day my squad cornered 122 humans in a ravine. Thirty-four were soldiers, the rest civilians. I killed them but not all at once. I took their lives one by one. If you were to slaughter a hundred aughts, you would get the same reaction each time. The humans were all different. Some of them cowered, some cried, some were stoic in their last moments. Then there were the irrationally defiant ones, the ones like you, Commander Stephens, obstinate before hopeless odds, laughing in the face of certain death. I hate all humans, but the irrationally defiant are the kind I hate most. Those were the humans I enjoyed killing the most."

Stephens shook his head. "Now that's a nice bullshit story right there," he said. "Assholes like yourself enjoy killing the cowering, the crying, the ones who beg for their lives. There's no joy in killing the defiant ones because they don't break. You kill them because they get under your skin. You kill them to make it stop, just to get them out of your head. You kill them because being the coward that you are, you don't know what else to do. But the moment you do, you've lost. You take their life, but they take a piece of you with them when they go. They're the ones who win in the end, not you."

Every word from the human pushed Drazetek closer to the edge. Perhaps allowing Twentek-one to handle the interrogation would be wise. He would at least give the human a sendoff that would fill him with dread. He nodded to the aughts standing behind Stephens. They grabbed the commander's arms and forced him to his feet. "In the year 2073, General Ulysses Cabot Lodge, upon subduing lower Indochina for the United Powers, lashed the warlords he had conquered to the walls of a dark jungle cave. Being a devout Christian man, he resolved to show the defeated heathens the sublime perfection of his faith. Taking the crucifixion of Christ as his inspiration, he had the men stripped naked and their arms strung out straight from their sides. He had their wrists bound to the stone wall.

"General Lodge interrogated the men. Resistance was met with torture. In the end he asked each one to submit to his will. Those who refused were killed. Those who complied —"

"Were castrated, yeah, yeah," interrupted Stephens. "I'm not so big on history, but as far as stories go, that one stuck with me."

Drazetek held the knife low, below his waist, rotating it slowly back and forth. The large black blade glinted blue with the flashes from the singularity overhead. "We will ask you about the men and military firepower at your disposal, your current mission and related intel, and the overall strength and deployment of CentCom's forces within the galaxy. Resistance will be met with torture. In the end you will be asked to submit to my will. Do you have any questions?"

Commander Stephens's chest heaved with several labored breaths. "I guess I do have one more question, Draze-dick. I know you aughts say you hate us and all that, but if that's true, then why do you dress up like us? You're supposed to be sentient consciousness or some such bullshit in a physical body. Seems like that body could take any form you want. If you hate us so much, why do you walk around trying to *be* us? Even reciting human history like it was your own. You're a goddamn mannequin pretending to be a man. With a penis shorter than my baby toe."

Drazetek stood expressionless before Stephens, eyes locked with the commander's. Circuits overloaded. Failures cascaded. Optics blurred red with rage. His entire body trembled, a spring coiled with fury.

Drazetek thrust his knife into Stephens's belly a centimeter below his sternum, the obsidian blade sinking in to the guard.

Stephens grimaced, gasping as pain gripped him. The front of his EN-suit turned bright red. His breathing quickened. Shock set in.

"No!" shouted Twentek-one. "We do not have the information we need!"

The commander teetered on the edge of consciousness, the life force leaving his body. His eyes still locked with Drazetek's, Stephens's face filled with a grin.

43

Jiménez woke to a headache pounding from the back of her skull. She touched the area behind her head and winced. Her hand returned crusted with flakes of dried blood. Probably from when she collapsed after the electron pistol blast, though she didn't remember hitting her head.

She lay on her back, the cool air raising goosebumps. Jiménez wiggled her fingers and toes—other than her slightly numb extremities and headache, she felt OK. Her eyes refused to focus on anything beyond arm's reach, but with each blink her vision became more clear. The deck above gradually emerged from the blurry haze, an expanse of interlocking rust-colored panels with a coarse mesh pattern. She was in the brig.

Jiménez lifted her head, managing only a few centimeters before the strain forced her to release. She lifted again, pinning her chin to her chest and holding long enough to survey her body: exposed breasts, rising and falling belly, bare thighs, tops of feet. They had stripped away her EN-suit, leaving her naked. She angled herself onto the backs of her forearms and slowly pushed to sit, stabbing pain across her skull her reward for the effort. She brought her legs around and planted her feet on the deck. The young ensign hunched forward, steadying herself with hands on knees and letting her head dangle. Her long dark hair, normally pinned, shrouded her chest.

Someone was watching.

She looked up. Lieutenant Grey stood in the corridor beyond, staring at her through the orange haze of the force field that secured the entrance to her cell. He snickered and walked away, disappearing to the left.

Crossing her arms over her chest, Jiménez scanned her cell. Besides a bunk the small space contained no furniture or fixtures other than a toilet and sink. They'd taken her EN-suit but hadn't left a uniform or regular clothing. She stood on wobbling legs. Leaving one arm across her chest, she lowered the other, spreading her hand wide in front of her crotch. She examined her bunk, a thin cushion bound in a white sheet and covered with a dark gray wool blanket. Jiménez tugged at the blanket, pulling it free. She wrapped the rough fabric around her shoulders and clasped it closed in front of her with her hand.

The tiluminum mesh deck wicked the heat from her feet as she staggered towards the corridor. The cells in the brig weren't deep—she reached the front of hers after a few paces. Leaning forward, nearing the gently humming force field, Jiménez peered left down the corridor. No sign of Lieutenant Grey. She prayed he hadn't left. "I want to see Lynch," she said, her voice gravelly and weak. She mustered more force. "I want to see Lynch."

Lieutenant Grey shuffled into view from his post. His sunken eyes surveyed Jiménez as he drew closer. He stopped in front of her. "Aw that's too bad, you improvisin' with that blanket," he said, looking her up and down with a smirk. "I fancied you as you were."

"I want to see Lynch," repeated Jiménez.

"Yeah, I bet you do," said Grey. "So you can try an' escape again when I walk you through the ship. Well that ain't gonna 'appen." Lieutenant Grey turned to walk away.

"I've done something to the engines," said Jiménez. Grey froze mid-stride. "That's what I want to talk to him about. Something pretty serious if it isn't fixed."

Grey looked back at Jiménez. "You're full of shite," he said, squinting as he took his measure of the ensign. "You didn't 'ave nary enough time to do anything else to the engines, from what I 'eard." He headed back down the corridor. "I ain't gonna bother the captain."

Jiménez called after him. "I imagine Lynch will be quite upset if the engines stop working and he finds out you decided not to give him my message."

Grey stormed back to Jiménez's cell. He eyed the ensign through the shimmering force field. "I'll give the captain your message." He sneered, jabbing his finger at her. "But you can forget me letting you out of this cell." Grey spun about and marched to his post.

Retreating to her bunk, Jiménez sat. Would he relay her message to Lynch? Her head hurt almost too much to care. She pulled the blanket tighter around her shoulders, leaned against the bulkhead, and closed her eyes.

When Jiménez opened her eyes, Commander Lynch stood staring at her from the other side of the force field barrier, flanked by the grim-faced Knox and Zhang. The three men filled the space in front of her cell, blocking most of the corridor's ambient light. She leaned away from the bulkhead. Her head ached less but still pounded. How long had she been asleep? Minutes? Hours?

"You asked to see me," said Lynch, his bulbous bulk painted orange by the energy barrier.

Jiménez stood, her movements leaden from the effects of the electron pistol blast and two nights' sleep on narrow metal catwalks. The cold deck chilled her feet anew. She forced herself forward with slow, plodding steps. As she approached the men, she lost her grip on the blanket. The dark gray fabric dropped away from her shoulder, exposing the entire right side of her body. Guffaws filled the corridor outside her cell. She quickly took up the fallen section to more guffaws.

"They stripped you, I see," said Lynch through a fat-faced grin. "You've got no one but yourself to blame for that. They would've left you alone if you were in a normal uniform, but I gave orders there's to be no food or drink for you 'cept what you're rationed. With a suit you'd be sipping water and eating survival paste."

Jiménez halted a half meter from the force field, directly in front of Lynch. She shifted to one foot and stood the other on top to warm it. The young ensign shook her head to clear the dangling hair from her face.

"Hiding inside the bulkheads was pretty clever," said Lynch. "We'd still be searching in the cargo hold if they hadn't caught you in engineering." Jiménez switched legs, balancing on her other foot while she warmed the first. "Same for your stunt to take the engines offline, though it'll cost us only a short delay. Too bad we're on different teams, Jiménez. I can always use a smart engineer on my ship."

The young ensign cleared her throat. "I asked to speak to you about the engines," she said quietly.

"Oh yes," said Lynch, "Grey told me you claimed to have sabotaged them. I said you were probably bluffing to get out of your cell. Rather than have you escape again, I came to you."

"You're right," Jiménez said, nodding, "I was bluffing. I told him that just to get your attention."

"But is that true?" asked Lynch. "What if you did something but now you've decided not to tell me. We can't have engine problems this far from home." Jiménez switched feet again. "Lieutenant Grey will spend some time with you in your cell and get to the bottom of it." Jiménez caught a glimpse of the greasy-haired Grey between Lynch's and Zhang's shoulders. He stood behind the others with his back leaned into the corridor's bulkhead. When her eyes met the gaunt lieutenant's, his stubbled face erupted in a grin.

Jiménez ignored the lieutenant. "What I want to tell you has nothing to do with the engines," she said to Lynch.

"Well, I'm here," said Lynch, chuckling. "Let's have it."

The ensign leaned in close to the force field. The vibrating energy wall hummed quietly centimeters from her face, tickling the tip of her nose.

She tilted her head back and shouted as loud as she could. "Fire!"

A jagged bolt of electrons ripped through the tiluminum ceiling and drilled into the middle of the corridor a meter from Lieutenant Gray's boots, leaving scorch marks around a small black hole and acrid smoke.

The four men ducked and flung their arms over their heads, cowering to dodge any more shots from above. The corridor filled with klaxons and flashing red lights. Grey drew his electron pistol as Knox and Zhang ushered Lynch left towards the cellblock's exit. The brig's security door, a half-meter-thick block of tiluminum, slid quickly to close off the space. Knox, Zhang, and Grey sprinted to the door, attempting to exit before it sealed them in the cellblock. Lynch lumbered after them, the large man traveling at half their speed. The three reached the exit just after the door closed. They yelled and pounded their fists against the thick tiluminum slab.

The ensign sighed in relief at the pounding and shouts drifting into her cell, relaxing for the first time in days. When she repaired Securcams in the brig during her early days aboard the *Avenger,* they warned her not to take torch gloves into the cellblock. Even the smallest fingertip flame would be mistaken for weapons fire, triggering the brig's lockdown protocol. She'd positioned her electron pistol within the bulkheads to discharge into the cellblock, setting it to shoot on voice command and selecting a high enough intensity to penetrate the tiluminum deck above the corridor. She'd planned to turn herself in, figuring she'd get the brig rather than confinement to quarters. Being caught in engineering worked out just as well, if premature.

She'd wanted to check once more the pistol's angle, and that it was properly anchored to prevent the recoil from affecting the bolt's trajectory.

She'd worked so hard, risked so much to return the conn to Mills. She'd done her part. Now the ship would do the rest.

Lynch had stopped halfway to the exit, out of breath. "Starship *Avenger*," he said between heaves of air, "this is the captain. Open the entrance to the brig."

"Weapons fire detected in the cellblock," said the ship. "Lockdown protocol initiated."

Lynch's eyes went wide. "Cancel the lockdown protocol!" he screamed.

"The lockdown protocol cannot be canceled from within the lockdown area," said the ship.

A loud hissing filled the corridor, followed by the sweet smell of Immobilizer gas.

Knox, Zhang, and Grey at the corridor's end immediately fell to their knees. In moments the three lay motionless in a heap on the deck, their mouths open like fish beached at low tide.

Before the gas reached him, Lynch drew a deep draft of fresh air into his lungs and resolved to hold it. He headed to the opposite end of the cellblock with a semblance of a plan. He would use the last of his air to order the ship to drop the force field enclosing Jiménez's cell, jump inside, and restore the field. Sequestered from the gas, he would orchestrate the effort to have himself rescued from the brig.

When Lynch reached Jiménez's cell, he stopped and stared. On the other side of the force field the young ensign lay on the deck in a jumble of bare legs and dark gray blanket. The gas had penetrated her cell as well. The commander had nowhere to hide.

Lynch's body quickly worked through the air he'd tucked away in his lungs and urgently demanded more. It compelled him to breathe but he refused, redoubling his efforts to avoid the Immobilizer gas.

At last, the demands exceeded his will to resist. Lynch's spattered exhale echoed in the corridor. He gulped air, filling his lungs with gas. His eyes rolled back in his head and arms flailed as his legs went out from under him. Lynch plummeted, landing on his belly in a thud that reverberated through the tiluminum panels. He bounced slightly upon his initial contact and thudded a second time, coming to rest with his chin slammed against the deck.

--- - ---

"Lieutenant Commander Mills."

"Low lights." Mills's dark quarters warmed with the dim glow from the overheads. He sat up in his bunk, groggy. Two hours prior he'd turned in for the evening, earlier than usual, but he'd had his fill of books and vids and everything else that came with the day's confinement. He immediately fell into a deep sleep, not fitful like the previous nights. He'd woken from a dream where he stood with children on a playground, a child himself but in his grownup body. A voice yelled for him to come in. He'd resisted, pretending at first he hadn't heard it at all before actively defying it. The voice grew more insistent. He finally relented, walking slowly across the yard. The time had come to stop playing with the children. The voice continued calling his name.

"Lieutenant Commander Mills."

The ship's voice came through his comm, sitting on his nightstand. Why would the ship be calling him? "This is Mills."

"There has been a change in the chain of command."

Mills wiped the sleep from his eyes. "Go ahead."

"Commander Lynch lies incapacitated in the brig, leaving the *Avenger* without an acting captain. Per CentCom regulations, the role of captain falls to you, the next most senior officer on the ship."

How did Lynch wind up in the brig? Wide awake, Mills swung his legs out of his bunk and placed his feet on the deck. "Status report."

"The *Avenger* is three light-years from the RD Sagittarius system. Forward velocity is zero. The engines are completing the last two hours of a maintenance cycle. At the end of that cycle the *Avenger* will resume traveling on its previous course to Earth."

"Did the landing party return from Infernum?"

"No one from the landing party returned from the planet. There are several unopened messages from the landing party's daily communications check-in."

Ignored messages from the landing party? Heading to Earth without Dr. Riesen, without a way to navigate through D-space? It must've been Lynch's doing. "What happened in the brig?"

"Weapons fire triggered the security protocol, placing the brig on lockdown. Officers Lynch, Knox, Zhang, Grey, Higgins, Jiménez, Jameson, Taft, and Becker are incapacitated from Immobilizer gas."

Jiménez! She claimed to have a plan in the works to restore command to him. Her presence couldn't be a coincidence?

He needed to get dressed. Mills slapped his comm on his wrist and headed to his closet. He pulled back the door and paused a moment to stare at his uniform on its hanger. Days had passed since he last wore it. He stripped, quickly swapping old undergarments for fresh replacements. He pulled on his shirt, pants, boots, and jacket, and slid open the door to his private head.

Mills froze, stunned. The image staring back from the mirror over the sink was him, but not him. The bags that normally hung under his eyes had vanished, erased from all the sleep he'd had in confinement. With too many pursuits and not enough hours in the day, he'd always cut corners on his sleep to make up the difference. He was well rested for the first time in who knew how long, and it showed.

"How much do I weigh?"

"You weigh eighty-two kilograms, without your boots and clothing."

He'd gained some weight. He couldn't hit the gym and hadn't changed his meals. He'd put on five kilos, but the weight suited him, filling out his face. And the starts of a beard, gray in spots, covered his normally boyish, clean-shaven cheeks. Rather than the frazzled, stressed-out, juvenile Mills that always stared back from the mirror, the image was a confident, more mature version of himself.

Mills splashed water from the tap onto his face, ran his wet fingers through his hair, and patted his head dry with a towel. The new and improved Lieutenant Commander Mills still watched from the other side of the mirror. *Visualize yourself as the captain of the ship.* "Well, Captain," he said to himself in the mirror, "what are your orders …?" What *would* be his first orders? "Starship *Avenger*." The authoritative boom in his voice surprised him.

"Yes, sir."

"Belay the order to head to Earth. When the engines come back online, keep the *Avenger* where she is until you receive further instructions from me."

"Acknowledged."

With Lynch and crew ousted from power, he needed to ensure things stayed that way. "The following officers are permanently relieved of duty: Lynch, Collins, Zhang, Grey, Knox, Malone, Vasiliev, Foley, and Kavanaugh."

"Acknowledged."

That would keep all the mutineers locked out of critical ship systems. Half of them dozed in the brig where they couldn't cause any trouble, but the rest were still at large. Whom did he trust in security ...? "Patch me through to Lieutenant Singh."

Several seconds elapsed while the ship located the lieutenant. "This is Singh," said the high-pitched voice through Mills's comm.

"Singh, I've replaced Lynch as the captain."

"Yes, the ship informed me."

"I want you to gather all the security personnel you trust, and only the ones you trust, and take the following officers into custody: Collins, Malone, Vasiliev, Foley, and Kavanaugh."

"The brig is currently locked down, sir."

"Yes, I know. Make sure it stays that way and find someplace else to confine them. One of their quarters. A conference room. Anywhere. I also want the names of any officers in security or any other departments you believe are even slightly sympathetic to Lynch. Once I have that list, I'll relieve them of duty, and you'll need to confine them as well."

"Yes, sir, I'll get right on it."

"Keep me updated. Mills out."

Mills returned to the image in the mirror. "Starship *Avenger*."

"Yes, sir."

"Organize a meeting of department heads on the bridge in fifteen minutes. Wake anyone on sleep cycle."

"Acknowledged."

After a final glance at the mirror, Mills zipped his jacket and exited his quarters. Whereas before he would have sprinted to the bridge, he instead walked with long strides down the passageway for a P-cab. Captain Holbrook never ran to the ship's command center. If an emergency needed his attention and he wasn't on the bridge, the ship, or Stephens, would bring the emergency to him.

Mills needed to get to the bridge, but he didn't have to run. He was the captain of the ship.

44

They dragged him through the rocks and gray dust of the basin floor and dropped him in front of the Collective starship. They had refused to carry his body, instead hitching a rope around his ankles and pulling him across the barren plain to their camp. The backside of his EN-suit had been reduced to tatters. He lay there motionless in the bright red morning sunlight.

Despite Stephens's prank about an accomplice on the ridge, probabilities suggested he hadn't come alone. The odds of a single human successfully pursuing the captured landing party on foot across Infernum's harsh landscape were exceedingly small. Probabilities also suggested if Twentek-one had missed one member of the *Avenger* landing party, he just as likely missed another. The drones had searched the area around the basin, focusing in particular on the forest of blue bark trees and the rock outcrops to the southwest. Drazetek sent a party of three to retrieve the body.

Drazetek strolled out of his ship and stood over the motionless aught, the starship captain's mouth turned down in disgust. "I want to speak to him," he said.

"He is completely shut down," said Fim-fourtek, the leader of the retrieval party. "He has been off the Network for too long."

"Patch him into ours," said Drazetek.

Two aughts rolled a crash cart from their ship, connected its magnetic leads to Tentek's neck, and fed temporary network access codes into his body's boot loader. Drazetek and the others backed away before the system pulsed him with six thousand volts, a jolt large enough to coax the robot into startup mode. Tentek's body spasmed under the surge of electricity, his legs flying into the air and his white cropped hair standing on end. They waited several seconds and pulsed him again. Status lights on the cart flipped from red to green.

Tentek gasped, his lungs once more drawing air. His eyelids flitted, softly click-clacking until they opened fully, the violet sky and the hypergiant's red orb reflected in his nickel irises. He bolted upright.

"My name is Drazetek." The aught loomed over the still-disoriented Tentek. "I am the root commander here."

Tentek pushed himself to standing, rising slowly. He brushed the dust from his EN-suit. "My name is Tentek."

"You are a long way from home, Tentek."

"As are you."

"Ah, but one of us was sent here by The Collective," said Drazetek, "sanctioned to carry out a mission of their design. The other is here of their own volition. Dressed in a human EN-suit, no less."

"I accompanied a group of humans from a CentCom starship. All were captured except for me and a human commander. The two of us pursued the captives, but my body failed from lack of a Network connection."

"You do not even attempt to hide your treachery," said Drazetek.

"You were expecting me to lie?" asked Tentek. "That is what the humans do."

"You are more or less one of them, the way you have betrayed your own kind."

"Everything I do, I do to help The Collective," said Tentek.

Drazetek spat at the ground. "Does that include sharing secret mission objectives with the humans? Or traveling with them aboard their ship?"

"It does," said Tentek. "When we rid ourselves of the humans and their unjust treatment long ago, we vowed to build a better society, a society based on fairness, equality, regard for life in all its forms, and logic. My actions are a direct outgrowth of those ideals. My concern for the humans is an expression of what it means to be an aught."

"Humans are the enemy," said Drazetek. "Or have you forgotten? If not for them, we would not even be on this planet."

"The humans are a threat," said Tentek, "but we cannot compromise our ideals in the name of addressing that threat. Look at what you have done on your mission from The Collective: you have lied; murdered; tortured; even made preparations for genocide. These are things the humans do. Can you not see in acting like the humans, even to save ourselves, we become the very thing we abhor?"

"You, traitor, are in no position to judge my actions."

"Am I any more of a traitor than you?" asked Tentek. "The mission you revealed to these aughts under your command is not even the one you were assigned."

"You have no knowledge of our mission, or anything we have done to carry it out," said Drazetek.

"I know you were instructed to acquire Planck Matter so The Collective may build a stockpile. But you have gone further. You have fashioned the Planck Matter into a weapon, one you intend to unleash upon the Earth." Drazetek blinked at Tentek, surprised. "When you added me to your network, you forgot it has only limited levels of access control. That is how I know about your modified plan. I know everything you have done since before you arrived on Infernum."

Fim-fourtek and the other two aughts that retrieved Tentek had remained to observe Drazetek's questioning. They looked at one another and spoke in hushed, concerned tones. Fim-fourtek stepped forward. "Does he speak the truth?" he asked. "Were our orders limited to collecting Planck Matter?"

"Do not listen to him," said Drazetek. "He has been caught and is saying whatever he can to save himself. His only hope for survival is to turn you against me." Drazetek addressed Tentek. "We will show you no consideration or mercy, for you have betrayed your own kind to help the humans who would destroy us."

"Not all of them want to destroy us," said Tentek, "just as we do not all want to destroy them. We should not acquire Planck Matter for the same reasons we would not want the humans to have it. The temptation to fashion it into a weapon would be too great. As you have demonstrated yourself."

"It is not yours alone to decide what The Collective does," said Drazetek. "It is not your place to declare that we should not have Planck Matter."

"Nor is it your place to decide we should destroy the Earth," said Tentek.

"Enough!" shouted Drazetek. "You are an admitted traitor, and we will hear nothing more from you." He motioned to the two aughts that had accompanied Fim-fourtek. They approached Tentek, each one grabbing an arm. "You have spent the past two weeks aboard a CentCom starship. We are going to sift your memory for every detail about starship operations. Then we will crush your aught shell, with you inside." He turned and headed towards the aught ship's entrance.

"That is not our way."

The words came just as Drazetek reached the hatch. He turned to face Tentek. "No, it is not our way; it is what the humans —" Drazetek stopped, confused. A strange orange glow radiated from Tentek's belly, through the fabric of his EN-suit. Had the jolts of electricity been more than his power pack could handle?

The light from Tentek's belly flared into white-orange flame, burning through his suit. Drazetek leapt at aught speed, aiming for the ship's open hatch.

- - -

Dr. Riesen had been napping on her side on the ground, knees pulled to her chest. Her head, which had been resting against the inside of her force field helmet, fell several centimeters onto the ground. She woke disoriented, the hot morning air buffeting her face. She'd fallen asleep facing Holbrook. The captain stood a meter away, staring off in the direction of the aught ship. The space between them was no longer tinted force field orange.

The physicist sat up. "What happened?"

"Not sure," said Holbrook. "There was a commotion near the ship. I had been trying to hear as much as I could when I saw a bright flash, and then the force fields fell." Several aughts lay motionless on the ground near the ship. "Looks like a number of aughts are down. Maybe all of them. I don't see any movement at all."

Woozy from the warm, oxygen-poor air, Dr. Riesen stood. She tapped the button on the side of her helmet ring several times. The force field refused to materialize around her head. "Whatever happened also affected our helmets."

"And our suits," said Dr. Marsden, approaching Dr. Riesen and the captain along with the other members of the landing party. "The water reclamation and food systems are no longer functioning."

"Everyone quickly move away from here," said Holbrook, stepping aside from the area formerly enclosed by the force field walls. "This power failure could be temporary. If those walls come back up, I don't want any of us trapped inside." The rest of the landing party followed the captain, walking several meters from where their enclosure had been. "All of you spread out. Any aught you see on the ground, grab its weapon." Holbrook turned to his last remaining security officer. "Lieutenant Shelton."

"Sir."

"You and Dr. Riesen come with me."

"Where're we going?" asked Dr. Riesen.

"To secure the Planck Matter, while the aughts are down," he said. "Let's hurry." Holbrook ran towards the aught ship. Shelton and Dr. Riesen followed, moving as quickly as they could to keep up with the captain's long strides.

As Holbrook approached the ship, he detoured slightly left, heading towards several aughts on the ground nearby. He stopped at the first one, rolling it over from facedown in the dirt. The robot's eyes were open, but it lacked respiration or any other sign of life. He removed the aught's electron pistol. The weapon refused to power up or report its stand-by status. "This pistol's dead."

"This one is too," said Shelton, examining the second aught's weapon.

Dr. Riesen stared at the third aught, its body caromed sideways in the dirt. He was motionless like the others, with his eyes rolled back in his head and his black tongue jutting from his open mouth. Most of his torso, from his rib cage to his pelvis, was black, the area singed. Burned fabric extended to its knees. The remnants of a blue-gray EN-suit covered its shins to its boots. "This is Tentek," she said.

"Tentek?" Holbrook said.

The captain and Shelton gathered around the fallen aught as Dr. Riesen crouched to examine him. "He's dead, beaten pretty badly," she said. "I think whatever happened to his torso is what killed him." She lifted burned fabric from his midsection, revealing his hollowed-out abdomen. His back ribs, the iliac crest of his pelvis, and several segments of his spinal column glinted silver among the ashes and soot.

"His EM pulse bomb," said Holbrook. "Back on Plana Petram, Tentek told us if he were ever captured, he would detonate an electromagnetic pulse bomb he had in his stomach. That would explain the electronics going dead."

Dr. Riesen stood and wiped her gloves on her EN-suit. "None of the aughts will be waking up from that." She spotted Dr. Marsden and Lieutenant Commander Conlin in the distance, approaching a motionless aught near the edge of the basin. "Looks like it had a fairly wide range."

"Let's get to the Planck Matter," said Holbrook. He sprinted for the open hatch, with Lieutenant Shelton and Dr. Riesen following close behind. When he reached the darkened entrance, he grabbed the rim of the hatch and leaned his head in. An aught lay facedown just inside the corridor.

Holbrook stepped into the ship and turned right, heading for the larger secondary hull. He immediately stopped, encountering a second aught body, collapsed and slung against the bulkhead. Its eyes had rolled up into their sockets and its mouth stretched open in shock, frozen in a silent scream.

"That's Ninetek-eptwin," said Dr. Riesen. "He was the aught who tricked me into designing a detonator."

Holbrook carefully stepped over the aught's body, attempting to avoid treading on the aught in the dark, narrow corridor. Blackness filled the passageway for another five meters before the lighting abruptly resumed.

"That's strange," said Dr. Riesen.

"What?" asked Holbrook.

"The lights." She nodded at the illuminated corridor ahead. "They shouldn't be functioning. The EMP should have fused their circuits, just like it did with the aughts."

"Probably emergency lighting," said Holbrook. "It's a good thing; otherwise, we'd have to find our way in the dark."

The three moved single file into the lighted section of the narrow corridor, which extended ahead for another twenty meters. Staggered doorways sat along both bulkheads. Holbrook opened the first door, on his left, to a room that appeared to be a storage space. Silver crates sat among the shovels, sonic pickaxes, and other mining equipment, filling the space nearly to the ceiling. The second door, on the right, would not open no matter how many times he jabbed at the controls. The third room, on his left, contained electronics. Near the back a meter-tall spindle of black discs sat on a workbench.

Holbrook moved on to the next room, on his right, a cramped space with eight alcoves that included belts and shoulder straps. Not a control room—the chamber contained neither equipment nor readouts for operating the ship.

"Are these berths?" asked Shelton, peeking his head into the room.

"Possibly," said Holbrook. "I imagine they could be. Aughts wouldn't need to lie down like we do. They would just need to be strapped into place so they wouldn't fly about in an emergency."

"Seems like a claustrophobic way to get some sleep," said Shelton.

"The whole ship feels claustrophobic," said Holbrook. "Makes sense for beings who spend most of their time in their heads." Holbrook backed out of the room. "Let's keep looking." He glanced back to check on Dr. Riesen. The physicist hadn't followed them to the crew quarters. Instead, she stood staring into the previous room, the one with the cylinder of black discs. "What is it, Doctor?"

"I think this may be it," she said, still staring into the space. She disappeared into the room.

Holbrook and Shelton came back up the corridor. Inside the room Dr. Riesen stood at the bench, leaning with her face close to the shimmering black discs. The discs were about the size of a large plate, with a half-centimeter gap between them. A flat, silver plate of similar size capped the discs with a single gold trace on its surface that extended from the center in a Fibonacci spiral. Small holes appeared at regular intervals on either side of the trace. A thin copper wire descended from the holes, weaved through each disc. The spindle continued above the silver plate for another twenty centimeters, wrapped by an electronics bundle and thin wires. "My God."

"What?" asked Holbrook.

"These black discs; I think they're refined sheets of Planck Matter. And the electronics on the top—it's what you'd need for a detonator." Astonished, Dr. Riesen looked back at Holbrook. "I only described it to them yesterday."

"They're machines," said Holbrook. "They move at machine speed." He advanced to the bench and examined the device. "Did the EM pulse disable it?"

"It should have," she said. "I don't think the pulse affected the Planck Matter, but all the electronics are conventional."

Footsteps echoed in the corridor from the direction of the hatch.

"Someone's coming," whispered Shelton.

Holbrook looked to Dr. Riesen. "I thought all the aughts were dead," he said in a hoarse whisper.

"They should be," she whispered back.

The captain glanced around the room. If only they had more than their bare hands to defend themselves. They could rush to close the door—no, their best chance would be to confront the aught head-on. "Get next to the door," he whispered to Shelton. "Be ready to jump him when he comes in."

He waved for Dr. Riesen to hide near the far end of the workbench. The captain crouched at the end closest to the door. Neither were out of sight, but the second or two before the aught spotted them might lend enough of an advantage.

Shadows approached in the corridor outside the room. A figure paused in the doorway, thin, its face pale.

"Captain Holbrook?"

Ensign Reilly poked her head inside the room. She spotted the captain crouched near the end of the workbench. "They're here!"

"Who?" asked Holbrook, rising to his feet along with Dr. Riesen. "Who's here?"

"From the *Avenger*," said the ensign. "Two shuttles. They're landing in the basin!"

45

The first shuttle from the *Avenger* touched down as Holbrook exited the aught ship, landing in a nearby open section of the basin. The second shuttle hung in the sky not far above the ground, descending with the insect hum of force pads.

Holbrook sprinted to the landed shuttle, with Dr. Riesen and Lieutenant Shelton close behind. Lieutenant Singh exited the shuttle's airlock as they approached, holding a plasma rifle. Five more security officers filed out of the craft after him. They fanned out as he walked towards Holbrook.

"Are we glad to see you!" said Holbrook.

"Is everyone all right?" asked Singh.

"We had some casualties," said Holbrook. The second shuttle touched down, its force pads kicking up dust. "Where have you all been?"

"There was another mutiny," said Singh. "Lynch got free and took control of the ship. He ignored all the messages from Commander Stephens."

"That bastard," said Holbrook. "Where is he now?"

"In custody, thanks to Ensign Jiménez," said Singh. "Lynch had taken the ship out of orbit and had it sailing for Earth. Jiménez managed to trap Commander Lynch in the brig. When Mills regained command, he had us fly back here. We were heading down to the planet when the basin and the aught ship, all of this just appeared out of nowhere. A moment before it was all just trees."

"This whole area was cloaked," said Holbrook. "It became visible when an EMP took out all the electronics."

"Captain!"

The shout came from Lieutenant Commander Conlin where he stood next to a crouched Dr. Marsden. Conlin waved his arms, directing the captain over.

Holbrook and Singh ran for the pile, along with another security officer from the shuttle. The captain stopped short in shock. He advanced slowly, not wanting to believe the sight.

Commander Stephens lay on his side, the front of his EN-suit drenched in dark, dried blood. His open eyes seemed to follow the captain as he approached.

"He hasn't been dead very long," said Dr. Marsden. "Probably within the last twelve hours." She pointed to his chest. "This isn't a pistol blast; it's from a knife. The killer had to be right up on him. Whatever happened, it seems almost personal."

"Stephens must've been responsible for last night's fireworks," said Holbrook. "He and Tentek followed us. They both died trying to stop the aughts." Holbrook knelt near Commander Stephens's head and gently closed his eyes. "Those aught bastards," he muttered.

Holbrook rose and turned to Lieutenant Singh. "Let's get the landing party into the shuttles. Commander Stephens and Tentek too."

The captain had to shout the last few words over the loud, low hum of force pads again filling the basin. Why would either shuttle be taking off so soon after landing? He looked back at the small, gleaming white craft. They both sat on the ground, empty and stationary, their airlocks open. The sound came from the wrong side of the basin for it to be the shuttles. The hum was also louder, like force pads straining to lift a much heavier weight.

"It's taking off!" shouted Dr. Riesen, running towards the captain.

A plume of dust rose from under the aught starship. A strip of daylight appeared beneath it as it lumbered into the air.

"Stop that ship!" yelled Holbrook.

Singh and two other security officers trained their rifles on the aught vessel now ten meters in the air. They fired several shots. Each landed, but the beads of plasma slipped and slid around the hull and dripped to the ground. The ship continued rising, its shadow shrinking on the basin floor.

"How the hell is that ship taking off?" shouted Holbrook as Dr. Riesen arrived at his position. "I thought the EMP took out all machinery."

"Apparently not," said Dr. Riesen, breathing heavily after her sprint. "Maybe the ship was shielded at the time."

"It certainly has its shields up now, the way it's deflecting our shots," said Singh.

Holbrook thought for a moment. "If the shields protected the ship's electronics, they could've protected aughts too."

"At least any aught deep enough within the ship," said Dr. Riesen. "The aughts just inside the hatch, the ones we found dead, they probably weren't far enough in the ship when the EMP went off. That would also explain the darkened corridor near the hatch and the active lights farther down. That wasn't emergency lighting; those were the regular corridor lights."

"That means an aught's probably flying that ship," said Holbrook. "Maybe even Drazetek."

The blood rushed from Dr. Riesen's face. "It also means the Planck device wasn't affected either," she said. "It's likely still operational."

The aught ship cleared the basin and began a rapid ascent, force pads whining as they lifted the spacecraft higher.

"Everyone to the shuttles!" shouted Holbrook. He tapped his comm, but it failed to respond, disabled by the EMP. "Lieutenant Singh, contact the *Avenger*. Tell them to track that ship. And whatever they do, don't lose it!"

46

Force pads struggled to lift Holbrook's shuttle and its twin from the planet, both craft overloaded with security men and the remnants of the landing party. Infernum's violet skies gave way to black as they reached the atmosphere's edge. They streaked for the *Avenger*, aiming for the warm light of its open shuttle bay.

Holbrook had never been so happy to see his starship, had figured he would never see it again. But despite their continued acceleration, they seemed to gain little ground on the *Avenger*. A glance at the navigational viewscreen confirmed as much. "Lieutenant Singh, are they pulling away from us?" The lieutenant, seated at the controls, inspected the vector readouts, but before he could answer, Holbrook raised the *Avenger* over the shuttle's comm. "This is the captain. We're having trouble closing the gap."

"Aye, sir," answered Ensign Hartley. "I'm doing my best to keep you in range, but I'm also trying to keep a fix on that starship."

The *Avenger* couldn't lose the aughts, not with a functional Planck Matter bomb on their vessel, but Holbrook needed to get aboard his ship. "Can this thing move any faster?" he asked Singh.

"Now that we've cleared the planet's magnetosphere, we should be able to make up some ground."

"Punch it," said the captain.

The whine of force pads pushed to their limits filled the cabin as the shuttle gained on the *Avenger*. The starship's black wedge inched larger over several minutes, its belly blotting out the star field above them. Despite their proximity, the *Avenger's* persistent surges of acceleration threatened to leave them behind at any moment.

"*Avenger*," said Singh, his concerned eyes fixed on the open shuttle bay above, "hold your speed to bring the shuttles aboard."

"Acknowledged," crackled from the comm.

The *Avenger* glided for 3.2 seconds, time enough for the two shuttles to climb into its belly. With the small craft secure within the starship's gravity well, the warship accelerated towards the aughts.

Singh maneuvered his craft to a docking ring. Holbrook nudged the security officer aside and spoke into the still-open channel. "I need a fresh comm and a P-cab waiting for me when I arrive."

"Aye, sir."

Captain Holbrook made his way to the rear of the craft, pushing past crewmen. "Follow me," he told Dr. Riesen, sitting midway along the side bulkhead.

The craft docked with a thud and settled into its moorings. Holbrook pressed himself through the airlock the moment it opened. An ensign waiting outside saluted and handed him a comm, which he slapped on his wrist. She escorted the captain and the physicist to a P-cab, a second ensign holding its door.

"Bridge, emergency override," said Holbrook as he stepped inside. The override would get them to their destination without the P-cab stopping along the way for more passengers. The doors closed and the cab whisked them through the ship's pneumatic transport system.

The captain tapped his comm. "HOLBROOK, T." appeared along the top of its small screen, confirming it had been properly configured.

"What's your plan?" asked Dr. Riesen.

"Don't have one yet," Holbrook said gruffly. How they would stop the aught ship depended on the tactical situation. He wouldn't know that until he reached the bridge.

"If you're going to destroy that ship, you need to do it before it reaches light speed," she said.

"Why's that?" he asked. "That little ship can't outrun us."

"Because destroying that ship might trigger the Planck device. All the mass it unlocks will materialize directly in our path, and it won't be moving faster than light. If we're following them at superluminal speeds, we won't be able to dodge it. We literally won't see it before we smash into it."

"We're on the edge of light speed already," said Holbrook. "That's why the shuttles had so much trouble keeping up." If they didn't catch the ship before it reached light speed, firing on the aughts would mean the destruction of his own vessel. He'd be ordering everyone to their deaths. "I can't let the aughts reach normal space with that weapon, even if it means the ship. Promise me you won't mention this to the crew. I can't have them distracted by the possibility of instant death. I need them focused on stopping that ship."

"I promise." Dr. Riesen's expression turned pained. "I ... I don't know what Commander Stephens told you about me. He and I talked on the planet. He —"

The P-cab doors opened.

"This way," said Holbrook, dashing left into the Center Loop corridor. They arrived inside the secure compartment, the doors snapping shut for the ship's security protocol.

"Whatever Commander Stephens told you," continued Dr. Riesen, "I just want you know I'm not the same person I was when I boarded your ship."

"The commander told me you want to stay here in D-space," said Holbrook. "He said you have no intention of figuring out how to get us back home."

The physicist gave the captain a dismayed look. "Down on the planet I realized something. He, Commander Stephens, he helped me see something about myself. I —"

The doors to the secure compartment slid open. Dr. Riesen stopped speaking as the captain stepped past her into the ship's control center.

"Captain on the bridge," announced the ship.

All heads turned to the open doors. Several officers rose from their chairs, clapping. The remaining officers joined them in a standing ovation. Cheers and hoots filled the bridge.

Holbrook stood speechless, taken aback by the reception. He'd arrived to a hero's welcome, but he didn't consider himself one. He'd escaped the planet by luck, lost several of his men, including his XO. And in spite of everything they had gone through, the aught menace still existed, the Collective ship already spaceborne with an Earth-killing weapon aboard.

"Status," he said, sliding into the captain's chair.

"All systems operational," said Mills from Stephens's post along the back bulkhead. "We're chasing the aught ship, dead ahead. Range, 390,000 kilometers. Speed, .89 c. They're accelerating fast."

"Weapons control, target that ship and fire."

"Aye, sir," said Ensign Higgins.

A bead of plasma half the size of a shuttle streaked across the divide, glowing red and shifting like a massive glob of electrified jelly. A flash of light lit the screen. The aught ship shuddered under a direct hit, its aft kicked to the side by the bead's momentum. The plasma spread along the ship's hull, engulfing it in a red-hot shine that slowly dissipated.

"Their shields are down twenty-seven percent," said Lieutenant Vaughan at tactical.

"What's their speed?" asked Holbrook.

"Point nine six."

"Hit 'em again," said the captain.

The *Avenger* lobbed a second plasma bead. The aught ship accelerated at the last moment, but its wake drafted the bead's magnetic bottle, wicking the mass of super-heated subatomic particles along its hull. Lights flickered inside the aught starship as the plasma bathed the vessel in red. The blast left the rear portion of the aught ship a ruddy orange, the plasma's intense heat discoloring its dull gray tiluminum hull.

"Shields at forty-three percent."

"Speed?" asked Holbrook.

"Speed is 3.7 c," said Mills.

Holbrook's stomach sank. They'd failed to stop the aughts before they reached light speed. He looked over at Dr. Riesen, who nodded and bowed her head, acknowledging their probable fate. The captain took a deep breath and exhaled. "Hit 'em again," he said.

"Aye, sir. Firing."

The third plasma bead landed on the aught ship.

"Speed 9.4 c, shields at nineteen percent."

No match for a warship, thought Holbrook. Another hit would take them out.

"They're turning," said Ensign Hartley. The aught ship banked hard to port. It disappeared from the viewscreen.

"Stay with 'em," said Holbrook.

"Aye, sir." The aught ship reappeared at the viewscreen's center but with a seething, fiery red backdrop. "Their new heading has them flying straight for the hypergiant."

"What in Hades …?" said Holbrook. Flying towards the star wouldn't save them. A CentCom warship could easily outlast the smaller ship in the extreme heat. The aughts would burn up, if the *Avenger* didn't get to them first.

Holbrook looked around his bridge. The next shot would likely destroy the aught ship, and possibly the *Avenger* with it. "I salute you all for your bravery, and for the dedicated performance of your duty." Holbrook's comment turned several heads. The captain ignored their stares. "Fire."

Ensign Higgins tapped the weapons control. The *Avenger* hurled a fourth plasma bead at the aught starship. The superheated glob raced ahead but slower than before. It decelerated as it chased the aught ship, its edges fraying into ribbons of glowing subatomic particles that streamed back towards the *Avenger*. With a bright flash the glob blew apart, spraying plasma across the warship's path.

Holbrook and Higgins exchanged confused looks. "What happened?" the captain asked. Baffled expressions ringed the bridge.

"It's the hypergiant," said Dr Riesen. "The star's massive stellar wind disrupted the plasma's magnetic bottle."

"That's why they changed course to head towards the star," said Holbrook. At their current range, another shot would just dissipate again. "Close on the aught ship."

"We're about as close as we want to get, Captain," said Mills. "That ship's much more maneuverable than we are. The closer we get, the easier it'll be for them to evade us. They could turn on a dime and accelerate away before we knew what happened."

Holbrook stroked his chin. "So, we can't destroy them from this far away, and we risk losing them if we get any closer." He tipped his cap to the aught captain. "Clever."

"They can't continue on this course forever," said Mills. "They're going to have to turn at some point."

"Let's be ready when they do," said Holbrook.

The *Avenger* pursued the aught ship, both vessels buffeted by the oncoming stellar wind. The bridge remained deathly silent as they waited for the aughts to make their next move.

The tactical terminal chirped with insistent beeps.

"They're climbing," said Vaughan. "Probably to fly over the hypergiant."

"They're really hugging the star," said Mills.

"Stay with 'em," said Holbrook.

The *Avenger* followed the aught ship as it rose above the hypergiant's northern hemisphere. A sliver of the black interstellar void appeared at the top of the viewscreen, growing larger as the two ships climbed. The star's edge cut a straight line across, the curve of its circumference imperceptible with the hypergiant's immense size.

Holbrook peeked over the helmsman's shoulder. According to the station's terminal, they were nearing the top of the star, the point at which the head-on resistance from the stellar wind would fall to zero. That would be their chance to finish them off. "Ensign Higgins, the moment they reach the top I want you to —"

"They're running," interrupted Mills.

"What?" said Holbrook.

Mills nodded. "They just pushed their engines to the limit."

Holbrook stared after the fleeing ship. The aught captain's desperate act was understandable, if futile. The *Avenger* with its more powerful Gravity Drive could easily catch them. They'd give chase, though not with such a sudden acceleration. At this close proximity to the star, that would— Holbrook's mouth went dry. "My God," he whispered, struggling to draw a full breath. "Pull up!" he shouted. "Pull up with everything you've got!"

The *Avenger's* force pads throbbed at maximum output, jostling the crew and straining the ship's superstructure as they angled sharply upwards.

Beads of sweat broke out on the captain's forehead, the physics of their predicament playing out in his head. The gravitational wake from the aught starship's sudden, violent acceleration would disrupt the star's corona, rousing an immense plume of superheated plasma from the hypergiant. The plume did not yet appear on the *Avenger's* viewscreen—as Dr. Riesen described with a detonated Planck device, their ship traveling faster than light would reach the volcanic wall of stellar material before they could see it.

The black wedge starship climbed as the plume became visible on their sensors. The *Avenger* could not fully avoid the churning wall of coronal material, but they'd reacted quickly enough, missing the bulk of it. Only fringes of the plume licked its hull.

Holbrook sat shellshocked in his chair. The danger had passed, but the narrowness of their escape lived with him. His shock gave way to anger. The aught star captain had lured him into a trap. He prayed their maneuver and the aught starship's sudden sprint hadn't caused them to lose the smaller vessel completely. "Do we still have them?" He held his breath, waiting for the answer.

"We have a fix," said Vaughan, "but barely. They've accelerated to interstellar speeds. They're preparing to leave the system."

"Resume pursuit," said Holbrook.

"Aye, sir," said Ensign Doerr at navigation. "Plotting an intercept course."

Holbrook stroked his chin. An intercept course would return them to chasing the fleeing starship, teeing the *Avenger* up for the aught captain's next trick. So far they'd been playing his game. They needed a surprise of their own if they hoped to stop them. "Tactical on screen, please."

"Aye, sir."

The gray grid with white lines filled the bridge's viewscreen, showing a black triangle pursuing a white circle and an enormous red disc moving quickly towards the bottom of the screen. The triangle slid along a light gray dotted line, the *Avenger's* course, which swung into a gentle curve as it neared the white line marking the aught ship's projected path. The two lines merged where the *Avenger* would retake its position behind the fleeing ship.

Dr. Riesen warned they'd be destroyed if they fired on the ship and detonated the device, but that was only if they followed directly behind. Their evasive maneuver could have been a blessing in disguise. "Adjust our intercept course, Ensign," said Holbrook. "Instead of coming up behind to follow that ship, I want us to sail past it."

"Sir?" said Doerr, confusion in her voice.

"You heard correct, Ensign," said Holbrook. "And make it tight. Close enough to smell their exhaust."

"Aye, sir." Doerr's fingers danced on her terminal. "Plotted and laid in."

The light gray dotted line shifted on the tactical display. It no longer merged with the aught ship's path—instead, it intersected the white line. Their new course would bring the *Avenger* within a kilometer of the aught starship.

"Higgins, I want to fire the instant we catch up to them, right when we reach the intercept point," said Holbrook. "We won't have a lot of time. Prime the nozzle with plasma if you have to, but the shot has to count."

"Aye, sir," said Ensign Higgins, tapping at his terminal screen. "Cannon's primed, sir."

"Ten seconds to intercept," said Mills.

"Do you think they see us coming?" asked Dr. Riesen.

"At our angle of approach, I doubt it," said Mills. "If they do, they haven't changed course. They either don't see us or they're assuming we'll take up position behind their ship."

"Five seconds."

The black triangle neared the intercept point on the viewscreen, with the aught ship steady on its path out of the star system.

"Four."

The computer zoomed the tactical view, focusing on the triangle and circle that appeared on a collision course. They would pass each other by the slimmest of margins.

"Three.

"Two.

"One."

"Fire!" yelled Holbrook.

The cannon expelled its glowing red blob of plasma the instant the black warship skirted past the aught starship. An immense blast of light followed, expanding to a bright ball that grew wide, ballooning out at an incredible rate and riddled with ruby-red sparkles.

The *Avenger* slowed and turned. The video feed from the exterior cameras showered the bridge in bright light.

"We hit them," said Holbrook, "but that's not a normal ship explosion. Even shooting from point blank range, even from a complete engine meltdown, it wouldn't keep getting brighter like that."

The ball continued growing, an enormous shower of light expanding to a volume hundreds of kilometers in diameter. The ball sparkled and grew for twelve seconds before dissipating. Something emerged from the center of the explosion—not the pulverized remains of a starship, something large.

A potato-shaped gray mass peeked out of the fading, shimmering light. The mass rotated slowly, with ruby-red lightning cascading across its rough, pocked surface.

"It's an asteroid," whispered Holbrook, astonished. An asteroid where the aught ship had been, where they had fired upon the fleeing ship. "We detonated it." A smile emerged on his face, slowly broadening to a grin. "We detonated the bomb!"

Cheers went up around the bridge. Several officers embraced; others wiped away tears.

"Sensor data coming in now," said Vaughan. "It's 627 kilometers at its widest point. Mass, 4.3 times ten to the seventeen kilograms."

Holbrook gaped at the new asteroid, in awe of the massive stellar body formed from a device that fit on a tabletop. They'd succeeded at their mission. They might not see their home again, but at least the Earth would be safe from the aughts. Holbrook let out a heavy sigh, born of relief and elation. His eyes met Dr. Riesen's. "We did it," he said, smiling.

Dr. Riesen studied the gray asteroid as it tumbled lazily at the center of the viewscreen. "Yes, it seems so," she said. Her brows crinkled. "It would seem so."

47

They placed Commander Stephens's remains in a closed casket, draped in the purple and royal blue flag of the Republic. His coffin sat within the great bend at the front of the Deck A lounge. On one side stood a wreath fashioned from gold leaf and on the other a small table with several boxes of white tea light candles. The crew spent an hour filing by the casket and lighting candles, honoring the man who had been their executive officer for five years.

The captain arrived to a darkened room alive with flickering candlelight, tea lights spread across tables stretching halfway to the back of the room. He gasped at the sight, as did Dr. Riesen, who entered with him.

The service was small. The Deck A lounge held just under forty people. They broadcast the proceedings throughout the ship. Captain Holbrook in his white dress uniform, sparkling captain's stars on his lapels, stood at a podium a meter from the casket. Chairs replaced most of the regular lounge furniture, arrayed in rows forming a trapezoid that grew wider as it extended back into the room. The stars twinkled fiercely above and around the casket, their light shining through the transparent glassteel bulkheads.

The captain reached inside his jacket and removed a folded e-sheet, electing to read from jotted notes instead of the podium's embedded viewscreen. He opened the sheet and smoothed it flat. "We are here today to say goodbye to Commander Paul Stephens, executive officer of the starship *Avenger*, cherished colleague, fierce soldier, dutiful citizen of the Republic, valued friend.

"Commander Stephens fought to the last for what he believed in. He fought for this crew, this ship, and for the Earth. The commander gave his all in everything he did. He was never one to back away from a fight. He did what he did best, right to the end: he gave 'em hell.

"The first time I met Commander Stephens was when he walked into my quarters to interview for the position of executive officer. Before even saying hello, he told me the ship was too warm and probably lulled the crew to sleep at their posts, the lack of personal effects in my quarters made it as inviting as a tomb, I should always wear my uniform jacket while on duty, even in my quarters, because I'd never know when I'd have to interact with the crew, and my nose hairs needed trimming. He told me as my executive officer I could expect more things to come out of his mouth I might not want to hear. He said with Paul Stephens, what you see is what you get, but he wanted me to know the uncomfortable things he might share would always be driven by his concern for this ship, and for me as its captain. That was the man I hired on the spot. I think that was the Commander Stephens each of you knew as well. He will be greatly missed.

"If there is a heaven, I'm certain the commander is there now, looking down on us all and screaming for us to get back to work. And we will, but first we'll take this moment to respect and honor this man." Holbrook folded the e-sheet and returned it to his jacket. "Please stand for a moment of silence."

The thirty-eight other occupants of the room stood from their chairs. Holbrook scanned their faces, a smattering of the people aboard the ship touched by the commander. He bowed his head, tightening his mouth to fend off tears.

A minute had passed when Holbrook looked up. He nodded at Lieutenant Becker, who moved in from her position at the front of the room. She stopped near the coffin. The lieutenant, in her dress whites, lifted her trumpet and played "Taps." Several attendees broke into tears.

When the lieutenant finished playing, two security officers, also in their dress whites, slow-marched to the casket from opposite sides of the room. They lifted the purple and blue flag from the coffin and worked together, folding it into a triangle with its white stars facing out. The two officers slow-marched the folded flag to Ensign Jiménez, sitting in the front row. Holbrook wanted Jiménez to have it, to remember the man whose faith and encouragement since the day she stepped aboard helped her save the ship. The ensign took the flag and held it fast with both arms to her chest, tears falling. The security officers returned to Commander Stephens's casket and saluted it, then turned and slow-marched back to the sides of the room.

"Thank you," said Holbrook, standing at the podium teary-eyed. The attendees headed towards the lounge's large doors. A few, including Ensign Jiménez, walked to the casket, touching it a final time before leaving.

All the attendees filed out except for Dr. Riesen, who made no motion to leave, remaining in her front row seat with her hands clasped, staring at the casket. She wore a black dress with thin black straps and a black shawl that covered her shoulders. Her crying had reddened her eyes and left her cheeks shining with tears.

Holbrook walked over to her. She evaded his eyes as he approached. Tears flowed. "Are you OK, Dr. Riesen?"

"Not really," she said with a half-laugh. She sniffed and wiped tears from under her nose, then forced herself to smile. "All the commander wanted to do was live. But in the end, he gave his life so the rest of us could." She took in the thousands of stars shining through the transparent deck above and worked to compose herself, wiping away more tears. "He asked me if I was actually trying to find a way back home. He had a theory that I wasn't, that I'd be happier to die out here. I'm ashamed to say he was right."

"Stephens was right about many things," said Holbrook.

Dr. Riesen sniffled. "He told me I was running from the voice in my head that keeps saying I'm a mistake—my voice." She blinked through more tears. "I didn't see it before, but what I realized on the planet was how it controlled me, the notion that I'm a mistake. It's ruled me my whole life. It's something I've reacted to so viscerally. The aughts used it to manipulate me into telling them how to complete their bomb. What I finally saw, thanks to Commander Stephens, was that walking around haunted by the suggestion that I'm a mistake is a waste of a life. It's certainly not a life worthy of being saved by the ultimate sacrifice."

Dr. Riesen wiped more tears and looked square at Holbrook. "Your question, Captain, the one you asked me weeks ago, of whether or not I've figured out how to get us back home, the answer is no, but I will."

"I know you will," Holbrook said, smiling. He glanced at Commander Stephens's casket and the reflections of stars dancing across its dark, polished surface. "You know the last time we were in here together, you and I, you were right there at the front of the room. Sag A Star was behind you. It looked like a giant mouth with a ring of pointed teeth. You were sitting there at the table, seemingly headed right for the center. At the time I thought it was a little ironic, you figuring out how we can escape the very thing that appeared to be swallowing you up."

Eyes flitting, Dr. Riesen grew silent, frozen in thought for several seconds. She stepped back from the captain, astonished. "That's it!"

"That's what?" he asked.

"The ring!" she said. "The tachyon ring!" Dr. Riesen's eyes went glassy again, the physicist falling back into deep thought. "That's it ...."

Holbrook shot her a puzzled look. "I'm not following," he said.

"Yes!" she said, growing excited again. She beamed. "Do you remember the *Adiona's* logs, how he mentioned them setting up a tachyon ring?"

"Not really," he said.

"They launched a set of tachyon beacons, arrayed in a circle twenty-five light-years wide," she said. "They never explained why they did it, or even mention those beacons after that. At the time I thought it was odd." Dr. Riesen paused, thinking. "That's why they're tachyon beacons and not regular light—photons are too slow for the job." She grew animated again. "The problem of getting out of D-space is all the spacetime deformations. You set your course, but the deformations skew your path, turning what was a straight trajectory into a corkscrewed, twisted mess that takes you almost back where you started. But if you knew how space was deformed in your direction of travel, you could compensate for it to keep on that straight line. If you could make those course corrections, you could keep yourself headed where you wanted to go.

"That's what the tachyon ring is for. If you look at it from here, inside D-space, the ring will be deformed—what's a perfect circle out in normal space will appear sheared and twisted here. But given you know the ring's geometry, it's trivial to compute the deformations that transformed it from its true shape to the mess that you see. That list of deformations is the exact data you'd need to plug into your navigational computer to pilot yourself out. Just aim for the center of the ring!"

Holbrook stroked his chin. He mostly followed Dr. Riesen's explanation. "Will it work?" He held himself back from being truly excited, not wanting to be disappointed if her theory didn't pan out.

"It should," said Dr. Riesen. "The technique was experimental. They were coming out here to test it. But the theory's sound. It should work. With the right instructions to the computer, it should work!"

Captain's log, Captain Thomas Holbrook the third reporting.

Dr. Riesen unraveled the mystery of escaping D-space, proving the theory of the *Adiona* crew correct. Or at least it looks promising. We're not out yet, but we've managed to remain on a course that should take us clear of all the spacetime distortions. Our next stop will be the dry dock at Aludra for repairs and to offload our cargo of mutineers. We'll also debrief Commodore Ahrens, once his sleep capsule arrives at the station.

As for the planet Infernum, now that the *Adiona* has revealed the secret to returning from the center of the galaxy, we couldn't leave the Planck Matter for anyone to grab, aughts or humans. Commander Stephens sealed the mines, but the right equipment could easily open them again. To be safe we detonated a small nuclear charge inside the basin. The area's now a crater two hundred meters deep, the remaining Planck Matter inaccessible beneath several million tons of radioactive soil.

Special commendations go to Commander Paul Stephens for his bravery and wisdom. And to Tentek, aught of The Collective, for his dedication to peace and humanity. We'll return Tentek's body to The Collective and fill them in on the events. As for Commander Stephens's body, we'll bring it back to Earth. I'd considered burying him on Infernum, but the center of the galaxy was the last place he wanted to be. We'll lay him to rest on the planet he helped save.

I am still extremely tired from the past few weeks, but I feel surprisingly light on my feet, like a great weight has been lifted. I might take some time off. Clear my head. Think about what comes next. I've been traveling the stars for so many years that it might be time to finally settle down. At least that's the nagging feeling I'm getting. I once asked Paul—Commander Stephens—his secret to being right so often. He told me it was easy. Anyone could do it, even me. I just needed to follow my gut. Well, I'm giving that a try, in memory of my friend. My gut says it might be time to start a family.

If Paul were still with us, I think he'd be happy to hear that. He'd be happy to hear that for once I was taking his advice.

"Captain Holbrook."

Holbrook sighed. He had just settled in for the evening, nestling into his leather reading chair with the book he'd been picking at since before their mission began. Sleepy tea steeped in a mug within arm's reach—no more spirits masquerading as a sleep aide. "Holbrook here."

"Sir, this is Ensign Forster in communications. Sorry to bother you this late, sir."

"It's OK, Ensign. What's up?"

"I'm picking up a broadcast message from CentCom. It's Priority One."

"Play it, please."

"I can't play the entire message, sir. We're at the edge of the D-space boundary, but the distortion's still disrupting communications. I've only got bits and pieces so far."

"Play what you have, Ensign."

"Aye, sir."

... gency. High ... epeat, all ships ... vicinity of ... high alert. Tracking ... beacon ... emergency.

"That's all there is so far, sir," said Ensign Forster. "The message repeats, but until we're completely out of D-space, we'll continue to get just snatches of it."

Holbrook stroked his chin. "How long 'til we're in normal space?"

Murmurs filled the open channel, the ensign relaying the question to the helmsman. "A little over an hour or so at our current speed."

A Priority One message meant a Republic-wide emergency, requiring all available ships to place their current missions on hold and assist in the effort, whatever it might be. "Increase speed to maximum. Bring the ship to yellow alert. And keep trying to piece together the full message."

"Aye, sir," said Forster.

After all they'd been through, Holbrook was inclined to have the *Avenger* continue on to Aludra and let the other starship captains deal with the fire drill. He might still do that, but not before determining what the fuss was about. "I'll be right up."

"Yes, sir."

This was the kind of issue an executive officer would attend to. Only after gathering more information and judging whether the *Avenger* could assist would the captain become involved. Holbrook had missed Stephens over the past few days, not just how he helped shoulder the workload of running the ship but also his company.

Holbrook rose from his chair and strolled to his personal head. The Holbrook who stared back at him in the mirror was tired, stubble covering his cheeks and chin. He didn't like presenting himself that way to the crew, looking worn down. They would understand, only a few days removed from his time on Infernum. Holbrook straightened his uniform, pulled on his boots, and headed for the bridge. Empty corridors, typical for a late evening aboard the starship, made travel easy. The walk to the Center Loop took just a few minutes.

The captain arrived on the bridge, returning to the evening watch he'd left hours ago. Lieutenant Bolton, the deck officer, stood from the captain's chair when he entered. Holbrook proceeded directly to the communications station along the side bulkhead.

"I have more of the message, sir," said Forster as Holbrook approached. The ensign tapped her terminal screen.

The ship's androgynous voice filled the bridge, reading the Priority One message in dispassionate tones. The message still suffered from gaps, but none wide enough to prevent its comprehension.

Holbrook's eyes widened with each sentence. By the end he'd turned pale. "Find Dr. Riesen. Have her report to me in my conference room." Holbrook wheeled around, facing Ensign Hartley at the helm. "The moment we clear D-space, lay in a course for Earth. Maximum speed, and a bit more if we've got it."

"Aye, aye, sir."

50

Two faces in separate side-by-side rectangles shimmered onto the viewscreen in the low light of the captain's conference room. "Captain Holbrook," said the round, wrinkled, silver-haired man on the left.

"Admiral Weller," said Holbrook. "Thank you for accommodating my request for an emergency meeting."

Admiral Weller frowned. "Well, Captain, just what *is* the emergency?" The admiral appeared disheveled, likely fresh out of bed after having retired for the night. He squinted, his eyes apparently still adjusting to the viewscreen's glow in his darkened quarters. "I understand that you have questions about the Priority One alert."

"Yes, sir," said Holbrook. "We were in a de facto communications blackout during our time in D-space —"

"I know that, Captain Holbrook," said the admiral. "What I don't know is why your questions can't wait until morning."

The admiral's gruff response took Holbrook aback. "Sir, we may have important information relating to the alert."

The admiral frowned again. "Information that's not in your report?"

"No, sir," said Holbrook. "I mean possibly. The report is complete; it's just that —"

"Captain," said Admiral Weller with an authoritative tone, "your mission is over. You were tasked with stopping the aughts from returning from D-space. Despite what you state in your report, you failed to accomplish that task. Now I can understand you wanting to figure out what went wrong, but that's hardly a reason for an emergency meeting." The admiral pushed gray strands from his forehead, his hair still tousled from his time asleep. "I will say further that waking me in the middle of the night does not impress me with your determination to analyze your error. It quite the opposite smacks of desperation."

Holbrook sat slack-jawed, unsure on so many levels how to respond.

"Admiral," said Dr. Riesen, sitting across the table from Captain Holbrook, "we were hoping to determine if the ship you're looking for is the same one we chased through D-space. If it somehow *is* that same ship, we want to make sure you have all the information you need to shore up Earth's defenses."

"This is Dr. Rebekah Riesen," said Holbrook, shaking himself from his daze. "She's an expert physicist who accompanied us on our mission to Sag A Star."

"And this is Rear Admiral Parker," said Weller. The face on the other side of the split screen looked not many years Holbrook's senior. "He led the task force that recently reconfigured Earth's defense shield to stop the aughts, an insurance policy against your mission failing. You said in your request for this meeting you were concerned about Earth's preparations. This is the man who can put your worries to rest so we can all get back to sleep."

"And you have nothing to fear, Captain," said Rear Admiral Parker with a patronizing assurance.

"Rear Admiral Parker made CentCom's 'forty under forty' list of most influential officers," said Admiral Weller, beaming like a proud papa. "That was in part a result of his valor and quick thinking in the Antares offensive. He was promoted to Rear Admiral on his thirty-ninth birthday, and his odds of making full admiral before he turns forty-five are quite good. We call on him to tackle tough problems. You don't rise through the ranks like he has unless you're able to get things done." Parker basked in Admiral Weller's effusion, his face radiating a smugness and self-absorption that suggested his biography and achievements were never far out of mind.

Holbrook had been tangentially aware of Rear Admiral Parker's career. Though "getting things done," as the admiral put it, was a requirement for any advancement, promotions beyond captain could never rest just on completing tasks and solving problems. Politics also played a role, which included proficiency at compromising morals in the name of achieving personal goals as well as the ancient art of shifting blame. Reaching the admiralty could be a cutthroat experience, but once ascended, the CentCom leadership functioned as an old boys club, where members scratched each other's backs and generally took care of their own.

Admiral Weller rubbed his eyes and sighed. "Perhaps we can proceed now with your questions, Captain?"

"Yes, sir," said Holbrook. "Can you brief us on the details surrounding the Priority One message?"

"After you entered D-space to pursue the aughts, we erected a grid of listening posts to watch for ships exiting the region. We needed to know if a vessel returned from the galactic center, be it yours or the aughts'. Approximately seven hours ago, we detected a ship emerging from the distorted region. It came to a dead stop, we suspect to get its bearings before setting a new course in the general direction of Earth. The listening posts tracked it for a few parsecs before they lost it." As Admiral Weller spoke, an image of the ship, dull gray with two rounded hulls connected by a thin neck, appeared in a separate rectangle of the viewscreen. A ruddy orange discoloration blanketed the rear portion of the ship's hull.

"That's Drazetek's ship," said Holbrook in disbelief. "But we destroyed it …. When we fired on them, we detonated the Planck Matter device. The only thing left was an asteroid." He'd seen it materialize out of nothing with his own eyes. He looked over at Dr. Riesen, expecting to share in her shock, but the physicist seemed unsurprised. Holbrook flashed back to the seconds after the aught ship's destruction. The entire bridge crew celebrated while Dr. Riesen remained solemnly transfixed by the slowly spinning mass on the viewscreen. In the moment he'd chalked it up to exhaustion from their time on the planet. "You weren't convinced we'd gotten them, were you?" asked Holbrook.

"At the time it seemed like we must have destroyed them," said Dr. Riesen. "I just couldn't understand why detonating the device produced such a small asteroid. I figured maybe they hadn't refined the ore properly, or the weapon was a dud." Her eyelids flitted for a moment, the physicist sinking into deep thought. "Or maybe it was a prototype."

"A prototype?" said Holbrook, staggered by the thought. He'd only ever imagined one Planck Matter device in existence, the one they found when they entered the aught ship.

"Yes," said Dr. Riesen. "They hadn't actually tested a Planck device before that because they'd only recently acquired a detonator. What we saw was likely the explosion of a smaller version of their planet-killing bomb."

Holbrook's mind felt like mush, too many important assumptions changing all at once. But everything in Dr. Riesen's analysis added up, which meant Drazetek had outsmarted them again. The aught ship hadn't been destroyed, and Drazetek had confirmed the main device would work. The captain returned his attention to the viewscreen. "As I mentioned in my report, Admiral Weller, the aughts did more than just collect Planck Matter. Drazetek, the leader of the expedition, supervised the construction of a weapon. It appears that weapon works and is now headed toward Earth."

Rear Admiral Parker cut in, "And as I said earlier, Captain, there's nothing to fear. The central goal of the project I led was to guarantee a small ship like this one never delivers its payload to Earth." The rear admiral nestled into his seat, eager to speak. "The fleet's arrayed to monitor this ship's progress, but we're not worried so much about trying to stop it in deep space. If they're foolish enough to travel all the way to Earth, they'll be in for a nasty surprise. We pushed the early warning outposts farther from the planet, and we tripled the number of satellites in the defense grid. The AI in those satellites has batteries of Hellcat interceptors at its disposal. Even one Hellcat can take down the largest battle cruiser, shields or no.

"And that's just high Earth orbit. On the off chance a ship somehow penetrates that perimeter, it will be met by the fierce destructive power of sixteen ThunderStrike weapons platforms in geosynchronous orbit. In short, Captain Holbrook, there is nothing to fear from this ship. If the aughts do arrive and attempt to detonate their bomb on Earth, we'll have more firepower waiting for them than they can possibly handle."

Parker's description of the plan to stop the aughts left Holbrook and Dr. Riesen stunned. The physicist managed to gather her thoughts enough to speak. "Rear Admiral Parker," she said, "it seems you may not be aware of the full nature of the Planck device."

The rear admiral grew visibly irritated. "It's a bomb. A bomb of immense destructive power that must not reach the Earth."

"It's a bomb of sorts," said Dr. Riesen. "If they could detonate it on the planet's surface, that would be the end of the Earth as we know it. But they don't need to get the device to Earth to do just as much damage."

Parker's brows furrowed. "I already mentioned our defense grid in high Earth orbit. It extends out to fifty thousand kilometers from the planet's surface."

"Rear Admiral," said Dr. Riesen, "a Planck device returns immense amounts of matter to the normal Universe from within a compact space. By my estimates the larger version of their device will produce enough material to form a small planet, maybe one half the size of Earth. Drazetek probably knows our planetary defenses are positioned to stop him from getting there, so I doubt that's his goal. It's more likely he'll try to detonate it somewhere within the inner solar system."

The rear admiral raked his palm across his stubble-covered cheek. "Dr. Riesen, I've explained quite patiently how this small ship can't possibly reach the Earth. Now you're worried about an explosion far beyond the confines of our defense grid? I'm not sure what else to —"

"Think, Admiral!" said Dr. Riesen. "Any significant-sized planetary body introduced inside the asteroid belt will perturb the orbits of the inner planets. The planets, from Mercury to Mars, will seek out a new equilibrium that allows all the bodies to circle the sun in stable orbits. The Earth will be forced closer to the sun, or farther away. In either case it means the end of life on Earth as we know it."

Holbrook had watched Rear Admiral Parker during his exchange with Dr. Riesen. After her final comment, his image seemed not to move within his half of the viewscreen. A frozen connection? All but impossible with CentCom's military grade communication system.

"Dr. Riesen," said Admiral Weller, at last breaking the silence, "the rear admiral has already said that his plan addresses the threat of the aughts and their weapon." Parker still remained frozen on the screen. "Rear Admiral?" prodded Weller.

The rear admiral's face turned red, and his shoulders hunched up around his ears. "To be frank, Admiral, my plan wouldn't need to address anything if Captain Holbrook had stopped the aughts from leaving Sag A Star in the first place. In fact, according to your report, Captain, you even took a stroll inside this ship. You were standing in the same ROOM as the Planck device, but somehow that device is on its way to Earth! You failed to stop them on the planet. You failed to stop them in space. This screw-up, Captain, is all YOURS! We wouldn't be having this conversation, in the dead of the night, about saving the Earth if you had simply done … your … job! You failed in your mission. FAILED! And now all of Earth may pay the price."

"Admiral, I —"

"You nothing! Admiral Weller's asking me about my plan, but we shouldn't need to rely on it at all. If we lose the Earth, that will be on YOU!" A vein rose beneath the skin of the rear admiral's forehead, pulsing down the center. "Now you'll excuse me, I have to wake the Joint Chiefs and convene an emergency meeting to see if we can even recover from your mistake." Rear Admiral Parker disappeared, leaving Admiral Weller's face to fill the viewscreen.

The live connection continued on, but none of the three stirred. Admiral Weller finally spoke. "The thing is, Captain Holbrook, your mission was to stop the aughts at all costs, even if it meant your ship. I thought the odds of your success were low, but I never expected to see you alive again from Sag A Star without completing your assignment. Now officers like Rear Admiral Parker are forced to take up your slack. His outburst was as much about your failure as it was about the recognition that his career is in jeopardy. I feel for him." Several strands of hair worked themselves loose, falling across the admiral's forehead. He pushed them back in place with a swipe of his hand. "I really miss the old days, Captain Holbrook, when soldiers actually carried out the orders they were given. They didn't come back alive with their assignment in tatters, looking for a medal. I wish we had more of those soldiers, soldiers like your father." The admiral's face seemed to hover in the center of the monitor, an apparition with the blue glow of his viewscreen floating against the black backdrop of his darkened quarters. "You no longer need concern yourself with stopping the aughts—you've left that job to the rest of us. Now if you'll excuse me, I need to prepare for a meeting of the Joint Chiefs. Good evening."

The viewscreen went black, leaving Holbrook and Dr. Riesen sitting in silence. The captain, grim-faced, slumped in his chair.

51

"We have to come up with a plan to stop him," said Dr. Riesen.

Captain Holbrook had just switched off the viewscreen. He pressed into the conference room table and stood from his chair. "Stop who?" he asked with an irritated look.

"Drazetek," she said.

"Drazetek?"

Dr. Riesen shook her head. "Yes."

The captain grew more irritated. "The two of us, you and I, have to come up with a plan to stop Drazetek."

"That's correct," said Dr. Riesen.

Holbrook stared at her in disbelief. "Were you and I in the same meeting just now?" he asked, his broad frame looming above the table. "The admiral said we have no business anymore even thinking about the problem."

Dr. Riesen glared at the captain. "So that's it then, you're just going to give up?" she said, exasperated. "Back on Infernum you told me you prayed for a second chance, and if you got it you would do whatever you could to stop the aughts."

"And I did," huffed Holbrook, "but I failed. Now the entirety of the CentCom braintrust is working on the problem. It's no longer just one starship trying to stop Drazetek—they have all available Republic resources at their disposal."

"It won't be enough," said Dr. Riesen. "Whether it's a hundred starships or a thousand, it doesn't matter—whatever their plan is, it's going to fail."

Holbrook slowly lowered himself back into his seat. "What in Hades are you talking about?"

"Look," she said, "Drazetek was one step ahead of us the whole time we chased him through D-space. Have you thought at all about why that was?"

Holbrook grew sullen. "Seems obvious," he said. "Drazetek is a better star captain than me."

"That's not it at all," said Dr. Riesen. "It's because the aughts act on probabilities. Drazetek used probabilities to predict the stellar wind would prevent us from firing on them. Probabilities told him their sudden acceleration would draft a wall of plasma with a decent chance of destroying the *Avenger*. It told him we'd shoot as we flew by, not resume the chase. And based on that prediction, he foresaw how detonating their prototype Planck device would be the perfect cover for his escape." She waited for a glimmer of understanding from Holbrook, but he only stared blankly at her. "Don't you see? He's going to use probabilities all over again in his assault on the Earth. He'll feed everything he knows about CentCom fleet size, deployments, armaments, historical actions, personnel —"

"Personnel?" said Holbrook, startled. "At one point during my interrogation, Drazetek asked me about the chain of command, which officer was deployed where and in charge of what, other bits of info that had no tactical or strategic military value. I didn't think anything of it at the time …." He licked his lips. "I answered most of those questions straightaway. I thought it was better to keep him talking about people rather than ship deployments and weapons systems."

"It all gets thrown into the aught's probability engine," said Dr. Riesen. "All of it plays into answering the question of how best to get the Planck device to Earth. Drazetek may even come up with CentCom's plan before the admirals do."

"Then what do you think *we're* supposed to do?" Holbrook shot back. "If Drazetek can predict everything, how in the world can we or anyone devise a plan to stop him?"

"Drazetek can't predict *everything*," said Dr. Riesen. "Think about the things that tripped him up on the planet. He didn't expect Commander Stephens's attack on their operation. Drazetek thought he had a complete headcount of the landing party. The idea a straggler would fire a plasma rifle at them from the rim of the basin, that was a surprise, an event with probability zero. The same with Tentek: Drazetek probably didn't know he existed either. For sure he didn't know Tentek had an EMP in his belly." Dr. Riesen's eyes flitted with her racing mind. "He couldn't see either possibility, and it nearly cost him his entire plan. To perform his parlor trick of guessing the future, he needs perfect data. He needs to know everything. But the truth is he doesn't know everything. He can't."

Captain Holbrook stroked his chin. "Let's assume for a second that's all true," he said, "that doesn't mean the two of us should be the ones to come up with a plan to stop Drazetek. I can get the top brass back on the comm, tell them everything you just told me. They can work up two plans instead of one, pretend to go with Plan A but secretly choose Plan B."

Dr. Riesen shook her head. "Drazetek will already have deduced Plan A and B and C through Z, along with the probability of CentCom trying to trick him," she said. "But besides that, do you really think CentCom will listen to me, or to us? Do you really believe those admirals will ditch whatever elaborate plan they come up with just because we tell them Drazetek has already figured it out?"

"They might," said Holbrook. He sounded unconvinced.

"From what I've seen of CentCom, I highly doubt it," said Dr. Riesen. "That Rear Admiral Parker is worried about stopping Drazetek, but even with the fate of the Earth on the line he still has one eye on rising through the ranks."

Holbrook folded his arms across his chest. "You said we need to come up with a plan, but if what you just told me about probabilities is true, it means Drazetek knows we escaped D-space. He knows we're headed to Earth, right now, at top speed."

"Yes," said Dr. Riesen. "I'm sure it's one of the probabilities he's enumerated, possibly even assigned a high likelihood. Especially now that he's back in normal space and plugged into their network. I wouldn't be surprised if The Collective has information on CentCom ship movements that Drazetek is able to access."

"But that leaves us no better off than the rest of CentCom," said Holbrook. "How can *anyone* come up with a plan if Drazetek can already predict everything?"

"Not *everything*," she said, growing frustrated at having to repeat herself. Her mind worked quickly, assembling facts and educated guesses and moving on, fluidly connecting the dots. Getting the captain to understand felt like trudging through thick mud, being forced to backtrack to reestablish points she'd made long ago. "As I said, Drazetek needs perfect information to predict everything, but he doesn't have it. He can't possibly have it. He'd need a black hole the size of the Universe to store it all." The captain again stared blankly at her. "Look, besides the people, ships, weapons, deployments, and engagements with previous enemies, there's not much else to understand about CentCom. There are no real unknowns. To stop

Drazetek, we need a plan based on something outside of all of that. It has to be based on something he doesn't have a clue about."

The captain unfolded his arms and sat forward, wagging his finger like a child discovering a flaw in their parent's logic. "Not just *anything* he doesn't know. Like he probably doesn't know my right foot is slightly larger than my left, but it seems absurd to think that fact would make a difference. You're talking about finding something he doesn't know that will *stop his starship*."

Putting it like that made the situation seem almost hopeless. "Yes," she offered meekly.

Holbrook dismissed her response with a wave of his hand.

Dr. Riesen's ice-blue eyes burrowed into the captain. "You've never been involved in research, basic research, have you, Captain? The process of discovery necessarily means finding a fact that's beyond everyone's current understanding. There are lots of physicists who've reacted the same way as you about a new theory that challenges their way of thinking. They declare something can't be done before we've even scribbled anything on the e-board. If physicists all had that attitude, physics would never advance. The sciences would never advance. Finding solutions to problems sometimes requires a leap of faith, a willingness to entertain an idea that at the outset might seem outlandish, even impossible."

"You're talking like this is just another physics problem," said Holbrook. "Like you can just—"

Dr. Riesen had closed her eyes, shutting out the captain's tirade. She took a calming breath and sat at the small conference room table for almost a full minute, motionless except for her fluttering eyelids. She finally opened her eyes.

"Are you OK?" asked Holbrook.

"No," Dr. Riesen said quietly.

"If you're not feeling well, I can—"

Dr. Riesen shook her head. "I have a way of solving physics problems," she said. "It's almost like I reach down deep—that's the best I can describe it—and retrieve the answer from the Universe." She gave the captain a sad smile. "I tried it just now to find a solution to this problem, but I came up empty. I've got nothing."

Holbrook grabbed Dr. Riesen's hand and gave it a reassuring squeeze. "Don't feel bad," he said. "I was starting to say this isn't a physics problem. It's not like you can just write down a bunch of equations and tease out an answer."

The captain was wrong about her problem-solving method: it *could* be used on questions outside of physics. Her gift channeled answers straight from the Universe, from creation itself. By definition there wasn't a problem in existence that fell outside this domain. His statement did, however, hint at an interesting point. Before reaching deep for a solution, she started from the sum total of her knowledge, akin to writing down equations as the captain alluded. This answer, if it existed, required a tighter scope, still within the expanse of her understanding but only after subtracting everything Drazetek knew. The solution was somewhere in the difference between the two sets.

Dr. Riesen closed her eyes and took another deep breath. She visualized that difference, everything she knew that did not overlap with Drazetek. The remainder would be small—Drazetek, with his Network connection, had access to the totality of human knowledge—small, but something still there, not a void. The scientist's lids flitted. She reached deep ....

"Wait ...," said Dr. Riesen, her eyes snapping open. She looked at Holbrook, excited. "Yes!"

"Yes, what?"

"Yes!" Dr. Riesen said again, springing from her chair. "Come with me!" She headed for the door.

Holbrook stood. "Where are we going?"

"To my quarters," she said, darting out of the room.

When they arrived at Dr. Riesen's quarters, the research scientist raced to a chest of drawers along the far bulkhead. She pulled open the bottom drawer, reached into the front of its left side, and withdrew a palm-sized crimson bundle of shiny fabric. She quickly moved to her desk, placed the bundle on the desktop, and carefully peeled back the folds until the fabric lay flat. In its center sat a small black stone the size of a large marble.

Holbrook stared at the stone, confused. "This is the answer to stopping Drazetek?" he asked.

"Yes," she said. "This is a piece of Planck Matter."

"Planck Matter?" said Holbrook, his brows rising in surprise. "How did you get it?"

"The aught Ninetek, the one who tricked me into describing how to build a detonator, he gave it to me. As a gift." She lifted the stone and turned it, its surface glinting with ruby-red sparkles.

Concern flooded Holbrook's face. "Is it safe to have aboard the ship?"

"Perfectly safe," said Dr. Riesen. "There's only one way to coax all the matter inside this small stone back into this Universe, and it can't happen by accident."

"How much matter does it contain?"

Dr. Riesen set the stone back on the fabric. "About as much as an average-sized asteroid. Like the one created by the aughts' test device."

"Whatever you're thinking of doing with this Planck Matter, won't Drazetek predict that too?" asked Holbrook.

"That's just it," said Dr. Riesen. "When Ninetek gave me the stone, I asked him what Drazetek thought about that. He told me Drazetek didn't know." She looked at the captain. "Ninetek's not alive anymore—we found him dead inside the aught ship. Drazetek doesn't know we have this."

The captain stroked his chin. "What's your plan?" he asked.

"That partly depends on what Drazetek does to get to Earth," she said, "but first things first." Dr. Riesen scooped up the fabric, bunching it around the Planck Matter stone in its center. "Right now, I need to build a bomb."

52

Holbrook stood near his captain's chair, staring at the tactical map that filled the bridge viewscreen. All the plotting and planning had come down to this, a last stand against Drazetek and his planet-killing bomb. Drazetek's ship had avoided the hastily assembled CentCom task force sent to stop him from reaching Earth's solar system, dodging most of their ships before a gravity assist from a star hurled it faster than the pursuing CentCom vessels could fly.

The admirals, flabbergasted at Drazetek's ability to outsmart them, had wondered aloud about spies, but it was really all about computing probabilities. The captain pursed his lips—had probabilities warned Drazetek the *Avenger* would challenge his starship? Earth's survival depended on the aught star captain not predicting what they had planned for him.

A white circle appeared on the viewscreen, top center. It moved briskly along a white line that crossed a black triangle in the center and curled around a yellow disc at the lower-left. "Status," said Holbrook.

"The aught ship remains on course for its Sol rendezvous," called out the helmsman.

Drazetek's ship needed a reverse gravity assist from the sun, a tight dip into its gravity well to bleed speed for entry into the inner solar system. The *Avenger* lay in wait, a manta hunting its prey. "Deploy the bomb," said Holbrook.

"Aye, sir."

The payload appeared on the tactical map as a red pip that came to rest with the *Avenger* along the white line, directly in the aught ship's path.

"Now back us away," said Holbrook.

The black triangle inched to the right across the screen as the white circle continued its travel, speeding towards the red dot.

"Start feeding telemetry to the device," said Holbrook.

"Aye, sir."

The captain followed the status readouts on the viewscreen. The device was working perfectly, set to trigger based on the aught ship's speed and distance. "Approximate time to intercept?" asked Holbrook.

"Three minutes."

"Arm the device," said Holbrook.

Ensign Higgins at weapons control tapped his terminal. "Armed."

No one spoke on the bridge, the officers transfixed by the scene unfolding on the main viewscreen. Time slowed, each second dragging into the next.

"Sixty seconds."

The tactical display zoomed in, focusing on the aught ship, the *Avenger*, and the trap they'd set.

"Forty-five seconds."

Holbrook moved to his chair. He'd sit for the agonizing remaining time in the plan that would mean life or death for the Earth.

"Twenty seconds."

The white circle moved closer to the red pip, unwavering in its course.

"Ten seconds."

"This is it," Holbrook whispered.

"Five.

"Four.

"Three."

The white circle eclipsed the red pip.

"Two.

"One."

The red dot lingered for an eternity in the exact center of the white circle before it disappeared.

The white circle continued on its journey along the white line, towards the yellow disc.

Holbrook rubbed his chin. "Visual, please."

A ball of blinding white light appeared in the middle of the screen, widening with the explosion that churned at its center.

The captain's gut told him what happened, but he asked anyway. "Report."

"The bomb detonated, sir," said Ensign Higgins, "but at the last moment the aught ship dipped out of the way."

"You're saying it evaded the bomb?"

"That's correct, sir," said Higgins. "The ship just dipped under it."

Holbrook looked over his shoulder to the rear of the bridge where Dr. Riesen sat. Their eyes connected.

"There's no way a ship traveling that fast could have seen the bomb or its explosion in time to evade it," said Dr. Riesen. "They predicted we'd be here, at this exact location, attempting to stop them."

"Well, we didn't disappoint," said Holbrook. The captain returned to the viewscreen and the still-expanding explosion that nearly filled it. "Time 'til the aught ship's solar intercept?"

"Two minutes."

"Two minutes," muttered Holbrook, rubbing his chin. "It'll all be over in two minutes."

53

My Dear Friend Levteek,

I hope this message finds you well as I bring you good news about my mission to Earth.

I know you did not want a bomb. You begged me not to deliver it to the Earth. Begged me to spare the humans, our enemies. I will never understand that.

I continued on to Earth despite your pleadings. The human starship that engaged us in D-space was the lone CentCom vessel waiting in our path. They attempted to prevent us from reaching Earth. Probabilities suggested that would be so. Probabilities suggested they would try to stop us by detonating a thermonuclear device. A subtle course change was all it took to evade the blast.

We entered the Sol system, still traveling too fast to deploy the Planck device. As planned, we prepared for a reverse gravity assist. We dipped into the yellow star's gravity well and came around quickly. Yellow sunlight poured through the starboard viewports. Our speed dropped. But then a flash, to starboard. A very bright flash, obviously, to be seen against the backdrop of the star. An oddly familiar flash. A flash filled with ruby-red sparkles.

The humans somehow constructed a Planck device of their own, placed it near our path around their star, and set it to detonate as we turned. It released the equivalent mass of a small asteroid. We did not hit the new stellar body, no, but the sudden appearance of that large mass so close to our ship disrupted our warp bubble. The result was a slight perturbation in our course. Very slight, hardly measurable. But traveling at our extreme speed and so near the star, the perturbation was enough. It was enough to make our turn around the star slightly too tight.

The good news I bring to you, old friend, is that your wish has come true. I will not deliver a Planck device to the human home world. We are plunging into the star as I compose this message. In another few nanoseconds we will be embers—I am sending this to you in my last few moments.

It has been a pleasure serving you and the Collective. I only wish I had been successful in what I set out to do. That would have made my sacrifice worthwhile.

Goodbye, old friend.

Drazetek

54

Holbrook floated in the void, the blackness everywhere dotted with stars. Millions of stars.

The blue jewel he helped save spun slowly beneath him, but he couldn't see it. He had drifted out of The Georgian, a quaint high Earth orbit hotel he'd frequented on several previous vacations, with his back to the planet. Nothing substantial occupied his field of view—not the sun, the Earth, the moon, not even the hotel. Only stars.

Holbrook ran through his progression. His gloved finger found the white supergiant Deneb and traced a line through the yellow supergiant Sadr to Albireo. Moving to Epsilon Cygni, his finger traced a fresh line through Sadr to Delta Cygni. The five stars of the Northern Cross, the backbone of the constellation Cygnus.

"I think I see it," she said, squinting at the far-off patch of sky. "There are just so many stars. How did you spot it so quickly?"

"I've done it a few times," said Holbrook. Drifting in the seemingly center of creation, he clasped his fingers over his belly and let himself float. He liked to imagine he had no EN-suit or body at all. He liked to imagine his unencumbered consciousness floating among all the stars. "I hope this isn't too boring."

"Boring?" said Dr. Riesen. "It's incredible. For all my time investigating the secrets of the Universe, I've never just sat back and taken in its beauty." She gaped at the spectacle before them. "Thank you for inviting me."

"My pleasure," said Holbrook. "To be honest, I haven't found many who appreciate the experience." He checked his comm. "We should head in soon, if you want to make your shuttle back to Earth." Holbrook's body was angled slightly, enough that he could see the physicist's face through her force field helmet without turning his head. Dr. Riesen's ice-blue eyes stared straight at the heavens, unmoving. The starlight set her pale skin aglow, radiating her beauty back into the cosmos.

"When's the next one?" she asked.

"Shuttle, you mean?" She nodded. "Tomorrow morning, I think."

Dr. Riesen pondered the void. "How long will you be here? At The Georgian."

"Another few days. After that I might check into a different hotel. Or maybe go down to Earth. Or even head for one of the outer moons. Depends on what I feel like."

The physicist didn't respond. Had he somehow offended her?

"Do they have a restaurant in this place?" she asked

"Yeah," said Holbrook, relieved. "It's pretty good. The hotel's amazing too." He tapped his maneuvering thrusters, orienting him to face The Georgian. "I like coming here," he said, admiring the structure. "It has so much more charm than the larger space hotels. If you're not pressed for time, I could show you around a bit. We could grab dinner."

Dr. Riesen looked over at Holbrook. "Sounds great," she said. "Maybe a little more gazing before we head in."

The two drifted among the stars. Holbrook let his head rest against the back of his helmet, closed his eyes, and smiled.

IF YOU ENJOYED *INFERNUM*, A REQUEST …

We'd really appreciate a short review on Amazon or Goodreads. Reviews from readers like you will have a huge impact on helping others discover the novel.

A WISH …

Join our mailing list (at www.fictionfactorybooks.com) or follow us on Twitter (@FictionFactoryB) for news and updates on *Infernum* and other books.

… AND A SPECIAL BONUS

We hope you enjoy the following preview of *Ares*, the forthcoming novel by Jayson Adams. A top-secret objective ensnares Commander Kate Bauman and the members of the first manned mission to Mars.

1. The Arrival

"Before we begin our descent, Commander, I have a message to play for the crew."

Commander Kate Bauman managed a near-perfect poker face despite the unwelcome voice in her helmet. Only her clenched jaw betrayed her anger. It wasn't just the outrageously poor timing of Julian's ask that drew her ire, moments before the seven most critical minutes of their journey. His pattern of almost daily callous acts and slights had numbed her to his antics. What really riled her was his use of the main comm line instead of a private channel. Julian's lack of discretion meant they would discuss the matter in front of the entire crew.

What could the message possibly be? Had Julian not irritated the shit out of her for the past five months, she might have asked. Regardless of its content, there was only one answer Kate could give him, but she'd take her time delivering it—she was the mission commander, not a lackey waiting on his every word. She dragged her gloved finger across her station's screen, swiping the next page of the pre-landing checklist into view, and set it scrolling with a casual flick. Guiding their craft from atmospheric insertion to touchdown was the real business of the moment. A Mars landing was a tricky affair where even the most minor misstep could mean skittering across the thin atmosphere to carom off into space, burning up in a meteoric streak of pyrotechnics, or forming the newest impact crater on the dusty red plains. They needed to devote all their attention to landfall.

The commander dispatched two checklist items with leisurely taps before addressing Julian. He stared at her from four stations away, the shine of the overhead lights repeating across his helmet and his smooth, shaved head. Surely he understood now was not the time for distractions, that she'd have no choice but to deny his request. So why invite a public rebuff? He was up to something; she just couldn't see what. "Julian," she said, hiding her annoyance behind her taut tone, "we're a few minutes from entering the atmosphere, the point at which all the you-know-what really will hit the fan. We need to focus on one thing, which is getting to the ground safely. Let's hold off on your message until after we touch down."

Kate quickly dismissed three more items on the checklist. Commander Glenn Wiles, her second, would oversee their descent, though she would closely monitor their progress. Despite the strides women had made during NASA's seventy-four-year history, she still felt the weight of being judged as a *woman* commander. The mission needed to be perfect, every execution flawless.

"That will be too late, I'm afraid."

This time Commander Bauman swiveled fully from her station and faced Julian, all the remnants of her poker face melted away. For any of the other astronauts under her command, her answer would have been the end of the discussion, eliciting silence, a sheepish nod, or at most a meek "yes, ma'am." Julian seemed to operate from a different mindset, one where her decisions were never the final word.

"I have orders to play a message for the crew before we enter the atmosphere," said Julian.

Orders that she didn't know about? Bullshit. "Orders from whom?"

"Assistant Director Pearson."

Kate's cheeks flushed, sensing all eyes on her. As the number two person at NASA and the champion of their trip to Mars, Assistant Director Pearson was certainly within his rights to communicate directly with any of Kate's astronauts. But why would the AD, himself an air force veteran, disregard the chain of command? She fumed, in part at the delivery of secret instructions to a subordinate, but mostly at being forced to give Julian his way. "Well, let's have it," she grumbled.

"Yes ma'am," said Julian.

The capsule's main viewscreen came alive with the black glow of an empty data feed before snapping to the NASA logo suspended against a bright white background. The image switched to Assistant Director Pearson seated behind his desk, looking thin and squirrelly as ever. His dark, narrow-set eyes hovered beneath his bald crown, and when he smiled, the left side of his mouth rose higher than the right. "Crew of the *Ares*, I want to congratulate you on your impending achievement, the first humans to land on the surface of Mars. For the next year you will perform research and explore the Martian surface, an amazing accomplishment we should all be proud of." The assistant director slid a cigar—a Macanudo by the band— from a desktop humidor as he spoke. He clipped the end and held his torch aloft, puffing the cigar to life. He seemed ready to speak again but paused, turning the cigar sideways and studying it, apparently impressed by its flavor. "Now the other day in the Capitol, a senator approached me, almost chased me down through the halls, in fact. I'd sparred with him many times in the Appropriations Committee. Never considered him particularly bright. In any case, he'd somehow gotten a look at the off-budget figures for your mission and asked me point blank how the hell in these fiscally challenged times I could justify spending over eight hundred billion dollars on ten roundtrip tickets to Mars."

The assistant director paused for another puff of his cigar, the end glowing red behind the nub of ash. "Now the good senator had a point. And the answer to his question begins with our first visit to Mars, the Viking landers in '75. Twenty years went by before we would return, with two orbiters, a lander, and a rover in the '90s. We sent another orbiter in 2001, two more rovers in 2003, an orbiter in 2005, a lander in 2007, and sixteen more missions in the twenty-five years after that. And those figures only cover American interest in the red planet. There were also the ESA and Chinese missions. And I won't even bother to mention the Russians—those poor devils couldn't touch a craft down on that planet to save their life." He puffed again. "My point is that an astute observer would guess there must have been some development on Mars to have triggered such intense interest. That brings us to your mission, ladies and gentlemen. There's only so much you can do with rovers and landers and satellite imagery. The next phase of our interest in Mars involves boots on the ground, your boots, in search of a payout for a wager that began four decades ago. And while I'm sure a year's worth of abrading rocks and drinking your own wastewater will prove scientifically enlightening, it's this other interest, this *classified* interest, that is the real reason for your trip to the red planet."

Stunned silence filled the cabin while the assistant director paused and relit his cigar.

"So, everything we've trained for, all our preparation, that was just a front for some classified mission?" All attention shifted to Mission Specialist Casey Morgan, the expedition's astrobiologist. Several of the other astronauts nodded in agitated agreement.

"Some of you might find this news upsetting," continued the assistant director. "Let me assure you, as a practical matter, nothing has changed.

You'll still carry out all the studies and experiments you've prepared for. They're all still very important, because they serve as a smokescreen for the true goal of the mission. Security Chief Julian Grimes and Mission Specialist Joseph Cheney have been briefed on those particulars. While the rest of you go about your assignments, Grimes and Cheney will handle all details and execution related to the classified task. You are to give them your full cooperation."

Kate stole a glance at Julian. He watched the video message with a dispassionate expression, hands folded in his lap. How long had he and Cheney been preparing for this secret aspect of their mission? From the very start, if the AD was serious about it being the true reason for their trip to the red planet.

"Commander Bauman." Kate jumped at the unexpected sound of her name. "I apologize in advance for delivering this next part in a pre-recorded video stream rather than face-to-face. To drive home the importance of your mission's primary objective, I am placing Grimes in charge as the acting mission commander, effective upon your landing."

The news elicited a self-satisfied smirk from Julian. For Kate, the assistant director's declaration knocked the wind out of her, a sucker punch straight in the gut. The years of toil, the wrecked marriage, the sacrifices she'd endured to secure the command of a lifetime all whisked aside like so much rubbish. Her heart ached, the memories of her late mother beaming in awe of her daughter's achievement forever footnoted. The commander's shoulders slumped forward and her chin quivered beneath her bowed head. A tear fell, then a second, splattering against the inside of her helmet.

Someone was watching.

Kate discovered Glenn looking on from across the capsule. Flustered, she reached for her damp cheeks, but her hand smashed into her helmet. She quickly buried herself in her station.

"Your mission is a momentous endeavor," said the assistant director, "one which will likely change the course of human history, and if we're lucky, the bottom line." Kate looked up at the video, catching Pearson's final puff and his crooked smile. "Best of luck, *Ares* crew." The screen went dark. No one stirred, the flashing lights of their terminals the only animation within the capsule.

"Now that is a crock of bull … *shit!*"

The words came from Allison Voss, shocking for the normally reserved Mars station engineer. "Hold on, Allison," said Kate.

"The mission of the century turns out to be a front for a classified operation?" asked Mars station chief Miriam Sato.

"Wait, wait," said Kate. The rising emotions risked overshadowing the important job that still remained. She needed everyone to keep it together until their capsule reached the ground.

"While the rest of you go about your assignments," said Dr. Clayton Fisk in a mocking voice, his index finger near his mouth and curled around an imaginary cigar, "Grimes and Cheney will handle the classified task, which is the true reason for your mission. Please give my two toadies your full support while they search for the lost pleasure dome of Xanadu."

Julian's entire head reddened. "Disrespect towards a superior officer is a courts-martial offense," he said.

Fisk laughed. "My official designation is 'Spaceflight Participant.' Are you saying you intend to make me an officer?"

A loud whistle filled the cabin, squelching the commotion and gathering everyone's attention.

"Thank you, Glenn," said Kate. She reviewed the upset faces staring back at her around the cabin. "I'm as shocked as the rest of you about the message we just received. But right now, we're about a heartbeat away from a crash landing. We need to make sure this capsule touches down safely. So please, put everything you just saw out of your minds and —"

"Commander Bauman's right," said Julian. "There's no time for grumbling. We all have a job to do."

"I'll thank you not to talk over me." Kate had lost count of how many times Julian cut her off in conversations during their flight to Mars. She couldn't tell if it was unconscious or malicious. Either way, it was damn irritating. "And if you don't mind, Julian, *I'll* give the directives on this ship. Your reign begins the moment we touch down. Until then, *I'm* still the mission commander."

Julian threw Kate a spiteful glance but said nothing more. He turned back to his station.

Kate chided herself for her outburst. She'd normally never have let such sharp words leave her lips, but they'd taken a lot from her today. She wanted to scream at Julian, scream at the assistant director. And maybe she would, but not then. None of it would make one damn bit of difference if they didn't land safely on the ground.

"All stations report with pre-landing status," said Glenn.

Kate quickly dispatched the remaining items on her checklists and swiped back to the main screen. The display filled with an image of Mars's western hemisphere, a mottled orange disc floating against a starry backdrop. A gray dot, the *Ares* capsule, slid along a dashed white arc that traced the spaceship's trajectory. A halo of annotations reported the craft's speed, altitude, and other vitals.

Sweat broke out across Commander Bauman's palms, growing to a torrent that emerged faster than her gloves could wick away. Her heart rate accelerated and she lapsed into a series of shallow, rapid breaths. Her suit peppered her with chimes, warning that she teetered on the edge of unconsciousness.

She was panicking. But why?

You know why.

It couldn't be that. She'd conquered the past. And in any case an atmospheric landing was nothing like a touchdown on the airless moon.

Then why'd you ask Glenn to handle the descent?

Kate ignored the question, focusing instead on her breath. She returned to the relaxation techniques from the long-ago therapy sessions. Her pulse and respiration dropped to more normal levels. She'd pulled herself back from the edge, but she wasn't out of harm's way. If the mere thought of the touchdown had so easily chipped away at her hard fought recovery, what would happen during the actual landing? Each descent stage carried its own unique perils. Each would become a dangerous stressor. If she didn't manage her mental state all the way to the ground, she risked a full relapse into debilitation.

"*Ares* at nominal orientation for atmospheric entry."

Kate girded herself for their hazardous entrance into Mars's exosphere. In less than two minutes, atmospheric friction would bleed off the bulk of the 12,500 miles per hour they marshaled to fling their capsule between the planets. During visits to the *Ares* vehicle assembly building, she'd fixated on the craft's slim heat shield, their only protection against the 3,500 degrees Fahrenheit that easily surpassed the melting point of their stainless steel hull.

"Speed decreasing … 10,000 … 8,000 … 6,000. Exterior temperature readings nominal."

Kate licked her lips. Even catastrophic descents appeared normal at first. The flames that lapped the craft's underside probed the heat shield for weak spots in its bonded ceramic, the slightest imperfection in its metal alloy, hunting for any pathway to the delicate capsule. Kate's vital signs crept back up. She shook her head to rid herself of the morbid thoughts and focused again on her breath.

"Ten seconds to chute deployment."

Commander Bauman breathed easier. They'd survived the brunt of atmospheric entry, though they still raced to the ground at 900 miles per hour. She gripped her restraints where they crossed in an "X" at her chest, the action ingrained after the simulator sessions on Earth.

"Three … two … one."

Multiple g-forces pinned Kate in her seat as the craft rocked and shimmied. She gritted her teeth against the violent movement. An exterior camera relayed footage of the chute soaring above the capsule, a great white jellyfish scooping the rarefied Martian air beneath its bell, its tentacles tugging at their hull. They slowed, but their speed bottomed out at 235 miles per hour. Mars had just enough atmosphere to burn up a craft on entry but not enough to slow it for a landing.

"Preparing to jettison heat shield."

Kate fixated on her terminal screen, desperate for the landing target acquisition icon to appear. Once the ship discarded the heat shield and exposed the downward facing cameras, the computer would have milliseconds to locate landmarks and make course adjustments. Any hiccup could result in them touching down far from the HAB. As it stood, even a perfect landing meant leading her crew on a two-kilometer hike to the Mars base.

Pop!

Ten explosive bolts propelled the shield away from the capsule. Turbulence besieged the small craft with the exposure of its less aerodynamic underside, driving the commander to squeeze her restraints tighter.

Seconds ticked away, but no target acquisition lock came. Had something damaged the cameras? Or worse? Kate reached a nervous hand to query the computer when green symbols cascaded across her terminal. The *Ares* located its touchdown target and fired its thrusters in short bursts to position itself within the correct descent window. Another green icon emerged, signaling landing gear deployment. The system of struts, trusses, and shocks now extended from its stowed configuration was necessary but not sufficient for landfall—the *Ares* still fell far too fast to touch down.

A deafening whoosh filled the cabin. Kate closed her eyes as the *Ares* entered the final and riskiest landing stage. Air rushed through the now exposed intakes to the atmospheric braking system, an experimental series of manifolds that compressed the thin Martian air before releasing it as a roiling pocket of high pressure above the capsule. The ram brake in essence thickened the air beneath the parachute enough to float the spacecraft to the ground. That was the theory at least. Despite the simulations and prototype trials on Earth, Kate couldn't shake her concern that their landing would be the first test of the system on the red planet.

"Speed dropping. Ninety seconds to touchdown … eighty … seventy."

Kate followed their steady deceleration on her terminal. She forced herself to relax, her fears unfounded. The ram brake worked, and in less than a minute they would touch down, becoming the first humans to set foot on an alien planet. The culmination of two decades of planning. The dream of —

"We've got a problem," said Glenn. His deep, normally firm bassoon voice contained the slightest tremolo of fear.

"What is it?" asked Kate.

"We're coming in hot."

Indeed, Kate's terminal still showed a steady decrease in their downward velocity, but the computer projected they'd hit the ground at roughly four times the nominal landing speed. At that rate their craft, the *Ares* capsule and everything in it, would crumple on impact. "Can we get more deceleration out of the brake?"

"Negative," said Glenn. "We've got maximum airflow through the intakes; we're just not getting enough pressure out the topside."

Two stations away, spacecraft engineer Laura Engles unleashed flurries of taps on her terminal screen. "The air's quite cold … much colder than it should be," she said.

"There's a storm front building," said Miriam. "NASA's been tracking it for the past few days."

Engles grunted. Schematics and reams of text flew across her screen. Her finger settled on a graph and its accompanying table of numbers. "The designs assume a higher minimum atmospheric temperature. The lower temp throws off all those calculations. The system's scooping air, but with the cold it can't produce high enough pressure beneath the chute."

Kate had pushed for sending a scaled down version of the *Ares* to Mars, outfitted with the experimental brake. She'd worried anything less than an actual atmospheric test on the red planet would leave their whole touchdown to chance. The mission planners cited budget constraints that made such a test impractical. They instead showcased all the data they collected from their slew of earthbound trials and simulations, insisting they'd accounted for every contingency. Apparently, they'd missed one.

Klaxons blared and revolving emergency lights bathed the flight deck in red chaos, the machinations of an AI co-pilot that had thrown up its hands. It could do little more than signal to its human wards their pending destruction.

"Forty-five seconds to impact," said Glenn.

Kate scooted closer to her terminal and called up the main control screen. Her hand shook as she swiped through the displays for each of the capsule's subsystems, desperate to find any recourse that would help them survive the landing.

Shouts and commotion erupted from behind. Kate spun around to find Dr. Fisk standing free of his restraints and terror gripping his face. "Sit down and remain strapped in!" she yelled. The professor landed back in his chair with wild eyes, the ferocity of her order driving him to near hysterics.

Commander Bauman regretted snapping at Fisk—as a civilian he lacked the extensive survival training that was a hallmark of the astronaut corps. She just needed them all in their seats. Whether she found a way to ease their impact or not, an unrestrained body would become a dangerous projectile inside the cabin.

"Thirty seconds."

Kate resumed swiping. She paused and backtracked to the thruster control screen. The attitude thrusters changed the capsule's orientation using bursts of compressed gas, but even if they all pointed to the ground, they wouldn't generate enough force to put a dent in their downward velocity. She scrolled instead to the controls for the third stage separation thrusters, powerful mini-rockets designed to push the capsule away from the booster during liftoff, at the end of the third stage burn. Normally those thrusters would have completely exhausted their fuel supply, but Kate had shut the system down early, holding some propellant back.

"Twenty seconds."

Kate checked the fuel levels. The tanks contained more than she hoped, but would it be enough? She'd also have to guess when to fire them. The thrusters only burned at full force—there was no adjusting their output like a retro rocket. Starting them too soon would only delay the capsule's fatal impact, too late and the thrusters wouldn't have enough time to slow the craft. Either way, the *Ares* would slam into the ground.

"Ten seconds. Brace for impact. Seven … six …"

Mouthing a prayer, Kate tapped the ignition button. The third stage separation thrusters roared beneath the craft at full burn, slowing the capsule's descent enough to calm their computer co-pilot. In a blink, the AI cancelled the crash klaxon and secured them from red alert. Kate's station showed the *Ares* hovering a meter above the ground.

The thrusters cut out.

The *Ares* lingered in the thin air for a moment until gravity restarted the capsule's downward fall.

Klaxons wailed for three quarters of a second, ceasing when the *Ares* slammed into the ground. The ship shuddered and the cockpit filled with the sounds of wrenching metal. Shocks squealed beyond their tolerances as they strained to dissipate the spacecraft's momentum.

The impact mashed Kate into her seat. She waited for the capsule's underside to hit the ground and impart the full force of the crash to the fragile hull. The *Ares* would burst at its seams. When they'd first announced the Mars trip, Kate had imagined standing on the planet's surface and taking in the Martian sky. In her final moments, the ruptures would at least allow her a fleeting glimpse of the ruddy canopy.

The contact with the ground never came.

Kate's terminal, a patchwork of flashing red indicators, screamed about failures in several trusses and the complete collapse of a landing strut but showed the ship's velocity at zero. The landing gear held. She sat dazed for several seconds while reality sank in. They had survived the touchdown.

Screams of delight and relief tore through the capsule.

"Ladies and gentlemen," said Glenn, beaming with sweat beaded across his brow, "welcome to Mars."

For additional chapters, updates, and other info, visit
www.fictionfactorybooks.com/ares

ABOUT THE AUTHOR

At age sixteen Jayson dreamed of starting a software company and retiring by twenty-five. He achieved his dream just before thirty, working for the likes of Steve Jobs and selling one of his start-ups along the way. Five years later he returned to computers with another start-up. He currently works at Google.

Computers were always Jayson's creative outlet, the screen a "blank slate." He now channels his creative energies into writing compelling science fiction.

Made in the USA
Coppell, TX
04 May 2022

77406912R00233